# Cayo Hueso/Cuba Libre

## A Political Thriller

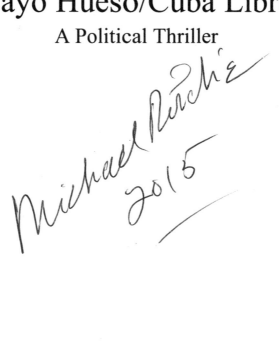

Michael Ritchie

SeaStory Press
Key West, Florida

Cayo Hueso/Cuba Libre

© 2008 by Michael Ritchie

Cover art by Martha dePoo; www.marthadepoo.com

Printed in the United States of America

ISBN 978-0-9799474-3-8

SeaStory Press
305 Whitehead St. #1
Key West. Florida 33040
www.seastorypress.com

# For the "Fox Family"

With special thanks to Emra Wagener Smith,
without whose help and encouragement,
this book could never have been written.

## Author and Publisher's Note

# *Prologue*

Long ago, before "civilization," there were great wars among Indian tribes in the Florida Keys. The final battle was fought on an outlying Gulf cay which is today known as Key West. The victors left the numerous bodies of the vanquished to rot on the shores of the southernmost, desolate, and mosquito-ridden cay.

Some time later, Spanish explorer Juan Ponce de Leon happened upon the series of Florida cays and claimed them for his native Spain. Setting foot on the southernmost of them, the Spanish were astounded and awed at the sight of vast expanses of coral rock littered with the skeletal remains of native-American Indians.

"Cayo Hueso!" the startled Spanish exclaimed, instantly naming the small island, "Cay of bones."

English settlers would later bastardize the name to "Key West."

Subsequent residents formed the first Key West Chamber of Commerce and proceeded to turn the vast expanses of coral rock into attractive sand beaches. They either ground the Indian bones for fertilizer or buried them deep beneath imported Bahamian sand.

Many skeletons remain in Key West. Some, though, are not buried so deeply.

# Contents

# CHAPTER ONE

# *Sea Changes*

Mac McKinney— reporter and senior political analyst for the *Key West Reporter*— sat alone at his usual corner table at Kelly's Caribbean Bar and Grill and rifled through the agenda for that night's city commission meeting. The quiet, dimly-lit venue had become his Algonguin Hotel, that of literary fame, his Table One at Chicago's Pump Room— where he had often shared drinks and gossip with Irv and Essie Kupcinet during his days covering the political antics of "Da Mayor," Richard J. Dalcy, as a reporter for the *Chicago Tribune*. It was his Riccardo's, where he had often shared "Nooners" with Mike Royko and Studs Terkel. It was his Billy Goat Tavern, gone south.

McKinney himself had gone south some 10 years before, longing for respite from harsh Chi-town winters and dreaming of sailing two-masted schooners— "the big blow boats," as the local old salts called them. He was pleased to have achieved both. During his first year in Key West, living off savings and profit-sharing from the *Trib*, he had signed on as crew aboard the 100-foot John Alden schooner *Constellation*. He would work for room and board, plus tips. His sparse accommodations included a three-by-six foot berth in the fo'csle. The tips from tourists— split among all the crew— afforded him $10 or $20 a day. It was enough for the essentials— cigarettes and a few beers a night at the Schooner Wharf Bar.

Then 38, McKinney was far older than most of his mates and a far less experienced seaman. He was also tall and sleight of stature— standing six foot and a weighing a meager 150 pounds.

1

But he worked hard and followed orders— something he had never in his life had to do.

The *Connie* was no day-sailer. With two 85-foot masts, she carried 3,000 square feet of sail. There were more than 200 feet of cap rails, which he had hand-sanded and varnished (including the nautically requisite four sandings followed by four coats of marine varnish).

His reward was a great loss of blood to the *Connie's* decks— mostly through the occasional mishandling of winches and running backstays— as well as a realization of the true "romance" of the sea. For there were times when he would position himself out at the tip of the bowsprit where he could gaze back at that magnificent vessel as she plied the blue-green seas of the Caribbean at a 14-knot clip, the waters parting port and starboard past her bow— showing a "bone in her teeth."

It was a world away from Michigan Avenue, Wacker Drive and the Chicago River.

But after a year before the mast— during which he gained both girth and permanently sun-bleached blond hair— the allure of the big blow boats and the romance of the sea gave way to the reality of McKinney's fast-dwindling savings. He would have to leave the *Connie* and get a job doing the only thing he was really good at— reporting. After piping himself off the *Connie*, he would occasionally see her massive sails rising above Key West harbor, off on another Caribbean adventure, and a powerful, empty feeling overcame him, commingled with an equally powerful desire to return to the sea. He knew those feelings would remain with him forever, his own personal *mal de mer.*

When the *Constellation* sank four years later off the coast of Spain, McKinney mourned her like a close family member.

Turning his back to the unpredictability and volatility of the sea, McKinney sailed into the far more tepid and tranquil waters of what was then Key West journalism. In Chicago he had been a noted political gadfly— a thorn in the side of corrupt politicos— and something of a "Gonzo" journalist. In Key West, the rule of thumb at *The Key West Citizen,* the southernmost city's daily, was "Don't rock the boat." The paper was a member in very good standing of the Chamber of Commerce. Stories which reflected negatively on local businesses or tourism were frowned upon, even disallowed. If someone leapt to his death from a local hotel— something difficult to do since most hotels were one or two stories— not only was the hotel not named, reporting of the suicide itself was prohibited.

"We don't want to encourage more of this," was the policy of the *Citizen* editorial board.

It took only one meeting between the *Citizen's* Editor and McKinney for both to realize that there was no journalistic compatibility. To add insult to injury, the Editor had to go and tell McKinney what reporters were being paid in Key West. Pondering the figure, combined with the paltry amount remaining in his bank account, he briefly considered suicide. But then he remembered that if he did take such drastic measures, he wouldn't even make headlines in the local newspaper.

*No way,* he thought. *If I'm going to off myself, it's going to be above the fold, in boldface.*

Key West journalism was indeed a world away from the *Chicago Tribune,* the *Sun-Times,* and the Michigan Avenue bridge— from which one might leap to one's final, watery rest and at least rate Page Two.

McKinney decided to ponder his options at his new watering hole, Kelly's. The atmosphere was tropical, laid back, Key West. And although Mac was a loner by nature and by choice, he was always fascinated by observing the eclectic patrons there. He was never anxious to engage in conversation. But neither would he be rude.

That night Mac happened to seat himself at the bar beside a bearded, balding gentleman who rested one hand on a pile of what appeared to be legal files and court records, and the other on the attentive head of a black lab dog. He was wearing a weathered Florida shirt, tattered black shorts and Kino sandals. Through his tortoise shell half-glasses, the curious stranger was poring intently over the legal files. Occasionally he'd lift his hand from the black lab's head— prompting the dog to stand on her haunches either in protest or the possibility that the pair might be going home for dinner— to sip from his Canadian Club. But his other hand and his eyes never left the bulging files.

As McKinney began to pay closer attention to the man, he noticed that he was muttering to himself as he read.

"God damned politicians. And they think they can get away with it!"

There would be a pause as the reader of legal briefs took another drink. Then would come another little tirade.

"They expect us to buy this bullshit? They really expect us to buy this bullshit?"

McKinney was taken aback when the man turned to look him in the eye and remark, as if he'd known him for years, "It's just bullshit… and they expect us to buy it!"

McKinney wasn't sure how or even whether to respond. This was, after all, Key West. Mac recalled his older brother's words of advice upon being advised that he would be moving to Key West.

"*Key West?* Why in the world would you move to *Key West?* There's nothing there but bars and bums!"

*Always listen to your older brother,* he thought.

But curiosity got the better of him and he turned his face to the man and asked, "You an attorney?"

"Naw, a journalist. Well, an editor. Naw, a reporter. I've just started a new newspaper… the *Key West Reporter.*

"David Conrad," he introduced himself, removing his hand from the lab's head and offering it to Mac.

"Mac McKinney. And you're not going to believe this…."

"Believe what?"

"I'm a reporter, too."

"With the *Citizen?*" Conrad wondered.

"No, currently freelancing, well actually unemployed," McKinney answered. "I've been at sea for a while."

Conrad closed his files for the first time since Mac had set down beside him and seemed interested.

"What's your background?" the man and his lab wondered.

Mac ran through his bona fides, including his stint at the *Trib,* ranging from covering Ward politics to walking down Dearborn Street arm-in-arm with Richard Daley during St. Patrick's Day parades, and finally his personal coverage of Da Mayor's funeral. It was the sort of reportage that a *Citizen* editor could neither comprehend nor appreciate.

4

Conrad dug it. Or so it seemed.

"Buy my friend here a beer," he called to the bartender.

"Thanks," Mac said.

The black lab stood and moved to the foot of McKinney's bar stool.

"That's *Chablis*," Conrad said. "She's my news hound."

The two laughed and conversation began to come easier for McKinney. He listened as Conrad told him about his history. He held a PhD in Communications and had worked primarily in public relations. As Mac, he had moved to Key West for the weather and the water. He had his own small sailboat and lived aboard. He had been working with a local treasure salvor. But his outrage with local politics and politicians had driven him to take a shot at his own weekly newspaper.

"You wouldn't believe what they're trying to do to the Key West Bight," Conrad explained. "The City wants to take over management of the bight. They want to run out all the classic schooners and the working shrimp boats. They want to run off Schooner Wharf bar and all the small shops. They want to turn it into some Disney cartoon seaport. They want to build hotels and bring in tourist head-boats and tour trains and trolleys."

Mac was getting infuriated just listening. He had personal knowledge of the bight. He'd lived there, aboard the *Constellation*— one of those classic schooners of which Conrad spoke. And he had been a regular at Schooner Wharf Bar.

"Point is," Conrad continued, "the City has no business managing a seaport. They don't know what in hell they're doing. They're just bending over for developers. And Mayor Jimmy Dailey is behind it all."

Even Chablis— shuffling restlessly beneath Mac's barstool— seemed offended. Or perhaps she was merely anxious for the steak which her keeper ordered for her dinner nightly.

"Well, if I can be of any help..." Mac offered.

Conrad took a long sip of his Canadian Club. He didn't like snap decisions. But he did like this McKinney guy. He wasn't sure why. Maybe it was because Chablis seemed comfortable with him.

"Do you know anything about PageMaker?" Conrad asked.

Mac knew the computer composing program like the back of his hand.

"I'm a pro," he answered.

So Mac McKinney joined David Conrad on the *Reporter*—inputting copy to the PageMaker program while Conrad pasted up the press flats. The two shared writing and reporting responsibilities.

The newspaper which had emerged from the fires of a burning debate over the Key West Bight grew and began to join in other crusades, including frequent skirmishes with autocrats at the Chamber of Commerce, dueling with avaricious developers, and battling bubbas bent on double-dipping their fortunes freely from city coffers.

Both the paper and McKinney gained a reputation for rooting out cronyism and corruption. Both he and Conrad used their city hall and police contacts as confidential sources, and they were able to sniff out stories that left the other media in town scratching their heads (or their asses) in disbelief. Their methods also made them as many enemies as friends. But most of those screaming the loudest protestations about "that damned *Reporter*" were also confidential sources.

Conrad called it "Journalism as a blood sport."

In a few short years, the *Reporter* was the most influential—some said the most feared— media outlet in Key West. Its coverage had expanded to include Monroe County and all of the Florida Keys.

McKinney now moved in the highest political and social circles. He enjoyed a power even beyond that he'd experienced in Chicago. Everyone answered his calls. And he was free to work his own political agenda, which was fervently anti-development and anti-growth. He also bristled at drunken tourists speeding down Key West's narrow streets on dangerous and uninsured rental scooters, and fumed over reckless jet ski riders hot-dogging in the island's near-shore waters.

McKinney fought editorially against threatened high-rise development and for the courting of a family-based tourist market— the specter of which incensed high-ups in the Chamber of Commerce and leaders of the island's sizable gay community.

But Mac was at his best when manipulating the city commission— Key West's small-time oligarchy. Over the years he had carefully cultivated personal, mostly friendly relationships with each of the six commissioners and the mayor. Favorable news stories written on their behalf and occasionally overlooked peccadilloes had served him well. He knew their passions and their foibles, their principles and perversions. And he deftly used that knowledge to spin votes one way or another on issues of major concern to him— and, in his mind, to Key West. All the while, each of the commissioners chortled at the thought they had their own personal reporter tucked in their pocket. McKinney was a master of the political tap dance.

The agenda for the evening's commission meeting was starkly brief.

> *A resolution allowing for the closure of city streets; providing for the funding of police officer overtime; for the cost of providing city services such as cleanup; waiving of the city's noise ordinance; and establishing community standards for nudity and/or body-painting; and other provisions for Fantasy Fest 2008.*
>
> —

Only one item on the agenda. But, as in every previous year leading up to Key West's annual Bacchanalian flesh festival, it promised to be both contentious and entertaining.

Mac ordered a beer and began to mentally choreograph his moves.

## CHAPTER TWO

# *Viva Raúl!*

The flamboyant city commissioner toweled dry his hair and leaned forward into the face of the ornate Rococo bathroom mirror, closely scrutinizing the effects of his latest Lady Clairol blonde treatment.

*Mirror, mirror on the wall...* he muttered to himself... *Oh my God, I'M the fairest of them all!*

Rustling through his massive, walk-in closet, Tommy Whitemoor searched for his favorite Florida shirt, the one with pink flamingos.

"Mother!" he cried out, "Where's my flamingo shirt?"

He heard his mother's footfalls on the Dade County Pine stairs as she craned her neck up the staircase to answer him.

"At the cleaners," Maria Whitemoor sang out. "It's at the cleaners with your blue chiffon gown!"

"Mother, how could you? You know I have a commission meeting tonight. How could You? Oh, hell, I need a drink!"

With considerable disgust, he chose his second-favorite Florida shirt, resplendent with green palm trees and pink Conch shells. He slipped the silk shirt over his shoulders, buttoned it up with some difficulty due to his bothersome paunch, then slipped into his lightweight, summer khaki pants.

As Tommy sat at his computer, Maria entered with his frozen mango margarita. She placed it delicately on his desk, next to the computer screen.

"You're too good, Mother," the commissioner cooed.

"It's so true," she remarked as Tommy's mother left her precious 45-year-old son to return to her painting— the fruits of which had allowed her and Tommy to live quite well since she had left her obsessively macho husband 30 years before. She didn't actually leave him. Rather, she threw him out of the lavish Key West home his "old money" had paid for and settled in there to raise her baby boy alone. Maria was quite happy with the fact that there was not a macho bone in her son's body. She had done a good job, she thought.

With a brush of his wireless mouse, the commissioner reluctantly wiped away his beloved Aaron Carter screensaver. Immediately he noticed the flashing AOL Instant Message icon.

*Frenetic little yellow man,* he thought, *always running like that.*

Tommy clicked on the icon and saw a familiar screen name— Raúl. Next to it was a beaming yellow smiley face.

*Oh my God, it's the Cuban queen!*

He reached into his desk drawer and retrieved a much dog-eared Spanish/English dictionary.

Clicking on the icon, he quickly typed *Buenos Noches, mi amigo!*

A soft bell tone accompanied the response…

*Greetings, my honest and much esteemed and blonde-haired friend,* Tommy quickly, and liberally, interpreted the instant message.

*How are things in Havana?* Tommy asked in broken Spanish.

*Good… but I have much news, Tommy.*

*Do tell, bitch!*

*Tommy, I must ask that you preserve our security of conversation. This matter is of the most importance.*

*Did you ever know me to kiss and tell, Raúl?*

*LMAOROTF,* accompanied by another smiley face, came the reply. Raúl was proud that he had learned the American IM shorthand for "Laughing my ass off and rolling on the floor."

Tommy thought back to the first time he had met Raúl, in a darkened bar at the *Saratoga Hotel*— at the intersection of Havana's central Paseo del Prado and Dragones Street, opposite the capitol building. It had occurred before the latest severe U.S. crackdown on visits to Cuba. Key West commissioners being what

9

they were, Whitemoor had not even carried his passport with him when he sailed down to meet his friend.

The two had downed numerous Mojitos over the course of an evening and ended up cruising for young boys in Raúl's Mercedes along the Malecon, on the northern coast.

*You know what you tell me goes no further,* the commissioner typed.

There was a long pause.

*My brother is gone,* Raúl messaged.

Tommy took a deep breath. He knew the import of what he was reading.

*I'm sorry, Raúl. Has this been announced yet? And should we be talking about it on IM?*

*My people and the world do not know yet,* the Cuban responded. *It will be some time before this news is known— except to you and my inner circle. Much remains to be done. And no I am not worried, AOL is the only outlet I have which is not being listened to by your officials. And, after all, how many named Raúl have AOL and how many of those have lost brothers? I do not worry about listeners here.*

Tommy wished that he had another mango margarita, but did not dare interrupt the startling conversation in which he was engaged. His maniacally egotistical mind was already racing to figure out ways in which he might turn this epic event to his own personal advantage.

*Is there anything I can do?* he typed.

*Events will move quickly. I am already engaged in talks with your president. Much will change. Much of that change will be good. But This may not be an easy transition. Not everyone here will be happy. And I know many in your Miami will not be pleased with our plans for the future. I may ask for your help dealing with the Miami Mafia. I also have a plan to help secure the confidence of my people, through an alliance of our two cities— Habana and Cayo Hueso. More on that later. We will talk much more, my friend.*

Whitemoor pondered the thought.

*Whatever you need, all you have to do is ask,* the Key West commissioner responded.

*Good, thank you amigo. I must go now and I know that this is your political meeting night and you must go too. Before you go, check your email. You have a message from the president of Cuba.*

*Viva Raúl!* Tommy typed.

*Adios, my friend,* came the response.

The commissioner signed off IM and quickly clicked on his email Inbox.

*Something for you,* the email read. There was a JPEG attachment.

Tommy opened the file and gasped with prurient delight. Pictured was a striking Cuban boy of 14 years or so in very revealing Speedo-type swimwear posing with one hand provocatively grasping his privates.

The photo was captioned, *"Ernesto— staying at my villa for the weekend. Much love, Raúl."*

*A message from the president of Cuba,* the commissioner chuckled to himself.

*Cuba Libre!*

## CHAPTER THREE

# *The Orphans of Old City Hall*

Mac McKinney was always an admirer of the structure that was Key West's Old City Hall, if not so much the structure of the governing body to which it played host. It was a grand brown stone Victorian edifice, replete with bell and clock tower. Observers of the many and varied political functions held there— including city commission meetings— made their way up a great and wide granite staircase to the second floor commission chambers.

Commissioners, city staffers, politicians and others in the know entered the less-traveled and more secretive Anne Street entrance and rode a small, intimate elevator one floor up to the cavernous meeting hall. Most common journalists used the front steps. But Mac had long ago included himself among the glitterati who made their entrance through the rear doors. He had even managed to convince the city manager to provide him with a "reporter's table" right up on the political platform, adjacent to the dais at which the commissioners and mayor sat. While other reporters could have insisted on sharing the table, most said that they preferred to observe the proceedings from the audience. In fact, they just didn't have the *cojones* to encroach on McKinney's territory.

Key West commission meetings were political rituals. Prior to the six p.m. opening gavel, lawyers, developers and others with influence wandered freely about the dais whispering into the ears of their favored commissioners. Mac would merely wink or give a nod to whichever commissioners he'd already conferred with about the evening's meeting. Those he had not contacted would

12

often come up to him to quietly ask why not and to seek input or curry favor.

There were those among the local media who viewed Mac as power hungry and manipulative— far from the Bristol image of a true journalist. It was a perception McKinney did little to refute. But, in fact, any power he had arose from his strong desire to effect change for the better. It was born of the fact that he had his finger on the pulse of the community, the pulse of the voter. Other reporters filed their stories and went home to watch *Friends* on TV. Mac's waking moments, and often most of his sleeping moments, were consumed with politics and political maneuvering. He lived it, even to the exclusion of female companionship— except for a semi-drunken, one-night affair with a former city attorney. Aside from that, Mac considered himself one of the world's few living asexual men.

Mac broke his focus on the commission audience to quickly stare at the high ceiling as Tommy Whitemoor minced past his table to take his seat on the dais. An unmistakable air followed McKinney's least favorite politician.

*God,* Mac wondered, *when will someone ever tell him that Patchouli oil went out 20 years ago?*

With a great flourish, Whitemoor threw himself into his overstuffed, high-back leather chair and adjusted his microphone.

Mac resisted the temptation to gag. He was not in the least homophobic, he just couldn't stand a flaming queen. And Whitemoor even embarrassed the highest order of local drag queens.

While Mac didn't always agree with every city commissioner, he gave the office of each the highest respect. But Whitemoor was the antithesis of what he respected in elected officials. He was a joke. Worse, in McKinney's mind, he seemed just a little too interested in young boys. Mac maintained a manila file stuffed thick with allegations— to his chagrin, mostly unsubstantiated— of Whitemoor's misbehavior with young actors in local theater, as well as misspent weekends with the sons of prominent Key West developers and attorneys— interestingly, the very ones who had supported his run for the city commission. There were also stories of Whitemoor's involvement with internet pornography. Mac knew that Whitemoor would fall sooner or later.

*The sun eventually shines on every dog's ass,* he thought.

Mac desperately wanted to be the reporter who broke the story.

The intrepid journalist set those thoughts aside to focus on the night's main agenda item: Fantasy Fest. The annual event— Key West's biggest tourist attraction and money-maker— was six months away, and city officials and city staff, as well as the police department, had to make provisions for crowd control, the enforcement (or more typically non-enforcement) of nudity laws, and so forth. The audience, as every year when the Fest issue surfaced, was packed with religious zealots who would decry the debauchery. They would be shouted down by perverts already tugging at their zippers in anticipation of the event. Liberals and Chamber of Commerce representatives would defend the rights of the latter and Fantasy Fest would once again fill the tiny island's main street with countless thousands of 40 and 50-year-old drunks baring fat paunches and droopy tits. The bar owners would be happy. The hoteliers would be ecstatic. And the Chamber would scratch its corpulent, corporate belly with avaricious glee.

Mac had always believed that parades were meant for children. The Fantasy Fest parade, on the other hand, was no sight for a child's eyes. In fact, many adults were forced to look the other way.

Mayor Jimmy Dailey tapped his gavel on the imposing Oak dais and called the meeting to order.

"Would the City Clerk read the agenda, please?"

Josephine Woods read the single item in her distinctive monotone voice:

"A resolution allowing for the closure of city streets; providing for the funding of police officer overtime; for the cost of providing city services such as cleanup; waiving of the city's noise ordinance; and establishing community standards for nudity and/or body-painting; and other provisions for Fantasy Fest 2008."

"Do we have a representative present from Fantasy Fest?" Mayor Dailey asked the clerk.

"Ann Richardson is here speaking for the festival," the clerk replied.

"If Mrs. Richardson will take the podium..." the mayor asked.

"Yes, Mr. Mayor," Ann Richardson replied, as she stepped to the lectern.

"Ann, why don't you just outline for us what you're asking from the City this year. And if you'd state your name for the record..."

"Yes, Mr. Mayor, I'm Ann Richardson, Fantasy Fest Director. We're looking forward to an exciting Fest this year, with perhaps a record number of participants and visitors.

"As usual, for the parade on Saturday night, we will be asking that the City close and cordon off Whitehead Street— from Southard to Front and Duval Streets— together with the length of Duval Street up to South Street. Duval Street will be designated as a "party zone" for the final two nights, including parade night, and in that zone we are asking for the suspension of the noise ordinance as well as open container laws— provided that alcohol is transported in and consumed from plastic cups.

"We are also requesting that the City provide up to 200 hours of overtime for police and emergency workers. The festival marketing organization will provide the balance of funding.

"We are also requesting that the City's nudity law be relaxed, as it has in past years, to allow for the public display of 'body painting,' provided that said body paint is applied only to the upper portion of the anatomy and that neither female nor male genitalia be exposed."

*Ah, now we're getting to the nuts and bolts,* Mac noted to himself.

Richardson, a tall, graying woman in her late forties, was rather prim and elegant— belying her longtime directorship of one of the country's raunchiest block parties. But she was also a sharp businesswoman. Fantasy Fest made big bucks for both her marketing firm and the bars, restaurants and hotels in Key West's Old Town district. She had seen commissioners come and go. And she had seen public opinions swing drastically from year to year. One year there would be wide-open, rampant nudity in the streets. The

15

following year would produce an overly-reactive crackdown on partying. One year, in fact, there had even been armed police helicopters circling over the parade, shining bright search lights on the crowd to observe any hint of exposed flesh or other impropriety. The result was a hue and cry about "police state" tactics. The following year's Fest found police officers bending over backward, as it were, to avoid enforcing nudity laws.

If things held true to form, Richardson anticipated that this year's Fest would most likely see a relaxing of rules in response to some perceived overreaction by police and city officials in a few cases the previous year. Some "rogue officers" had once again attempted to reign in body-painting on public streets— in full view of passersby, including children.

"And so, Mr. Mayor and city commissioners," the director continued, "We ask that you approve these requests and join us in providing both the city of Key West and thousands of visitors with yet another fabulous and profitable Fantasy Fest.

"If you have any questions, I'll be happy to answer them."

With that, Richardson stepped respectfully from the podium and returned to her front row seat, facing the assembled body of city officials.

"I'm sure there will be some questions," noted Mayor Dailey. "We'll get to that later. But for now, are there any public speakers?"

A titter floated through the overflowing audience.

"There are 52 speakers signed up, Mayor," Mrs. Woods replied, bending over her microphone.

*This is going to be such a long night,* Mac thought. He was already thirsty for a beer.

"Considering the large number of speakers, and with the consent of the commission, I suggest speakers be limited to three minutes, for this item only," the mayor suggested. "All in favor?"

*Viva voce,* the commission agreed.

A grumble of discontent rumbled through the overflow audience.

"I would also encourage speakers, if your point has already been made by a previous speaker, please don't waste all of our time repeating the same point," Dailey added. "We all want to get out of here before midnight."

*Nice try,* McKinney applauded silently.

The first public speaker, not surprisingly, was the Reverend Theodore Adams, leader of the local Baptist Convention.

Tommy Whitemoor covered his face. Mac wondered if the action derived from disgust or shame.

"Fantasy Fest is the personification of the devil himself!" the fiery preacher began, his voice booming through the commission chambers. "And those who condone the work of the devil shall burn in the fires of Hell!"

One drunk in the rear of the commission chamber felt compelled to respond with a resounding "AMEN!"

McKinney chuckled.

*Welcome to Key West,* he thought.

Unperturbed, the good reverend continued, "More importantly, there is the matter of orphans…"

*Orphans?* Mac wondered.

"I could parade before this commission hundreds of pitiful children," Adams continued, "orphaned by the Mephisthophelean corruption that is alcoholism…"

*Oh,* those *orphans.*

"Not to mention the sin that pervades this so-called festival!" the reverend added. "I have provided to each of you commissioners copies of photos that were taken during last year's Fantasy Fest parade. As you view those disgusting photos, I think you must all agree with me that never has there been seen such a blatant display of prurient nudity in our small island community!"

*Obviously, he hasn't viewed my internet collection,* Commissioner Whitemoor giggled to himself.

"I urge you to reign in this sin and debauchery… to enforce the nudity laws which are among our city ordinances… to put a stop to the public drunkenness and open displays of *homosexual* behavior— an insult to God—and to think of the orphans!"

There was raucous applause from exactly half of the audience at Old City Hall. Boos of contempt erupted from the opposing half.

17

Mrs. Woods tapped the small, silver bell on her desk, signaling the good reverend's sermon had exceeded the 3-minute fire and brimstone limit.

"Think of the orphans!" Adams shouted once more, with his last desperate breath. He then stormed away from the podium and out of the commission chamber. As the doors of Old City Hall slammed behind him, Adams knew, as did everyone else in the chamber, that his appeal had fallen on deaf ears.

McKinney tapped a few brief notes into his laptop:

*Adams decries drunkenness, nudity and homosexual behavior...sanctifies orphans.*

"The next speaker is Victoria Pennekamp," the city clerk intoned.

The prissy president of Key West's Chamber of Commerce paraded, with much presumed pomp, down the central aisle of the chamber. As she marched to the podium, the pounding of her trademark red high heels reverberated in Mac's ears.

McKinney disliked Pennekamp almost as much as Whitemoor. She was the driving force behind the ever-increasing hordes of tourists making their way onto the island paradise—building condo/hotels and driving countless Conchs and their families out.

Even worse, she was the long time paramour of Mayor Jimmy Dailey. The thought of the two together in the sack gave the reporter the heaves. In satirical columns, McKinney had tagged her "Vicky Pantyhose."

"Mister Mayor and city commissioners," the deceivingly petite Pennekamp began, brushing her ebony hair away from one eye and to the side, "I am here tonight representing the Key West Chamber of Commerce, which wholeheartedly supports Fantasy Fest as an event which brings a considerable amount of tourism dollars to our town at a time of year which has traditionally been very slow economically."

*Pantyhose at her best,* Mac murmured under his breath.

"This has never been defined as a 'family' event. It has always been intended for adults. Over the years we've all seen attempts to limit behavior such as body painting during Fantasy

Fest. And it has always been met with opposition from both our locals and tourists.

"This festival is an annual cash cow for the city of Key West— its businesses and its service industry workers. Any attempt to 'water down' Fantasy Fest would severely impact us from both a fiscal and a public relations standpoint."

*Horse feathers,* Mac grumbled.

"I encourage you," Pennekamp charged, "to fully endorse this year's Fest and to provide all of the services and variances at the city's disposal."

The Chamber president received the same divided response of applause and boos afforded her evangelical predecessor. But she also received a number of wolf whistles as she shimmied her way back to her seat.

*Slut,* Mac thought.

*Slut,* Tommy Whitemoor thought.

*My slut,* the mayor grinned.

By 10:30 p.m., more than 25 citizens— representing business, religion, those of varied sexual orientation, varied gender and transgender, and varied states of sobriety— had expressed their opinions before the commission. At least one of the commissioners had nodded off more than once. And Mac was more than desperate for a beer.

His nemesis on the dais, Commissioner Whitemoor, could also virtually taste his overdue mango margarita. And the secret with which he had been entrusted earlier in the evening was beginning to make him nervous and fitful. He'd never been good at keeping secrets. But he knew that he had to hold this one close to his breast.

*All in good time, my pretty, all in good time...* he purred to himself.

Fortunately for all involved, the remainder of the 52 scheduled speakers had abandoned their right to be heard in favor of prime-time TV or a good night's sleep.

"That concludes the public speakers," Mrs. Woods informed the mayor and commissioners.

"Public comment being closed," Mayor Dailey said, tapping his gavel, "the commission will now move to discussion.

"Due to the late hour, with the consent of the commissioners, I would move that we approve the closure of streets and waiving of noise ordinance provisions, in order to expedite these proceedings."

"I second the motion," Whitemoor chimed in.

"Will the city clerk call the roll?"

The items were quickly and unanimously approved. But that was the easy part.

*I smell a continuance,* Mac thought. It was an occurrence that "due to the late hour" as well as his need for a Budweiser fix, he would not oppose. It was also not unexpected. It was a classic city commission tactic when controversial issues came before them. Get all the public speakers out of the way in a first meeting, maybe throw them a crumb or two like closing the streets… and save the really contentious issues for another meeting— when far fewer speakers would be likely to sign up to speak or even attend. Then they could appease the special interests without having to deal with the messy business of public input.

"That done," Mayor Dailey said, "I suggest that we continue discussion of police overtime funding and community standards until our next scheduled meeting."

The mayor's suggestion was seconded and approved without dissention.

*Go figure,* Mac thought.

## CHAPTER FOUR

# *Cigar Smoke-filled Rooms*

The two men who sat sipping Bucce in La Cantina, a small Cuban coffee shop in Miami's Little Havana, were both known and unknown to all of the elderly Cuban exiles who peopled the popular breakfast spot. It was their way: Known when they need to be known; unknown when they needed to be unknown.

Still, many necks craned to catch morsels of the men's conversation as they whispered quietly under the rhythmic strains of Latin Salsa music.

"We have received word," the slender, more aged and distinguished-looking Cuban began, "that change is under way."

Pausing only briefly to brush away gray cigar ash which had fallen from his Monte Cristo onto the sleeve of his blue pin-striped suit, he continued, "We have no details. Raúl has shut down all communication, throughout the capital. But from what we know, either El Diablo is dead or unable to exert any further control over his brother."

The eyes of his portly, balding companion flashed with excitement. His belly oozed out of his dingy white guayabera shirt as he leaned over the table in anticipation of further details.

"Are we sure, José?"

*"We* are sure of nothing," the elderly Cuban replied. "I have what I have heard from my sources in the capital. It is up to you and your sources in the streets of Havana to confirm what little we have heard and to provide us with more solid information.

"We are confident that Raúl is making his move. I don't need to tell you, my friend, that we must know his plans. We must know everything he knows... and more importantly, what the U.S. gov-

21

ernment knows— and plans to do. Our liaisons in Washington are in constant contact with us. But the jackass Raúl may have already begun negotiations with them. I need your people in Havana working night and day, Manuel. We must have this information and we must have it yesterday."

"Does Ramon know of these events?" Manuel asked.

"He does," José Castillo replied firmly. "He knows and he is anxious—as we all are."

Manuel "Manny" Caballero scratched his ass nervously. This could be the moment they had all waited so long for. He dreamed of returning home— returning in victory.

## CHAPTER FIVE

# *Lap Dancing Above the Fold*

It was nearly midnight by the time Mac's aging scooter sputtered to the crest of the Palm Avenue bridge, and the flat roof of his rustic houseboat came into view. As he pulled into the Garrison Bight parking lot and slid into his tiny space, he spotted a KWPD patrol car parked directly behind him. As soon as Mac turned off the ignition, the patrol car's overhead red and blues flashed on. Just as quickly, the lights were extinguished. It was a signal familiar to the reporter.

"Hey, John, wassup?" Mac asked, opening the passenger door of the police car and sliding onto the front seat next to KWPD Sergeant John Hardin— his best police department source.

"Well, I just got off Special Duty and thought I'd stop by and say hi."

"Special duty?" McKinney asked, knowing full well that Hardin had something to tell him.

"Well, right after the Commission meeting, I got the call to escort Juan-Carlo to the BareAss bar and park behind his car so he wouldn't get a ticket while he was enjoying his lap dances."

Mac laughed out loud. He was well aware of City Manager Juan-Carlo Valdez's penchant for the lap dancing establishments on Duval Street. But in the past, to Mac's knowledge, Juan-Carlo had always relied on City Code Enforcement toadies for backup.

Sargeant Hardin was clearly not happy with his latest assignment.

"I'm only here 'cause I bullied a newbie motorcycle cop into babysitting for me. Man, we really gotta put a stop to this crap!"

Mac had a good deal of respect for John Hardin. Not only was he the reporter's best source, he was a truly dedicated cop. He believed in law and order, truth, justice and the whole American thing. He was a family man, with two daughters about to start college. It was too bad, Mac thought, that he worked for a corrupt department headed by a do-nothing Chief who answered to lap-dancing, chicken-chasing city government officials.

Hardin had worked in the KWPD Detective Division for nearly 10 years. During that time, he had solved some of the city's most notorious crime cases. He dogged local criminals, tracking them even to other states via the internet. He was one of the few officers who cared.

Just a year ago, newly-appointed Chief Ray "Cuz" Dillard had returned Hardin to patrol duty suspecting that he might be leaking department "secrets" to the *Reporter* and other local media outlets.

Hardin didn't grouse or protest the demotion. He simply became more determined to try to clean up the police department, if not city government. But the more he tried, the more frustrated he became.

Sergeant Hardin was a lot like McKinney. And Mac felt fortunate to have him on his side.

"So what does 'Cuz' have to say about your special assignment?" Mac asked, fidgeting in his seat and fumbling awkwardly with the barrel of the unfamiliar shotgun which stood locked at attention in the seat between him and his friend.

"Shit, he's the one who made the call!" Hardin growled.

"Fuck."

"Yeah, fuck," Hardin agreed.

The thought of "Cuz" Dillard usually made Mac laugh. He had arrived in Key West from his native Alabama, where he had been a Boss Hogg sort of State Highway Patrol officer specializing in bogus speed traps. The City of Key West— looking for a "tough" Chief— had offered him more money than he'd ever dreamed of in the back woods of Alabama, as well as a few other quirky perks he had demanded.

"Cuz" refused to wear the Police Chief uniform, opting instead for Ralph Lauren polo shirts and green or yellow golf slacks.

He also declined to carry a weapon.

"I'd rather win the respect of citizens and criminals with my strong law enforcement presence," Dillard told the city manager at his hiring.

But the general consensus among KWPD officers had been quietly expressed by Hardin in an aside at a morning briefing.

"He's afraid of guns."

The Chief was also granted a special dispensation to live outside the city limits, up the Keys. So he saw or heard little of any crime at all in Key West. When he was in town, he lunched or supped with city officials, Chamber of Commerce types, or a small cabal of higher echelon officers with whom he had surrounded himself.

"Cuz" Dillard had moved to Key West to retire with benefits at a relatively young age. He wanted to wear the Chief's gold badge and ride around in the Chief's conspicuously unmarked patrol car. And he wanted no part of any negative press notoriety which might rock his comfortable boat.

But Cuz's lucrative contract with the City had included an unwritten clause. It was made clear to him shortly after his hiring that he was expected to be a "team player"— to provide cover, or look the other way when it came to certain minor failings of certain city officials and commissioners, as well as a few designated developers and local business leaders. A few county commissioners and even some magistrates fell under his tacit blanket of personal protection.

It was a lot of responsibility for one man, afraid of guns, to bear.

"I've got pictures," Hardin announced proudly.

"Huh?" Mac wondered.

"I used my digital to sneak photos of Juan-Carlo entering BareAss. Can you use 'em?"

He handed a small, black digital memory card to his trusted friend.

"It's good," Mac offered. "But you know he'll just claim he went in to check the bar's license or some other bullshit. We need more. Any way to get some shots of him inside… with a bimbo on his lap?"

"Jeez, you really want blood, don't you?"

"That would be nice," Mac said, laughing, "but a little bare tit would be even better. That'd be front page, above the fold. "

"Maybe we could pay Code Enforcement," Hardin joked. His mood had lightened a good deal since talking to McKinney.

"I don't make enough money," Mac replied. "Only those guys who run the T-shirt shops can afford that."

Hardin heard only half of what McKinney had said. His ear was bent attentively to the police receiver strapped to his shoulder. Mac could discern only scratchy garbled noise.

"Gotta go," Hardin said abruptly. "Important call. Drunks fighting on Higgs Beach."

"Hope you're wearing a vest," Mac joked.

"Yeah, they can be dangerous," the sergeant agreed. "More likely I'll end up with two of 'em puking in my back seat."

"I'll download the pics and get the memory card back to you," Mac said. "I'll hold 'em 'til we get some tit shots."

"Good," Hardin said. "I'll figure something out. See ya, Mac."

Mac exited the patrol car and Sergeant John Hardin, KWPD, sped off, red and blues flashing and siren blaring.

The reporter retrieved his laptop from the basket on his scooter and walked slowly down the narrow, floating dock toward his houseboat. He was rarely up that late and so took a moment to listen to the sound of croaking tree frogs and the night wind rattling palm fronds on the near shore.

*It's good to live in Key West,* Mac thought. Even though there's nothing but bars and bums.

His spirits rose even more as he entered his houseboat and felt the floor beneath his feet stir soothingly with the motion of the gentle waves of the Bight.

He took a beer from the 'fridge and settled into a comfy chair to watch a little *Fox News.*

Mac watched distantly as U.S. fighters bombed resistance positions in North Korea and he listened, inattentive, as Hillary denied the latest accusations that her presidential campaign had accepted donations from middle-eastern oil interests. But his real thoughts were of John Hardin.

He wasn't worried about Hardin dealing with drunks on Higgs Beach. He worried more that this sincere law enforcement officer was seriously jeopardizing his career and his family in a futile struggle against police department and city government corruption. And he worried that that he was helping him do just that... for a good story.

It was a constant struggle for McKinney— trying to balance the people's right to know with innocent victims who might fall by the wayside.

Mac's internal ethical struggles always ended with the same conclusion. He inevitably fell back on one Jeffersonian quote which had driven him into journalism and seen him through its emotional throes.

"The informed citizen," Jefferson said, "is the cornerstone of democracy."

Mac finished his beer, turned off the TV and went to bed. The waves lapping against the hull of his houseboat lulled him to sleep.

## CHAPTER SIX

# Gateway to Havana

Commissioner Whitemoor knew that he had a limited amount of time before his secret information exploded as a news alert on MSNBC. He had already read rumors and rumblings on internet blogs and witnessed chat room conversations perilously close to guessing what he already knew.

Whitemoor was intent upon getting his piece of the publicity pie. He just had to figure out the best way to do it.

His friend Raúl Castro's IM screen name had appeared as "offline" for two days. Whitemoor worried that he might lose control of news that could put him and his face on TV broadcasts around the world.

*Not bad for a tubby little queen from Key West,* he thought.

Whitemoor briefly considered simply calling the news networks and telling them what he knew. But he quickly abandoned the idea. Once the news was out, he figured, he'd be lost in the media shuffle. He knew that he had to come up with a plan that would make him, and perhaps Key West as well, *part of the news—* part of the opening of Cuba.

His mind raced in circles. He was in over his head, and he knew it.

The commissioner placed a call to his close "girlfriend," Victoria Pennekamp, at the Chamber of Commerce.

"You have to meet me for lunch at Latitudes," Whitemoor begged. "I need to pick your brain. I'm going to see if Ted will join us, too."

"You buying?" Pennekamp asked, quite seriously.

"Hell no!" Whitemoor shrieked. "What good is it being a city commissioner if I can't at least get free lunches from the Chamber of Commerce?"

With some reluctance about paying, Pennekamp agreed to lunch.

"Eleven forty-five boat," the commissioner advised her.

"Okay," she replied. "But maybe Ted will pay. He's got more money than the Chamber."

"We'll see."

Ted Lively grimaced when he saw the name *Tommy Whitemoor* appear on the incoming call screen of his private cell phone.

*Shit,* he muttered to himself.

Lively— the sole owner of Island Tours, Key West's predominant and highly profitable tour train operation— despised Whitemoor. But he viewed him as a necessary cost of doing business. He had even contributed heavily— more heavily than election laws permit, truth be known— to Whitemoor's commission campaign. He knew that Whitemoor was a simpleton. But he figured that should he by some outside chance win, he'd be one more vote added to those he already owned on the city commission. A few grand was a small price to pay, he figured. Again, just part of doing business.

"Hey, Tommy!" Lively answered the unwelcome call.

"I need you to join me and Vicky for lunch," the commissioner announced. "And you're paying!"

Lively laughed. While Whitemoor was a dunderhead, he was amusing.

"Eleven forty-five boat," Whitemoor told him.

"Okay. See ya there," Lively agreed.

Tommy Whitemoor chose the restaurant Latitudes for his luncheon meeting because it was the most secretive spot in Key West, being located on a tiny, privately-owned out-island named Sunset Key. The island and the restaurant could be reached only by a launch from the pier behind the fashionable Westin hotel, operated by the same owners of the island.

Native Conchs and long-time locals still called Sunset Key by its original name, Tank Island— a moniker derived from its original use as a fuel tank facility for Naval vessels in earlier years. When the new owners purchased the islet, they figured "Tank Island" would summon up few romantic vacation images and thus renamed it Sunset Key— despite the fact that its development partially blocked the previously unimpeded shore view of Key West's famous sunset.

When Tommy Whitemoor arrived at Pier B behind the Westin, his luncheon companions were already aboard the small launch which would carry the party to Sunset Key. But their departure would be delayed because of the concurrent arrival of a giant cruise ship, the Disney *Magic*.

Not only had the developers of Sunset Key managed to block the view of the sunset, they'd also figured out a way to block the view of their own development by using their pier as a port facility for cruise ships. Offering lucrative, low-maintenance disembarkation fees, cruise ships provided a huge cash cow for both the resort and the city.

As the commissioner gingerly stepped aboard the launch, the *Magic's* calliope-style ship's horn blared out the first bar of Disney's signature tune, "When you wish upon a star."

"Is that for me?" Whitemoor asked as he took his seat on the launch beside his friends.

"Well, this boat *is* called the *'Little Princess,'*" Pennekamp noted cattily.

*"Bitch!"* the commissioner snarled.

The launch to the restaurant could not depart until the *Magic*— dubbed by locals "the Mouse Boat"— had secured its lines to the dock. But after ten minutes, the three were winding their way toward Sunset Key. It was a short trip of seven minutes to lunch on the exclusive islet.

The three sat at a beachside table, on its own raised, wooden deck. Surrounded by pristine, white Bahamian sand— unlike any native to Tank Island or even Key West itself— they ordered drinks and talked small until Tommy Whitemoor was ready to broach the subject matter for his meeting.

"Here's what I wanted to talk about," he began abruptly. "I want to know how each of you feel about the possibility of Cuba opening and what it will mean to Key West. I mean, how will it affect our tourism economy and, well, quite frankly... the three of us."

Ted Lively was unaccustomed to discussing such weighty, geopolitical issues with low-level public servants of Whitemoor's ilk. Still, the topic was one in which he had a great interest, both personal and financial. And he was especially curious as to why Whitemoor was raising the question. Did he know something?

Pennekamp, on the other hand, was more interested in devouring her shrimp cocktail.

"That's a complex and debatable question," Lively answered quite seriously. "If you read and listen to the opinion of political reporters like Mac McKinney..."

"I **don't**!" Pennekamp interjected with a distinct note of disdain for McKinney.

"Horse feathers!" Lively chided her. "You may not like him, but you read him. Just like we all do. It's called knowing your enemy.

"But as I was saying, McKinney is always on a soap box about the opening of Cuba. He predicts that it will be a death knell for Key West."

"How so?" Whitemoor wondered.

"His premise is that after 40 years of being prohibited from visiting Havana, hordes of curious Americans will descend on Cuba. I think he's absolutely right about that. There's a great deal of curiosity among baby-boomers who remember seeing Cuban night spots in old movies and remember the Cuban TV character Ricky Ricardo.

"But his theory continues that tourists from New York, Chicago, L.A. or Atlanta will fly to Miami and from there, directly to Havana... completely bypassing Key West. He proffers that Key West has nothing to offer tourists when compared to Cuba. That's the part of his theory I disagree with— sort of."

"Sort of?" Pennekamp asked.

Whitemoor sipped his mango margarita and listened intently.

"Well, it's true that Key West has just about exhausted its uniqueness. We're pretty much a Disneyland destination now. Havana will undoubtedly offer all the sin, vice and gambling one

31

could imagine— much more even than Key West. And it's true that many airlines will schedule direct flights from Miami to Havana. But if we have time to develop things our way, we can create the image of Key West as the 'gateway' to Havana... the way it used to be. At one time, there was regular ferry service between Havana and Key West. And I think that we'll see that again. In fact, I have my money on it."

"Do tell," Whitemoor begged.

"Are we on the record here?" the tourist entrepreneur asked.

"Hell no, it's just us guys," Whitemoor advised.

"Beg pardon?" Pennekamp growled.

"And ladies," the commissioner corrected himself.

"Well, truth is I'm counting heavily on Cuba opening up soon," Lively said. "I've already lined up space at the ferry terminal here and I've made certain arrangements with contacts in Havana to provide the first tour train service as soon as the opening occurs. I hate to brag, but I'll be up and running tourists all over that island before Fidel feels the first effects of rigor mortis."

"Big surprise," Pennekamp intoned. "I think we all knew that. And since when do you hate to brag?"

"Gateway to Havana..." Whitemoor repeated Lively's words. "I like that. It sounds like a good way to go. It could save our asses."

"It could be the only thing that will," Lively noted ominously.

Victoria Pennekamp sat twiddling her thumbs and frowning.

"You don't agree with Ted's analysis?" Whitemoor asked.

"No," she answered bluntly. "And I certainly don't agree with that asshole McKinney. Key West will always be a prime tourist destination. We'll always have that great unwashed— the camper crowd and that trailer trash from the cruise ships— those people who can't afford or don't want to leave the U.S. just to go snorkeling or gambling."

"Hey, that trailer trash bought me a five million dollar house on Shark Key!" Lively laughed.

"Indeed," the Chamber maven agreed. "As long as cruise ships continue to stop here and as long as the great unwashed continue to max out their MasterCards on our $200-a-night hotel rooms, we'll all do well. I don't see any end to that in the immediate future. Unless Tommy knows something we don't know."

"But will cruise ships still stop here when they can just go directly to Havana?" Whitemoor pondered.

"It's a good question," Lively noted. "That's why I, for one businessman, am prepared to cover that shortfall should it occur."

"Well, I guess you've both answered my question," Whitemoor said. "I think I've picked up some pretty good advice."

He meant what he said. He was particularly interested in the "gateway to Havana" concept Lively had presented. And as he stared past the beach and the swaying palms of Sunset Key, the imposing figure posed by the Disney *Magic* docked just across the harbor gave him the germ of another idea.

"Okay, Tommy," said Ted Lively, "Now tell us what this is all about. What do you know?"

"Oh, nothing, Ted. I just figure that the opening can't be far off and I'm just feeling out how I should vote on any issues that might be coming up."

"That's a no-brainer, Tommy," said Lively, "You vote the way we tell you to vote."

All three laughed. But all three knew that what Lively had said was true.

The waiter presented the $250 lunch tab to Whitemoor, who casually slid it across the table to Pennekamp. She, in turn, handed it demurely to Lively.

"Thank you so much for lunch," she purred.

"It's always a pleasure, my dear Vicky."

Whitemoor chuckled.

The three Key West movers and shakers made their way back to the mother island. As the small launch shrunk in the shadow of the massive Disney cruise ship, Whitemoor thought again that this great leviathan might be of use to him... of great use in the very near future.

## CHAPTER SEVEN

# *"Just leave out the bimbo part..."*

Tuesday morning— two days before the *Reporter* went to press— nearly always found Mac McKinney scrambling for a lead news story. David Conrad, his editor and publisher had come to rely on him for blockbuster, above-the-fold pieces— preferably involving corruption in city government. Some grew into long-term investigative reports. Occasionally he could get away with a commentary about Key West's burgeoning chicken population, or a "think piece" examining the potential effects of computer voting, or some of his ponderous pontificating regarding the opening of Cuba.

Somehow, between Mac and his editor, the two always managed to place a story or two on page one that kept the city talking. It was a source of pride for the veteran reporter. He had even named his new 22-foot McGregor sailboat— his one luxury in life, purchased for the grandiose sum of $3,000— *Front Page.*

But McKinney was a procrastinator by nature. There were weeks— though rare— when he kept Conrad sweating bullets until press morning. This Tuesday found him no further ahead with a lead story than usual. And it was no mystery to him who was on the other end of the call that set his cell phone ringing so early in the morning.

"Whatcha got?" Conrad asked, the usual tone of desperation in his voice.

"Hot!" Mac answered, the usual tone of bullshit in his voice. "It's really hot. Still working on it, though. Gotta talk to a couple more sources."

"Goddammit, Mac, it's Tuesday. You know we go to press on Thursday. What have you got? I don't care if it's tightened up yet— just give me some idea so I can save the space. We've got a lot of ads this week. How many words?"

"Jeez, David, we go through this every Tuesday. And every Thursday we have a great front page. Gimme a break. How many words? How the hell would I know 'til I've written it?"

"Okay, okay. Just give me an idea of what you're working on. It'll make me feel better. I won't have to drink so much tonight."

*Time for some tap dancing,* Mac thought.

"Okay, I've got some good stuff on Juan-Carlo and the lap dancers."

"Pictures?" Conrad asked anxiously. "What's the angle?"

"Well, some weak pics. But it's really more about how he's using city personnel, mainly the KWPD, to stand guard for him."

"Hmmmm," Conrad pondered. "We've covered this before. But if you've got something concrete about him using the cops, then that could put him in the hot seat. More importantly, it could put Chief Dillard in the hot seat. I like it."

McKinney actually felt better about the scrap of a story he had.

"I told you it's hot, didn't I?"

"Sure, sure. You got confirmed sources?"

"Rock solid," Mac assured his editor. "The usual 'reliable source close to...'"

"You mean Hardin?"

"Yeah. He's hot about it, too."

"Good. Flesh it out and get it over to me as soon as you can. Try to get some comment from Juan-Carlo and the Chief, too."

"Already in the works," Mac fibbed. "I've got calls into both of them."

"Cool! Get it to me as soon as you can."

"Yeah. By Thursday," Mac said, abruptly ending the conversation.

Sergeant Hardin would be happy. The gritty reporter would whip the lap-dancing incident into a front page story. He plugged Hardin's memory card into his computer and brought up the photos the officer had taken. They were dark and grainy. But using Photoshop he was able to clean one up well enough to make clear the image of Key West's ever-horny city manager shuffling into a well-known sex spot.

Before contacting Cuz Dillard and Valdez himself, there were a couple of issues that McKinney wanted to clear up first. He placed a call to Hardin.

"Sergeant Hardin," a familiar, authoritative voice answered on the first ring.

"Mac here, John."

"Hey, bubba."

"Listen, we're gonna run with the Juan-Carlo story, pics and all. But I wanted to check with you on a couple of things..."

"Yeah?"

"The photo of Juan-Carlo shows the front of your patrol car. Any way the Chief or Internal Affairs can identify it as yours?"

The officer thought for a moment.

"I'll have to take a look at how you're cropping it, but I don't think so. But that really doesn't make any difference, 'cause Cuz assigned me there."

"Shit, that's right."

"Besides, IA already has a pretty good idea who your source is," Hardin added. "And there's not a lot they can do to me at this point."

*"Oh yeah,* all they can do is cut your cojones off!"

"It'll take a better man than Cuz Dillard to do that," Hardin replied.

McKinney stared at the photo on his computer screen.

"Listen," he said, "I think I can crop this so tightly that no one can tell it was shot from a patrol car. We'll lose a little of the signage on the BareAss Bar, but that's okay. Everyone will recognize the venue. And it'll keep you somewhat safer. Okay?"

"Cool," the sergeant replied. "I'm heading into the station for the morning briefing now. Call me if I can help with anything."

"You've already helped," Mac told him. "Now I've just got to try to pull some bullshit out of Juan-Carlo and Cuz."

"That shouldn't be hard," Hardin offered.

"You're so right, pal."

"Oh, by the way…" the sergeant added, "A bike officer told me he spotted the pedocommish heading over to Sunset Key last Sunday for lunch with Ted Lively and Vicky Pantyhose. Wonder what that was all about."

"Damn, that is interesting," Mac agreed. "Ted's probably building another million-dollar-per-unit 'affordable housing' condo project. Who knows. But I'll check into it.

"Meantime, John, keep your head down."

"You betcha, pal," Sergeant Hardin agreed. "My mama didn't raise any fools."

Mac suddenly, and quite unintentionally, found himself in reporter mode. He placed a call to the city manager.

"City Manager's office, this is Debbie," the call was answered promptly and politely.

"Hi, Debbie. It's Mac McKinney. Juan-Carlo available?"

"Oh, I'm sure he'll talk to you, Mr. McKinney. Hold one second, please."

Mac poised his fingers on the computer keys.

"Mac! What's up, bubba?"

Juan-Carlo Valdez's glad-handing, spin-conscious, "One Human Family" voice was unmistakable to the reporter.

"Oh, just the usual crap," Mac replied, "Looking for a story, stirring the shit."

Even over the phone, the reporter could hear Juan-Carlo's booming laughter resound throughout City Hall.

"That's why I like you, Mac. No bullshit with you."

In fact, Valdez really did like McKinney. At the same time, he was confident that he could manipulate him with calculated misinformation as long as he threw him an exclusive news crumb every now and then. It was something of a symbiotic relationship. McKinney knew more about him than any other reporter because the two shared a mutual alliance with District Two Commissioner Henry Becker, the most powerful bubba on the city commission. It was a quid pro quo relationship that occasionally made McKinney's Gonzo form of journalism somewhat uncomfortable at times— times such as this.

"Sources tell me…." Mac introduced the topic.

"Uh oh, I'm in trouble," the city manager volunteered with humor. "This have anything to do with the chickens?"

"Naw, I'm saving the chickens for next week. This week I'm hearing about you spending some time at BareAss after last Tuesday night's commission meeting. I don't want to get pushy, but you got any comment?"

"Aw come on, Mac. You're not gonna publish that, huh? My wife's been giving me hell about it lately. She's got that hot Cuban temper, ya know. Can't you just lay off this one?"

The cocoa butter— a Key West Conch term for extreme schmoozing— was flowing palpably through the phone line.

"Hey, Juan-Carlo, you know I would if I could. But hell, even the *Citizen* is starting to ask questions about the lap-dancing business. You haven't exactly kept it a secret."

"Mea culpa," Valdez cried. "Can I get away with checking occupational licenses?"

"If it were just me, fine," Mac said. "But there are witnesses this time. One says you used police backup. That complicates the issue."

"Hey, that wasn't *my call!*" the city manager protested. "I can't help who follows me around."

"Can I quote you on that?" Mac asked.

"Fuck. No. Say that I routinely have a police escort after commission meetings."

"Taxpayers covering the cost?" Mac pressed.

"Shit. Okay, I routinely have a courtesy police escort after commission meetings. Maybe you can add that it's for protection against asshole reporters!"

Mac could once again hear Valdez's laughter bouncing off the City Hall walls.

"Just kidding about that last part, off the record," the city manager added.

"Sure," Mac noted. "Just let me get this on the record. You're acknowledging that you were at the night spot in question, with an unnamed bimbo bouncing on your lap and the cops were out front in a routine escort capacity. Right?"

"Well," Juan-Carlo chuckled, "you word it best for both of us. I'll trust you. Just leave out the bimbo part and make me look good."

"Did I say I have photos?" McKinney asked.

"Fuck. Hope it's my good side."

"Yeah, it's your ass going into BareAss."

"Strictly city business," Valdez said. "It's a tough job, but somebody's gotta do it."

McKinney laughed.

"Okay, Juan-Carlo. I'll go easy on you, but I'm gonna have to lay into Cuz for calling out the troops. You got a problem with that?"

"No, none. Truth be known, he's probably trying to set me up."

McKinney knew that Chief Dillard had found himself on a short leash of late. The Chief had tried to assume a little too much power and Mac could tell that the city manager was more than happy to put him on notice publicly. Valdez would happily deep-six Dillard to save himself.

"Okay, that's it," Mac told Valdez. "I've gotta call Cuz, then I'll see ya in the paper on Friday."

"Sonofabitch, you're good," Valdez said. "I'm gonna have to have the Port Authority raise the rent on your houseboat slip!"

*Fuck,* Mac thought, *he's probably not kidding.*

McKinney had Debbie transfer him back to the city hall switchboard where he asked for Chief Dillard.

His call was answered by the PIO, the Police Public Information Officer— a tight-assed witch named Sheila.

"Mister McKinney, the Chief has requested that I take your call in the hope that I might be able to answer your inquiries," the PIO bleated in an irritating voice.

"Nope, I want to talk to Cuz," Mac informed her.

"Well, sir, I can only pass your questions along to the Chief. If you'd like to fax them to my office, I'll be glad to do that."

"So the Chief is refusing to answer questions from the media? Has he informed the city manager of that position? The city attorney? Is he anxious for a First Amendment debate in the media? Are you willing to be named as a complicit party in a lawsuit?"

Mac knew well how to intimidate underlings and he relished in the practice.

"If you'll hold, Mr. McKinney, I'll see if the Chief will speak with you."

Mac utilized his time on hold to closely crop Hardin's photo of Valdez to the point where his patrol car might be unidentifiable.

"Chief Dillard," a pompous voice boomed in Mac's ear.

"Good morning, Chief. It's Mac McKinney. Thanks for taking my call. Wondered if you might have a minute to talk about a story I'm working on for this week's edition of the *Key West Reporter*."

"I'd really prefer that reporters fax any questions to me and I'll respond," the Chief snapped.

"I'm sure I appreciate that," Mac responded, doing his best to restrain his ire, "But I find that paper trails, such as facsimile documents, can come back to haunt one... either you or myself. So I'd rather just ask you the questions while I have you and take down your responses for the record. That okay with you, Cuz?"

"Go ahead, sir, how may I help you?"

McKinney could feel the bile in the Chief's voice two miles away.

"Well, sir," Mac began his interrogation, "can you confirm that, following last Tuesday night's city commission meeting, at least one KWPD patrol car and possibly a motorcycle officer were dispatched to guard the city manager's vehicle while he was present at a Duval Street nightspot featuring a popular activity commonly referred to as 'lap-dancing'?"

Mac grinned as the length of the pause between question and answer grew.

"Sir, I would have to have my PIO obtain dispatch tapes to confirm or deny any such assumption of fact. Again, if you will fax me the inquiry in detail, including date and time, I will attempt to supply you with an adequate response."

*No wonder he doesn't carry a gun,* Mac thought. *He'd only shoot himself in the mouth.*

"Chief, you can check the tapes all you want, but isn't it a fact that you, yourself, ordered a patrol car to escort Juan-Carlo Valdez from Old City Hall to the BareAss Club last Tuesday night?

And do you consider that a prudent and cost-efficient use of taxpayer dollars?"

"Look, punk..." the Chief started, then gathered his limited wits, "Mr. McKinney, city commission meetings often run late and I do consider it prudent to provide a certain amount of police protection to our city officials. For security reasons, that is the extent to which I will comment regarding your inquiry. Any other questions you may have will be responded to in a timely manner through the requested method of facsimile. Good day, sir."

"Then I can't ask you why you won't wear a gun?" Mac managed to squeak before being hung up on.

The intrepid reporter leaned back in his chair and chortled to himself. He had his story. He had his man— page one, above the fold.

## CHAPTER EIGHT

# *Cuba Libre!*

Manny Caballero was enjoying a cold, longneck Hatuey beer and playing an intense game of dominoes with friends when he caught sight of José Castillo walking through the ornately carved teak doors of La Cantina. The old man was wearing a flawlessly pressed white suit and sporting a white panama hat, which was cocked to one side.

The impeccably-dressed Cuban cast a meaningful eye toward Caballero as he took a seat in a secluded booth near the back of the bistro. Manny knew that his presence had been requested.

The old man looked especially anxious, Caballero thought. He would be asking about what Manny had learned, which wasn't one hell of a lot. Havana was sealed off, as tight as a rum barrel.

"You should cut back on the Hatuey, Manuel" Castillo remarked as his friend forced his substantial belly into the tight booth. "You may soon need to be down to your fighting weight."

"You have news?" Caballero asked.

"My friend, you are the one who was to deliver news to me. Have you heard from your sources in Habana?"

Caballero shifted nervously in his seat.

"The whole island is sealed off, José. I've never seen it like this. From the mountains of the Sierra Maestra to the Malecon, I can't squeeze a word out of my sources. In fact, I can't even reach most of them."

"I'm not surprised, my friend. Raúl has issued a gag order unprecedented even by Habana standards. Our friends speak on pain of death.

42

"But in fact I do have news, Manuel. Big news."

Caballero sensed the excitement in Castillo's voice. At the same time, he perceived foreboding in the old Cuban's eyes.

"Tell me, José. Is he dead?"

Castillo enjoyed the pleasure of a long, sensual puff from his Monte Cristo.

"Is he dead, damn it?" Manny squeaked anxiously.

"You rush me, my friend. Our business here is multifarious. It is both pleasurable and deathly. Such business, my friend, must be savored, as a fine port wine."

Caballero hated being toyed with. He slurped down the remaining *Hatuey*.

"We are convinced— that is the movement and Ramon Sanchez— are convinced that Fidel is dead."

Even as his spirits soared, Manny's heart sank into his stomach. The news he had waited 30 years to hear filled him with so many emotions that he could barely contain them. Nor could he discern one from another. Hate, nationalism, regret, pride and fear flew through his psyche and collided with one another in a whirlwind of confusion.

Manny's mind flashed back to his boyhood on his father's tobacco farm at the foot of the Sierra Maestra. He recalled the excitement surrounding Castro's revolution— the excitement among the people that the brutal dictator Fulgencio Batista would soon be overthrown. And his mind flashed then on his father's tears, and his own, upon hearing that the family's land would be seized by Castro's communist state. He remembered his sense of total loss and bewilderment as his weeping parents had reluctantly loaded their only son onto the *Pedro Pan* "freedom flight" headed for America.

Tears flowed from Caballero's eyes and he rested his head in his hands on the bucce-stained table.

José Castillo felt Manny's pain.

"Cry, my friend," he comforted Caballero. "Cry freely— for it is free that our people may soon be. God willing, the tyrant is dead. And God willing, we will soon see the return of our homeland."

Caballero composed himself and looked into the old man's eyes.

"Are you sure?"

"We are 99 percent sure that Fidel is dead. The story of how we found out is quite interesting, even funny, given the history of events."

"Tell me, José."

"One of our operatives serves as a limousine driver for the party. He told of being ordered several days ago to pick up young Elian Gonzalez and his father, Juan-Miguel, in Cardenas and drive them to the capital on a matter of utmost importance.

"After more than an hour, his passengers returned to the limousine. Our operative reported that both the boy and his father appeared distraught, grief-stricken. The boy was sobbing and repeating the words, 'Muerte! Muerte!'

"It is somewhat ironic that news of Fidel's death would come from the mouth of a child— the very child he chose to represent the future of his 'revolution.'"

"And this has convinced you of Fidel's death?" Caballero wondered.

"That report, plus others from sources deep within the regime. We even have reports from Key West that Raúl has made contact there.

"Also, we have received word from our Washington sources that Raúl has begun negotiations with U.S. officials. What we are not sure about is how Raúl and those U.S. officials will handle the transition."

"The administration is on our side," Caballero noted.

"They *appear* to be on the side of the Cuban exiles," Castillo agreed. "But appearances can be deceiving, my friend. We saw how they handled the affair of the Gonzalez boy. For that very reason, we are concerned that the administration may cut a deal with Raúl which would allow him to maintain control of land seized by his brother during the revolution— in exchange for what will be called 'Democratization,' and will be perceived as a victory for the administration here in the U.S.

"That, my friend, is something we cannot allow."

"Never," Caballero concurred. "But tell me, José, what are our plans now? What can we do?"

"For now we must await the official announcement from Havana. And we must await the official response from Washington. In the meantime, Raúl Sanchez is on his way to the U.S. capital now to represent the expatriates. We are hoping for a meeting with the president.

"But you and I, together with our own forces, must be prepared for the worst. We must begin planning now to fight for the recovery of our land. Raúl Castro must not be allowed to steal it once again from us."

"Never," Caballero agreed. "Never."

*"Cuba Libre!"* José Castillo whispered.

*"Cuba Libre!"* Manny softly returned the wish, while grasping his old friend's hand and pressing it tightly.

45

## CHAPTER NINE

# *Tips from the City Manager*

Juan-Carlo Valdez stopped for his ritual cafe con leche at El Siboney. The strong Cuban coffee cleaned out the cobwebs remaining from the evening before, and he was always among friends. It was the way the city manager chose to start his day. But this Friday morning he was greeted with a great number of titters and sniggers from the local patrons as he approached the breakfast counter.

"Hey Juan-Carlo!" his old friend, federal magistrate Lou Morgan, called to him from a window booth, "What's wrong, you not getting enough at home?"

The titters turned to open laughter and the sniggers grew to generous guffaws.

Juan-Carlo knew immediately the source of the widespread hilarity among the El Siboney regulars.

*That fucking McKinney and the* Reporter.

Rosita handed Valdez his con leche and subtly tucked a copy of the dreaded newspaper under his arm.

"Thanks, Rosita," he said. "Should I read it?"

"Is all lies," Rosita comforted him. "But still, it make me laugh."

Valdez took the time to shake a few hands and greet a few friends before seating himself, alone, in a dimly-lit corner booth. Following a few fortifying sips of the strong coffee, he cautiously unfolded the tabloid-style newspaper.

*Please, not front page…*

There it was— page one, replete with photo, above the fold:

46

## KWPD CHIEF WATCHES CITY MANAGER'S BEHIND; VALDEZ LAPS IT UP
### By Mac McKinney

Following last Tuesday night's city commission meeting, City Manager Juan-Carlo Valdez was given a police escort while he visited a Duval Street night spot dedicated to an activity known as lap-dancing. According to a reliable source, the KWPD officer was assigned by Police Chief Ray "Cuz" Dillard.

"I was there checking occupational licenses," Valdez told *The Reporter.* "And the police escort wasn't my call. You'd have to ask Cuz Dillard about that."

Contacted on Tuesday for comment, Chief Dillard was reluctant to respond to any questions not submitted in writing. But when pressed, he told *The Reporter,* "City commission meetings often run late and I do consider it prudent to provide a certain amount of police protection to our city officials."

Asked if Dillard thought providing police protection for city officials visiting sex emporiums might be a good use of taxpayer dollars, Dillard declined further comment.

"For security reasons, that is the extent to which I will comment regarding your inquiry," he said.

Sources told *The Reporter* that a rift has grown between Valdez and Dillard and that the Chief's assignment of an officer to accompany the city manager may not have been purely for his protection.

Valdez seemed to agree, saying, "Truth be known, he's probably trying to set me up."

Following interviews with both Valdez and Dillard, *The Reporter* uncovered and contacted the lap-dancer who had "serviced" the city manager. She agreed to comment on the condition of anonymity.

"He's fun!" she said. "He's always a gentleman— well almost always— and he tips great!"

Stay tuned for more on how well Valdez tips.

—

The city manager laughed out loud, causing heads to turn throughout the restaurant.

"You gotta love this paper!" he declared to anyone who might be listening. And he meant it.

Valdez reread and analyzed every word and sentence in the news story. He was pleased. While he knew he'd be in minor trouble at home, he'd managed to feed McKinney just what he wanted published. He'd known that the reporter would quote his "set up" remark, and that was exactly what he wanted. It served two purposes. Firstly, it shifted overall responsibility for the whole incident to the Chief's shoulders. Secondly, it laid the foundation for his plan to eventually oust Dillard.

"Uno mas con leche, Rosita!" Valdez called to his favorite waitress. "And an order of Cuban bread."

## CHAPTER TEN

# *Bogey and Bacall*

Trying desperately to awaken his thoughts—any thoughts whatever— on this placid, Spring Key West morning, Tommy Whitemoor delicately sipped a mimosa from its Lalique crystal flute as he lolled languorously in a well-worn, wicker chaise lounge at the edge of the mosaic-tiled pool. The sun was just beginning to cut multi-angled slats of light through the Traveler's Palms, which arched high above the lush central garden of Casa Whitemoor.

To amuse himself, Whitemoor was indifferently tossing sunflower seeds to his pet twin peacocks, *Bogey* and *Bacall*. It was one of the few ways he had found to quiet their interminable morning cat-calls.

"The neighbors will be grateful," his mother observed, handing her son the morning newspapers. On top of the small pile of one daily and two weeklies, lay the *Key West Reporter.*

"Oh mother, must you ruin my morning?"

The freshman commissioner was a fan of neither the *Reporter* nor Mac McKinney, but he read both religiously. Anyone involved with or interested in Key West politics would have been foolish not to.

"It's best to know your enemy," Maria Whitemoor warned her wayward son.

"Whatever," Tommy replied nonchalantly. "This is one divine mimosa. You've outdone yourself, mother."

Ignoring his indolence, Maria disappeared through the lush foliage in the direction of her artist's studio. She prized painting with the diffused garden light of the morning sun.

Downing the remainder of his wake-up mimosa for courage, Tommy retrieved a chic pair of red enamel-rimmed reading glasses from the pocket of his bathrobe and cautiously glanced at the front page of the *Reporter*. He was ever fearful that his name would appear in the banner headline.

He was delighted to see that McKinney had chosen the police chief and city manager as this week's targets.

"My god, that tacky Juan-Carlo and her lap-dancing again!" he shrieked to himself and, by happenchance, *Bogey* and *Bacall*. The birds seemed unfazed as they continued to peck at the seeds cast carelessly about the pool's edge.

Whitemoor chuckled to himself as he read. He secretly relished the misfortune of others.

## CHAPTER ELEVEN

# *The Big Guns*

Two blocks away in his City Hall office, Police Chief "Cuz" Dillard was not so amused.

"I want Toler and Newly in here *now*," he growled through the intercom to his secretary.

Captain Andy Toler was the Chief's friend and closest adviser. Captain Allen Newly served as Chief Internal Affairs Officer.

Both officers had already seen the *Reporter*, and neither was surprised to be ordered to Dillard's office.

Newly shook visibly as he sat in one of the two oversize leather chairs facing the Chief's massive Oak desk. At five foot-two, he felt lost in the enormous chair. He knew that he was about to be called on the carpet because of the story in the *Reporter*. But he wasn't sure how he could be to blame. Newly had made the rank of Captain by default when Dillard fired his predecessor, and he had barely passed the captain's exam. On top of that, he was gay— a fact which he knew irritated the Chief. Newly knew quite well that the city's official slogan, "One Human Family" was merely P.C. lip service to the large gay community— a population truly *tolerated* by the old-time Conchs.

Captain Toler, a moose of a man, was not so easily intimidated by the Chief. He sat confidently, adjusting the twin .45's strapped to his waist. For effect, he tugged at the cuff of his right pant leg, partially revealing the hidden .38 police special. It was rumored among the force— even strongly considered fact— that Toler was routinely armed with a total of *five* weapons. He never revealed the type or caliber of the remaining armament, nor where it might be concealed.

51

"The really big gun's between my legs," he liked to rag junior officers.

Chief Dillard ceased the incessant shuffling of papers on his desk and stared grimly at the two officers seated before him.

"I want to know McKinney's source," he barked. "I want to know who it is and I want to know *now*."

Newly shifted nervously in his chair.

"We've known for months who it is," Toler said. "It's John Hardin. Only thing is, we can't document it. He won't confess to I.A. And if we try to bump him from the force, he'll go running to the Civilian Review Board."

"What about the dispatch tapes?" Newly asked. "Since you assigned Hardin, Chief, wouldn't that prove he was the one?"

Dillard bristled at the naïve remark.

"That particular tape was accidentally erased," Captain Toler noted quickly. "It's not clear who assigned Hardin to watch the city manager."

He knew what Cuz Dillard wanted to hear.

"Newly, I want Hardin in your office being grilled today," the Chief warned, leaning ominously over his desk and lecturing the young officer. "I want this leak sealed. As Chief I.A. Officer, that's your job. Do it. You're dismissed for now. But I want to briefed at the end of the day."

Captain Newly stood and saluted, relieved to be freed from the Chief's wrath. He wasted no time charging toward the door.

"Nail the sonofabitch!" Dillard called after him.

"Now, you..." the Chief turned his gaze to Toler. "You're sure that tape is taken care of?"

"It was erased five minutes after I leave your office," Toler assured him. "You can count on it."

"I will. And I want you to bypass Newly, too— unofficially. He hasn't got the cojones to strong-arm Hardin. I need you to do that. Catch him someplace outside HQ and make it clear that we're not happy with his performance."

"What about Valdez?" Toler asked.

"He wants my ass, Andy. He's building a file. But this time he's involved and I won't let him forget that. I'm gonna keep the focus of this one on him— even if I have to call that damned reporter myself. I've got far more dirt on him than he's got on me."

Toler wondered about that. Valdez had a reputation as a ruthless hatchet-man. If the title fight came down to Valdez and Dillard, Captain Toler was prepared to put his money on the city manager. He had already made that clear— in closed-door meetings— to Valdez. If Cuz Dillard got the axe, Toler was poised to assume the position.

"Not to worry, Cuz, I've got your Six," the Chief's friend and number one adviser assured him.

*And I'm damn close to having your job, Toler thought to himself.*

# CHAPTER TWELVE
## *"I Am Cuba"*

Mac McKinney quickly scanned the front page of his Friday morning edition. Having proofread it before publication, this was a surface perusal, focused only on the general cosmetics of the paper— were the photos right-side up, was the masthead legible, and so forth. Mac was pleased with the photo of Key West's city manager entering the lap-dancing club. While it was dark and somewhat blurred, that obscurity actually added to the perceived surreptitiousness of the whole sordid affair.

*What a slime ball,* Mac thought.

Satisfied that another delectably controversial issue of The Reporter had hit the streets, seedy bars, and deal-cluttered desks of corrupt city officials throughout Key West, Mac returned to his primary focus of attention, *Imus Returns* on the newly-established Trump Network.

The acerbic curmudgeon and his political observations and biases had always appealed to the reporter. Don Imus— a.k.a. The I-Man— was for sure an acquired taste. Mac was certain that he was one of only two people in the entire city of Key West both politically astute and diabolically twisted enough to appreciate and religiously watch the early morning talk show.

Mac had suffered withdrawal when the I-Man was fired from MSNBC and CBS for his "nappy-headed ho" remark. And he was delighted when, only months later, Donald Trump purchased the floundering CNN network, renamed it Trump Network and immediately made Imus his morning headliner. He was less excited but equally amused that Trump had also given Rosie O'Donnell her own afternoon talk show.

54

This morning, Imus was lecturing his toady sidekick, Charles McCord, on the immorality of Hillary Clinton.

"She's EVIL!" he screamed into the mike, feigning the fervency of an evangelical preacher. "She's THE DEVIL!"

McKinney was just beginning to enjoy the mischievous diatribe when a TRUMP BREAKING NEWS graphic and accompanying blare of newsy trumpet clatter interrupted the acid merriment.

A starkly-lit, Armani-suited, perfectly-coifed and pancake made-up talking head replaced Imus and McCord on the screen. Behind him was a large projected image of Fidel Castro.

"This is Trump breaking news," the on-camera announcer began. "The Associated Press is reporting that Cuban President Fidel Castro may be near death."

*Oh shit,* Mac groaned.

"According to the AP, the 83-year-old Cuban dictator has missed two previously-scheduled public appearances and has not been seen in public for more than a week.

"Castro was hospitalized for several months in 2006 for unspecified abdominal surgery. Speculation was widespread, then, that Fidel might be suffering the ravages of cancer.

"The Cuban leader's younger brother, Raúl, assumed control of the communist government until Castro resumed his duties as president in late 2007.

"We take you now to our reporter in Havana, Miguel Diaz."

The screen image shifted to that of a Cuban-American reporter standing on a nondescript street corner in Havana. The local residents appeared to be going about their usual daily routines. Cubans were still ingenuously unfazed by network or cable TV reporters standing on their street corners.

"You can see the concern and the apprehension in the eyes and on the faces of the Cuban people," the reporter droned dramatically. "Unsure of their future, they mill aimlessly, zombie-like, through the streets of Havana."

Mac laughed aloud.

*More likely they're trying to figure out which Bolito numbers to play today,* he reflected.

"While still unconfirmed, the rumors increase that Fidel Castro lies near death in the capitol building, just blocks from here. Indeed, there is speculation among high-placed sources in the Cuban government that the revolutionary leader may already be dead."

*God forbid,* Mac prayed.

The specter of Raúl Castro assuming the presidency of Cuba troubled him greatly. He knew Fidel's brother— the domineering head of the island nation's military— to be an alcoholic schizophrenic, with homosexual tendencies. Unlike his brother Fidel, Raúl held little respect for the Cuban people— and vice versa.

"Further information about Fidel Castro and his possible declining health or even demise remains a closely-guarded state secret as of this moment," the news reporter observed ominously. "Reporting from Havana, this is Miguel Diaz."

The TV image reverted to a commercial for "Head-On," the alleged headache reliever. The commercials gave Mac a headache.

Mac switched off the TV. He knew that Imus would bitch about yet another Castro death report interrupting his comic routine. He simply didn't feel comfortable with that.

While far from a communist sympathizer, McKinney held Fidel Castro in high esteem. His respect was born of years of personal study of Cuban history, from Spanish domination to the decadence and corruption of the Batista regime and its ultimate ouster at the hands of the upstart Castro and his ragtag band of revolutionaries. He studied the evolution of Cuban-American relations, which had shifted over a few short years in the 1950s from allied and symbiotic to aggrieved and contentious.

McKinney had also interviewed countless Cuban nationals who sang Castro's praises— belying the boisterous, political protestations of self-interested Cuban exiles who had come to be known as the "Miami Mafia."

As he mused quietly about the future of the Cuban people, Mac felt the need to review some of his commentaries in *The Reporter.* Maybe it was time for a redux.

In one corner of the upstairs bedroom of his houseboat, Mac maintained three rather high, yellowing and wobbly stacks of old

*Reporter* editions. Rummaging through the stacks, he came upon what he considered one of his better commentaries.

*Dateline, February 21, 2000:*

## DON'T LOOK FOR ANOTHER
## REVOLUTION IN CUBA
### *By Mac McKinney*

There's a lot of talk these days— particularly among aging and bitter Cuban exiles in Miami— about the inevitable, impending revolt of the Cuban people against the totalitarian rule of President Fidel Castro.

Well, don't hold your breath.

Despite what the estate-deprived Miami Mafia would have you believe, Fidel Castro is quite comfortable and secure in his position as President. He is revered by the people of Cuba as a father figure. He is admired and loved. The Cuban people would no more give up Fidel than we would give up Coke.

Under Castro's leadership— albeit in the shadow of the communist manifesto— educational opportunity, scientific study and medical care have placed the small island nation at the world fore.

If you fall ill in Cuba, no matter your station— be it farmer or party member— you will be afforded some of the best medical treatment on earth. And you won't have to deal with insurance companies or HMO's or co-pays. *You are Cuba.*

Your child will receive a quality education without preference for parental income or status. He or she will likely speak a second language fluently and will be taught to respect his or her elders. Indeed, what we consider social niceties will become second nature. Yes, your child will be a member of the Young Pioneers— a political cobweb lingering in the vacuous alcoves of Soviet occupation— but the Pioneers, replete with their starched white shirts and blue neckerchiefs, will serve as a source of pride for your child, and for you. *You are Cuba.*

You also share with your leader, Fidel Castro, the memory of a Revolution which galvanized the classes— from sugar cane farmer to student to businessman— to overthrow the *truly* dictatorial and sadistic regime of former Cuban President Fulgencio Batista. *You are Cuba.*

Strong Cuban nationalistic viewpoints? Indeed.

To better understand the genesis of such emotions, and to better comprehend how and why Fidel Castro Ruz and 80 or so revolutionaries were able to overthrow Batista, his army and his air force, get your hands on the poetic documentary titled *I Am Cuba.* It's just now becoming available on DVD in the U.S.

Mihail Kolatozov's classic 1964 Russian-Cuban co-production, *I Am Cuba* is part epic, part agitprop, part poetry and part drama. In harsh black and white, with many scenes being shot on infrared film for even more dramatic contrast, the stirring film depicts conditions in Batista-era Cuba and tells of the struggle of real people to maintain the land, their land, against corrupt influences.

From his secret camp in the Sierra Maestra, a young Fidel Castro heard the pleading voices and felt the growing pain and loss of his fellow countrymen. He tapped into those emotions to instill a strong nationalistic desire in the Cuban people until small skirmishes with his enemy, Fulgencio Batista, grew into full-fledged revolution— the Cuban Revolution.

A pause here for those among you screaming *Communista!* at this commentator— and a bit of

58

a history lesson, based in fact rather than political hysteria.

Believe it or not, Cuba was once a U.S. possession. But that came only after 400-plus years of Spanish domination and the infamous Spanish-American war. The sinking of the battleship *USS Maine* in Havana Harbor was first broadcast across telegraph wires to Key West. The occurrence was the genesis of the clarion cry of that war, "Remember the Maine." U.S. sailors who served on the *Maine* rest today in the Key West cemetery.

Cuba was ceded to the U.S. by Spain following its loss of that war.

In 1902, Cuba was granted independence by the United States. The small country flourished, trading cigars and sugar from its abundant sugar cane fields.

The Cuban and American governments were allies— economic allies. But it didn't take long for U.S. interests to turn the economic alliance into a one-sided affair. American companies began buying up Cuban land and companies, taking control of their operation. By 1926, U.S. companies owned 60 percent of Cuba's major sugar cane industry and imported 95 percent of the crop.

In 1952, General Fulgencio Batista used his army to seize control of government. Immediately, Batista began to award supporters and close friends with political favors, including land and money. He was "elected" president in 1954.

During Batista's years as president of Cuba, he increased the country's economy significantly, primarily due to the infusion of Yankee dollars— much of the money being used to buy the land of poor Cubans. A good deal of the land in Cuba was also parceled out to Batista cronies who rapidly became the "landed gentry" of that nation.

Cuban families were being driven from their farms by U.S. corporations while Batista and his American pals partied in elegant night clubs and palatial hotels in Havana.

The late Wilhelmina Harvey, former Mayor of Monroe County and the wife of C.B. Harvey, former Key West Mayor, once spoke to this reporter of the Batista years.

"We often took the *City of Havana* ferry down there to attend Batista's parties," she said. "They were truly lavish affairs. The Bacardis and other wealthy families were all in attendance. There were 10 servants for every one guest. There was Salsa music and Camparsa dancing. The artwork on the walls of the presidential palace was stunning. And the food was plenteous and delicious. We were put up in the premier hotels of the time and provided with the best of accommodations.

"I'll tell you a story. I admired one of those paintings on the wall at the palace. I mentioned it to Fulgencio. Two weeks after I returned to Key West, a large plywood frame box arrived at our house. It contained that painting I had admired.

"We *loved* the Batista years."

Indeed, a number of moneyed Americans enjoyed the Batista years. But even more Cuban farmers and peasants lost their meager lands to the political favoritism of Fulgencio Batista. Those peasants came, quite naturally, to view American capitalism as a cancer, morbidly devouring their land and their nation.

Batista forbade any dissention, including free speech. Student opposition was crushed, often by outright murder at the hands of Batista army troops or secret police.

The streets and the land of Cuba belonged to the close political *familia* of Fulgencio Batista. But Fidel was hiding in the hills. Batista could hear Fidel's voice— the voice of the people— through scratchy broadcasts made from deep in the Sierra Maestra on radio equipment commandeered by Castro and his band of revolutionaries. Batista grew to fear that voice, those voices.

In July of 1959, Castro came down from the hills. He was no longer alone or accompanied by a mere 80 troops. He had the support of a nation.

Cuban President Fulgencio Batista resigned and fled the country. And General Fidel Castro Ruz assumed control of a provisional government.

Interestingly, the United States was the first nation to recognize Castro as Cuba's new leader. But the love affair was short-lived.

One of Castro's first actions was to institute the Agrarian Reform Act, allowing for the expropriation and/or nationalization of large, largely American-owned Cuban land holdings. Compensation was offered by the Castro government, but was rejected by American interests as inadequate.

Those American interests were not pleased. And they set out, using their political lobbying influence, to loosen Castro's hold over the Cuban people— and over their land holdings.

In 1960, hoping to strangle Castro and his country economically, the U.S. reduced the import quota of Cuban sugar by 700,000 tons.

In 1961, stepping up the pressure on Castro, U.S. President Dwight Eisenhower broke off diplomatic relations with the island nation.

But there was another player in the political game that the U.S. had not considered. Anxious to gain a foothold in the Caribbean, the Soviet

Union stepped in and made Castro an offer he couldn't refuse. The USSR offered Cuba "preferential trade prices" for its sugar exports and agreed to provide them with Soviet crude oil at the same preferential prices.

The Soviet-Cuban rapprochement allowed Castro and his Cuba to become independent from American control. It allowed him to fulfill his dream of returning Cuban land to the Cuban people.

The price was high: Embrace Communism.

Castro did not hesitate. Socialism was not a far stretch from his own personal ideology. And he hungered for an independent Cuba.

Castro expanded his policy of the expropriation and nationalization of Cuban land owned by American interests and friends of Batista. Deprived of their ill-gotten gains, most of the former land-holders fled the island like lemmings, relocating primarily in Miami. A few settled in Key West. But all shared two common interests— their hatred for Castro and their determination to retrieve the land which the bearded despot had "stolen" from them.

The Cuban exiles established businesses and rapidly grew fortunes in the U.S.— fortunes which they used to buy political influence.

On Feb. 7, 1962, Castro received word of *El Bloqueo*— literally, the blockade. The Cuban Trade Embargo had been instituted by the United States. It effectively cut all trade and economic tries with Castro and his country.

For 30 years, at the behest of the "Miami Mafia," the U.S. held Fidel in its economic strangle-hold. In the 1990s, the collapse of the Soviet Union added to the economic pressure on Castro. Suddenly he found himself and his country truly isolated. This period of economic deprivation was known to Cubans as the "special period."

The Trade Embargo was codified and strengthened in 1992 and again in 1995. Principal supporters of the stronger legislation were Cuban-heritage Miami politicians Lincoln Diaz-Balart (R-Fl) and Ileana Ros-Lehtinin (R-Fl), among others. The curious thing about those actions is that none of the Miami Mafia politicians have sought similar economic restrictions on other Communist nations such as China or Vietnam.

It is clear that America has held the Cuban people hostage for more than 40 years based solely on the word of a comparative handful of disgruntled former land-owners determined to get their pound of flesh, or their acre of Cuban soil. They want their land back and they don't care what the cost might be, as long as they don't have to pay it.

This same relative handful of malcontents have managed to convince a number of Americans that the Cuban people despise Fidel Castro and that it is only a matter of time before they rise up and overthrow the violent dictator.

We're back where we began. While there might be sizable numbers of Cubans anxious to raft their way across the Florida Straits to Miami for economic reasons— resulting primarily from *El Bloqueo*— one would be hard-pressed to find even a handful of Cuban nationals anxious to take to the Sierra Maestra and lead a revolution to overthrow Fidel. It's simply not going to happen. And that fact continues to frustrate the Miami Mafia. They may be winning the propaganda war in the U.S. But in their motherland, they are persona non grata. No one is interested in their whining.

In fact, in the ensuing years since the Embargo and the "special period," Castro's Cuba has grown stronger economically, thanks to the infusion of tourist dollars from Canada and Europe, as well as trade with other Latin-American countries. The country is rapidly regaining its independence. The Embargo is having less and less effect every year that passes. In the final analysis, it may not be Castro and Cuba who lose the embargo war.

Americans are clamoring to travel freely— as do tourists from around the world— to Cuba, and to spend U.S. dollars there. The Miami Mafia will go to any lengths to prevent that. But their influence is weakening.

Cuba will open to free travel and trade with the U.S. And it will be an economic boon for both countries. But the exiles will never get their land back.— not as long as Fidel Castro or his dream of a Cuba owned by the Cuban people is alive.

*Castro is Cuba.*

—

It was a good piece, Mac thought. It buoyed his spirits. But typical of his emotional mood swings, he quickly sank into depression at the thought of the passing— be it present-time or future— of Fidel.

McKinney was confident that Raúl Castro would be able to assume control of the Cuban government, at least on a temporary basis. But would he be able to ever win the confidence of the Cuban people? Was he even worthy of that confidence? Would he sell out to the Miami Mafia in exchange for quick bucks and the attendant support of the U.S. government for his presidency?

One way or another, Mac knew that the opening of Cuba to U.S. trade and tourism was coming and coming soon. And it was his worst nightmare. In his view it meant the demise of an innocent and peaceful population. It meant the muddying of still gin-clear waters by armadas of pollution-belching cruise ships. It assured that tranquil, narrow Havana streets, peopled only by small groups of cheerful old men playing dominoes and small children playing ball, would suddenly grow pregnant with tour trains overflowing with camera-laden tourists, and rental cars and rental mopeds. The farms dotting the countryside would be cleared for high-rise hotel and condo development. And the simple, happy lives of thousands of Cuban families would be forever changed. Perhaps, with the help of some man-made snow, the Sierra Maestra would make for great skiing.

Mac knew that there was little he could do as a Key West journalist to influence geopolitical developments. But he was determined to try. If worst came to worst, he had often thought of emptying his savings account of its marginally five-figure cash fortune and sailing his tiny sailboat 90 miles south to Cuba and the comforting waters of Marina Hemingway— while he could still afford dockage fees.

Perhaps there he could have a positive impact. Perhaps he could help stop the unstoppable.

As always, reality crept over Mac and he resigned himself to doing the best job he could of covering the events which seemed to be closing in around him, Key West and Castro's Cuba.

He wondered whether Fidel was really dead. He wondered if he might be able to find out before the AP. He had strong Cuban sources in Key West and also in Havana.

Reaching for his blackberry, McKinney engaged reporter mode.

# CHAPTER THIRTEEN

# *The Bag Man*

Two weeks and not a word from Raúl. Now speculation about Fidel Castro was all over the network and cable news. Whitemoor was beginning to wonder if perhaps something had happened to his friend. Had Raúl Castro been arrested or even murdered by his own military? Tommy knew little about the internal politics of Cuba. In fact, he barely understood Key West politics. He had run for city commissioner on a lark. He never expected to actually be elected. Once seated, he found himself befuddled by the complexities of such things as Land Development Regulations, Rate of Growth Ordinance units and city charter amendments.

Whitemoor had realized only a high school education, and his experience in the business world had been limited to managing a gay night club or helping to sell his mother's paintings. The paintings were mostly sold at social functions held by the Key West Woman's Club, of which Tommy was a valued member. When he found himself elected to the commission, Whitemoor took the course of least resistance— he voted the way he was told to vote. He took his voting instructions from developers, attorneys representing developers, and, most importantly, from the Bag Man.

Whitemoor had known the Bag Man all of his life— this was an individual who was, after all, one of the most influential and respected figures in Key West. But prior to Tommy's announcement as a candidate, he'd never known him under that dark alias. He knew him only as a gentle, kindly, soft-spoken and accomplished figure who seemed to be appointed to all important local boards and was omnipresent at significant social functions.

So when Tommy held his candidate's announcement party— at the Woman's Club, of course— he was not surprised to see the Bag Man in attendance. He was not even surprised when the good-natured personality approached and greeted him warmly.

"Tommy," the Bag Man whispered, "I was so glad to hear that you would be running. I know that your mother is very proud of you. And I know she'll be even more proud when you win."

"Oh, don't count on that!" Whitemoor protested. "I'm running against one of the most important architects in Key West. He knows everybody and he already has ten times the contributions I'll ever get."

"He's also got a few enemies. But that's neither here nor there. Let me buy you a drink, Tommy."

"Sure, I'm easy."

The two made their way through a host of bedecked and bejeweled drag queens, as well as a few matronly and totally aghast club members, to the bar, where Tommy had arranged for free and free-flowing frozen mango margaritas.

"Now, let's step out on the veranda," the Bag Man suggested. I have a little advice for you."

Whitemoor wondered for a moment if the elderly gentleman might be after his body.

*Definitely not a queen!* He rapidly dismissed the thought.

The sweet aroma of frangipani blossoms diffused and perfumed the warm, Spring night air. Tommy welcomed the respite from the din of the socialites and socialite wannabes. At the same time, he felt oddly uncomfortable with this at-once familiar and unfamiliar presence.

"Don't underestimate your ability to win this election," the Bag Man began. "You have friends who can and will help you."

Whitemoor liked the direction in which the one-sided conversation seemed to be going. He savored sips of his mango margarita.

"We need a solid fourth vote— a controlling vote— on this commission. You can offer us that vote, Tommy."

*Who is "we?"* Whitemoor wondered, ever so briefly.

"Well, you can count on me if I can count on your vote," Whitemoor declared clumsily.

*Shit, that sounded really stupid.*

"This has nothing to do with votes, Tommy. It has do with money and power. That's where votes come from— they're bought. We're going to buy them for you. Oh, that advice I promised you... not all contributions have to appear on your campaign treasurer's report."

"And in return for this support?" Whitemoor asked naively.

The Bag Man smiled.

"You simply remember your friends," he answered.

From somewhere within his blue blazer, the Bag Man produced a folded copy of the *Key West Citizen,* which he handed to the commissioner-elect.

"If there's anything I can do to help your campaign— anything all— just call me. In the meantime, read this newspaper. It will tell you all you need to know. Good luck, my friend."

With that, the enigmatic and charismatic figure was gone.

Whitemoor unfolded the newspaper, revealing a stack of $100 bills. While only high school-educated, Tommy could count to 50. The folded newspaper contained $5,000 in cash.

Whitemoor gulped the remainder of his mango margarita.

He knew that, under election law, individual campaign contributions were limited to $500 and that all contributions had to be reported on his treasurer's report. But then he also knew that the age of consent in Florida was 18, and that had never bothered him. He didn't think twice about pocketing the cash.

Following his peculiar meeting with the Bag Man, Whitemoor's campaign received numerous "legitimate" $500 contributions from local developers and attorneys. Most were cloaked as personal checks from the secretaries or personal assistants of the real parties in control. Contributions from Key West Tours showed up on his treasurer's report as contributions from Liz Smith, Judy Wasserman or other nondescript "supporters." He would come to learn this practice was simply the way things were done in Key West elections.

To Whitemoor's surprise, the *Citizen* endorsed him. To no one's surprise, the *Reporter* trashed him, warning that he would be "the wag who would tail the development dogs."

To everyone's surprise— except perhaps that of his mother, who drank and believed that congregations of free-roaming chickens and roosters were perfectly appropriate and acceptable in Key West— Whitemoor was, indeed, elected.

Following a somewhat drunken and inept acceptance speech at his victory party— again at the Woman's Club— Tommy scanned the crowd searching for the Bag Man. He expected him to appear and claim his political markers. But while developers and their attorneys were plenteous, his secretive benefactor was nowhere to be seen.

The Bag Man never worked that way. He was known by everyone, but no one knew his name— not *on the record*. He remained cloaked in benign obscurity until called upon by *his* benefactors to deliver his subtle, yet Machiavellian influence.

*No matter,* Tommy thought. *I'm the commissioner now, and I'm in control.*

# CHAPTER FOURTEEN

# *Web of Deception*

It was not Peter14's first visit to the chat room. It was merely his first visit under that nick. He knew the screen names and online personae of most of the posters at Boy Chat. Many had emailed or IM'ed him personal information, pics and even presents. He was good at what he did— which was, being a boy.

This night he was looking for one poster in particular. He was a "regular" who posted under the nick, *Peacock.*

*Hi! I'm Peter and I'm new here. I live in Florida with my mom. I'm 14 and into PS-3 and b-ball. Any of you guys players?*

*Peter14* hit "post" and waited for reactions. He knew the routine. First an administrator of the board would check his ip addy— his internet provider address— and issue a warning.

*Hi, Peter. I'm Admin. Welcome to BC. If you're truly 14 and this is truly your first visit to this chat room, you should know a few facts. First, I've removed the mention of your home state from your post for your protection. This is a chat room comprised mainly of boylovers— men interested in boys for love and even sexual enjoyment. If you think you've landed in the wrong room, I'd encourage you to move along. Thanks for your interest— Admin.*

*Peter14* wasn't worried about the ip search; he always posted using a proxy, an anonymizer to veil his internet provider. And he knew perfectly well the sort of men who frequented BC. He carefully crafted a response to the admin.

*Hi, Admin. Thanks for the warning— LOL! But I have an older friend who has posted here for a long time and he's the one who asked me to come. His nick is Screech. But if you don't want me here, I'll go.*

70

*Peter14* knew that the name he'd provided as a reference would be immediately recognized and that he would be viewed by most as a YF— young friend— of *Screech*, a longtime and respected poster. Again, he hit "post."

A familiar thread began to take shape. One or two skeptics posted warnings to other posters to ignore "another fraud." *Peter14* ignored their posts. Then newer posters like *Moose* joined the thread.

*Hi, Peter. I'm Moose. Welcome to BC. The Admins mean well and you should listen to them. Never post personal information (like where you live, etc.). But you can ignore the nervous Nelly old queens who want to drive you away. Far as I'm concerned, you're welcome here. Take some time to meet people and tell us a little about yourself! Are you Screech's YF?*

Bait taken. *Peter14* switched proxies and screen names. Using the BC-registered, password-protected nick *Screech*, he hit "post."

*Sorry, I should have warned you guys, and the admins that Peter would be stopping by tonight. He's been after me to let him post here. Yeah, he's a YF I've known since he was 10. Naturally, I won't go into details— LOL! But you can trust him. Just don't try to hit on him. And that means you, Peacock!!!*

*Peter14* returned for a few cursory, "thank you for the welcome" posts and then watched the screen and waited for the response in which he was most interested.

***Bitch!*** Tommy Whitemoor screamed aloud at the screen. He hated to see his name, well his nick, used in vain. Quickly entering his password, he dashed off a response directly under *Screech's* post.

*So, Miss Screech… you looking for a bitch fight? I'll have you know that the Peacock has plenty of boys without hitting on yours— if he really IS yours! 14? ROTFLMAO! He's prolly more like 41! He should be banned just like you! Of course if he is 14, I'd do him! Cya… your pal, Peacock.*

*Screech/Peter14* had watched *Peacock's* posts for months. He had become convinced that this was someone he knew. He had done intricate ip searches and tried to approach him under several nicks. None of his efforts, so far, had managed to flush out his quarry. But he felt that he was getting close.

The thread was growing by the minute, with BC regulars battling amongst themselves over whether *Peter14* was "real" or not. Many were taking shots at *Peacock* for going off on *Screech*— and the "boy." He bided his time, let the thread grow. Then *Peter14* posted a response to *Peacock*.

*Hi, Mr. Peacock. I think you're mean and nasty. Screech is my friend and you don't need to talk about him like that. And besides he's gone out and he can't read what you wrote. Yeah, I'm 14 but I'm not dumb. You should be nicer to people. Screech warned me about you. But you could IM me. I'm PETER14 on IM. And I'd tell you about me and Screech. You might even like me. Cya... your pal, Peter14.*

*Peter14/Screech* knew that the admins would quickly delete the "boy's" IM address. But he also knew that Peacock would have made note of it long before its deletion. It didn't take long for the little yellow man to start jogging at the bottom of his screen, signaling an Instant Message.

*PEACOCK is calling. Add him to your friends list?*

Bingo.

*Hi, Peter. Is that your real name?*

*Peter14* considered blocking *Peacock* to help build credibility, but he was losing patience. He wanted to win this poster over. He wanted to know for sure.

*Are you really a peacock???*

*LOL! Well said! If you're 14, you're a very clever 14 y.o. No, I'm not a peacock.... I'm a 29 y.o. guy who likes boys... especially clever ones. I think maybe I'd like to get to know you better.... Or do you belong to Screech? BTW, you should stay away from BC.... Just a bunch of pervs there. You're better off on IM.*

Excitement welled inside *Peter14/Screech*. He felt confident that he could pull this off. But he had to remain in control of the conversation. And he had to be patient.

*I don't belong to Screech or anybody. He's my friend, though. And yeah I'm 14. You afraid of that? And btw, you really 29?*

*LOL! No, if you're 14 it doesn't scare me. I've got younger friends than you. I'm really 29. I'm pretty good looking, too. Naturally blonde.*

Tommy lied.

*HA! I'm blonde too! But I don't have YFs. All my friends are older.*

Peter14 lied.

*So, Peter... you said in your first post that you live in Florida....*

*Yeah, with my mom. She's divorced and.... Hey, how'd you know that? They deleted that.*

*LOL! I was watching before it was deleted. Just like I was watching before they deleted your IM addy.*

*They deleted that too???*

*Yeah, the admins are like that.*

*Hmm, maybe you're right. I should stick to IM.*

*Yeah.*

*You seem nice. How come you got so pissed at Screech?*

*Aw, Screech and I argue all the time... it's mostly a joke. I really like him. And you seem nice too. What part of Florida?*

*I dunno if I should say that.*

*Well, it's okay 'cause I live in Florida too.*

*Yeah?*

*The IM bell tone alerted Tommy Whitemoor to another messenger...* **RAÚL.**

*Hey, Peter, I gotta go. But I've got your IM. List me as a "friend" and I'll get back to you. Okay? I'd really like to get to know you.*

*Sure, IM me anytime. I think I like you peacock.*

*Peacock signed off Peter14s IM board.*

*Shit, so close,* Sergeant Hardin thought.

## CHAPTER FIFTEEN

# *Fidel on the Rocks*

*Raúl!* Whitemoor typed anxiously. For sincerity, he added a yellow smiley face. It's good to hear from you! I was getting worried.

*Hello, Tommy. I apologize for the delay in communicating with you. There has been so much to do here.*

*I understand, Raúl. It's hard enough being a city commissioner. I can't imagine suddenly becoming president of a nation.*

*Fortunately, my friend, I have access to large quantities of Bacardi Rum.*

*ROTFLMAO!* Tommy hooted onscreen. *Yes, I suppose when one owns Cuba, one owns all of the Cuban rum!*

*If it were only that easy. To tell you the truth, the Bacardi family probably has more power than the Castro family! Especially now.*

The commissioner could tell that his friend was uneasy assuming the mantle of presidency.

*Tell me, Raúl, how is the transition going? The networks here are speculating wildly about the situation there. Will you be making an announcement soon? Will there be a State funeral? How can I help?*

*So many questions, my friend. And there are so few answers. I will attempt to inform you— again, in confidence. Yes, a State funeral will come. But for now my brother lies in a walk-in freezer in the basement of the old presidential palace, guarded by my most trusted military officers.*

Whitemoor pictured the once-powerful Cuban leader lying frozen amongst woven cane baskets of papaya and guava fruit. He shuddered at the thought.

Raúl Castro continued his message. He was willing to talk and Whitemoor was anxious to listen.

*I know that news of my brother's death has leaked to the U.S. media. The leaks come from your own government officials who have known the truth for more than a week. I laugh that your news reporters are unable to confirm their stories, as I have locked down the capital. Even the Miami Mafia scrambles to find the truth. This lockdown was necessary for me to secure the support of the military. Now I must secure the support of the Cuban people. And I am working to renew diplomatic relations with the U.S.*

*You have already been in contact with Washington?* Tommy asked.

*Your president was contacted by Felipe Perez Roque— our prime minister— the night that Fidel died. I ordered him to make the contact.*

Whitemoor was genuinely shocked. The thought that the U.S. government had known of Castro's death for two weeks and not informed the people astounded him. He wasn't exactly sure why that thought should astound him, it just did.

*Raúl, I'm grateful to your for taking me into your confidence. I'm just a small town city commissioner. And here I am IM-ing with the president of Cuba!*

*LOL! Would it make you more comfortable if I emailed you some filthy pictures, my friend?*

*You know my weakness, Raúl. No, right now I'm more interested in what's going on there. Does this mean that America will relax the Embargo? Will there be free travel to Havana? I'm anxious to troll the Malecon with you once more!*

*Ah, this is the most of complex questions, Tommy. I do not want to bore you, but I will continue to inform you on this, because I do need your help, as I mentioned to you before. Travel and trade between the U.S. and my country has been held political hostage for more than 30 years by the Cuban exiles— the so-called Miami Mafia— led primarily by the Miami-based Democracia movement, together with your republican representatives such as Ileana Ros-Lehtinen and Lincoln Diaz-Balart, among others.*

Whitemoor had met and dined with Ros-Lehtinen during one of her political stops in Key West. He had found her rather bitchy— much like Victoria Pennekamp of the Chamber of Commerce.

*The Democracia movement cries for "democracy" in my country. What they really cry for is the return of the land they stole from the Cuban people with the help of Fulgencio Batista— may he rot in hell. They use their wealth to influence Washington politicians to continue El Bloqueo until Cuba agrees to democratic elections.*

*Is that possible?* Tommy *asked. Or will Cuba remain a Communist country?*

*LOL! My friend, Cuba has been Communist in name only for a decade or more. My brother instituted a socialist society here to end the private ownership of land and the exploitation of Cuban workers. That is why we have no homeless. No one goes hungry. And no one wants for medical care. Fidel embraced the name of communism for the benefit of the Soviet Union, who was supplying us with wheel-barrows full of money and oil that we needed to grow independent.*

Much of this was flying over Tommy Whitemoor's head. He felt intellectually impotent.

"Mother," he called out, "Bring me a mango margarita!"

*Now we have our independence...* Raúl continued to explain... *The truth is that we do not need the U.S. International tourism is making us quite wealthy. And our friends in Latin America provide us with all the oil and trade opportunities we need. There could come a day when each and every Cuban will be driving a Mercedes, as do the peoples of the oil-rich middle east. But I personally want to end the chilled relations with America. It is something Fidel always longed for but would never admit publicly.*

Maria Whitemoor dutifully delivered her son's margarita.

"Who are you chatting with?" She inquired innocently.

"Just a friend, mother, just a friend. It's politics. You wouldn't understand."

"Oh. Forgive me," she muttered, leaving the commissioner alone with his computer. "Political Science was only my minor in college. You've heard of college?" Her voice trailed behind as she left her son's bedroom.

*Bitch*, Tommy grumbled.

*I do bore you, Tommy?*

*No, no, not at all, Raúl. I'm just dealing with my mother here. She can be such a pain. But she makes a hell of a margarita. Please, continue. And tell me how I can help you.*

*I will be brief, for now. Let me tell you, our secret talks with your leaders have gone extremely well. The opportunity now exists that we could see the restoration of diplomatic relations between our two countries within six months.*

*That's awesome!* Tommy typed exuberantly. *You've accomplished in two weeks what your brother couldn't accomplish in 30 years!*

*Don't give me too much credit, my friend. Talks with your president began before my brother died. Shortly after resuming power following his surgery, Fidel approached Bush with what your politicians call an election year "October surprise" that your president could not resist— the establishment of a so-called democratic Republic of Cuba under Bush's regime, before he leaves office.*

*Shit, that would knock the legs from under Hillary!* Whitemoor correctly observed.

*LOL! Yes. There remains only one block— the Democracia movement in America. They will offer the only opposition to our joint plan.*

*But why would they oppose democratic elections, Raúl?*

*Ah, my friend, there are democratic elections and there are democratic elections. My government has placed certain conditions on any free elections. While your government has tentatively agreed to such conditions, it is unlikely that Democracia will feel so disposed. And that is where I need your help.*

*Tell me what to do, Raúl.*

*I want your Key West to be the centerpiece for the opening of relations between the U.S. and Cuba. That would steal away the voice of the Miami Mafia. It would focus attention on your president and on me and also place it on Havana and Key West.*

*Key West— Gateway to Havana!* Tommy typed excitedly, recalling his luncheon with Pennekamp and Ted Lively.

77

*Exactly, my friend! As a start, I need you to convince your city commission to name Havana as a "sister city" and to return your San Carlos Institute building to the ownership of the Cuban people. Those would be good first diplomatic steps.*

*Consider it done, Raúl.*

In truth, Whitemoor had no idea how he might convince the city commission to approve either of those requests.

*Good. I am also dispatching Felipe Perez Roque to meet with you in your city. The arrangements are being made and he will be there by May 1.*

*He's coming here? He can get into the U.S.? How? Where? My God, the media will be all over it!*

*Things are moving quickly, my friend. And you must learn that not all is accomplished in the spotlight of the news media. Perez Roque will travel on an unmarked American transport plane, escorted by U.S. fighter aircraft, and will arrive at your Boca Chica military base— with no public knowledge. You— and others— will meet with him there under the tightest of security. He will explain to you what you must do to help facilitate our plans. All this depends, of course, upon your agreement— and your confidence.*

Whitemoor's hands shook as he typed his response. The scope of his small significance had suddenly expanded and he found himself thrown into the midst of events far greater than he had ever imagined possible.

"Mother, I need another drink!"

*Of course, Raúl... he typed... Just let me know the details of your prime minister's arrival and what I am to do. In the meantime, I'll start to work on the ordinances necessary for the sister city and San Carlos business.*

*Good. One final word, and it is a word of warning. If Democracia and the Miami Mafia learn of your efforts on my behalf, they will try to stop you. They will do anything in their power to prevent détente between America and Cuba. If you are able, be sure that you have police protection.*

*Don't worry, Raúl... the police chief is a friend.*

*Good. You will learn far more from Perez Roque when he arrives. For now, I thank you for your help. I will be in your debt.*

*Just give me 15 minutes alone with Elian Gonzalez!* Tommy quipped.

*ROTFLMAO! Consider it done, my friend. If we succeed, both you and I will benefit. Your Cayo Hueso will become the gateway, as you say, to a free Cuba.*

*Cayo Hueso, Cuba Libre!* Tommy typed, uncharacteristically aware of the import of his words.

## CHAPTER SIXTEEN

# *"You show me yours and— well, just show me yours"*

Sergeant Hardin had sworn off of Cuban coffee weeks before. It had begun to make him jumpy, and he tried to resist any foreign substance which might interfere with his animal instincts. But breakfast at Pepe's without Cuban coffee just didn't cut it. The second cup he justified by convincing himself that he needed to be on his toes for a looming meeting with "the boys."

After years of undercover work with the FBI, Hardin was quite comfortable dealing with the feds and was on a first-name basis with most of the agents. Still, he always felt somewhat like a kid visiting the principal's office whenever he entered the portico of the federal building. It wasn't a feeling of guilt for some malfeasance; rather it was a feeling that they always seemed to know more than he did— even though Hardin considered the Key West office of the FBI on a level with the KWPD in terms of competence. There were only two full-time agents, assisted when needed by "floaters" from the Miami or Fort Lauderdale FBI offices. They got no cooperation from the local State Attorney's office— save for one idealistic senior investigator— or local magistrates, all of whom were deep in the back pockets of the local bubbas. And they dealt daily with a local population more interested in the overabundance of chickens than exposing political corruption. Still, they were the only federal game in town.

Sergeant Hardin was planning to leave his patrol car parked in front of Pepe's and walk the two blocks to the federal building. He didn't want it to be seen there. But as he stepped out the front door his sharp eye immediately caught sight of Captain Newly's unmarked vehicle in the Waterfront Market parking lot. The windows of Newly's patrol car were tinted, but Hardin knew that the I.A. officer was inside, watching. Dillard was having him tailed—not very effectively.

*Shit, this guy couldn't tail my grandma in a wheel chair,* the adroit sergeant chuckled to himself.

Hardin strolled confidently to his patrol car, seemingly oblivious to his "tail." Tossing his cap on the seat, he stood at the door and called Dispatch on his shoulder mike.

"Unit 51— I'll be 10-7 at 205 Duval Street, the legal offices of Michael Savage, for a scheduled deposition."

"Unit 51, 10-4," the voice at Dispatch crackled back.

*Quick on your feet, Hardin,* he complimented himself. He also made a mental note to renew his love affair with Cuban coffee.

Sergeant Hardin parked his patrol car directly in front of the attorney's office. Glancing in his rear view mirror, he saw Newly pull to the curb four cars behind him.

*Jeez, could the guy be any more clumsy?*

He was buzzed into the second-floor, private, office of Michael Savage, one of Key West's most successful attorneys. Savage had recently been named Acting City Attorney following the unfortunate conviction and imprisonment of the former city attorney for accepting bribes from developers. It was not an appointment Savage had sought.

Savage maintained the sort of clients that allowed him to make more money by any given Noon than city attorneys make in a year. Also, the notoriety provided by the public office was in direct opposition to the advice he most often gave to his most valued clients: "Keep your head down."

Ironically, it was the Bag Man who had prevailed upon Savage to take the job.

"There are a number of projects we need to see move through the commission in the coming months," he told Savage privately. "And the Feds are swarming all over City Hall and the city attorney's office. You're the only attorney in town clean enough to fly under their radar."

Savage agreed to serve as Acting City Attorney on two conditions. One, it would be for a period no longer than a year. Two, the shrewd attorney insisted that his services would be provided *pro bono*— there could be no appearance of impropriety. Also, Savage would work out of his own office. Most of the day-to-day legal work of the city would be performed by assistant city attorneys, with Michael's oversight. He reluctantly agreed to be present for city commission meetings, provided they didn't run too long.

The city commission approved Savage's appointment gleefully. They knew all too well that the Feds were sniffing around and that Savage could provide a sort of "cloak of invisibility" to much of their machination.

The popular and affable attorney was also a friend and ally of the *Reporter's* Mac McKinney— though he didn't advertise the fact. And he had long enjoyed a friendship with Sergeant John Hardin.

This day, Hardin was greeted at the top of the office stairs by the attorney's legal aide.

"Hey, John!" The officer was greeted by Donna Merrill from top of the stairs. "Come on up, where the hell you been? We haven't seen you forever."

Merrill hugged him warmly. She was tall, middle-aged and very attractive. She was also devoted to her boss. Both were highly trustworthy.

"What's up?" she asked Hardin. "It's too early for Michael, were you supposed to meet him here?"

"Naw, I just need to use your back door, Donna."

"Huh?"

"The Chief's got somebody on my tail, so I need to slip out the back for a meeting with the boys. Cover for me if anyone calls. Okay?"

"Not a problem."

She led him down the back stairs to a rear door which opened behind Old City Hall, just catty-corner from the federal building.

"Sorry I can't stay and chat," the officer said, giving Merrill a quick peck on the cheek. "Thanks for your help."

"Anytime, officer. I've got a couple parking tickets I need fixed."

"Tear 'em up, Hon."

Within minutes Sergeant Hardin was inside the federal building. Captain Newly sat patiently two blocks away, watching the legal office door and the parade of handsome college frat-boys in tank-tops and surf shorts passing by his unmarked patrol car. Newly loved Spring Break in Key West.

Twin gold-embossed American Eagles flew to either side as the ornate elevator doors in the federal building opened. Alone in the huge elevator, his head down, blonde hair falling over his eyes, stood Mac McKinney.

"Assume the position, you're under arrest!" Hardin called out.

Clearly surprised, Mac jumped backward against the wall of the elevator.

"Shit, Hardin, you scared the piss outta me!"

"Guilty conscience?"

"Hell, yes... I'm a friggin' reporter!"

McKinney stepped off the elevator and joined Hardin in the lobby.

"So what drags you down to this level?" the officer asked.

"Just sniffing around to see what I can find out about this Castro rumor," the reporter replied. "I took a shot at questioning the boys, but you know that if there were 200 bodies lying beheaded and bloody on the front steps here they'd give me a 'cannot confirm or deny.'"

Hardin roared with laughter. He appreciated FBI humor.

"So true, pal."

"How about you, Sarge? Something hot here I should know about?"

"I've got a meeting with the boys, too. It's about your favorite commissioner."

"Yeah?

"Yeah. But I can't talk about it now. When I have more, I'll talk to you."

"I'll count on it," Mac said. "Good luck with the boys."

"Thanks. I'll call you later. Maybe we can talk about the Chief, too. He's putting the heat on."

"Shit. Real heat?"

"Naw, just the same old crap. He can't touch me."

"Okay, pal. Just be careful. I know you like pushing the envelope but these bubbas can play pretty rough."

"Police work as a blood sport," Hardin joked.

"Call me!" Mac shouted as Sergeant Hardin disappeared behind the closed elevator doors.

Shit, the bubbas are gonna nail his ass sure as shit...

Hardin instinctively swung his right hand to his holster to grip his weapon as he walked down the dimly-lit, third-floor hallway. But the holster was empty. Not even cops were allowed to carry side arms onto this floor of the federal building. His eyes darted from side to side at the numerous ceiling-mounted CCTV cameras which lined the dull gray, nondescript passageway. He had been watched since he exited the elevator.

Hardin counted 50 steps— a nervous detective habit he had— to the single, closed doorway on the entire floor. There were no markings on the door. No official seals, no "Department of" classifications.

He knocked the requisite three times.

*Silliness,* Hardin thought.

The tiny peephole in the center of the gray door went dark as someone within peered out.

*Like they don't know who's out here!*

The ca-chunk of a deadbolt echoed down the hall as the door opened wide.

"John! How you been? Come on in!"

Special Agent Tim Smith belied the stereotypical FBI agent. His diminutive stature, balding head and bespectacled, bookish appearance was more that of a CPA. But it was hard to ignore the .357 magnum resting comfortably in his shoulder holster.

"Have a seat, make yourself comfortable, tell me what's going on!" Smith directed the KWPD officer to his stark, steel-gray, steel desk.

The venue was familiar to Hardin. The agent's desk was pristine, void of any papers, files or photos of the wife and kids. A monitor linked to an unseen computer mainframe was the only outstanding feature present.

"I'm onto something, I think, with Commissioner Whitemoor," Hardin began. "It's not there yet, but I'm sure he's soliciting boys online. I've almost got him tagged. And I wanted you to be aware of what I'm doing… mainly 'cause it's not official police work."

"I understand," Special Agent Smith replied. "You're here as a friend of the Bureau. That's where it stops. Goes no further. And we cover your ass. So, what've you got?"

Hardin handed the agent a manila folder containing a transcript of the brief IM encounter he'd had with Whitemoor, while posing as *Peter14.*

The agent scanned the page intently.

"You're sure he's *Peacock?*"

"As sure as I can be with my limited tracing capability," Hardin said. "Truth is, I'd need your facilities to make a concrete ID. Meantime, I'm sure he's ready to open up to *Peter14.* My guess, he'll spill his guts and ask for a meeting."

"You think?" Smith asked.

*FBI 101,* Hardin mused. *They never tell you what they're thinking. They just want to know what you're thinking.*

"Yeah, I think so."

Tim Smith hated having to play "the game" with Hardin. He had been a good source for the Bureau and the agent had a great deal of respect for him. In fact, he wished he had 10 John Hardins working for him. But rules were rules. You give nothing, take everything— except culpability on the part of the Bureau.

"Keep me informed, John."

Hardin knew that was the most he could expect. He had done what he had come to do— cover his ass.

He shook Smith's hand and made his way out of the Bureau catacombs.

Special Agent Jill Andrews left the monitor where she had been observing the Hardin interview and joined Smith in his office.

"Anything new?" she asked.

"A transcript of his IM with Whitemoor," Special Agent Smith replied.

*"Peter14?"* Special Agent Andrews wondered.

"Yeah."

"You think he can hook him?"

"I'd bet on it. But we've got to be careful it doesn't happen too soon. The Castro business takes priority."

"Do we have clearance yet?"

"No. I can't get a straight answer from upstairs. There's a lot of politicos involved here somewhere. Can't figure that out yet."

Sergeant Hardin tapped on the window of Captain Newly's patrol car.

"Hey, John!" the surprised and somewhat embarrassed IA officer announced, rolling down his window. "I didn't see you come out..." He stopped mid-sentence.

"You didn't see me come out of Michael Savage's office? Well, that's 'cause I was behind you writing you this ticket for parking in a No Parking zone."

Hardin handed his fellow officer the quickly-scribbled citation.

"Funny, John. Real funny. But you won't be laughing so hard when the Chief cans your ass. Just keep pushing him, keep it up, and that's what's gonna happen."

"You're probably right, Allen. But that's only if Juan-Carlo doesn't get him first."

Hardin turned and walked to his patrol car with a smile on his face.

Captain Newly tore up the citation and threw it out his patrol car window onto the street.

*Problem is, the sonofabitch is probably right,* he thought.

## CHAPTER SEVENTEEN

# *A Get Out of Jail Free Card*

Yet another annoying Tuesday morning found Mac McKinney, once again, scratching around for a lead story. He wanted to do a follow-up on the Valdez lap-dancing story, but he'd been unable to garner enough calls among his friends on the commission for a censure of either Valdez or Chief Dillard. The most he could hope for was a mention of the incident or a slap on the wrist for either the city manager or the Chief at that night's city commission meeting. Hardly worth pursuing as a lead story.

The commission agenda held no promising leads either— only what promised to be the rubber-stamp approval of myriad variances, special favors and funding for Fantasy Fest 2008. Nothing there, he thought. Merely another year of the city bending over for the interests of the Chamber of Commerce, Duval Street bars and T-shirt shops.

*We can always hope for another Hurricane Wilma,* Mac wished sanguinely.

Mac pulled a hardened, somewhat stale, raspberry scone— his favorite breakfast— from the fridge, lathered it up with enough butter to clog Mother Teresa's arteries, and zapped it in the microwave. He needed brain food.

Munching on the buttery-soft pastry and washing it down intermittently with gulps of Dr. Pepper, Mac began to peruse his "pending news" file. The grandiose designation belied what was in reality a manila folder crammed full of yellow, or yellow-turned-brown, post-it notes which had, through time, coagulated into a mass similar to day-old oatmeal.

87

*Let's see,* the reporter mused, reading the scribbled notes to himself...

*Cruise ships increase to six per day despite commission's promise years ago to limit them to "a few ships a week"...*

Promising, he thought, but it would require time to pressure or cajole the city clerk into searching for minutes from a meeting too long ago for him to be able to provide a date specific— just what the commissioners had planned at the time of that meeting. The Key West City Commission had long relied on the forgetfulness of the public— and in most cases, the media.

Mac scraped that note loose from the pile and set it to the side for further consideration. But he continued to dig...

*...phone interview... city attorney said— off the record— he will appeal latest "Ducks" decision against the city to Supreme Court. Total amount now owed by city, with interest, $37 million...*

Too much work. In addition to the court decisions against the city, the living members of two previous city commissions were now under subpoena for a new grand jury investigating a possible RICO indictment by the feds over the whole affair— violation of antitrust laws and such. That would add to the complexity. Maybe next week, Mac thought.

*... fed up with noise, irate city residents threaten to lay bodies across U.S. 1 to block Harley Hogs with illegal pipes during onset of annual "Poker Run"...*

Never happen— too many city cops own personal Harleys. McKinney dug further into his "file."

*... stray chicken poisoning on the increase... 15 pullets found chicken-feet-up behind Custom House... former city attorney now living in Truman Annex suspect...*

Wouldn't fly. No wings. The reporter was beginning to feel desperate.

*... Wisteria Isle— a.k.a. Christmas Tree Island— cleared for development. Owners plan 20-story luxury hotel... promise lawsuit charging city charter's height restriction doesn't apply to out-islands. Fallback for developers... Pirate Land Water Park...*

Mac set that one aside also. It was promising, he thought. Perhaps he could pull some information out of the city planner. He continued to dig.

*...another former county attorney charged with bribery, con-spiracy granted 10th trial extension by feds... too busy with per-sonal land-use cases to appear... primary witness died a year ago... remaining witness charged with bestiality... testimony unlikely...feds watch another one walk...*

McKinney sighed. It was one of the most frustrating cases the Key West reporter had ever covered. The only thing worse than corrupt local government officials, in his opinion, was inept feder-al prosecution. He had seen it time and again. The feds spent years investigating local officials, conducting grand juries and obtaining indictments (that being the easiest part, as with the proverbial indictment of any given "ham sandwich"), only to blow their cases in the prosecution phase.

It seemed the only way the feds ever won was with a plea bargain, and only then when given overwhelming evidence... such as a commissioner, state senator or governor standing over a blood-ied corpse with a butcher knife in his or her hand and "guilty" writ-ten in the corpse's blood across the alleged perp's forehead. Even in that happenstance, successful prosecution seemed "iffy," he had come to learn.

Mac gave up on his "pending news" file. He decided, instead, to pay an unannounced call on City Hall. Maybe he could rattle a few skeletons. Before leaving, he stuffed the few post-it notes he'd culled as possible stories into his pocket.

Mac's face was a familiar one at City Hall. The reporter picked up his city commission and press information package every other week from the city clerk's office. Mac was also some-thing of a hero to Marilyn Lee, the city hall receptionist. She read his news stories voraciously and viewed him as a journalistic Paul Revere, valiantly shouting out the news of government corruption to a sleeping public. While Mac appreciated the idolatry— he saw so little of it— he considered Marilyn overly-idealistic, even Pollyannaish. At the same time, she was frequently a good infor-mation source for Mac. He also welcomed the way she provided him with easy access to most closed doors at city hall.

Marilyn beamed as Mac paraded through the front doors of Josephine Parker City Hall.

"Mac!"

"Hi, Marilyn. How's my favorite source?"

"Oh my, he's barely in the door and he starts with the cocoa butter! Who you want see, Mac? After that story about Juan-Carlo's lap-dancing— my God it was *so* funny— I can get you in to see anyone but the Chief."

"No big loss, Marilyn. The Chief has never given me an audience anyway. He only sees cub reporters from the *Citizen*— the ones who suck up to him."

"You're so bad, Mac! Of course you're right, too. Now who can I sic you on today?"

"Let's start with Juan-Carlo, Marilyn. He available?"

The gate-keeper of city hall pushed a button on her pbx console.

"Debbie, it's Marilyn. Listen, that reporter Mac McKinney just sped by me and yelled back that he was on his way up to Juan-Carlo's office. I'm just warning you. Boy, does that guy have some cojones!

"You're welcome Debbie… and he won't get by me again!"

Marilyn disconnected from the line.

"You can go right up, Mr. McKinney," she said with a grin. "Juan-Carlo's expecting you."

"*Who's* bad, Marilyn?"

"I guess I am, honey. That's why you love me."

"Thanks, I owe you," Mac called back to Marilyn as he raced up the central stairway to the city manager's office.

"Tell him I'm up to my butt in city budget numbers!" the city manager called to his secretary just as Mac arrived at his door.

"No you're not," Mac observed, leaning into Valdez's office, "you're looking at internet porn!"

The city manager's notorious laughter filled the office and adjoining hallways.

"Okay, okay you caught me. Come on in, Mac."

Unlike his editor/publisher, McKinney actually liked Valdez. He was fully aware that the guy was the definitive bubba, a philanderer and a back-stabbing sonofabitch. But he was always straight with Mac— at least to his face. And Mac respected that.

"So what kind of dirt are you scattering about this week?" Valdez asked, stepping halfway onto his second floor balcony to light a genuine— and quite illegal if one followed U.S. Embargo laws— Cuban Monte Cristo cigar.

"I was hoping you'd tell me," Mac replied honestly. "Anything you want pushed this week?"

Valdez placed his large hands behind his back as he paced back and forth, stepping further out onto the balcony and staring out across his tiny island city. Without turning to face the reporter, Valdez replied, "I figured you were here to ask me about the Chief."

It was a not-so-subtle hint. Mac quickly picked up on the cue.

*No flies on this reporter!*

"Sure, Juan-Carlo… let me ask you this… is Chief Dillard in hot water for assigning officers to tail you when you visit sex clubs?"

Valdez continued to pace and puff on his cigar.

"Well, I'd put it differently, Mac. But between you and me— that's to say off the record— I've had some problems with the Chief's behavior ever since he was selected by the commission."

"Not a big secret," Mac noted. "Did you call him on the carpet about the tailing incident? '

"Officially— and on the record— I discussed the assignment of officers with Chief Dillard."

"Would you classify the discussion as a reprimand?"

"A letter of reprimand was not issued, officially. But I made note of the incident in a small file I have been maintaining on the Chief."

Valdez tossed the remainder of the contraband Monte Cristo onto Angela Street. Sliding open his credenza, he withdrew a huge, blue folder and handed it to McKinney. On the cover was a white label which read, "Chief Ray "Cuz" Dillard: Professional Issues."

"Damn, this must weigh 10 pounds!" Mac observed.

"That's an extra copy, Mac. You can take it with you, if you like."

*Wait a minute, why is Valdez handing me this package of dynamite?* Mac wondered. Easy answer, he wants me to leak it.

"Did I get this from you?" Mac asked candidly.

"Hell, no. But if asked, I won't deny its existence."

91

"You want me and the paper to back you on this."

"You scratch my back, I'll scratch yours, Mac."

The city manager's cell phone interrupted the unusually blunt tête-à-tête.

"This is Juan-Carlo..." he answered. "Oh, hi, Tommy. What's up?

"Yeah. You mean Havana? That's gonna be a tough sell, pal.

"Tonight? Well, it would have to be advertised... but check with the city attorney and see if Josephine can bring it up as a discussion item. That'd work. Okay, later Bubba."

"Your favorite commissioner," Valdez enlightened McKinney.

"Shit, Whitemoor? What did that Nelly whore want? Uh, I mean if you don't mind me asking."

"He wants to ask the commission to name Havana as a 'sister city' and return the San Carlos Institute building to Cuba."

"What the hell's that all about?" Mac probed.

"I haven't the vaguest idea," Valdez responded. "You know Tommy. One day it's approving variances for drag shows at Mallory Square, the next it's naming Havana a sister city. Who the hell knows what he's up to?"

"I guess I'll have to pay closer attention to tonight's meeting than I'd planned to," McKinney quipped.

"Just keep me out of it, whatever you do," Valdez chuckled. "I'm still in hot water with Rosalita over that lap-dancing story."

"I think your blue book on the Chief buys you a free pass this week, Bubba."

"Sort of a get out of jail free card, huh?"

"I wouldn't go that far. If Cuz ever gets you behind bars, you'll never see the light of day again!"

"I could say the same about you, Mac!" the city manager observed ironically.

"Yeah, I guess you're right."

Both men laughed... a rather uncomfortable laugh.

Mac stood to leave but, reaching into his pocket and finding crumpled wads of paper, he remembered his other questions.

"Oh, while I have you, Juan-Carlo..."

Picking a wrinkly post-it at random, Mac took a shot at developing another story.

"Tell me how cruise ship arrivals have quietly increased to six and more a day when the city commission promised years ago that there would only be 'a few cruise ships a week'? When was the increase approved?"

"Cruise ships are an economic boon for the city," Valdez declared, reciting the party line almost as though he believed it. "They're low maintenance from a City-service standpoint. The City budget benefits from significant disembarkation fees which allow us to avoid increases in ad valorem taxes. Passengers spend an average of $30 per person in our local shops, and a large number return to stay in our hotels and spend more money in those shops and restaurants."

"They're floating trailer parks," Mac retorted. "The ships dump crap into our waterways. They block the view for residents and tourists alike. And the passengers buy one bottle of water, a T-shirt emblazoned with some example of high-school locker room humor, and a refrigerator magnet or a souvenir spoon with 'Key West.' scribbled on it."

Valdez roared with laughter.

"That's what I love about you, Mac. You never let your personal opinions influence a story!"

McKinney knew that he had crossed the line journalistically, but then no one had ever accused him of being the least bit impartial, much less fair and balanced.

"Of course— off the record— you're right," Valdez added. "But the cruise ships are a fact of life now. There's nothing you or I or the city commission can do it about it. It means too much money to certain parties. And you don't even want to go there."

"Ted Lively and his tours," Mac acknowledged. "Twelve bucks a head to transport the passengers on his vehicles to his businesses."

"You said it, I didn't," the city manager tacitly confessed.

"So where does it stop? I mean the number of cruise ships?"

"There are some Caribbean ports that harbor 20 cruise ships a day," Valdez told the reporter.

"Is that a warning?" Mac asked, fuming.

"It's the specter of Key West future," Valdez observed, almost plaintively. "Hopefully, I'll have taken my money and run by then."

McKinney knew that was the way most Conchs in city government felt. They'd sell the cherished burial plot in Key West cemetery from under their blessed grandmothers for enough cold, hard cash. It was inbred, he figured. Their "wrecker" forebears had built the economy of the island with booty gained from the misfortune of ships which had grounded on the reefs in the shallows of the southernmost Cay.

*The only difference today,* Mac thought, *is that they don't have to bother going out to retrieve the booty from the wrecked ships— Carnival Cruise lines now brings it right to them.*

Mac gave up on pursuing any cruise ship story with Valdez.

"So I'll see you at the meeting tonight, huh?" he closed the discussion.

"Sure. Look forward to it, Bubba."

Mac again stood to leave and again had an afterthought.

"Hey, should I try to talk to Cuz Dillard about the blue book business?"

"He won't talk to you, Mac. In fact that's one of the charges in the file... 'fails to openly communicate City and Police Department issues with media.'"

"Oh. Well, maybe I'll give it a shot."

"Knock yourself out, Bubba."

## CHAPTER EIGHTEEN

# *Lock Up Your Children!*

McKinney abandoned the thought of trying to leech a comment out of Chief Cuz Dillard in favor of a beer or several at Kelly's before the city commission meeting. He needed a bit of a buzz to sit and listen to two or more hours of banal political platitudes of yet another gathering of that august group.

At precisely 4 p.m., Mac strolled through the back gate at the Caribbean bar, laptop under arm. He was not surprised to see his editor and Chablis, the news hound, already seated at his private, corner table. As Mac approached, Chablis wagged her tail and welcomed him with a modest curtsey and a cordial "arf!" Conrad merely harrumphed and took another sip of his Canadian Club.

"Well, at least Chablis is happy to see me," Mac said, placing his laptop on the table and signaling the bartender for his usual Bud.

"I'm happy to see you if you're got some good stuff," Conrad replied with a grin. "What ya got?"

"It's hot, real hot," Mac teased his editor. "And you're gonna love it!"

He withdrew Valdez's blue book of accusations about the chief from his brief case and dropped it next to Conrad's CC glass.

"What's this?"

"Only a file of accusations Juan-Carlo's been building against Cuz Dillard."

The editor was aghast at the sheer size of the blue binder.

"You're shitting me!"

"Nope, David, it's all there— a plethora of both factual and fanciful charges— including the Chief having him tailed to his lap dances."

"Sonofabitch. Is it on the record?"

"Yes and no. He's leaking it. He won't deny its existence, but he's not ready to say that he's going to use it to can Dillard."

Conrad leafed quickly but intently through the blue book.

"Dynamite!" he whispered to himself repeatedly as he read.

"Does that mean I can skip the commission meeting tonight?" Mac asked.

"Hell, you might as well. They're only going to be approving the Fantasy Fest business."

Tempting as the offer to pass up a meeting was, McKinney actually intended to go.

"There may be something else going on," he noted. "Whitemoor called Juan-Carlo while I was in his office. Something about naming Key West as a sister city to Havana and returning ownership of the San Carlos building to Cuba. Might be interesting."

"What's that all about?" Conrad wondered.

"I don't know. Could be nothing. Could be something to do with the possible opening of Cuba. But it doesn't sound like something he'd come up with on his own. Somebody's put him up to this. I smell Key West Tours or some other interest like that."

"You think Cuba's gonna open? Why? You heard something concrete about Castro? I mean if anyone would know, you would."

"Not a word. Raúl's got Havana sealed like a rum barrel."

"But what's your feeling?"

"I think Fidel's either on his death bed or already dead."

"And you think there's a nexus between Castro's death and Tommy Whitemoor?"

"Does sound stupid, doesn't it?"

"It's Key West, Mac. Stupid is the norm."

"True. At any rate, I guess I'll go just to see what the hell Tommy's up to."

"Well, I suppose I should buy you a beer for digging up the blue book business."

"That'd be good," Mac smiled agreeably. "Two beers would be even better."

"I can see the headlines," Conrad envisioned, "*Reporter reporter staggers into Commission meeting.*"

"The *Citizen* doesn't have the cojones!" Mac laughed.

"True," his editor agreed.

Chablis wagged her tail approvingly.

At 5:45, Mac packed up his laptop, retrieved his copy of Valdez's blue book from his editor, patted Chablis and began the short walk down Caroline Street to Old City Hall and yet another stimulating city commission meeting.

As he turned the corner onto Anne Street, Mac spotted Sargeant Hardin's patrol car parked at the curb. Nearing the vehicle, he could see that the officer was intently working his dashboard-mounted computer.

Mac tapped on the window of the patrol car.

"You babysitting Juan-Carlo again tonight?" the reporter shouted through the window.

Turning casually from his computer screen, Hardin lowered the window and flashed a big grin at the reporter.

"Nope," Hardin replied, "I got promoted. Cuz put me on the mayor tonight."

"Oh, so you're on Vicky Pantyhose watch."

"Yep, I guess," Hardin chuckled. "If it's a short meeting, I'm sure he'll be headed for her condo."

"I expect it will be short," Mac said. "Just some Fantasy Fest crap and a couple add-ons by Miss Whitemoor."

Hardin's countenance grew solemn at the mention of Tommy Whitemoor's name.

"Keep your eye on that one," he warned Mac. "There's a lot going on with him. I'm working on some stuff that could put him away for a long time."

"From your mouth to God's ear!" Mac pleaded. "Can you give me any background?"

"Not yet. In time. Just watch him."

"Cool. Meantime, I've got something for *you*."

McKinney handed the sergeant the file with which Valdez had supplied him.

"I'll need it back tomorrow, but I think you'll find it interesting reading tonight."

Glancing at the heading on the cover and the gauging the heft of the blue book, Hardin laughed and shook his head in disbelief.

"It's going to be interesting to see which knocks the other off first! But Juan-Carlo appears to have the advantage on sheer weight."

"My money's definitely on Valdez," Mac agreed. "He didn't earn the title 'hatchet man' for nothing."

"Well, it doesn't matter much to me which one walks," Hardin said. "They're both equally corrupt."

Mac nodded concurrence.

"Hey, Sarge, I gotta head on up to the meeting. Don't want to miss any of the action. I'm anxious to see how many drunken nudes they'll allow on the streets this year."

"Yep, see ya later, Mac. By the way, like I told you last year... no way the department's equipped to handle a crowd the size they're expecting for the Fest this year. Not the KWPD. Not rescue. Not even Homeland Security. But that's another story, my friend."

"Yeah, I definitely want to do a piece on that— even though, as you know, no one will listen. Gotta run now, though. See ya, Sarge! And, hey, don't go doing any body searches on Pantyhose tonight. You don't know where that thing's been!"

"Later, Mac."

"Later."

McKinney arrived in commission chambers late enough to make a dramatic entrance right in the middle of Josephine Woods' reading of the agenda. He loved doing that. The sharp resonance of the crisp soles of his Weejuns— a preppie fashion anathema to the Kino sandals worn by most present— on the hardwood floor caused Josephine to glance in his direction. Her reaction, in turn, prompted the cable TV cameras to focus their attention on the tardy reporter as he flung his laptop on the press table and began to gather his wits about himself.

Mac enjoyed playing to the camera.

As soon as the city clerk finished reading the resolution providing for Fantasy Fest variances and special provisions, Mayor

Dailey asked if there was any public comment. Seeing none— a three-week delay in consideration of the item had silenced even the religious right— he moved for approval of the resolution.

Fantasy Fest Director Ann Richardson, who had been standing at the podium prepared to give yet another presentation and once again defend the variances and city funding, was taken aback.

*It's your lucky night, Ann,* Mac thought. *Jimmy has a hot date.*

The vote in favor of the resolution was unanimous. Once again all of the city's ordinances and all of the community's standards— such as they were— would be thrown out the windows and down the front steps of Old City Hall. The city would be turned over to 60,000 or more intruders whose sole purpose was to get drunk and do or see things they would never be allowed to do or see in the streets of their own hometowns. Taxpayers would cover the cost of overtime for police coverage— no matter how inadequate— and for the resultant cleanup— a task tantamount to hurricane recovery. Of course much of it was done in the name of "charity," just as with the annual island-wide roar of the Harley Poker Run. Nothing whatever to do with lining pockets.

*Lock up your children, Key West residents*— Mac typed into his notes —*Fantasy Fest is coming to town.*

Acting City Attorney Michael Savage, whose desk was situated directly in front of Mac's press table, craned his head backward and whispered over his shoulder to the reporter.

"The good thing is we didn't have to listen to Pantyhose again!"

Mac laughed.

"Yeah, now Jimmy will have to listen to her speech in bed tonight."

"Poetic justice," Savage observed. "As long as she's performing, he won't have to!"

Both tried to keep straight faces as Josephine Woods introduced the only other item on the agenda.

"Commissioner Whitemoor has requested an add-on discussion item proposing that the City of Key West enter into a formal "sister city" agreement with the Cuban city of Havana. Further, Commissioner Whitemoor proposes for discussion that the San

Carlos Institute building, located on Duval Street in Key West, be returned 'to the people of Cuba.' Discussion is at the will of the Commission..."

Mayor Dailey gently tapped his gavel on the bench.

"I would first like to ask the acting city attorney if we're allowed under the provisions of the Sunshine Law to consider this item since it was an add-on and unadvertised."

Dailey always liked to cover his ass, and was behaving particularly saintly with the Feds watching it.

"I see no problem," Savage advised, leaning forward to his microphone, "as long as the items are for discussion only and no formal vote is taken. But I would further advise that the question of ownership of the San Carlos, as well as the legality of any transfer of said property and/or ownership of it under the existing restraints imposed by the U.S. Trade Embargo against Cuba, would present a number of legal issues and entanglements which the City may not be prepared to pursue."

"May *I* speak now?" Whitemoor whined. "It's my discussion item."

A subtle but palpable current of amusement buzzed through the commission audience.

"What's the whole idea behind this?" Commissioner Henry Becker interrupted. "I mean why in the world would we even consider naming a Communist city a sister city?"

Becker was the commissioner Whitemoor feared most. He was mortally intimidated by the elder city official. While he was thinking of how to answer, Becker's voice of obvious opposition was joined by that of Commissioner Carmen Burana— who was born in Cuba, of African descent.

"I'd have considerable difficulty supporting such a proposal, Commissioner Whitemoor," she said. "As one whose family lived under the thumb of Fidel Castro, I can see no circumstances under which this commissioner could ever name Fidel's Havana a sister city...

"Unless there's something in it for us," Burana quickly added.

McKinney chuckled silently to himself.

"Let me explain what I have in mind..." Whitemoor pleaded.

"Well, *is* there anything in it for us?" Mayor Dailey joined the skirmish. "I mean is Castro going to die and give us transfer of development rights in Cuba?"

From the floor, City Manager Juan-Carlo Valdez felt moved to add his two cents.

"Will they take our chickens?" Valdez joked.

The audience roared with laughter.

Tommy Whitemoor appeared near tears. But he was not about to be walked on by the likes of Valdez.

"Well, I suspect that Castro could do a better job of controlling wild chickens than you have, Mister City Manager!"

*"Ooooooooooooh!"* a response of ironic appreciation wafted through the audience.

*Score one for the drag queen,* Mac noted.

"I move to close discussion on the item," Becker interjected. He had endured enough of Whitemoor's silliness. The Conch tattoo on his forearm, which heralded his manhood, was even beginning to itch.

"Is there a Second?" the mayor asked the assembled officials.

"Second," Commissioner Burana replied.

"Hold on a minute!" Whitemoor protested. "This is serious. I have a serious discussion item on the table!"

"Well, a motion has been made to remove the item from the table," the mayor said. "That motion has been seconded. Will the city clerk poll the commission?"

The vote was a foregone conclusion. Discussion closed.

"Meeting adjourned," Mayor Dailey announced with a stern wallop of his gavel.

As he gathered up his papers and the tattered remnants of his pride, Whitemoor began to panic and wonder how he would explain the fiasco to his friend Raúl Castro. Stepping off the dais, as fortune would have it for Whitemoor, he bumped right into the Bag Man. Instantly he knew what he had to do.

"Well, hello!" he greeted his enigmatic friend.

## CHAPTER NINETEEN

# *Voodoo Politics*

The commissioner and the Bag Man sat at a small table in a darkened corner of the Chart Room— a noted locals' watering hole frequented by politicians, Literati and more than a few scoundrels.

"This place reminds me of the West Indies Lounge," the Bag Man said, lifting a chilled martini glass to his lips. "It was Emery Major's favorite meeting spot. He met Mac McKinney there to supply him with all his inside information. It was a good choice, I guess. There were never more than three people in that bar in all the years it was open."

Emery Major was a city commissioner in the early Nineties, before being caught accepting a bribe in one of the few successful FBI stings ever conducted in Key West. Defending his friend, McKinney always claimed it was a setup.

"They were after a big developer, an attorney and, more importantly the Bag Man," the reporter told friends in confidence. "They picked the weakest link in the chain— Emery. The Feds knew they could suck him in, scare him to death and convince him to flip on the others.

"Well, he was sucked in sure enough. A hidden camera showed him taking money, stuffing it in his shirt pocket and exclaiming, 'God is a good God!'

"It looked like he would flip, too. He stood before two of the three targets of the investigation and told them, 'If I go down, I'm taking everyone else with me. The Greyhound bus is loading now, boys!'

"It was fear, bravado on Emery's part. When push came to shove, he refused to flip. But he did give the Feds a lot of cocoa butter. *Har!*"

While convicted and removed from office, Major never served time. He returned to serving his community of Bahama Village as an ombudsman for many of the old blacks of Bahamian and Cuban descent, until his death.

He was never rewarded for his silence.

"I went to commission meetings hungry because I couldn't afford to eat," Major once told McKinney. "I'd manipulate approval of multi-million dollar development deals for those guys, but I'd still go home hungry. And people wonder why I ever took a bribe."

"You remember the West Indies, Tommy?" the Bag Man asked.

Whitemoor had been recalling Major's misfortune. He hoped that by engaging with the Bag Man, he wasn't headed for the same.

"Sure, I remember it well. It was in the old Santa Maria Motel, hidden behind the Queen's Table restaurant. My mom used to take me in there when I was a little boy. She'd point out the monkeys hidden in the mural on the wall behind the bar. It was a cool place, but it scared me. It was so dark and there were all those Haitian voodoo people dancing on the beach in that mural."

"Shame to see it go under for a condo/hotel," the Bag Man lamented. "But, like selling out the old fairgrounds, we do what we have to do."

Whitemoor gulped his mango margarita nervously.

"What is it you want from me, Tommy?"

"I need your help on this Cuba thing," the commissioner said. "It's important that I get Havana named a sister city. I'd like to pull off the San Carlos thing, too. But that may be more difficult, at least for a while. At any rate, I know that you can make a few calls and get this passed by the commission."

The Bag Man ordered another martini.

"Why is this so important?" he asked Whitemoor.

Whitemoor was desperate. He had to let somebody in on his secret.

"Fidel Castro is dead," he blurted out. "Cuba is going to open up with his brother, Raúl, as president. I know this, and I also know that Key West stands to benefit big time financially— if we act now to be the gateway to Cuba."

"When you say that Key West will benefit financially, what do you mean? *Who* will benefit? That's something I need to know."

The commissioner was surprised that the commanding power broker had not questioned the content of his shocking information. He seemed to accept it merely on faith.

"Well, we all, we all will…" Whitemoor stammered.

"But what's in it for *me?*"

The Bag Man cut quickly to the chase.

"Well, you and Ted Lively. I mean you work for Lively, right?"

"I don't work for anyone, Tommy. Ted is a friend, just as you are."

"But when Cuba opens up, he can take his tour trains down there, and he'll benefit on this end from Cuban tourists— that'll be big! And there's the development all your friends can do down there. They can buy the land for dirt and build hotels and high rises 'til the cows come home! They'll make money, you'll make money."

"And you? Will you make money?"

"I will be powerful," Tommy declared. "I'm in very tight with Raúl. He's going to make me his point man here in Key West. Hell, I may even move there and live in the presidential palace."

*So naïve, so silly,* the Bag Man thought to himself. He had chewed up and spit out so many like Whitemoor.

"Let me offer you some advice, Tommy. Firstly, if you are playing with Raúl Castro Ruz, you are playing with fire. How do I know this?

"I know Raúl. I have dined with him and his wife, Vilma, at the Tropicana Hotel in Havana— on many occasions."

"Vilma? You knew her?" Whitemoor queried. "He never talks about her."

"Yes, I knew her— in better times. Vilma Espin was the aristocratic and strikingly beautiful daughter of a wealthy rum distiller. When she agreed to marry Raúl, she signed her own death warrant. That death would be slow. Vilma, once beautiful and admired by so many men, has wasted away to a lonely and bitter old woman. Her marriage was barren, empty of love or desire. It was a marriage of convenience for Raúl. But if you know him, I'm sure that doesn't surprise you."

"No, it doesn't," Whitemoor replied.

"Back to the point," the Bag Man continued, "Raúl is not to be trusted. I'm not even sure that he will be able to hold power once the people learn Fidel is dead. The only thing in his favor is his control of the armed forces— and an iron will. If you're relying on Raúl Castro, Tommy, you're relying on an empty promise."

Whitemoor was becoming antsy, and he was tired of being lectured to.

"Look, maybe you knew Raúl a long time ago, but I know him now. And I trust him. He's made promises to me and I think he'll keep them.

"You once told me I could ask you for anything. Well, I'm asking for this. And if you want any more support from me on your projects, I expect some support from you, as well."

The faint-hearted commissioner immediately regretted what he had said to the powerful Bag Man. But if his companion was angry, his countenance and demeanor revealed no sign of it. He simply sipped his martini and glanced at his Rolex.

"It's late," he said. "I should've been home an hour ago. Damn those commission meetings!"

"Is that a yes or a no?" Whitemoor pressed.

"I have advised you against this course of action, my friend. But since you are determined, I will make some calls. You will get what you want. Then, I will have no further debt to you. And you will have no further debt to me. Do you understand that?"

Whitemoor breathed a sigh of relief. He knew that the Bag Man would deliver on his promise. But he also worried that he may have cut off his hand to spite his face. Politics was far too complex a game for him, he thought.

"I understand," he answered.

"We never met tonight," the Bag Man said as he stood and left Whitemoor alone in the Chart Room.

## CHAPTER TWENTY

# *Of Secret Flags and Secret Friends*

The old Cuban waited impatiently for his friend and inexpert operative. The Democracia movement in Little Havana was not the CIA. It depended heavily upon dedication and determination. Castillo had no doubts about Manny Caballero's dedication. His determination, however, was sometimes impaired by his sheer mass and his habitual beer consumption. Manny was no alcoholic, Castillo knew, but he did enjoy a beer and a heated game of dominoes. Still, José Castillo trusted Manuel Caballero as his own brother.

Castillo had just ordered a second Cuban coffee when his friend appeared in the bistro.

"Good evening, my friend," Manny greeted the aged Cuban as he nudged his way into the small booth. "Cuba Libre!"

"Si, Manuel. Cuba Libre! We continue to hope."

"You have news?" Caballero asked excitedly.

"I do indeed, my friend. I also have a critical assignment for you."

Caballero was anxious to help the movement. Of late, he had done little more than pilot small boats in protest armadas to the fringes of Cuban territorial waters.

"I am ready," he pronounced earnestly.

"Let me outline the assignment for you, then. I will begin with some background— at least what we know to this point. We have a Democracia follower working in the Naval Air Base at Boca Chica, in Key West. He learned some days ago that the base will be

106

placed on its highest level of security on May 1. Training missions will be halted for two days. Special meeting rooms are being prepared. And our source has learned of at least one flight which will arrive at the base from Washington, D.C. That flight will be escorted by fighter jets and a second plane will carry secret service agents."

"How did he learn all this?" Caballero wondered aloud.

"Operatives learn to watch for departures from the norm," the older Cuban told him. "The very lifeblood of a Naval Air Station is normalcy. Everything from breakfast to laundry to flight departures and arrivals depends on 'the norm.' Any major departure from that norm sends shockwaves throughout the facility. An operative need only listen and observe to ferret out the source of the upheaval. Loose lips at the base BOQ are generally most helpful.

"Beyond that, our source stumbled upon a more important piece of information."

"What's that?" asked Manny, enrapt with Castillo's relating of the espionage.

"Just yesterday he passed a senior officer's desk and saw a FedEx box marked 'Security Level: Top Secret'. The box was open and sticking out was the edge of a flag. He immediately recognized it as a Cuban flag. Being alone in the office, he took a chance and pulled the flag further out of the box. He found that there were, in fact, two Cuban flags— both large, the size that would adorn flag stands in a meeting room."

"What does it mean?" Caballero asked, more curious than ever.

"We think it means that someone important from Washington is coming to Boca Chica to meet with someone important from Cuba."

*"Jesús!"*

"Indeed. It is ominous news, my friend. We fear that the transition may already be underway. And it is becoming increasingly clear that the U.S. government will ignore the rights— the birth rights— of Cuban exiles in favor of political advantage."

Castillo banged his empty coffee mug on the table in outrage, prompting several domino players to turn their heads in his direction. He cast them an icy stare and they quickly returned to their own business.

Caballero had rarely seen his mentor behave so heatedly. Castillo's deportment was usually one of calm control, combined with an air of elegance.

"I lose my temper, my friend. I apologize."

"You are right to lose your temper if it is true, José. Now, what can we do. Tell me what I must do."

"I am sending you to Key West, Manuel. You leave in two days. You will be my eyes and ears in Cayo Hueso."

"But I can't get on that Navy base, José."

"I know that. But you can meet privately with our operative and debrief him before and after any meeting. You are familiar with all the high-level members of Castro's regime. He will describe to you anyone he sees arrive at Boca Chica. He may even be able to secretly secure photos. You will recognize who that figure might be."

"Do you think it will be Raúl?"

"No. He would never leave the security of Havana. But it will be someone at a high level— someone Raúl trusts.

"Beyond the May 1 meeting, there are also other things going on in Key West which are of concern to us. Your days there will be filled with important work, my friend. I promise you."

"I assure you that I will not let you or the movement down, José. I will not fail you."

"Good, my friend. Your dedication and service to the movement will be rewarded when our homeland is returned to us. Meanwhile, here are your plane tickets and hotel reservations. Upon arrival you will meet with my personal contact there. His name is Juan-Carlo Valdez."

"Valdez...isn't he..."

"Yes, he's the Key West City Manager. He is also a son of Cuba and a dedicated partisan of Democracia."

Caballero was impressed. He had no idea that the movement had such powerful supporters so far from the Cuban community in Miami.

"Again, I will not let you down," Caballero said. "And I dedicate my assignment to the memory of José Martí and the original Revolución Cubano!"

"Cuba Libre," the old Cuban whispered. *"Cuba Libre."*

## CHAPTER TWENTY-ONE
# *Gotta Catch 'Em All!*

*Peacock* opened his buddy list and clicked on the nick *Peter14*. Just a few miles away in Key Haven, John Hardin saw an IM alert appear on his computer screen.

*You have an IM message from **PEACOCK**.*

Hardin entered AOL IM and became *Peter14*, complete with the boy's own unique signature.

*Hiya, Peacock.*

*Hiya, Peter. Wassup?*

*Not much, just watchin b-ball.*

*Forgot to tell you last time... I like your siggy!*

*Peter14* used a graphic of Ash, the young boy featured in the Pokemon game, as his signature.

*Yeah, that's Ash. He's my hero— "gotta catch 'em all!"*

*Peacock* knew the catch phrase from Pokemon. Most adults wouldn't know it. The boy certainly seemed to be legit.

*So who's your favorite Pokemon figure? Pikachu?*

*Naw, Pikachu's a wimp. I'm actually into the Ancient Mew.*

Oops, *Peacock* didn't know that character. He'd have to brush up on his Pokemon details if he wanted to get to this kid.

*Yeah, Mew's cool. But let's talk about you. We know you're 14... You said you're blonde?*

*Yeah.*

*Muscular?*

*Not really.*

*Cute?*

*That's what they tell me.*

*You into other boys, Peter?*

*Not really. My best friend and I played around, but I really like older guys.*

*How much older?*

*Aw, I dunno... maybe 20.*

*20, huh? How about 29?*

*Shit, he's about as close to 29 as I am,* Hardin thought.

*I guess it depends on the 29 YO. LOL!*

*I think you'd like me, Peter. I'm kinda hunky... into swimming and scuba diving.*

Hardin noted the scuba diving remark. It was significant.

*Diving? That sounds cool. What do ya do for work?*

*Peacock* thought for a moment about how much to tell the boy. He wanted to impress him, but one always had to be cautious.

*I'm sort of in politics.*

*Way cool! You the governor or something?*

Hardin began an IP trace. In seconds he'd matched *Peacock's* BellSouth IP with others he'd done on the poster. He copied it to the guy's file. Hardin knew that Peacock was in South Florida. How far south?

*Naw, I'm not the governor. I'm just sort of involved in politics. But I do know the governor.*

*You do? Cool! You live in Florida, too?*

*Yeah.*

*Where?*

*Peacock* began to feel a little apprehensive about the direction of the conversation. The boy seemed to be asking explicit questions.

*Just Florida, or near there anyway... could be Cuba.*

*Nobody lives in Cuba! They don't have internet.*

*Sure they do. I IM there all the time.*

Hardin made another note.

*What about you, Peter? Where are you?*

*I told you, Florida.*

*It's a big state. Where in Florida? If you're close enough, I could take you diving.*

*I'm on the west coast.*

*Okay, that's a start. Tampa?*

*Screech told me not to tell anyone where I live.*

*But haven't you ever met anyone from the net IRL?*

*Naw, real life is scary. Haven't you ever seen those Dateline shows where the guy catches the pervs?*

The kid was right, *Peacock* thought to himself. Real life *is* scary. But if you're desperate, or confident, or horny enough, you just leap and hope a net shows up.

*Have you ever been to the Keys, Peter?*

Sergeant Hardin lifted his fingers from the keyboard, cupped his hefty hands over his mouth and breathed deeply, in and out. Slowly, he thought, take it slowly.

*I think when I was a kid,* he typed. *You mean Key Largo?*

*I mean all the Keys, Peter. They're all pretty nice for diving. If you're somewhere like Tampa, I could send you a bus ticket and you could come down and go diving with me. Would that be cool?*

*I don't know how to dive.*

*I'd teach you. Of course I dive with no swim suit. That okay with you?*

*I dunno, I guess.*

*You ever go skinny dipping, Peter?*

*Yeah. With my friend.*

*Is he cute like you?*

*I dunno, I guess.*

Hardin was playing the part of the boy so well that he felt sympathetic nausea under the intense sexual scrutiny of this *Peacock*. He knew that *Peacock* was sitting at his computer screen getting off on a boy's naïveté and innocence. And he felt more determined than ever to catch the pervert.

*You still there, Peter?*

Hardin's nausea and thoughts of disgust had obviously caused a noticeable lapse between his posts. He had to watch that.

*Yeah. Sorry. My mom was calling me.*

*That's okay. You gotta go?*

*Yeah, soon. Homework, ya know.*

*That's cool. I'll IM you again soon and we'll talk about getting together maybe. Would you like that?*

*Sure. It's kinda lonely, just me and my mom.*

Those were the words Tommy was looking for. He was convinced this boy was real. And he became determined to get to him.

*Gotta catch 'em all*, he thought.

## CHAPTER TWENTY-TWO

# *Interview With The Vamp*

Buoyed by his promising online flirtation with *Peter14*, Tommy sang a very falsetto "Somewhere Over the Rainbow" to himself as he sat before his vanity mirror and delicately daubed on blush, applied a stunning violet mascara, and lavishly spread Oprah's favorite brand of plumping gloss onto his lips. He was just pulling up his hair to accommodate his finest bouffant wig when his mother fairly burst into the room. She was clearly agitated.

"Tommy, there are some men here to see you. They're with the Secret Service! And one of them has *a gun!*"

"Ohmigod!" the commissioner near drag shrieked. "How do you know he has a gun?"

"He pulled back his jacket to show me a badge and I saw it—in a leather holster on his shoulder. Have you done something wrong?"

"No, mother, I haven't done anything wrong. At least nothing that I can think of right now."

"Well, they're waiting for you downstairs."

"Oh bother, I'm due onstage at the New Copa in an hour and I haven't even done my hair. Hell, tell them I'll see them in the garden."

With some difficulty, the two government agents maintained a stoic demeanor as Whitemoor appeared in the lush garden before them, wearing a chenille bathrobe and a large, silk scarf wrapped neatly about his head.

Bogey and Bacall briefly stuck their heads out from beneath the bougainvillea, cackled loudly, and then returned to rooting about the dense garden foliage.

113

"What the hell was that?" one of the stone-faced agents shouted, his hand reaching nervously for his shoulder holster.

"Oh that's just those nasty peacocks of mine," Tommy intoned. "They have no taste whatever."

"You Whitemoor?" the other, seemingly more stable agent asked.

"I'm *Commissioner* Whitemoor," Tommy snapped with the velocity of a coiled spring let fly. "What can I do for you?"

Each of the black-suited men flashed very official gold badges in Tommy's face, causing him to step back just a bit.

"I'm Agent Black and this is Agent Gold. We're with the United States Secret Service."

"I'm impressed," Whitemoor said, seating himself demurely in his wicker chaise lounge. "Do take a seat, gentlemen. And tell me what you're here for. Have I broken any laws?"

"We'd rather stand, thanks," Agent Black replied solemnly. "We're here, Mr. Whitemoor, because your name has appeared on a list of persons scheduled to be present at a high security-level meeting on a closed military base in the near future. Are you familiar with the scheduling of this meeting, Mr. Whitemoor?"

"Well, Raúl told me something about a meeting at Boca Chica..." Whitemoor began to answer.

"Sir," Agent Black interrupted him tersely, "It would be better if you do not mention the names of any of the parties involved, nor specific locations. Perhaps you do not appreciate the gravity of this area of concern."

"Sorry," Tommy squeaked.

*Now here's a guy who really needs to get laid,* the commissioner thought to himself.

"Considering the political significance of personages with whom you are scheduled to meet, Mr. Whitemoor, and given the secure location, we need to conduct a brief personal background interview with you. Naturally, a more thorough vetting by our office will follow this personal interview. Is this acceptable to you, sir?"

"I have a choice?"

"Not really, sir."

114

From darkness beneath the shrubbery, Bacall nipped affectionately at Agent Gold's pant leg. The agent nervously shook off the advance.

"Well, I'll tell you anything except my true age!" Whitemoor joked.

The agents were not amused.

"We could begin with your passport, Mr. Whitemoor. We'll need that."

"Don't have one," Tommy answered.

Appearing perplexed, Agent Black leaned toward Agent Gold's ear and whispered something inaudible to the curious commissioner.

"Did you not visit Havana, Cuba on one occasion, sir?"

"No, on *several* occasions."

Black again whispered to his compatriot.

"Mr. Whitemoor, are you not aware of the Embargo against Cuba, and were you not aware at the time of your visit, or visits, to Cuba that a U.S. passport is requisite for any international travel?"

"I know people in high places," Whitemoor responded curtly.

Agent Gold whispered something to Black.

"Let's move on, Mr. Whitemoor. Are you now or have you ever been a member of the Communist Party?"

"Are you kidding me?"

"Sir, we do not kid."

"Well, it's just that the Soviet Union went belly-up years ago. And that McCarthy queen is rotting in her grave. You boys still beating that dead whore?"

Neither agent bothered whispering to the other.

"Again, let's move on, Mr. Whitemoor," Agent Black attempted to continue the interview.

"I'm glad to tell you anything you want to know, within reason, Agent Black. But I'm due at a benefit concert at the New Copa in less than an hour. So I'd appreciate it if you could speed this thing up a little."

"Do you carry or are you licensed to carry a concealed weapon, Mr. Whitemoor?"

"My God, No! Who would I shoot— except maybe Mac McKinney!"

"Do you belong to any fraternal organization which could pose a threat to the security of the United States?"

"I'm a longtime member of the Key West Woman's Club."

Bogey cackled at Bacall in the underbrush.

"Mr. Whitemoor, I'd like to once more stress the importance of this matter. You are scheduled to be in the presence of some very highly-placed government officials. It is our job to protect the security of those officials. You need to understand, sir, that we are empowered to prohibit your presence at any event involving national security."

Whitemoor was incensed.

"Listen, bitch!" he shouted, adjusting his robe about him as he stood. "Without me there will be no meeting. I'm the one who arranged all this… with my Cuban friend. I don't think you want me telling him that the meeting was cancelled because of a couple of petty government agents. I don't think you want to tell your superiors that the president's October surprise was ruined by the two of you!"

The agents stared at each other in bewilderment.

"Now," Tommy continued, "I have a drag show to do. You two put your heads together and figure out whether I'm a threat to national security or not and then I'll let Raúl know what you said. Anything else you want to know?"

"One thing," Agent Gold answered. "What *is* that gloss you're wearing?"

"Oh honey, it's *Big Lips*— Oprah's favorite!"

116

## CHAPTER TWENTY-THREE

# *Two Things You Never Want To See*

Mac McKinney glanced unenthusiastically through the upcoming commission meeting agenda as he meandered down the steps of City Hall toward his scooter.

"There's not really much exciting this week," City Clerk Josephine Woods had advised him as she provided him with his bi-weekly copy of the press document. Mac was confident that she would be proven correct.

"Consent agenda... blah, blah..." he read to himself. "Next... An ordinance providing for ridding Key West of feral chickens... An ordinance approving a development agreement for Pirate World theme park on Christmas Tree Island, a.k.a. Wisteria Island... Closed Session to consider settlement of the City of Key West vs. Robbins lawsuit..."

The reporter stopped reading and returned hastily to the first page, the consent agenda.

"What the hell was that?"

*A resolution declaring the City of Havana, Cuba to be a "Sister City" to the City of Key West; providing for diplomatic relations and the mutual exchange of ideas and principles; and the furthering of economic ties between the two municipalities.*

"Huh? Wasn't that killed two weeks ago? What the hell's it doing on the consent agenda?"

He read on, vowing to stop talking to himself.

*A resolution establishing a blue ribbon commission to study the feasibility of transferal of the Key West property known as the*

*San Carlos Institute to the ownership of the people of Cuba; providing for the facilitation of such transfer.*

Mac bounded back up the steps and through the portico into City Hall, and slid across the marble floor to Marilyn Lee's reception desk.

"Hot story, honey?" Marilyn wondered.

"Could be, Marilyn. Could be. I need to see Juan-Carlo."

"He's not in yet."

"Hell, it's too early for him to be getting a lap dance!" Marilyn chuckled.

"He's probably still at El Siboney having his Cuban coffee," the receptionist confided.

"Shit!" McKinney pronounced, turning to leave.

"Give 'em hell," Marilyn Lee called to him as he flew out of the building.

He stopped by his scooter and dialed Commissioner Henry Becker on his cell phone.

"Hey, Henry... what's this on the consent agenda? This sister city business was trashed at the last meeting..."

"Some of us have had a change of heart, Mac." the gravelly voice on the other end of the line responded. "I'm beginning to think that it might be a good thing to normalize relations with Havana. It could make economic sense."

Something was up. Mac could feel it in his reporter's soul.

"What aren't you telling me, Henry? You're going to support an off-the-wall resolution proposed by that asshole Whitemoor? Why?"

"It's nothing," the commissioner replied. "Nothing at all. Let's just say I'm taking the advice of a friend."

"Who are we talking about, Henry?"

"Trust me, Mac, you don't want to go there."

"Juan-Carlo?"

"No. He's against it. Hell, his family lost land when Castro took power. Look, Mac, you know I never discuss this kind of stuff on the phone. Just trust me, a mutual friend wants this passed."

*The Bag Man.* Mac knew it. But why would *he* have any interest in the issue?

Convinced that he was on to something big, McKinney drove to the Duval Street office of Michael Savage.

The reluctant city attorney greeted Mac with a big hug. The two had been friends for 10 years. Savage was even the reporter's personal attorney off-record.

"What's up, Mac? Sit. Let's talk."

The high-power attorney instructed his secretary to hold his calls.

"What's this item on the consent agenda all about?" Mac asked, passing the document across the lawyer's desk.

"Hmm," Savage mused, "I hadn't read the agenda. I see they didn't mention your name under the closed session discussion."

"Huh?"

"Surprise. I'm calling you into the closed session as a special witness."

"The Robbins suit? How am I involved in that?"

"Off the record?" the attorney asked.

"Sure, it's just us guys."

"You advised the City on numerous occasions in the past— in print— to require scooter rental agencies to provide proof of insurance."

"Yeah, I warned they could face a wrongful death lawsuit when some drunk or inexperienced tourist got splattered all over Duval Street."

"Well, that's what we're facing. The Robbins family has a solid case, Mac. The City is liable because they did not exercise reasonable caution or take reasonable action— particularly when repeatedly advised to do so— to provide for the health and safety of residents and tourists, as related to potential scooter accidents involving inexperienced drivers. The Robbins girl ended up under a delivery truck and the City's liable through legislative negligence."

"I know, I saw her body," Mac lamented. "I talked to her parents in Iowa."

"Yep. That's what I need you to tell the commissioners. They need to settle this one quietly— no matter what it costs. And it's gonna cost a lot."

119

"Then they have to move to require the insurance," Mac pressed.

"That's what I'm going to recommend," the city attorney agreed.

"Good. Now how about this consent agenda business. Who the hell is behind that?"

"You don't know?"

"The Bag Man?" McKinney asked.

"Yep. It's a done deal."

"Well, I really can't say I'm against the resolutions. It's just that I can't bear to see the pedocommish get something through. And I can't understand where it all came from. What's his interest in Havana? And why the hell is the Bag Man behind it?"

"You got me, pal," Savage said, turning in his chair to stare out his back window at Old City Hall. "Lyndon Johnson once said, 'There are two things you never want to see being made...'"

"Sausage and legislation," Mac finished the quote.

"Yep."

"Still doesn't answer my question. Why is the Bag Man supporting this?"

"Between you and me, I think he's just giving Whitemoor enough rope to hang himself," Savage answered frankly.

"The boy's on the outs with the Conchs?"

"It would seem so."

"Couldn't happen to a nicer guy," Mac observed.

"No argument from me." Savage shared McKinney's opinion of Commissioner Whitemoor.

"I guess we'll just see how it plays out."

"Yep."

"So I'm being called to the closed session tomorrow night? Didn't you always advise me to keep my head down?"

"Hey, you'll be making history. You'll be the first reporter ever allowed in closed session of the city commission!"

"Oh, the Citizen will love that! They'll have me branded as a Conch sympathizer quicker than you can say *Bum Farto!*"

The city attorney grinned.

"It'll be the first thing they ever got right," he replied.

# CHAPTER TWENTY-FOUR

# *Spy vs. Spy*

"Do you have any idea what's going on here, Tim?"

"I think we're being left out of a very big loop, Jill," Agent Smith answered.

He sipped at his Cuban coffee as he studied the transcript before him. The document was labeled "Subject: Whitemoor; Location: Quadrant 4, Rear Garden"

"Did we receive any notification at all that the Service would be interviewing Whitemoor?" Agent Andrews asked her boss.

"None."

"Were we told anything about this meeting at Boca Chica?"

"Not a thing."

Agent Andrews paced anxiously in front of her superior's desk.

"Shouldn't we tell them what we have on Whitemoor, boss?"

"Not until we know what they're up to, Jill. Let's talk to Kilpatrick over at Homeland Security and see if he's received any storm warnings."

"I'll get on it now, boss."

"Don't give up anything, Jill. Let him tell us what he knows. My guess, it's nothing more than we know."

"Well, given what we have," Agent Andrews warned, "we can't allow this subject to meet with any high level officials. We'll have to inform the Service. Hell, maybe we should go ahead and bust Whitemoor now. We've got enough on him."

"What we have is a lot of warrantless surveillance," Smith said. "Yes, it's internal Bureau information, obtained legally under provisions of the Patriot Act. Still, I wouldn't want it splashed all

121

over the front pages of the local press. And that's exactly what that whiny little bitch would do if we nail him. I'd rather let the S.A.'s office handle it through a grand jury. And there's plenty of time for that.

"For now, let's just contact Homeland and keep up the surveillance."

"And the Service boys?" Agent Andrews asked.

"If they want to keep us out of their loop, then god damn it, I can sure as hell keep them out of our loop."

"Your call, boss," the agent said, turning toward her office.

"One other thing, Jill..."

"Yeah?"

"Get me profiles on those two Service Agents... Gold and Black. Start with their real names. I want to know their histories, their bona fides. What are their career specialties? Protection or political? Do they speak Spanish? Did they wet the bed as children? Tell me everything about them.

"I want to know what they're doing here and why the Service assigned them to this meeting. Which government officials are they assigned to protect?"

Agent Andrews returned to her office and dutifully placed a call to Ron Kilpatrick at the Key West office of Homeland Security. It was not something she was comfortable doing. She didn't like involving other agencies in her investigation. It wasn't professional and it wasn't Bureau procedure. There was too much going on at too many levels— and Agent Andrews didn't like the way things were playing out. She wondered if maybe her boss had been in Key West too long. And she wondered if maybe she had, as well.

"Meeting? What meeting?" the local Homeland Security director asked curiously.

"We can't go into specifics, Ron. You know that. But we're just trying to find out if you've picked up anything on your radar involving Latin-American movements on or about May 1."

"Lemme check some files here, hold on a sec," the director answered.

There was a long pause. The FBI agent used the time to dash off a secure email to the home office requesting information on Secret Service Agents Black and Gold."

*Black and Gold, indeed!* She thought. *They sound like cigar labels.*

"Agent Andrews... here's what I got on Latin-American movements. We have rumblings of Hugo Chavez— Venezuelan president— being in Havana near that date. The way things are going, that could be for a Castro State funeral. But we also have reports that he may travel from there to a destination unknown. That could be Haiti, or it could be Shea Stadium for all we know... that's you guys' job. Other than that we're showing no unusual activity.

"Tell me, though, Agent Andrews... anything else we should know about? Should we step it up a notch down here?"

"Naw, Ron, we're just following a few leads. Nothing to write home about. But if anything develops, I'll send up a flare."

"Thanks, I'd appreciate it. By the way, you guys got any confirmation on Fidel?"

*Don't bother to send him a Christmas card this year,* Jill considered advising him.

"We can't confirm or deny any information regarding that subject," the agent answered in the approved manner.

## CHAPTER TWENTY-FIVE

# *The Commission Meeting From Hell*

Adhering to his Tuesday night routine, Mac met with his editor at Kelly's to fill him in on the agenda and what to expect in the way of potential headlines. Chablis, the news hound and accepted Kelly's regular, sprawled at David Conrad's feet and listened attentively, as well.

"What ya got?" Conrad asked his star reporter.

"It's sort of an interesting night," McKinney responded. "There are a couple of juicy agenda items. First off, that business about Havana being named a sister city has popped up again— on the consent agenda."

"What the hell?" the reserved editor snapped, nearly choking on his Canadian Club. "I thought they laughed Whitemoor down the front steps over that proposal. How'd it get on the consent agenda?"

"Interestingly, the city manager is listed as the sponsor— which takes the heat off of Whitemoor," Mac explained. "But in truth, Valdez is totally against the resolution."

"You lost me," Conrad replied.

Chablis softly barked what might have been a note of confusion. More likely, she wanted a pat on the head— which her owner supplied as a matter of habit.

"With Valdez sponsoring the resolution, Conchs like Becker can vote for approval without endorsing another Whitemoor debacle," Mac explained further. "And word is, the approval is a done deal."

"Who's behind it?" Conrad wondered.

Mac uttered the name of the Bag Man.

"Shit, what's his interest in this?" Conrad probed.

"Dunno yet," Mac answered candidly. "Michael Savage told me he thinks the Conchs are out to bury Whitemoor— the Bag Man's just giving him enough rope to hang himself."

"You gonna break it?" his editor asked hopefully.

"As best I can," Mac replied. "Of course, you know I won't name the Bag Man."

The gruff editor harrumphed as he ordered another CC. He understood McKinney's reluctance to give name to the Bag Man. This was a person who was so highly respected, even loved, that he enjoyed tacit immunity from media scrutiny. He understood it, but he didn't like it. When it came to the journalistic coverage of politicians, their hidden agendas or their lackeys, Conrad maintained a strict Scorched Earth policy. But, frustrating as it was, even he could not bring himself to expose this individual.

"You said there were a *couple* of juicy items," the thwarted editor reminded Mac. "What is the other?"

"It's a closed session discussion on the Susan Robbins suit. Looks like the city's going to settle. Here's the twist, though... Savage is calling me in as a witness."

"That's a quasi-judicial hearing, right?" Conrad noted.

"Yep."

"So you'll be, in effect, under a gag order."

"Yep."

"Then what you're telling me is that you have two juicy stories that you won't be able to write about."

Mac laughed aloud— something he rarely did.

Raising one ear, Chablis took note.

"Not really," he answered. "I'll cover everything about the Cuba story. I just won't mention the Bag Man. And I'll 'speculate' about the closed session business under your byline. '*Reporter* reporter testifies in closed session,' yada, yada, yada. You'll have the 'inside' angle."

"I guess that'll work," Conrad agreed. "It'll really piss off the *Citizen*."

Conrad was pleased anytime he could scoop the big daily in town— something which his paper did on a regular basis.

"Hell, I'm late for the meeting!" Mac yelped. "I gotta run."

He chugged the remainder of his Bud and vaulted out of the bar.

"Get me a headline!" his single-minded editor called after him.

Josephine Woods was just completing the reading of the commission agenda as McKinney fairly crashed through the rear doors at Old City Hall. As he threw his laptop on the press table and tried to compose himself, he was met with knowing sniggers from the dais.

The city attorney smiled and, leaning backward toward McKinney, whispered, "If you'd like, we could arrange to have these meetings at Kelly's."

"Kiss my ass," Mac growled good-naturedly.

"Move to approve the consent agenda," Mayor Dailey motioned.

McKinney expected opposition to the Cuba item from the floor, but saw none. Or surely one or more commissioners would insist on removal of the resolution from the consent agenda. Only one voice of opposition was required to do so. But suddenly all of the commissioners seemed to be fumbling with paperwork or carefully "looking the other way."

Only Carmen Burana spoke up.

"I just have a small question about the sister city resolution," she said.

"Are you asking that the item be removed from the consent agenda?" Dailey queried.

"No, I just want to verify who sponsored the item."

*Carmen's freaking clever,* Mac thought. *She's gonna cover her ass.*

"The item is sponsored by City Manager Juan-Carlo Valdez," the city clerk intoned.

"Is that true, Mr. City Manager."

"Yes, it is," Valdez replied matter-of-factly.

"Fine. I second the motion to approve."

The motion to approve the consent agenda— including Tommy's Cuba resolutions— passed unanimously. From his seat at the south end of the dais, Whitemoor smirked like the proverbial cat with canary feathers protruding from its mouth. Mac was floored with disbelief. The meager audience in attendance seemed unaware of any significance in the item.

*Such is the way of the consent agenda,* Mac thought as he peered in frustration at the politically vacant faces of the onlookers.

"I would request the city manager to proceed with all due haste to prepare the necessary papers and procedures for Sister City status for Havana, Cuba," Whitemoor pronounced with much flair.

It was rare that the oft-ostracized commissioner got to have his way with the powerful and notorious Conch leadership.

"The city manager is so directed," the mayor ordered with a bang of his gavel. "Will the city clerk read the next item on the agenda…"

"An ordinance providing for ridding Key West of feral chickens. Whereas…"

Ms. Woods was interrupted by another rap of the mayor's gavel.

"As the sponsor of this ordinance, I am requesting that it be removed from the agenda pending further study by the legal department," Mayor Dailey announced. "I'm not happy with the wording. I think there are too many legal loopholes."

*Read: I got a call from a wealthy campaign contributor who doesn't want us to touch the chickens,* Mac interpreted the mayor's comments to himself.

"The item has been withdrawn by the mayor," Josephine Woods continued. "Moving on to the next item on the agenda… An ordinance approving a development agreement for Pirate World theme park on Christmas Tree Island, a.k.a. Wisteria Island."

"Are there any speakers?" the mayor asked the city clerk.

"Tim King, attorney for the developer, has requested time to speak," Woods answered.

The youthful, red-haired lawyer— known for his fiery defense of developers' relentless attempts to bypass land development regulations— approached the speaker's podium as though he owned it.

"Mister Mayor, Commissioners... and don't let me forget the lovely Ms. Josephine Woods..."

The prudish city clerk flounced her blonde wig to mask the ruby red flush which had infused her cheeks. King was known as a charming sycophant, but he couldn't sway Ms. Woods.

Mac made a note: *Cocoa butter fails King.*

"Commissioners," the indefatigable lawyer continued, "You have before you our latest development agreement. I see no need for any real discussion here, as we've incorporated all of the suggestions provided by yourselves and the planning board..."

"What I see," Commissioner Becker cut King short, "is that the developer has reduced a 40-story hotel facility, which was illegal under the height restrictions in the city charter to a 10-story hotel facility which is equally illegal under those same restrictions. And what's this business about a 200-foot 'Booty Slide?'"

Chuckles erupted in the audience.

"The 'Booty Slide' is part of the Pirate World theme park which we are planning for the island, Commissioner. Water parks have proven to be extremely attractive to the family tourist market— and the 'Booty Slide' will be the largest water slide this side of Orlando. We're confident it will provide the city with megabucks in tax revenue."

"And mega-bucks for the developer," Becker noted.

"Well, that's the name of the game, Commissioner. Now, as far as the height of the Morgan's Castle hotel, we have made every effort to comply with requests of the commission and the planning board. However, the commission should know that I have filed notice with the city attorney— on behalf of the developers— of intent to pursue a lawsuit seeking to prove that 'out islands' do not fall under the restrictions of the city charter of the City of Key West."

"Is that true, Mr. City Attorney?" Becker directed the question to Savage.

"I received the notice late this afternoon, Commissioner Becker."

Ominous, dark clouds seemed to gather around the old Conch's seat on the dais. Lightning could almost be seen flashing behind him as he seethed.

*Oops, counselor— your bad!* Mac sniggered to himself.

"I see no need for any further discussion of this development agreement," Becker erupted. "This commissioner has no intention of playing footsie with any shyster who walks into these chambers asking for approvals when he's just filed a lawsuit against the city. *Move to deny.*"

"Commissioner, my time is not up!" the summarily unmasked shyster protested.

"It is as far as I'm concerned," Becker growled. "Move to deny."

"Mrs. Woods, do we have any other speakers?" the mayor asked.

"No, sir."

"We have a motion to deny the development agreement; is there a second?"

"I'll second, Mister Mayor," Carmen Burana spoke. "I don't often agree with Commissioner Becker, but in this case... I'm not anxious to discuss niceties with a gentleman who's suing us."

"You can take the 10 stories now or live with the 40 stories when the height restriction is ruled inapplicable to our project," King snuck in a parting shot.

"Let me tell you what you can do with your Booty Slide and your whole damn project..." Commissioner Becker began to erupt once again.

"Order!" Mayor Dailey banged his gavel. "Order, please."

"Shyster!" Becker managed to pipe in under the second gavel.

"We have a motion to deny and a second," the mayor continued. "The city clerk will poll the commission."

Only Tommy Whitemoor opposed the denial.

*No surprise,* Mac thought, *the project's developers were big-time contributors to his campaign. Maybe they should have sent some cash Becker's way.*

It was an oversight that Mac was sure the attorney and the developer would rectify in the very near future.

The reporter was quickly developing a thirst for a cold Bud. *Damn, there's still that closed session,* he remembered.

As if on cue, Ms. Woods announced, "The commission will now close public session and meet in closed session to discuss legal matters pending before the commission."

After a brief intermission to clear the audience from the chamber, the mayor gaveled the commission into closed session.

Mac noted how much larger and oddly peaceful the room seemed with only the commissioners, the city attorney, city manager and himself present.

"The city commission will is now in order under closed session," Dailey announced with a tap of the gavel. Madame City Clerk, will you read the agenda..."

"Discussion of the status of and possible settlement of the pending lawsuit titled 'Robbins Estate vs. City of Key West'"

"Mr. Savage, you have the floor," Dailey opened the meeting.

"Mr. Mayor, I wish to advise the commission that after reviewing the merits of the Robbins lawsuit, I and the assistant city attorneys agree that we are on very thin ice in this case. I fear that the court will hold that the city was negligent in providing for the safety and welfare of its citizens and tourist visitors by not legislating a requirement of insurance for rental scooter businesses licensed by the city.

"A major part of my concern stems from the fact that there is a paper trail to support such a judgment. Present here in closed session is Mr. Mac McKinney, reporter. Mr. McKinney has been called by counsel to provide testimony relevant to the case. With the consent of the commission, I call Mac McKinney..."

Mac appeared openly nervous. He never was a public speaker. From age five, he had written all his thoughts.

The reporter reluctantly assumed a position at the podium. Fidgeting, he adjusted the gooseneck microphone.

"Mr. McKinney," his friend Michael Savage began, "you understand that this is a quasi-judicial hearing and that your are prohibited from disclosing the content of the hearing in any public media?"

"Yes," Mac squeaked. "I understand that."

"Fine, sir. The city clerk will swear you in."

"Do you swear to tell the truth, the whole truth and nothing but the truth?" Josephine Woods read the requisite oath to the reporter. Mac thought he detected a slight smile on her pursed lips. He had long been her favorite reporter.

"I do," he responded.

He did really want a cold Bud.

The mayor and commissioners, with the exception of Whitemoor, seemed rapt in anticipation of seeing and hearing a real, live reporter on the stand, as it were, before them. Mac, on the other hand, was hoping desperately that he could remember everything which took place and report it accurately under his editor's byline— quasi-judicial oath be damned.

City Attorney Savage stood and walked to the podium to stand by his friend, literally and figuratively.

"Mr. McKinney, have you, as a reporter for the local newspaper, the *Key West Reporter*, ever editorialized on the issue that proof of insurance be required by the City for scooter rental businesses?"

*Piece of cake.*

"Over and over again," Mac answered honestly.

"Could you be more specific about the number of times you've raised this issue in your editorials?"

"Well, I've brought copies of five editorials with me— they span a period of five years."

"So you've editorialized on this topic approximately once a year?"

"No, probably a lot more. Five were all I could find rooting around in my pile of old papers."

"Okay, if we were on trial, we'd stipulate that you've editorialized on numerous occasions about this topic. Without reading all five of your editorials, can you summarize the content for the commission?"

Mac suddenly felt like a kid in a candy store. He was being afforded the opportunity of telling the commission face-to-face what he had been brow-beating them with in print for years. And they were a captive audience.

131

"From Day One," Mac began to speak confidently, "I and my paper have contended that scooter rental companies— perhaps among the most callous and unscrupulous merchants in town, if one disallows T-shirt shops— should be required by the City to provide evidence of casualty insurance adequate to cover potential accidents involving their rental scooters.

"While the City requires proof of insurance from virtually every other business seeking an occupancy license from the City, scooter rental businesses have never had, nor do they currently have any insurance whatsoever to cover renters of their scooters. The inequity seems obvious."

"May I question the witness?" Commissioner Burana asked Savage.

"Indeed, go ahead Commissioner Burana," the city attorney allowed.

"Mr. McKinney, have you been able to determine any reason that previous city commissions have been unwilling to legislatively require that scooter rental agencies provide proof of insurance?"

McKinney cleared his throat.

"You want the truth, Commissioner?"

"You *are* under oath, sir."

"The scooter rental agencies have been major contributors to the political campaigns of a number of city commissioners," Mac testified truthfully. "There's one seated here tonight who's totally on their payroll."

The mayor pounded his gavel anxiously.

"Mr. McKinney, please restrict yourself to relevant testimony and not personal opinion. I must tell you that I opposed your presence in this session for fear of just such comments."

"I wasn't talking about you, Jimmy" Mac snapped back. "You're only on the Truman Annex payroll."

The mayor's gavel pounded order once again.

"Mister Mayor, I beg the indulgence of the commission," Savage pleaded. "Mac McKinney has a lot to say which could be of use to us in this case and I would ask that you hear him out. At the same time, I advise you, Mr. McKinney, to stick to the pertinent material."

*My bad,* Mac conceded under his breath.

"I have a question," Commissioner Becker said, twirling a pencil on the commission table. "Can you tell us why the scooter rental agencies resist providing insurance?"

"Simple," Mac answered without hesitating, "They can't get it."

"They can't get insurance?"

"Not at any price," Mac proclaimed. "Well, not at any reasonable price. I surveyed a number of insurance agencies and to the company, they told me that they would not provide insurance to any scooter rental operation because the liability involved with inexperienced and untrained drivers is astronomical.

"There are some foreign companies— like maybe Acme Insurance of Arabia— that will provide some faux insurance papers for perhaps several hundreds of millions of dollars. I exaggerate only slightly. Truthfully, these scooter rental operations simply cannot buy insurance at any cost. If you required them to have insurance, they'd have to close.

"That's what I've been trying to get the City to understand for years. Why can't they get insurance? Because no reputable insurance company is going to insure people who take those scooters and drive them— the first scooters they've ever driven— straight to Sloppy Joe's to get drunk. Then they do 'wheelies' down Duval Street until they run into a light pole, a pedestrian or another idiot on a rental scooter.

"At best they get a sickening case of raw road rash up and down their legs and arms. At worst, they die. I've seen too many cases of each here in Key West."

Mac spoke with a passion which was real, deep within him.

"Susan Robbins, the girl whose parents brought this lawsuit against the City. Let me tell you about her..."

Mac waited for what he was sure would be an objection from either an irate commissioner or his friend, the city attorney. Seeing none, he carried on.

"Susan was 23 years old— a beautiful girl with bright brown eyes and a bubbly personality. She was a nurse at a hospital in Des Moines, Iowa. She traveled to Key West on a cruise ship with her fiancé— her high school sweetheart. They were so excited about being in Key West...

"When the young couple disembarked, the first site they visited was a scooter rental business on Greene Street— yes, just catty-corner from this very building. Neither Susan nor her boyfriend had ever ridden a motor scooter. But following two minutes of cursory 'instruction', they rode off on rental scooters. They had a great time riding the scooters— for one block. One block they drove to Greene and Simonton Streets. Then Susan turned right too wide and skidded under the rear wheels of a beer delivery truck."

Mac paused. He was close to the story. He had spoken with the parents. He remembered it all too well.

There had been no interruption. And his friend Michael Savage winked approval for him to continue.

"Susan's head was crushed under the multiple rear wheels of the vehicle. She died instantly— one minute and thirty seconds after renting a scooter from an uninsured scooter rental company."

"Excuse me for interrupting, Mac," Commissioner Becker said, "but aren't people required to sign a waiver of liability when they rent those scooters?"

"Yes," Mac answered. "But the waiver only protects the rental company— not the City, nor even the renter or his or her relatives."

"Mister City Attorney?" Becker questioned Savage.

"Mr. McKinney is correct, Commissioner. The waiver is solely for the protection of the proprietor of the scooter rental operation. It does not indemnify the City in any way."

"Harrumph," Becker commented.

"Let me ask you, Mr. McKinney, were you present at the accident scene?" Savage asked the reporter.

"I was. I heard the call on the police scanner and was only a couple of blocks away. I arrived as the rescue paramedics were covering Susan's body with a yellow tarp. I still can see her bare feet protruding from under the rear bumper of the huge truck. Her bright pink flip-flops had flown off on impact—and lay there on the street, some 10 feet away. Her fiancé had collapsed in grief on the hood of a patrol car."

There was a hush in the chambers of Old City Hall.

"Mr. McKinney," Savage broke the stillness, "did you have occasion to speak with the parents of Ms. Robbins— the plaintiffs in the lawsuit under discussion here?"

"I did. You see, I was deeply moved by Susan's death. I felt somehow responsible because I had not been able to convince the City to regulate scooter rentals. I waited about a week following the accident. I wanted to spare their feelings— a pushy reporter calling during their time of grief and all that. As it turned out, I reached them on the day their daughter's body arrived back in Iowa."

"Can you tell us the content of your conversation with them?"

"I spoke with her father first. But when I explained that I wanted to talk about the unnecessary death of his daughter, he was unable to speak. He put his wife on the phone. Funny, I thought it might have been the other way around.

"Anyway, Susan's mother was very composed, very polite. She told me that there had been some difficulty getting Susan's body released from the Key West funeral home. But Susan was home, she told me.

"I informed Mrs. Robbins that I was writing a story about the accident and, more importantly, the problem with inexperienced drivers being allowed to rent those scooters with little or no training. I asked her if she held any animosity toward the rental agency or the City."

"How did she answer that question?" Savage interjected.

"She told me that she and her husband were too emotionally distraught to think beyond the recovery and burial of her daughter's body. She said that Susan had called her on her cell phone and told her how excited she was to be in Key West.

"It was difficult speaking with her.

"I asked her how much information she had been given about the accident. 'None,' she told me. A police officer had called and told her of the death of her daughter and that was it. She later received a call from the funeral home asking how she wanted to dispose of the body.

"These are good people. I could tell that from both their voices. They didn't care about the how or why, only that their daughter was gone.

"That made me all the more furious that the girl's death was not only unnecessary… but bordered on murder."

"Did the parents indicate to you at that time any intention to sue the City?" Savage pressed.

"None whatsoever," Mac replied. "I, however, encouraged them to do just that."

"Excuse me, Mr. McKinney, are you saying," Mayor Dailey asked incredulously, "that you *encouraged* them to sue the City?"

"I did. And they were not the first parents that I have encouraged to sue, Mayor Dailey. It was and is my opinion that there is no other way to ensure that the needless injury and death of innocent victims at the hands of scooter rental operations in our city ends. The city has been warned of its liability time and time again— by myself and others. Legislation was never forthcoming. Now, maybe…"

"Thank you, Mr. McKinney," the city attorney said. "Your testimony will be of great assistance to the commission and I'm sure that they're grateful."

With that, the mayor dismissed Mac. He would not be allowed to hear the settlement discussion. He considered making a scene and demanding to be allowed to stay, but he knew that he'd be able to glean all the particulars from Savage later. He left the commission chambers and made his way toward Kelly's and a much deserved cold Bud.

His words, however, still reverberated in Old City Hall.

"I am certain," the city attorney advised the Commission, "that Mac McKinney will be called by the plaintiff's attorneys as a material witness in this lawsuit. Can you imagine him giving that emotional— and frankly biased— testimony on the stand before a judge or jury?

"Combine his testimony with grisly traffic homicide photos, the further emotional testimony of the girl's parents, and the *fact* that we *have* failed to adequately regulate scooter rentals, and we're facing a disastrous judicial scenario.

"It is, therefore, my recommendation as city attorney, that we begin settlement talks immediately."

"Do you have any idea how much we're talking?" Commissioner Becker asked.

"It's going to be a sizable amount," Savage advised him. "If we settle out of court, I'd say in the $2 million to $3 million range. If we try the case, it could be much higher, however. We could be talking $10 million."

"Jesus Christ, *settle!*" Becker bellowed, shaking his head in disgust.

"There's more," Savage added, pacing before the dais for added gravitas. "It would benefit the City's case if we had legislation regulating the scooter rental industry in place at the time of settlement, or before having to appear in court."

"You're saying we should pass an ordinance requiring insurance now?" Commissioner Whitemoor asked, scowling.

"They'll scream like stuck pigs," Becker warned.

"I would suggest, Commissioners, that we can deal with a few squealing pigs," Savage told the squeamish city officials. "What we can't deal with are any more dead 23-year-old nurses from Iowa."

The city attorney was directed to immediately begin settlement negotiations with the Robbins's and to prepare a city ordinance requiring that all city-licensed scooter rental businesses provide proof of insurance— in time for the next meeting of the city commission.

Mac sat alone at Kelly's and wondered if his remarks before the commission had been effective. He was becoming increasingly frustrated with city and county governments that had to be sued before doing the right thing. More and more his thoughts wandered to his small sailboat and a short 90-mile cruise to Cuba.

## CHAPTER TWENTY-SIX

# *The World Learns*

Tommy Whitemoor was blow-drying his hair and sipping his first frozen mango margarita of the day when his PC chimed, *You have email.*

It was Thursday morning and Mac McKinney was doing a final edit on his story about his closed session testimony. It would be bylined as the work of his editor. In the background, Don Imus ranted about Hillary's latest primary victory.

Manny Caballero was fast asleep in his room at Key West's La Concha Hotel. He was dreaming of black beans and rice, washed down with a cold Hatuey beer. The phone woke him from his feast.

"Manuel, it's José. Turn on your news."

"Huh?"

"Turn on your TV, my friend. There is news you need to see."

Whitemoor opened his email. It was from *Raúl.*

*It is done,* the email read. *Now we move. More later.*

Tommy wasn't sure what the message meant.

"Oh well, if it's important, he'll IM me later," he told himself.

Mac was finishing his edit when the familiar TNN Breaking News alert sounded on his HDTV. He had almost become immune to "Breaking News" alerts on cable TV since they'd become as frequent as commercials. Still, perforce, he turned his head to see which Hollywood starlet had been caught not wearing underwear or kissing another Hollywood starlet this time.

"This is Trump Breaking News," the news anchor declared. "Cuban Prime Minister Felipe Perez Roque has issued a statement confirming the death of Cuban President Fidel Castro. The statement appeared with little fanfare on the website of Granma, the Cuban national newspaper. The statement included no mention of a State funeral and made no mention of Castro's brother, Raúl Castro Ruz, being officially named as the new Cuban president."

Mac stared at the screen in disbelief and sadness.

Manny Castillo's pulse raced as he watched Channel 7 News from Miami.

"Moments ago, a U.S. State Department spokesman confirmed the authenticity of the Cuban Prime Minister's statement. It appears that Fidel Castro, the world's longest-ruling dictator is dead at age 83. Details of Castro's death were not disclosed in the government-issued announcement."

*Our long battle is over,* Manuel Caballero mused as he stared out his hotel window onto Duval Street. *The new revolution begins.*

"The president will address the nation from the Oval Office in 30 minutes," another TNN reporter continued his network's coverage of the event.

*Well, that's it,* Mac told himself.

He dialed his editor's cell phone.

"Hey, it's Mac," he told Conrad. "Banner headline— *Fidel Dead.* There's no time for a long think piece, but I'll dash off a couple of quick background 'graphs and email the text over before press time."

Mac typed a short history of Castro's life and his revolution into his laptop as he listened to the wall-to-wall news coverage in the background and awaited the president's statement. He wondered if, based on Raúl Castro's recent olive branches to the U.S. government, the president's speech might be conciliatory toward ending the embargo and opening diplomatic relations with Havana. As ever, he continued to be torn about the possible opening of Cuba. It was a beginning; it was an end.

"The President of the United States," a nondescript voice announced as George W. Bush appeared on Mac's screen.

"Early this morning, the United States Department of State received confirmation of the death of Cuban President Fidel Castro," he began.

"This is a day of promise for the Cuban people."

*Asshole,* Mac grumbled.

"In the wake of the Cuban dictator's death, an influx of Cuban refugees may be expected along the shores of Florida. The Department of Homeland Security, together with Immigration and Customs has implemented emergency plans to handle any such influx. I have directed immigration authorities to waive the U.S. "wet foot/dry foot" policy for a period of 30 days— during which time the United States will welcome Cuban immigrants to our shore."

*Don't hold your breath, W.*

"The Cuban men, women and children who have suffered under the Communist Castro regime will be welcomed to our democratic form of government.

"While the Fidel Castro regime has ended, however, the United States government has received no word of who will now assume power in the island nation of Cuba. It is assumed that Fidel's brother, Raúl Castro, will take control. To date, we have seen no indication that such a power shift would lead to the release of Cuban political prisoners or the establishment of democratic elections.

"Until we receive word that Cuba is ready to join the United States and most of the world in the pursuit of democracy, our policy toward Cuba will remain the same. The embargo against U.S. travel and trade will remain in effect."

*Further asshole.*

"This is a time of dramatic change and decision for the Cuban people. While, as a nation, we pray for a smooth transition to a democratic government in Cuba, the United States is prepared to back Cuban dissidents and revolutionaries in their struggle to regain control of their nation.

"Good morning, and God bless you."

Mac could not believe that Bush was continuing his hard-line stance. Worse, he had publicly offered to finance insurrection.

*Damn, he's one hard-headed sonofabitch.*

140

On his way out to the garden to feed Bogey and Bacall, Tommy Whitemoor switched on the downstairs TV in time to hear the CBS reporter state, "That was the president speaking from the White House."

"Damn, I hope I didn't miss anything important," Tommy sang to himself as he continued out the French doors to his garden and his precious peacocks.

## CHAPTER TWENTY-SEVEN
# *The Occupation*

With the news of Fidel Castro's death resounding over network and Miami news broadcasts, an air of nervous anticipation wafted through Cayo Hueso, Havana's closest American neighbor.

Naval Air Station Key West (NASKW) was immediately placed on a state of alert. FA-18 Hornets buzzed the shoreline in noisy swarms. Orange and white Coast Guard helicopters hovered over cruise ships as they entered the port of Key West. Homeland Security vehicles— compact, ecologically-friendly models— roamed the streets, bars and T-shirt shops in search of Cuban immigrants and/or potential terrorists. National Guard troops— replete with automatic weapons— stood on street corners and before hotel entrances normally occupied by bums seeking handouts or spray-paint artists and palm weavers also seeking handouts.

It was not the first time Key West had reacted— or over-reacted— to political events in Cuba. During the Cuban missile crisis in the 60s, missiles— aimed at Havana— had actually been deployed on the beach at the fashionable Casa Marina Hotel. Rooms normally filled with well-heeled Florida politicians and notorious notables such as Bebe Rebozo and even Jimmy Hoffa were occupied instead by U.S. troops.

The reaction of local residents to the current occupation was mixed. The bums and spray-paint artists grumbled in protest. But Victoria Pennekamp and the Chamber of Commerce were thrilled. Hotels, bars and restaurants were being filled by all sort of military and government types during an off-season period.

The Chamber president even had colorful, seemingly supportive decals printed for storefront windows. "We welcome the death of Castro and our military" the decals declared.

When Mac McKinney pointed out to her, in a printed interview, that the statement could be read to mean that Key Westers supported both the death of Castro and the death of our military, Pennekamp pooh-poohed the whole supposition.

"Picky, picky, picky! You just don't want us to profit from anything!" he quoted her as replying. "We're just saying that our members support the military presence, just like we support local people shopping locally. If your newspaper belonged to the Chamber, you'd understand better what we try to do."

Mac pointed out that his newspaper had been uninvited from membership— though it had never applied.

"I have no further comment," Pennekamp had scoffed.

Mayor Dailey and Commissioner Whitewood took turns doing round-the-clock, on-camera interviews with news reporters in front of the La Concha hotel. It was a tradition born of news coverage of the frequent hurricanes in Key West.

"I view this as a positive occurrence," Dailey told one reporter. "I think it means that Cuba will open to trade and that can only be good for the city of Key West. In fact, I proposed some weeks ago that we renew old alliances with Cuba. We're even planning to name Havana as our 'Sister City.'"

Fortunately for his honor, the mayor, Tommy Whitemoor did not see that particular interview.

But Whitemoor was busy feathering his nest with promises of lucrative compensation for his assistance in facilitating business ventures in "the New Cuba." Whitemoor had abandoned any secrecy regarding his relationship with Raúl Castro. Indeed, he had begun to trumpet his closeness to the emerging Cuban president.

"Key West will be the 'Gateway to Havana'!" Whitemoor told one reporter in a La Concha interview. "I've had contact with certain high level Cuban officials and have been assured that Havana will be open to tourism by the end of October— by the time of our annual Fantasy Fest!"

FBI Special Agent Tim Smith cringed when he saw the interview on Channel 7. This asshole had clearly been told more by

143

either U.S. or Cuban officials than had his own agents. He was understandably pissed at being left out of the loop, but was more upset that such sensitive information had been entrusted to such a clearly loose cannon of a local politician.

Agent Smith decided that it was time to call Whitemoor in for a Bureau interview.

*Soon,* he told himself.

The Commissioner's mother, Maria, dutifully TIVO'ed all of her son's on-camera interviews. When Tommy viewed the Channel 7 piece, he was struck with not only his dashing appearance— the result of a recent, intensive Miss Clairol treatment— but with what he had quite inadvertently said.

*...Havana will be open to tourism by the end of October— by the time of our annual Fantasy Fest!*

The easily excitable commissioner quickly punched the number of Ann Richardson, Fantasy Director, into his cell phone.

"How firm is the theme for this year's Fest?" he asked the surprised festival director.

"It's locked," she answered firmly. "'CocoNUTS in Cayo Hueso.' We announced it months ago, and the artwork's in preparation."

"But could it be changed if the Commission requested it?"

"No. Not at this point. Why?"

"Don't fight me on this, Ann. Something big is going to happen and I'll need to change the theme. I've got a great idea and it's going to make the Fest even bigger and better than ever! I'll get back to you. Byee, now!"

At the La Concha Hotel, Jimmy Dailey was smiling for yet another news interview. In room 412 of the same hotel, City Manager Juan-Carlo Valdez was sharing warm, buttered Cuban bread and café con leche with Manny Caballero.

"My sources in the police department have confirmed that they will be escorting our Commissioner Whitemoor to the Naval base at Boca Chica on May 1," Valdez told the Miami operative. "The U.S. Secret Service is also in town— which means that unnamed government officials will be present at the meeting."

"And I know," Caballero interjected, "that Cuban officials will be present as well.

"The question is, my friend, what will be the topic of discussion. And, how close can you get me to that meeting?"

"It's clear to me," Valdez answered, "that the topic is the opening of Cuba. What our dear Commissioner Whitemoor has to do with it is beyond me. You should know that he's a complete idiot. But he has, in fact, told me that he's friendly with Raúl."

"Whitemoor is a homosexual?" the Cuban asked.

"Yes. In fact, he's a drag queen three nights a week."

Caballero sipped his con leche and smiled.

"That would fit, my friend. It has long been known that Raúl has an interest in boys."

"He's interested in Tommy Whitemoor?" the city manager asked incredulously.

"No, no, much younger. I suspect that the two men share a similar interest."

"Jesus!" Valdez shook his head.

"It could be good for us, my friend— if we need to force information from your commissioner. Now about this meeting, can you get me anywhere near it? Or can we get one of your operatives in there?"

"This is big-time military stuff— I can't get you anywhere near it," Valdez answered quite honestly. "I can't get anywhere near it. And I don't have any 'operatives'— only a few sycophants and Conch-friendly reporters. I guess we'll have to rely on whatever Whitemoor lets slip."

Caballero knew that his superiors in Miami— mainly his friend José Castillo— would not be pleased if he returned empty-handed.

"I think that the U.S. government is negotiating with Raúl Castro," he told Valdez frankly. "We desperately need to know what is being offered by both sides."

He stood and walked to the window. Below he saw the glare of floodlights illuminating news reporters speculating about his Cuba and its future, sharing their thoughts with the world. Most of them knew nothing of Cuba, its present or its past, or of its people— the beating heart of Cuba.

"If the U.S. is going to make a deal, we need to know it, my friend," he reiterated to Valdez. "Get me whatever you can. I will do what I can from my end."

"Cuba Libre!" Valdez declared, taking Caballero's hand.

"It is our hope, my friend," the Cuban agreed.

# CHAPTER TWENTY-EIGHT

# *Habana Dreams*

Calle Tejadillo, Calle Obispo, all of the narrow streets of Old Havana had become filled with Cubans— tired old men and their devoted wives, fretful mothers nursing infants, students and musicians— all poring over and discussing the latest news disseminated via *Granma*. The national newspaper was one of their most reliable sources of information about the death of Fidel.

Impromptu, simple feasts— chicken and meat empanadas and bocaditos, with yuca con mojo— had been set up in the streets, where most residents now spent their days and nights. Together, they shared the desperately sparse news and mourned their loss.

At the ancient tobacco mill of Partagas, behind the capitol, hundreds of cigar makers listened intently to a radio placed on the old reader's platform as they sat at their small desks and caringly rolled and cut precious Cuban tobacco leaves.

The voices of wailing women floated palpably on the breeze through the small, yet comfortable two-room apartment which Raquel Zavala shared with her young son, Fidelito, in the Habana Vieja district. She had named her now nine-year-old for the late Cuban Premier.

"Mother, why do they cry so, the old ladies?" Fidelito asked as he clung to his mother for comfort.

"They cry for what we have lost and for what may come, Fidelito. They mourn for your namesake, the great leader of our revolution, Fidel. And they cry for you, my son— for what is to become of you."

"Will we die mother?"

"No, Fidelito. We will live, we will love. At school, you will continue to learn. And we will prosper. Fidel is gone, yet his soul lives on in the Cuban people."

Thus Raquel Zavala comforted her young son.

Dressed in his omnipresent green military uniform, 78-year-old Raúl Castro Ruz paced the floor of his elegant new office at the presidential palace— hastily restored by Raúl to the glory it had enjoyed in the time of Batista. His was a stride of confidence. In one hand he clutched a tumbler of Bacardi dark rum, which he consumed at regular intervals as he surveyed the seemingly stone countenances of his two comrades— Vice President Carlos Lage and Prime Minister Felipe Perez Roque.

"What is the atmosphere?" Castro abruptly asked his prime minister.

The diminutive Cuban snapped to attention in his chair.

"It is good, it is clear," he answered. "There is no unrest in the nation."

Raúl smiled. It was what he wanted to hear.

"And on the American front?" he queried further.

"It is also good," Roque replied proudly. "The vice president and I continue to receive positive responses from the Bush administration. The meeting at Boca Chica will be attended by top State Department officials, and we are confident the discussions will bear fruit.

"The only obstacle we face is— as usual— the Miami Mafia. Ileana Ros-Lehtinen, Lincoln Diaz-Balart and the rest of the Cuban rejects, backed by the so-called Cuban-American lobby, are poised to fight any initiative on the part of the U.S. administration."

"What do they know of our plans?" Castro asked, gulping the remnants of his Bacardi and pouring another tumbler-full from the bar adjacent to a remarkable marble statue of his older brother, Fidel.

"The *Democracia* movement has operatives already in the Florida Keys," Roque answered. "We have learned this from their relatives here, most of whom are patriots.

"But we do not believe that they know any substance of our plans."

"Good," Raúl replied. "The less they know, the better."

148

"What of the plans for the State funeral?" Carlos Lage asked, changing the subject to one with which he felt more comfortable.

"I have received several designs from our leading architects for an addition to the José Martí monument at the Plaza de la Revolución," Raúl announced. "One I am particularly pleased with includes a small, white marble mausoleum enshrining my brother in a glistening crystal sarcophagus— permanently preserved in state, to be viewed by many future generations.

"The funeral procession— comprised of one million plus of our citizens— will follow Fidel's body down the Malecon to the Plaza. Leading the procession will be young Elian Gonzalez and his family."

"It is *inspirational!*" Lage gasped.

"Yes," Raúl beamed. "He would be proud."

"Indeed!" Roque agreed.

"I'm even thinking of stuffing a half-smoked Partagas in his mouth!" Raúl joked, lightening the mood.

The three Cuban leaders shared Bacardi and continued to plan for the transition of their country.

"I have prepared a letter for you to carry to Boca Chica for your meeting with my friend Tommy Whitemoor," Raúl told the prime minister. "It will be your introduction and you must share it with no one but him."

"I understand, Señor Presidente."

"You will like him," Castro added. "You may not understand him— he is unnerving, even flamboyant. But you will like him, Felipito."

"If he is your friend, I am sure I will like him."

"He is my friend, though I have not seen him for many years. I trust him to plead our case in South Florida. Support in that region is essential leverage in our negotiations with the administration."

"I have recently received a letter from the Key West City Commission inviting Havana to become a 'sister city' to that town," Rogue advised Raúl. "It appears that your friend is busy at work already."

"Yes. Respond that the City of Havana would be honored."

"I shall do that, and I will carry a formal document with me to Boca Chica."

Raúl Castro raised his Bacardi in a toast to the memory of his elder brother.

"Viva Fidel!" he declared.

"Viva Raúl!" Roque and Lage responded.

In her small, two-room apartment in Habana Vieja, Raquel Zavala tucked her precious little boy into his bed. She hugged him and kissed his forehead.

"Sleep well, Fidelito," the young Cuban mother whispered. "Dream of Fidel. He dreams of you."

## CHAPTER TWENTY-NINE

# *The Tangled Web He Weaves*

Sergeant John Hardin was dutifully writing a citation for a Harley with an altered muffler when he noticed Juan-Carlo Valdez leaving the La Concha hotel with a short, fat Cuban man in a white Guayabera shirt. The officer quickly stepped to the other side of the offending motorcycle so that his face would be obscured by the rider.

"Hey man, you gonna write the ticket and let me go or what?" the bearded Detroit physician, clearly suffering midlife crisis, as well as midriff bulge, demanded.

"You're only three blocks from Sloppy Joe's," the officer replied courteously. "You've got plenty of time."

Hardin scribbled illegibly on the citation form he kept his eyes locked on the two subjects across the street from him. He watched as Valdez shook the man's hand, then embraced him as an old friend. Hardin took a mental mug shot of Valdez's companion. The two then parted company. The Cuban re-entered the hotel, while Valdez pulled off in his car, which had been illegally parked in the La Concha's loading zone.

"Aw, you cops just like to pick on Harleys!" the surly biker growled at the distracted officer. "You think your 80-buck ticket is gonna break me?"

John Hardin had long ago raised his level of consciousness high above the ill-tempered insults of indignant perps.

"I seldom pick on Harleys, Dr. Rhodes," Hardin informed the biker in a calm voice. "Fact is, I own one myself. So do most of the officers on the force. I only 'pick on' Harley riders who have to reinforce their manhood by revving their engines to discharge

151

raucous exhaust blasts from their straight pipes. Altered exhausts are illegal in Florida, as are they in most states."

Hardin was tired of talking. It was having as much effect as addressing the city commission, he realized. He tore up the citation— which was really unreadable at any rate— and stuffed it in his back pocket.

"Let's call this one a warning, sir. Just try to keep the noise level down. It's a small island."

Taken aback, the biker smiled and, quietly as he could, started his engine.

"Hey, you're a straight guy!" he told the sergeant. "Stop by Sloppy's when you get off and I'll buy you a beer."

"Yeah, sure."

Hardin returned to his patrol car and switched off the blue lights. He sat still, zoned out the cacophony of Duval Street, and visualized the face of the man in the white Guayabera shirt. It was a familiar face, he had seen it somewhere— not in Key West, the man was not a local. He felt that he had seen the man's face somewhere on the internet. He mentally utilized association and his photographic memory— tools which had made him the most effective detective in KWPD history.

*Miami,* he thought.

*Democracia, something to do with Democracia.*

The web page appeared in his mind.

*Raúl Saul Sanchez hunger strike protesting wet foot/dry foot policy... aide to Sanchez comforts him...*

There was the man in the white Guayabera shirt.

*Democracia and the city manager? What the hell does that mean?*

Hardin glanced at his watch. Fourteen-thirty hours. He knew where Mac McKinney would be— two blocks away at Kelly's. He radioed himself out of service and parked on the Caroline Street side of the restaurant, just below the window adjacent to Mac's regular corner of the bar. The officer could never meet with McKinney at a public venue in uniform. He punched the reporter's number into his cell phone.

"You at Kelly's?" he asked.

"Yeah, what's up?"

"Meet me outside on Caroline."

Within minutes, Mac was seated in the patrol car beside his friend.

"We've got to stop meeting this way, John. People are going to talk."

"It wouldn't be the first time they've talked about us!" Hardin chuckled.

"So what's up in the KWPD?"

"I just saw your pal Juan-Carlo meeting with a member of the Miami Mafia."

"The Cubans?" Mac asked.

"Yeah, *Democracia*, I think."

"At City Hall?"

"Naw, at the La Concha. It could be nothing, but with the Castro thing and all these military and Homeland Security people in town, Juan-Carlo meeting with dark figures raises a red flag for me."

"Yeah, you're right," Mac agreed. "I just don't see the link—unless Valdez is working to get his family's Cuban land back. But then there are 50,000 expatriates in Florida after the same thing. Why's the Miami Mafia here in Key West?"

"There's something else," Hardin said. "There's a special detail being set up, a police escort for some government officials attending a hot meeting at Boca Chica on the first of the month."

"You think there's a nexus?" Mac asked.

"Dunno. Just seems there's a lot going on that we don't know about."

"Let me see what I can dig up," McKinney replied. "I'll feel Juan-Carlo out and get back to you. And let me know anything more you hear about that meeting, okay?"

Mac was about to leave the patrol car when he saw Tommy Whitemoor stroll into the back garden of Kelly's, arm-in-arm with Victoria Pennekamp and Fantasy Fest Director Ann Richardson.

"Shit, what's *he* doing here?" he shrieked. "Doesn't he know Kelly's is *my* office?"

"Want me to arrest him?" Hardin joked.

"Yes, in fact. Arrest him now. No, never mind, I'll just go back in and pee on his table… mark my territory."

153

"Careful, Pantyhose might like that," Hardin warned.

"Yeah, you're right. Maybe I'll just watch and listen."

"See ya," Sergeant Hardin said, placing his patrol car in gear.

"See ya," Mac replied, stepping out and slamming the car door.

McKinney re-entered Kelly's through the front entrance, hoping to avoid his nemesis. He was relieved to see that Whitemoor and his companions had been seated for dinner in the garden. He could observe from a safe distance, from his secluded corner in the bar.

Mac was not close enough to hear what was being said, but there was no mistaking Whitemoor's colorful cackling or the limp flailing of his wrists as he attempted to entertain the two women— each of whom appeared as though they would rather be in Cleveland.

"I've been on three cable networks just today!" Whitemoor bragged to his companions. "CNN, Fox News and MSNBC! They all wanted to know what I know. But I didn't tell any of them. Oh, I hinted around and dropped clues, but that's it."

"Well, Jimmy told one interviewer that he knew Cuba is going to open and that's why he proposed the sister city resolution," Pennekamp told the boastful commissioner. She knew that it would get under his sensitive skin. It did.

"That bitch!" Tommy wailed. "He had nothing to do with that resolution. That was all mine."

Whitemoor was about to spew forth a litany of vulgar epithets about the mayor when he remembered that Pennekamp was Jimmy's paramour.

"But he's welcome to take some of the credit," the commissioner tap-danced. "This is going to benefit us all in the end."

Ann Richardson fidgeted in her seat. A cultured lady with urbane tastes, she was uncomfortable with the gauche, unrefined personages in whose company she found herself. She tolerated Whitemoor because of his political position. She needed his support for city variances and such. Pennekamp she considered just another foul-mouthed slut from New Jersey. She needed the Chamber of Commerce for nothing— her Fest funding came from the TDC, the Tourist Development Council.

Pennekamp, at the same time, felt intimidated by the Fest director. Richardson wore conservative suits, was clearly more intelligent and sophisticated than herself, and never showed one hint of upper thigh.

Victoria took comfort, as well as a bit of delight, though, in one thought:

*I make twice the money the old bag makes!*

"What exactly is the story, Commissioner?" Richardson asked Whitemoor. "And what does it have to do with Fantasy Fest?"

The commissioner interlaced his delicate fingers, forming a childish steeple, and rested his chin on them for dramatic effect.

"The story is, Ann... and Vicky... that Cuba is definitely going to open to trade with the U.S. And it's going to happen this October."

Pennekamp could not contain her laughter.

From his dark corner in the bar, Mac McKinney bristled at the grating sound of Pantyhose's wicked laugh.

"You seriously think this Republican administration is going to lift the Cuban Embargo within six months— right before the election? What have you been smoking, Tommy?"

"Victoria has a point," Richardson found herself agreeing with the Chamber maven.

"That is not what I think, that is what I know," Whitemoor said, gesturing to the waiter for drinks. "I cannot tell either of you all the details, but I am in contact with both Raúl Castro and officials of our government. A deal is being cut and the embargo will be lifted by October. And when that happens, Key West could become the gateway to Havana— if the three of us act now."

"This is what you were talking about at lunch with Ted Lively," Pennekamp reminded Whitemoor.

"Yes, though I wasn't as sure then as I am now."

"I still don't understand the role of the Fest in all this," Richardson said. "If Cuba opens at the same time as Fantasy Fest, won't that draw tourists away from Key West?"

"Not if we make it a *Key West* event," Tommy pointed out. "That's why I want you to change the Fest theme. It's got to be Cuba-oriented."

Pennekamp remained silent, buying less than half of what the wacko commissioner was saying.

"I've been thinking," Whitemoor continued. "Something like 'Cayo Hueso/Cuba Libre!' would work nicely."

"It's just not something we can do," Richardson said resolutely. "It's too late to change all the preparations that have been made based on the current theme. There are graphics, artwork, etc. We can't just scrap all that based on a vague promise."

"It's not a promise, it's a guarantee!" Tommy protested.

"So what good will a new theme do you? How will that make us the gateway to Cuba? It's not going to have that much impact."

"I agree," Pennekamp chimed in. "What's the big deal if the Fest is Cayo Hueso, Cuba whatever? That's not going to drag in the national media."

"That's not all I have planned," Whitemoor replied, beaming with pride over his own cleverness. "I am going to have international dignitaries here to celebrate both the 'opening' and the Fest. And there's one *giant* secret event that I can't even tell you about yet. But if you'll go along with this, Ann, I promise you that this will be the biggest extravaganza in Key West history. That means money for your company, for the city, and, yes, Vicky, for the Chamber."

Pennekamp wondered if Whitemoor might be planning a drag queen invasion of Havana.

"Everything you're telling me may be true," Richardson said. "But I'll need something more concrete before I can justify a change that major to my own board."

Tommy didn't have time to dicker. He was two days away from the meeting at Boca Chica and he wanted to walk in with the promise of a huge event in his pocket.

Desperate, Whitemoor dropped the name of the Bag Man.

"He wants this," he told his doubting audience.

It was a lie. He was lying to two of the most powerful women in Key West. But he figured that neither would actually question the Bag Man as to whether or not he was behind the proposal. And his lie had the desired effect.

"If I go along with this, I'll have his backing, as well as all the variances and all the city funding we'll need?" the Fest director questioned Whitemoor.

156

"Absolutely," Tommy replied, smiling. "Scout's honor."

"Hah!" Pennekamp yelped. "Like you were ever a boy scout!"

"Well, I've certainly done my share of camping!" the brassy commissioner quipped.

"How will I break this to the media?" Richardson asked. She was far from satisfied with the proposed arrangement.

"Don't, not yet," Tommy advised her. "I'll know much more in two days. Then I think we should still keep all of this under wraps until the last possible moment— that's when it will have the most impact. I'll let you know when the time is right."

"But I've got to rework graphics now if we're going to do this."

"Do it. Just don't advertise it yet."

"Have you told Ted about this?" Pennekamp asked. "I'm sure he'd be interested."

"I'll include him in all our future meetings," Whitemoor replied. "He may be able to help me with the big finale I have planned. Girls, I swear you won't *believe* what I have in mind!"

Ann Richardson cringed. She was not accustomed to being called "girl." Nor was she accustomed to anyone interfering with her Fest plans. She determined then to consult with the Bag Man before making any substantial changes.

"Now, let's do dinner!" the self-satisfied commissioner proclaimed.

"By the way, Tommy, you did notice who's been watching us?" Pennekamp asked, motioning her eyes upward toward corner of the bar where Mac McKinney sat, desperately trying to avoid her knowing gaze.

"Well isn't she the nosy one!" Tommy snorted. "Not to worry, though. McKinney will get nothing from me. And I trust he'll get nothing from you either, Vicky."

"He has a way of rooting out stories," Pennekamp observed.

"Yeah, 'cause he's in bed with Valdez. When the Chief and I take Juan-Carlo down, he'll go down right along with him."

"From your mouth to God's ear," Pennekamp prayed.

## CHAPTER THIRTY

# *"We've got a file on every one of them!"*

Special Agent Tim Smith mouse-clicked his way deep into local Bureau files as he did his monthly Subject updates.

**Subject Name: Mac R. McKinney**
**Alias: None known**

Despite his personal fondness for and basic trust of the reporter, Mac McKinney remained an enigma to the veteran FBI agent. He had helped the local Bureau on several investigations— primarily background subject information he'd gleaned from journalistic interviews. He was reliable and always showed at the office when called upon. Mac was also candid with the agents, apparently far less interested in the protection of confidential sources then some more junior, less-jaded reporters. At the same time, he had a rather nasty—some would say illegal— habit of taping his phone calls to city officials. Smith had unofficially looked the other way on several occasions when Mac had supplied him with copies of his illicit tapes. Officially, he had always warned him of the illegality of such activities.

What bothered Smith most about McKinney's Bureau file were the huge personal information gaps in it. They were the sort of gaps that typically showed up when a subject was angelically pious, unbelievably pedestrian, or maniacally Machiavellian. Mac had never been arrested, though he had rolled and totaled three cars during his fraternity years in college. Interviews with Mac's University of Virginia contemporaries had reported a penchant for dark rum and moneyed debutantes.

But following his graduation, Mac McKinney seemed to drop off the edge of the earth, as far as personal contacts and history. Smith had been able to track successful careers in advertising and journalism in Chicago, as well as some local history involving sailing. But for the most part, McKinney was a complete loner— an attribute which left FBI agents like Smith desperately out in the cold, as they relied on background interviews with past friends and associates.

Mac McKinney could be either a saint or a sinner. Smith had no way of really knowing which. He suspected that the truth lay somewhere in between.

The agent really didn't give a damn where Mac was coming from. He liked him. He entered his requisite monthly report on McKinney:

***Subject Activity: No illicit taping incidents reported. Surveillance level, minimum.***

Smith was about to dig into his Commissioner Whitemoor file when his phone rang. He was shocked to hear the voice— a rather pretentious and condescending voice— of a U.S. Secret Service agent on the line.

Would Smith be able to meet with a couple of Service agents within the hour, the voice wondered.

"Sure," Smith agreed. "Just knock three times and say the president sent you."

The voice hesitated, wondering if it had indeed reached the FBI.

"Do me a favor and email me an encrypted confirmation," Smith added.

That seemed to please the voice and the conversation ended.

In less than 20 minutes, there were three tentative knocks on the office door and Smith was peering out his official, secure peephole at two unbelievably "Men-in-Black" looking figures.

"Agent Black."

"Agent Gold."

"Special Agent Smith."

Following the exchange and dramatically scrutinizing examination of badge/Id's, the three sat at Smith's desk.

There was a noticeable chill in the air. These were Secret Service agents from the Beltway, where they were treated with respect and even awe. This whole Key West zeitgeist— from Jimmy Buffett to feral chickens and drag queen commissioners— found them completely out of their element. They also viewed FBI agents as pencil-pushers and interviewers of snitches. Still, they had a job to do.

"Special Agent Smith, we are here to seek your help in the vetting process of a subject of interest. His name is Thomas Q. Whitemoor. His occupations are listed as— harrumph— drag show manager and city commissioner."

Smith steeled his jaw to forestall almost uncontrollable laughter.

"Can you give me some idea of the nature of your interest?" he asked the agents. "I've been provided with no background, although this Bureau knows that you are here for a high-level meeting."

"That is the nature of our interest, Agent Smith," Black answered. "This subject is scheduled to be included in that meeting and we have been assigned with the vetting of the subject. We would appreciate it— the United States Secret Service would appreciate it— if you would share with us any background information you might have on Whitemoor."

Agent Smith glanced at the Whitemoor file which was serendipitously up on his computer screen, then at the two Service agents.

"Suppose you tell me what you've already uncovered and that'll help me fill in the gaps."

The Service agents exchanged nervous glances.

"Frankly, Agent Smith, we've only had one personal interview with Whitemoor upon which to base our vetting. We don't have a background file on him— he's small-time local government, you know."

Smith let one small chuckle escape his steel jaw.

"Yeah, he's no Alger Hiss," Agent Smith agreed. "On the other hand, I can tell you that he has been under serious investigation and surveillance by this local Bureau for some time now."

Black shot a concerned look at Gold.

"Can you tell us the nature of the investigation?" Agent Gold asked.

"For the most part, our investigation of him suggests that Whitemoor is indeed a small-time politician, taking small-time bribes for development projects and the like. Frankly, I don't think he'd be a threat to any high-level government officials... unless he's attracted to them."

Black and Gold exchanged knowing glances.

"Is that it?" Black asked.

"No, it's not," the FBI agent answered in a suddenly serious voice. "Mr. Whitemoor is under intense investigation by my office for suspicion of felonious online solicitation of minors— male minors."

"Shit," Gold grumbled. "We don't like to hear that sort of stuff. Has there been any physical contact with minors? And how imminent is an arrest, prosecution?"

"Certainly not within 24 hours, which means your meeting at Boca Chica can go off without a great deal of concern, I think," Smith informed them, letting the Secret Service agents know that he was fully aware of their meeting and its locale.

"We would certainly welcome both yourself and Special Agent Andrews as part of our backup team at the Boca Chica meeting," Black offered.

*Ah, at least they've done their homework on me and Jill,* Smith thought to himself.

"To tell you the truth, we'd rather keep our heads down on this one, Agent Black, since we're so close to the Whitemoor investigation."

"That's fine, we understand your position," Black noted. "Can you just confirm for us one more time that it is the opinion of the local Bureau that Whitemoor poses no threat to any high-level government officials with whom he might have immediate contact?'

"Tommy Whitemoor is no threat to any adults," Smith said.

"Thanks, Special Agent Smith, that helps us. We do have some further concerns, however. Whitemoor's involvement with certain government officials may extend beyond the Boca Chica meeting. Do you have any idea of when your investigation of him may conclude and when an arrest, if any, might take place? And could you give us a future heads-up on that?"

"When you called I was pulling up his file with the intention of calling him in for an intense interview," Smith told Black and Gold honestly. "I can belay that in the interest of your meeting. Beyond that, he continues under investigation, which includes online monitoring and a surreptitious sting operation.

"His indictment and prosecution will depend on how quickly he responds to bait placed before him. It could be weeks, it could be months. That's the best heads-up I can give you."

"You've been a big help, Special Agent Smith," Black said. "We'll try to keep you fully in the loop on this Boca Chica business. And I apologize for not including you up front— it was just a matter of the limitations of national security. You know the game."

Both Secret Service agents seemed genuinely appreciative for Smith's time and information.

"We all work for the same boss," Smith said, standing to show the two men to the door. "If I can be of further help, just call. We're pretty informal around here, as you've probably learned."

"Thanks," Black said, firmly shaking Tim Smith's hand in parting.

"One more thing," Gold asked the FBI agent, "What's with all the chickens roaming the streets here? Haven't you guys ever heard of Bird Flu?"

"Don't worry," Smith answered, laughing, "We've got a file on every one of them!"

## CHAPTER THIRTY-ONE

# *Honey and Flies*

It wasn't every day that Mac McKinney was invited to the city manager's office for a private one-on-one. Of course he always had access to Juan-Carlo, but personal invitations were rare— so he arrived early. Seated alone in Valdez's office as he waited, the understandably cynical reporter wondered what Valdez had in mind, or more likely, up his sleeve.

Mac studiously surveyed the trappings of the spacious office. Central on Juan-Carlo's desk was a eight-by-ten, framed photo of Juan-Carlo, his wife Rosalita and their four children— three well-fed, devilish boys and a timid, yet subtly sensual young Latino girl with long, lustrous black hair and giant brown eyes. The happy family were pictured gathered around a roast pig in a pit in Juan-Carlo's back yard. Mac supposed that the photo might been taken in any back yard in Cuba.

Scattered about the desk were gold-colored, plastic trophies featuring Little Leaguers in batting positions— mementos of Juan-Carlo's boys' baseball prowess. The desk was not unlike that of any other proud father.

Mac turned his eyes toward the door as he heard the sound of Valdez's rapid footsteps down the hall. The pace was unmistakable. Juan-Carlo always moved with a purpose, a quality he strove to instill in all city hall "associates." He was a big believer in "motivational" management.

"Mac!" the city manager declared as he entered the office, his arms laden with files and papers. "Sorry I'm late— I was busy busting the Chief's cojones."

"Anything I should know about?" Mac asked.

"Naw, I just like to do that to the Chief on a daily basis. Helps keep him in line."

Valdez threw his armload of files and papers onto a side credenza and threw himself into his large, leather chair.

"Cuban cigar?" he offered Mac. "They're real Partagas."

"No, thanks. Cigarettes are enough of a vice for me."

"Cigarettes will kill you," Valdez warned. "Cuban cigars will raise your libido!"

"Reporters don't have libidos," Mac answered. "We're too busy exposing politicians' libidos."

The city manager laughed from the depths of his oversize belly.

"Gotta love ya, Bubba!" he bellowed.

*Okay, enough coca butter, Juan-Carlo. What's up?*

"So what's up?" Mac asked. "Why am I here?"

Lighting a long, elegant cigar and deftly rolling it between and through his fingers, the city manager leaned forward over his expansive desk. His countenance became one of seeming paternal concern.

"We have a problem, Mac— and you're that problem."

"Huh?" McKinney was completely taken aback.

"It's the Susan Robbins business," Valdez told him.

"I thought that was settled," the reporter said. "The commission agreed, the City's going to settle."

"True enough, Mac. They all agreed on that. We'll give the family a lucrative settlement. Included in that will be a non-disclosure clause. We— and more importantly, the media— will never hear from the girl's family again."

"So what's the problem?" Mac asked. He then answered his own question. "Oh, I see... the commission doesn't want to pass the follow-up ordinance requiring rental scooter insurance."

"Bingo," Valdez replied candidly. "I've been asked to remove it from the next meeting agenda."

"So the whole thing is supposed to just go away?"

"Bingo again."

"They never learn," Mac lamented. "They freaking never learn."

164

"It's business, Mac. If we clamp down on all the scooter rental places, we're screwing with the TDC, the Chamber of Commerce, the hotels, the whole enchilada. There's just too much money involved, my friend."

"And you want me to lay off the issue in the paper?"

"It would be a special favor to the Conchs," Valdez carefully chose his words. "And remember, like my sainted mama always told me, you attract more flies with honey than with vinegar."

"I'm not a big fan of flies," Mac advised Valdez. "Aside from that, how does Michael Savage feel about this? He told me, as well as the commission, that an ordinance needs to be passed. And he is the city attorney."

"Michael is completely on board."

McKinney could not believe that his good friend had sold out to the Bubbas and the scooter agents. The disbelief quickly passed, being replaced by the sudden awareness that high-power attorneys don't become high-power attorneys by messing with the system.

"This is *Cayo Hueso,* Mac. You've been here, what, 10, 15 years or so? I've been here all my life— nearly 50 years. The Peso speaks louder than the conscience, my friend."

"I'm not ever going to abandon my attacks on the rental scooter agents," Mac told the city manager bluntly. "The Peso means nothing to me— something affirmed by the salary for which I work— not when unknowing tourists like Susan Robbins are being killed on our streets."

Valdez knocked a lengthy accumulation of ash from his cigar, stood and paced by the sliding door onto his Angela Street balcony.

"This is something you should agree to," he advised. "The Conchs can be very vindictive."

"Meaning what?" Mac asked.

"In the old days, anyone who caused problems for the Conchs disappeared in the mangroves— just disappeared," Valdez said. "Of course that doesn't happen anymore. At least I don't think it does. Now, if you don't play ball, you're simply painted out of the picture— persona non grata if you will."

Mac was not used to being lectured to or threatened. And he didn't believe that Valdez spoke with the voice of the full cadre of commission Conchs.

"Shall I report this threat in this week's edition?" he asked pointedly.

"No, I have something better for you to report," Valdez said with a grin, his attitude shifting 180 degrees.

*"Huh?"*

"Well, back to my mama's old adage about the honey and the flies…"

*Again with the flies!*

"Like I said, laying off that story would be a favor— and I've got a much bigger story for you in return."

"I'm listening," Mac replied, clearly unwilling to commit to any deal involving honey and flies.

"You've noticed all the increased security in town?" Valdez asked.

"Well, I've seen a bunch of Homeland Security cars and it's kind of hard to ignore the troops with the automatic weapons," Mac replied. "Word is, they're scared of an influx of Cuban refugees."

"It's more than that," the city manager said, returning to his leather chair across from the reporter. "Now this is totally off the record— I never said a word to you. That understood?"

"Naturally," Mac answered.

"This time off the record means totally off the record. There's a top secret government meeting taking place tomorrow at Boca Chica Naval Base."

"Topic: Cuba?" Mac asked.

"Very much Cuba," Valdez answered. "I don't know the full extent of what will be discussed there, but I know that high-level U.S. officials, as well as high-level Cuban officials will be present."

"Cuban officials *here?*" Mac asked. He was hooked.

"Yes. Now I've got to tell you the truth… I'm not even supposed to know about this. The Chief knows because some officers were needed for backup security and escort. The FBI knows. And the Secret Service is in town. One city commissioner knows, as well. Other than that, no one— except you. That's my favor."

"One commissioner?" Mac wondered.

"Whitemoor," Valdez answered with a grimace.

"*Whitemoor?* You're shitting me."

"Hey, don't shoot the messenger, Mac. It's just what I've heard. Why he's invited, I have no idea. I've heard that maybe he has friends in Havana. He *did* propose that whole sister city business."

"I knew he was up to something!" Mac observed. "So how do I get into this meeting?"

"Not possible that I know of," Valdez answered. "I can't get in. I figured maybe you could— you're good at that sort of stuff."

"I don't know. I've got some pals in the Bureau, but I doubt that they can pull this off. All I know is, if Cuban officials are here, it has to do with the transition. And that's *big.*"

"Well, I know I'd love to be a fly on the wall," Valdez said. *More flies!*

"What time's this meeting?" Mac asked.

"Noon tomorrow, I think."

"Not a lot of time. I've gotta jump on this now."

"You'll let me know what you hear?" Valdez asked.

"I'll let the world know," McKinney answered.

The reporter stood to leave.

"About our deal…" Valdez pressed.

"I don't make deals, Juan-Carlo," Mac replied. "But I do appreciate this lead. And if it pans out, I'm sure it will overshadow any story about the scooter rental stuff."

The city manager understood the reporter's veiled message. "Thanks, Mac."

"Don't thank me, get me a free house in Truman Annex."

As soon as McKinney had left his office, the city manager placed a call to his friend at the La Concha hotel.

"Hello, my friend," Valdez greeted Manny Caballero. "I believe we may have a good source of information on the Boca Chica meeting."

167

## CHAPTER THIRTY-TWO

# *Boca Chica— Classified*

Mac's phone rang early on the morning of May 1. He knew that it was his editor's weekly call of desperation.

The reporter had been up most of the night working his sources in a concerted effort to worm his way onto the Boca Chica Naval base and into the top-secret meeting about which the city manager had informed him. At least, he had hoped to secure a good source who did have access to the meeting. His efforts had produced little more than a promise from Sergeant Hardin to monitor the KWPD secure communications channel for information. He found himself the storied spy left out in the cold.

"What ya got?" Conrad growled predictably.

"David, you wouldn't believe me if I told you," Mac replied.

At the same time— just two small islands East of Key West— a combined team of three NSA and four Secret Service agents waved a multiplicity of electronic wands over leather chairs and pressed an assortment of sensing devices to floors and walls in a windowless conference room at NASKW— Boca Chica.

"I told you boys," Command Master Chief Charles Cole reminded the industrious team of electronic communications specialists, "You could set off a nuke in this room and ain't nobody outside gonna hear it."

The crusty Master Chief was not pleased with Beltway-types second-guessing the security work of his men.

"We're not big fans of nuclear bomb jokes," one stone-faced agent advised him. "Our job here is to protect against any such devices."

*Jeez, what a bunch of assholes!* the Master Chief thought. *You'd think Fidel his self was comin' to town.*

At his compound-like home in Old Town Key West, Tommy Whitemoor was busy selecting his attire for the imminent soiree. He considered a white guayabera shirt in hope of fitting in with the Cuban visitors, but rejected that fearing over-exposure of both his gut and his ample man-boobs.

*The Prime Minister might not be ready,* he thought.

Back at Boca Chica, a young Naval air controller guided a nondescript, military C-130 air transport on its final approach to the westernmost runway, which had been uncharacteristically cleared of all support personnel. The controller advised the pilots of two FA-18 Hornets flanking the C-130 to break off at its touch-down and remain in flight for surveillance over the secure area.

As the landing wheels of the huge transport screeched onto the steaming tarmac of NASKW, the same controller advised his civilian counterpart at Key West International Airport that general aviation flights could resume arrival and departure patterns at that facility.

On the easternmost runway at Boca Chica, a gray Air Force Lear jet landed with not so much elaboration. On board was U.S. Deputy Secretary of State John Negroponte, along with several of his Staff, translators, and a cadre of Secret Service agents.

In line with the well-coordinated effort, a black SUV with dark-tinted windows and bearing government plates arrived at the front door of Commissioner Whitemoor's Old Town home. Agents Black and Gold exited the vehicle. The two looked both ways, literally, then over their shoulders and behind several bushes before advancing to the door and knocking softly. Both agents tugged nervously at the bulky weapons suspended in shoulder holsters beneath their black suit coats.

"Oh, my God, it's you two!" Whitemoor squealed as he flung open the door. "I'm so late, I know. I just didn't know what to wear!"

With that, Whitemoor performed a pirouette in the doorway as the impassive agents stared at his wardrobe choice. He was wearing bright madras shorts, a pink shirt and a white dinner jacket. His eyes fairly beamed through pink-lens sun glasses, one lens of which bore the gold signature, *Elton John.*

"Oh, the glasses were a personal gift from Sir Elton himself!" Whitemoor informed the agents proudly. "What do you think, boys? Too hot, or just right?"

"You're not late, sir," Agent Gold told the commissioner. "We're right on schedule."

Across the street, from the cover of his personal vehicle, a tan Hummer, Sergeant John Hardin snapped telephoto shots of the unlikely trio. His police radio was tuned to the secure communications frequency. Hardin noted that two unmarked KWPD patrol cars had pulled into place fore and aft of the black SUV.

Whitemoor and the agents entered the government vehicle and pulled off, led and followed by the patrol cars.

Hardin placed a call on his cell phone as he followed the procession of official cars.

"Mac, it's John."

"Hey, what's up, pal?"

"I'm riding in a parade," Hardin answered.

"Huh?"

"Two Secret Service agents just picked up Whitemoor at his house and they're on their way to Boca Chica— two unmarked KWPD patrol cars in escort. One car I know belongs to Cuz Dillard. The other, I think is Capt. Toler. All the big brass."

"I just can't believe it!" Mac McKinney replied. "They're really escorting that clown to this big secret meeting? What the hell are they thinking?"

"That's not all," Hardin said. "I've been listening to the secure channel. All air traffic at Key West International was suspended for an hour while Navy air controllers guided something the feds called 'Cigar Transport' into Boca Chica airfield."

"Jesus Christ! This thing is starting to sound scary, John!"

"Hey, remember where we are," Hardin laughed into the phone. "Nothing scary or even serious ever happens in Key West."

"Wait a minute, don't you remember former Commissioner Harry Powell threatening to blow up the planned military housing at Peary Court?"

170

"Yeah, but all he really had was a bag of horse shit, and we never even considered using snipers to blow ole Harry's scalp off.

"Hey, pal, I gotta go— they're speeding up as we turn onto U.S. One."

"Cool, John. Keep giving me the heads-ups if you can."

"You got it, bubba."

The Diplomatic Conference Room at Boca Chica was beginning to fill with high-level U.S. government officials, aides, translators and military. The setting and seating had been carefully arranged by Protocol officers. There was no "head" of the table. Officials from the U.S. and their Cuban counterparts would face each other across the long, Oak conference table, which had been tastefully accented with vases of Bougainvillea sprigs— a colorful, woody plant common to both Key West and Havana.

In the center of the table lay a mahogany humidor filled with genuine, hand-rolled Partagas cigars. On either side of the humidor were placed gold DuPont lighters, molded in the shape of American Eagles.

On the wall behind the U.S. side of the conference table was a historical, pre-Revolutionary map of America. Backing the Cuban flank was an early— ante-Batista— map of the island nation of Cuba. Both had been attentively chosen to avoid political sensitivities, such as the observable and unsettling presence of the U.S.-held Guantanamo Bay on the Cuban map.

At opposing ends of the conference table stood large flags of both the United States and the Republic of Cuba.

The Deputy Secretary of State was already seated at the U.S. side of the conference table. He studied papers filled with talking points and listened as various sycophantic aides struggled to catch his ear with varied bits of last-minute advice about protocol, politics and strategy.

Negroponte paid little attention to his advisors. In his sixties, a Washington veteran, balding and stoic, he was a no-bullshit guy. He was there to get two promises— free elections and freedom for Cuban political prisoners.

From intelligence briefings, he had learned that Felipe Perez Roque, the Cuban Foreign Minister with whom he was about to meet, was of a similar nature— no-bullshit, up front. He was also reported to have a good sense of humor. Negroponte looked forward to meeting the gentleman.

Prime Minister Roque entered the conference room with little flourish. He was, indeed, wearing a trademark white Guayabera shirt, and dress pants. A man in his early seventies, Roque was diminutive of stature. He had jet-black hair, styled in a "butch" cut. At his side strode his personal translator and a much younger Cuban man, dressed in a pin-striped suit which was clearly of Brooks Brothers origin.

With a large smile and a parade-like wave to all present, Roque shuffled quickly to his place opposite Negroponte. The Deputy Secretary stood and shook his hand.

"It is my honor, Prime Minister Roque, to welcome you to Naval Air Station Key West— Boca Chica, Key West and the United States," Negroponte greeted the Cuban dignitary through a U.S. translator.

"I hope your flight was enjoyable. I apologize for the transport, but we have made every attempt to maintain security and preserve the secrecy of our negotiations."

"I too am honored, Deputy Secretary Negroponte," Rogue responded through his translator. "As for the transport, I found it a thrilling ride— quite impressive machinery. And I can assure you, my friend, that it was far more comfortable than the inner tubes and rafts utilized by some of my countrymen to visit Key West!"

Slightly uncomfortable laughter was exchanged among the U.S. contention.

"I would like to introduce to you my diplomatic associate, Otto Rivero Torres, Vice President of the Executive Committee of the Council of Ministries and a Deputy in the Cuban National Assembly of the People's Power."

The man in the pin-striped Brooks Brothers suit extended his hand smartly to the U.S. Deputy Secretary. With a strong background in Economics, Torres was a rising star in the Cuban government hierarchy. While many in the Assembly of the People's Power— the equivalent of a Cuban Parliament— leaned toward securing Cuba's financial future through Venezuela and the growing Socialism in Latin-American countries, Torres saw Cuba's future linked inevitably to tourism— primarily American tourism.

As Roque, he was a true Socialist and a Cuban patriot, but he was also an economic pragmatist.

"President Bush has asked me to extend to you, Raúl Castro Ruz, the Castro family and the Cuban people his condolences on the passing of President Fidel Castro," Negroponte told Roque.

"Thank you for the kind words, Deputy Secretary Negroponte," the prime minister responded diplomatically. "Despite what was published in the world media, Fidel always held a warm spot in his heart for the people of America. He was particularly fond of the New York Yankees."

A much more comfortable laugh arose from the U.S. assemblage.

"I have also been authorized," Roque continued, "to invite President Bush and a full delegation from the United States to Fidel's State funeral, which will be held in coming days."

"You must understand, Prime Minister, that we must move closer to renewed relations with small steps, my friend.," Negroponte told Roque candidly. "There are important political considerations…"

"The Miami vote in your current election year," Roque suggested.

The Deputy Secretary chuckled.

"I was told that I could lay my cards on the table with you, Prime Minister. I'm pleased to see that I was well informed. I think that we can do business."

"I am not so good at cards, Deputy Secretary. But like most Cubans, I relish a good game of dominoes.

"And, please, my friend, call me Felipe."

A senior Naval officer took advantage of the relaxed atmosphere to tap Negroponte on the shoulder and whisper in his ear.

"Yes, I see," he responded. "Have him wait for just a bit while we discuss a few classified issues."

With those instructions, the officer left the room.

"I apologize, Felipe. Your contact here, the Key West city commissioner has arrived. I have asked that we be allowed to have some limited private discussions before bringing him into our meeting. I hope that will be acceptable with you."

Felipe Roque conferred inaudibly with Otto Torres and their translators.

"That will be fine," Roque said. "While Commissioner Whitemoor is a trusted friend of Raúl, I believe that his use to us is of a localized, limited nature. And to put you at ease, I have already been informed of his rather unusual personality."

"Yes, indeed," Negroponte agreed. He was relieved that the Cuban Prime Minister understood that a local city official— a wacky one at that— had no place in geopolitical negotiations.

Negroponte opened his brief case and spread a pile of communiqués on the table before him.

"To get down to business, Felipe, these are copies of our confidential correspondence to date. Our government has informed the Republic of Cuba that we maintain two non-negotiable prerequisites to any relaxation of the U.S. embargo and any possible renewal of diplomatic relations between our countries. Those prerequisites are the establishment of free and open elections by the Cuban government, and the release of approximately 1500 political prisoners now being held in Cuban prisons.

"You have agreed, in principle, to those terms."

"In principle, yes," Roque agreed.

"What is not written in these communiqués is what we in America call 'wiggle room' in both our interests. The administration is clearly anxious, at this time, to see these negotiations come to fruition, Felipe. It would be advantageous to us both to be able to announce the normalization of diplomatic relations and the resumption of commercial trade in the very near future."

"That is our desire, Deputy Secretary."

"John, please, call me John."

"Thank you, amigo. Let me now lay my cards on the table, as you say. My government is prepared to facilitate free national elections by a simple revision of our existing electoral process. Our general elections are held every five years, to elect Deputies to the National Assembly and delegates to the Provincial Assemblies of People's Power. Our National Electoral Commission, the CEN, has already begun to institute computerized voting. This will replace some of our archaic vote-gathering methods such as transportation by horseback, cart and even carrier pigeon!

174

"We are prepared to establish a Cuban Republic National Party— a nationalist party, if you will— which will be faced by an opposition party, the Cuban Democratic Party. Both political entities will present candidates for Deputies, Delegates, First and Second Vice President and President of the Republic.

"Raúl Castro Ruz will be the first candidate of the Cuban Nationalist Party, candidate for President of the Republic. The opposition candidate will be freely elected by delegates to a national convention of the Cuban Democratic Party.

"In the general election, voting will be open to all Cuban citizens, in all provinces. And the process will be open to scrutiny by United Nations representatives."

Negroponte stared Roque in the eye. Neither flinched.

"May we read this as a rejection of Socialism in favor of Democratization?" he asked.

"As you said, my friend, we must move with small steps. My nation is not prepared to summarily abandon Socialism. It is a system which has worked well for our people. However, to your advantage, you may feel free to describe— publicly— the revisions in our political process as 'a move toward democratic elections.' The Cuban government will confirm any such statement to the international media."

The U.S. official conferred with aides on either side of him.

"The administration is prepared to accept such election changes as meeting our first prerequisite," he announced.

The Cuban in the pin-striped suit smiled.

"Naturally," Negroponte continued, "we will need to formalize all details in a formal agreement. We'll leave that to the pencil-pushers.

"Now, about political prisoners…"

Roque laughed openly.

"My dear John, you may count any of our prisoners your Miami Mafia consider to be 'political' in nature to be immediately released upon our formal agreement. We are more than happy to be rid of them.

"Any 'political' prisoners will be offered free passage to the United States, or assimilation back into the Cuban community, provided that they have not been proven guilty of murder or sexual crimes against children."

This is too easy, Negroponte thought. He knew that there must be another Cuban shoe waiting to drop. Instead of waiting for that shoe, he decided to drop another of his own.

"There's one more thing," he said. "It is the question of the return of land and businesses appropriated by the Castro regime following the Revolution of 1959."

*The voice of the Miami Mafia speaks,* Felipe Roque mused.

"Any discussion of repeal of Cuba's Agrarian Reform Act of 1959 is out of the question… it is simply not something we will ever consider," Otto Torres growled. He spoke without consulting his superior, the Prime Minister. But Roque voiced no opposition. He clearly yielded the conference table to his friend in the Brooks Brothers suit.

"Lands and businesses that were appropriated from mercenary American corporations and friends of Fulgencio Batista were justly returned to the Cuban people. Compensation was offered and was refused at the time of appropriation. We will never ask the Cuban people to ever again surrender what is rightfully theirs."

"Is this your position, Prime Minister?" Negroponte asked.

"It is our firm position, my friend. You may feel free to convey it to the Miami Mafia."

Negroponte had been hoping to present the president with a "Lucky Strike Extra," but he saw that it was not going to happen.

"Well," he said, "that's why we have our local commissioner friend— to help smooth the way with the Florida electorate."

The two Cuban representatives waited for a further response from Negroponte. They knew that Cuba's refusal to return appropriated land and businesses could be a deal-breaker.

"The administration is prepared to accept the Republic of Cuba's position that compensation for lands and businesses appropriated under the Agrarian Act of 1959 was offered and refused," he said. "Therefore it cannot be considered a prerequisite to normalization of relations."

The statement— though not yet made public— constituted a home run for Team Cuba. It also signaled "game over" for the Miami Mafia.

*Here's your payback for inviting anyone to kill Fidel Castro, Ileana Ros-Lehtinen,* Roque gloated to himself.

He knew, however, that the Miami contingent of Cuban expatriates would never give up their fight simply because of a weasel-worded statement by U.S. officials.

"Let me offer you a genuine Cuban Partagas cigar, gentlemen," Negroponte said, taking two of the long, elegant cigars from their mahogany humidor and presenting them to Roque and Torres. "To affirm and celebrate our preliminary agreement.

"Just don't ask me how I got them through Customs!"

Both Cubans grinned as they lit the flavorful and famous symbols of their homeland.

"U.S. Customs has never been a problem for Partagas," Rogue joked. "Every presidential administration since Eisenhower has been provided with similar mahogany humidors of the product."

Negroponte laughed aloud.

"That's what I'd heard, Felipe."

"Our government also supplied Elvis and Charlton Heston— *Moses!*" Torres bragged further.

"Well, gentlemen, I believe that we are one step closer to normalization and the resumption of trade," Negroponte advanced. "I congratulate you. Should we now bring in our Commissioner Whitemoor?"

"Just one more thing," Roque said. "The Republic of Cuba does have one prerequisite."

Negroponte had not expected any curve balls from Roque. He steeled himself for the pitch.

"It concerns the illegal seizure by the U.S. of Guantanamo. It would be a sign of good faith on the part of your administration to return the property to the Cuban people."

The Deputy Secretary fairly beamed with delight.

"As you would welcome the departure of your dissident prisoners," he said, "we would be delighted to surrender Guantanamo Bay. It's been an albatross around our neck for years— and that liberal witch Cindy Sheehan nosing around there certainly didn't help matters. When we formalize our agreements, Guantanamo will be part of the deal."

Roque puffed proudly on his Partagas as he shook Negroponte's hand.

"There's nothing like a good Cuban cigar, Juan," he purred.

# CHAPTER THIRTY-THREE

# *Boca Chica— Unclassified*

Deeming himself a virtual prisoner held by armed military officers in a very tastelessly-decorated anteroom, the commissioner was not a happy camper. He had asked three times for a frozen mango margarita— or at least a mimosa— only to be rudely informed each time that alcohol was limited strictly to the B.O.Q. Whitemoor was preparing to turn on his heels and storm off the base when the conference room door opened and he found himself face-to-face with the U.S. Deputy Secretary of State.

"Commissioner Whitemoor, I'm John Negroponte," the imposing figure announced, taking Whitemoor's hand.

The commissioner wasn't really familiar with the man's face, but recognized his name from the nightly news. He found himself somewhat intimidated by the sheer gravitas of the individual.

"First let me say, Commissioner, that the United States government is grateful for your participation in this very important meeting. I sincerely apologize for the delay, but there were certain matters involving national security which needed to be attended to. Very boring business, I assure you."

Whitemoor knew that he was being patronized, but he didn't mind. He relished any sort of attention.

"Well, John, I'm just glad to do my part," Whitemoor answered.

"Please join us now in the conference room, Commissioner. Prime Minister Roque and the Cuban delegation are anxious to meet you."

The deputy secretary was nauseated at the thought of escorting a grown man wearing madras shorts and a white dinner jacket into a vital geopolitical conference. He wondered if he might not be in the wrong job.

Less than a quarter-mile away, his Hummer veiled in the darkness of tangled mangroves, Sergeant Hardin kept his field glasses trained on the tightly-guarded main gate of the Boca Chica air base. With the aid of a hands-free headset, he continued to update Mac McKinney by cell phone.

"No traffic whatsoever," he told the reporter. "Nothing landing, nothing taking off. No vehicle traffic in or out of the base. It's a virtual lockdown. Been that way for an hour."

"So we know they're all in there, whoever they all are," Mac opined.

"Well, not all. The Chief and Captain Toady didn't even get on the base. The escort's cooling its heels outside the main gate."

"Jeez, Cuz must be pissed," Mac laughed.

"You betcha," Hardin agreed. "Of course it's no wonder they wouldn't let Captain Toler on the base. He's packing more firepower than half their FA-18's! Hold on... there's some activity at the gate... shit, it's Juan-Carlo."

"Valdez? He's there?"

"He's just pulled up beside Chief Dillard's patrol car. Windows rolled down. They're talking. Somebody in Juan-Carlo's car... who is it?"

"Don't ask me, you're the one watching." Mac interrupted the sergeant's narrative.

"I know who it is," Hardin responded. "It's the Miami Mafia guy."

"Sonofabitch!" Mac replied. "That Miami Cell's got some cojones!"

"They're desperate," Hardin answered. "And they're ruthless."

Felipe Roque's eyes widened with incredulity, but he managed an awkward smile as Commissioner Whitemoor pranced into the Diplomatic Conference Room with the deputy secretary.

Whitemoor did not wait to be introduced to the Havana dignitaries. In an extreme breach of diplomatic protocol, he simply toddled to the Cuban side of the conference table, grabbed the prime minister's hand and began shaking it energetically.

"Felipito Roque! I'd know you anywhere!" Whitemoor pronounced in broken Spanish. "Raúl described you perfectly! But you're much younger!"

Otto Torres laughed aloud. He had never seen a Cuban man blush.

The members of the American delegation looked on with mixed feelings— indignant disgust and resentful awe.

"And you, my friend, could only be Commissioner Tommy Whitemoor!" Roque responded, offering his own robust handshake. He thought that, perhaps despite his better judgment, he might actually like this gringo.

There could be no doubt that, for better or worse, Whitemoor could rule a room.

"Now…" the brash commissioner began, motioning to a statue-like Naval officer, "It's well past Noon in Key West and I for one could use a drink. Make mine a frozen mango margarita. How about you, Felipito— a Rumrunner for starters?"

"Do you have Bacardi dark?" Roque asked.

Cubans, as a people, never disrespect the hospitality of a host.

"Oh, I'm sure!" Whitemoor responded, turning to Negroponte. "Can you take care of that, John?"

Accepting the fact that he had clearly lost control of the situation, the deputy secretary motioned to Master Chief Cole, who dutifully— if somewhat dubiously— assigned one of his protocol officers to the task of quickly procuring a bar set-up and wait staff from the B.O.Q.

"How about you, Otto?" Whitemoor asked the Cuban in the Brooks Brothers suit. "Rum for you, too?"

"Oh, no, my friend, a Cuban coffee would be fine."

*I'll have a martini straight-up with two olives,* Negroponte thought to himself. Instead of voicing the thought, however, he opted for attempting to regain control of the meeting.

"Commissioner, we all thank you for your Key West hospitality. But our time with the Cuban delegation is limited. While we await the wait staff, let's try to resume this important meeting."

"My bad!" Whitemoor declared, patting Roque on the shoulder, then moving hastily to his assigned seat beside the deputy secretary. "I'm just so excited to have our Cuban brothers here."

"We share your excitement, Commissioner Whitemoor," Prime Minister Roque said. "Also I have some items for you and your city commission from the City of Havana. Otto..."

Vice President Torres opened his brief case and handed several items to the prime minister.

"First, in response to your city's kind offer, I have a formal document signed by Raúl Castro Ruz, as well as all the members of the Council of Ministers— our highest executive and administrative body, constituting the government of the Republic of Cuba— declaring Key West to be a Sister City of Havana, Cuba."

Roque passed the impressive, framed document across the table to Whitemoor, who accepted it with an audible gasp.

"Oh, it's so beautiful!" he declared. "We'll hang this in the mayor's city hall office. It'll replace the picture of Victoria Pennekamp!" Perhaps fortunately, no one present picked up on his quip.

"Second," Roque continued his presentations, "On behalf of the mayor of Havana, I would like to present your mayor— as well as all the wonderful people of Key West— with this Key to the City of Havana. I hope that all Key West citizens will consider it their welcome to our capital and to our entire island nation."

The prime minister passed the large, gold key— replete with a colorful seal of the Republic of Cuba and encased in Plexiglas like an insect in amber— to the commissioner.

"Oh, I have one of those for *you!*" Whitemoor exclaimed, fumbling about the pocket of his white dinner jacket. "Ah, here it is... the Key to the City of Key West— from our mayor and city commission to the charming people of Havana and of Cuba, who make such good coffee and rum... and the pristine Cuban beaches filled with those handsome, young...

"Well, I've never been one for speeches, just accept this with our thanks!" Whitemoor cut himself off.

*Make that a double martini, with four olives!* Negroponte reconsidered.

"Gentlemen, again, our time together here is limited."

"I'm so sorry, Deputy Secretary," Roque responded. "I just have one more item for the Key West commissioner. It is a personal letter from Raúl.

"It is for your eyes only, Commissioner."

Roque handed the note to Whitemoor.

"You may read it later in privacy, Commissioner," the prime minister added. "Now John, my friend, let us continue the meeting."

"Thank you, Felipe," Negroponte said, gratefully resuming control of the conference. "As we lead toward the resumption of diplomatic relations with Cuba, all of us understand the political sensitivity of such a move. There is the sizable Miami Cell and its significant political influence to be considered. To that end, we have mutually agreed that the opening of Cuba be softened by the initial resumption of relations with the City of Key West— which has a large population of residents of Cuban heritage.

"And that is why Commissioner Whitemoor is here."

Whitemoor smiled proudly.

"The commissioner has already begun the process by convincing his city commission to name Havana a Sister City. I understand that further public actions are under consideration. I'm sure that we would all like to hear of your plans, Commissioner Whitemoor."

Suddenly Tommy found himself in the spotlight— and on the spot. He had no concrete plans, only some grandiose ideas.

Fortunately, a rolling bar and a cadre of Naval bartenders arrived to provide him a few moments to think. Drink orders were placed and delivered to the conference table. All of the U.S. deputies, aides and translators opted, correctly, for soft drinks or coffee. Roque was served a dark Bacardi on the rocks. Whitemoor was pleased to see an expertly-crafted frozen mango margarita. And Negroponte did, indeed, welcome a double martini.

*Fortunately, there will be no record of this meeting,* he comforted himself.

"I do have a few ideas," Whitemoor offered, emboldened by several quick gulps of Tequila.

"We in Key West want to become the gateway to Havana. In addition to the Sister City declaration, I have consulted with the organizers of Key West's annual Fantasy Fest and gained their approval to make the opening of Cuba the focal point, the theme, of this year's Fest."

"Fantasy Fest?" Negroponte asked, unfamiliar with the annual event.

"It's like Carnivale in Rio or Mardi Gras in New Orleans— well, the old New Orleans," Whitemoor informed him. "Up to 60,000 visitors come to Key West for a week-long costume festival, culminating in a giant parade on Halloween weekend— around the time you've said we can expect the 'opening'.

"The Fest also draws media from around the world— it gets incredible press, most of it positive."

"Sounds good," Negroponte considered.

"I've convinced the festival organizers to use the theme *Cayo Hueso/Cuba Libre*— literally Key West, Cuban Freedom— to recognize the opening of Cuba. It will be utilized on all festival posters, ads, promotional materials, etc. It will also be the theme of the festival centerpiece, the finale parade. I think the theme will resound around the world."

"I am impressed," the Cuban prime minister said. "Not only are you a outstanding city commissioner, but a public relations guru, as well, my friend!"

"Thank you, Felipe, but that's not all..." Whitemoor said, signaling the bartenders, who were standing at attention by their station, with a wave of the empty glass in his hand. "I have also convinced festival organizers to name Raúl Castro and a Cuban delegation, including yourselves, as Grand Marshals of the parade."

Whitemoor lied about that part. But he considered it a small detail which could be handled at a later date.

"I think the idea is good," Roque said. "But I do not think that we could allow Raúl to travel to Florida so early in the period of transition. I do not feel that it would be safe."

"Indeed," Negroponte agreed. "I know that Homeland Security would have a problem with Raúl's attendance at any event with that many people in an uncontrolled public environment."

"Okay," Tommy concurred reluctantly. "You, Felipe and Otto, will be the Grand Marshals, and Raúl will be the focus of the Cuban end of the event…"

"There is a Cuban end of the event?" Negroponte wondered.

With the discretion of a spy transferring microfilm secrets, a waiter slipped a fresh mango margarita into Tommy's waiting hand.

"Ah, the Cuban end of the event…" the commissioner replied. "There's the real big idea! Immediately following the Fantasy Fest parade, the Cuban delegation will join a Key West delegation— including our mayor and city commissioners— onboard the cruise ship Disney Magic for a celebratory cruise to Havana!"

Whitemoor beamed with pride at his own pronouncement. But there was an air of uncertainty in the room.

"That would be rather costly and problematic, would it not?" the U.S. Deputy Secretary asked.

"Oh, no, it's already arranged," Whitemoor answered cavalierly.

He lied once again— another minor detail to be handled.

"What greater symbol of America and friendship than *Disney?*" Whitemoor pressed.

Prime Minister Roque clapped his hands softly in approval.

"Again I am impressed, my friend. The Cuban people would be quite happy to welcome the Disney cruise line to our island. The arrival of such a cruise liner would indeed present a grand symbol of the opening of relations between our two nations."

Tommy beamed once more.

Negroponte grimaced. He thought Whitemoor was a blustering braggart and quite full of shit. He felt an immediate need to scale back any official U.S. government involvement with the disturbing local politico.

"We may be getting a little ahead of ourselves," Negroponte cautioned. "Your idea, Commissioner Whitemoor, may have a good deal of merit, but we certainly cannot announce any such arrangements at this point in time. That is not to say that you cannot proceed with those arrangements, only that the U.S. government is not prepared to participate in such an event until agreements between our two governments have been finalized. While normalization is being fast-tracked for, well, political reasons, we are still weeks, perhaps months, from announcing that normalization."

Whitemoor smirked. He did not appreciate governmental wet blankets.

"Do not be deterred in your noble efforts," Roque told the commissioner. "I assure you that we look forward to welcoming Mickey Mouse to Habana's Revolution Square!"

"Gentlemen," Negroponte addressed the assemblage, "I am pleased that we have achieved so much in this brief but momentous conference. By way of tying up loose ends, Prime Minister Roque... in the papers provided to you earlier, you will find the URL for a secure web channel which the U.S. State Department will be utilizing in the coming days to videoconference with you and your aides. As we do not feel email secure, hard copies of our agreements will be transcribed and delivered to you, in Havana, via unmarked military jet. The confidential instructions for your air traffic controllers are included in your information package.

"For all parties present, I cannot stress enough the necessity for absolute secrecy regarding this conference, its context, contents and conclusions. At the risk of sounding like the voice from *Mission: Impossible,* the administration will vehemently deny the very existence of this meeting."

"You expect no leaks on your end?" Roque asked, clearly insulted by the Deputy Secretary's seemingly arrogant security warning. "I believe that a comparison between the security measures of our two governments will show that the Republic of Cuba is significantly more successful at preventing information leaks."

"You are so right, my friend!" Negroponte laughed. "And I apologize for sounding condescending. Of course there will be leaks on our end... I'm sure far more than on your end... but we will try to make sure that ours are controlled leaks. In fact, we will begin to disseminate suggestions of normalization through our NIE— the National Intelligence Estimate. These are official intelligence updates provided to the president, updates which often are deliberately leaked as trial political balloons, weather balloons if you will.

"When we have come to final agreement, the NIE information will be confirmed by administration officials.

"What I'm really saying is that no one here should rush off to meet with the U.S. press."

Negroponte looked deliberately at Whitemoor.

The commissioner appeared indignant.

"Honey, I guarantee you, these lips are sealed!" he assured the deputy secretary.

The deputy secretary felt less than confident in the commissioner's oath of confidentiality.

In the mangroves, John Hardin watched as a C-130 transport emerged from a secluded hangar and rolled onto an otherwise vacant runway. At the same moment, the black SUV which he had followed to Boca Chica appeared at the main gate.

"We have movement," he spoke into his cell phone.

"What've you got?" Mac McKinney asked.

"It looks like the meeting is over. Stand by…"

Hardin listened attentively to the transmissions on his secure police communications channel.

"Okay, air traffic at KWIA was just halted again. Must mean the Cigar Transport is ready to take off."

Hardin's Hummer shook as two FA-18 Hornets flew by, low, on either side of the runway occupied by the transport. They were signaling escort readiness.

"Yep, they're definitely on their way out."

"But we still don't know who *they* were?" Mac asked, disappointed.

"No idea," Hardin replied. "But Tommy's leaving the front gate. I'd bet you a box of Dunkin' Donuts he'll spill his guts to someone before the day's out."

The heavy, deliberate drone of huge C-130 engines drowned out the conversation as the Cuban delegation's transport lifted off from the runway.

"I wonder if it was Fidel," Hardin told Mac.

"He's dead," the reporter answered.

"You sure?" the KWPD officer asked.

187

# CHAPTER THIRTY-FOUR

# *Fallout*

Police Chief Cuz Dillard pulled his unmarked patrol car in front of the black SUV containing Whitemoor and the two Secret Service agents and escorted the vehicle away from the Boca Chica Naval Air Base. His escort instructions had been specific: Blue lights only, no siren; adhere to speed limits. The agents did not want attention drawn to the entourage.

Tommy Whitemoor peered out the rear window of the SUV to view the giant transport carrying his new Cuban friends rise into the sky and bank southeast toward the island nation of Cuba. As he watched, his hands caressed the precious Key to the City of Havana. It was, he felt, a quite impressive object d'art— one which belonged in Casa Whitemoor. He would retain possession of the gift to prevent its becoming lost in the bureaucratic labyrinths of City Hall. The Sister City document he would present with all due flair, and to much personal acclaim, at the next commission gathering.

The commissioner pulled the personal note from Raúl Castro from his pocket and began to unseal it.

"We'll need to impound that as contraband, under the Homeland Security Act," Agent Black, who had been watching Whitemoor closely in the rear view mirror, informed him.

"It's personal!" Tommy howled indignantly.

"It's *intelligence*," Black replied sardonically.

"In a rat's ass!" the commissioner shot back.

Whitemoor quickly pressed the button which lowered the rear window of the SUV, just as the vehicle crossed over the Cow Key Channel bridge. Almost without thinking, he flung the letter to the wind, which carried it up, then down into the depths of the Cow Key Channel.

It was the most noble thing Whitemoor had ever done.

He immediately regretted it.

Agent Gold hastily radioed for following patrol cars to break off and search for the discarded "contraband." Whitemoor turned to watch and chuckle as two KWPD officers jumped from their vehicles and scrambled down the banks of the Cow Key Channel— desperately dodging the countless vagrants who called the area home.

Sergeant Hardin drove slowly by the ruckus, craning to see what might be occurring. He decided not to stop, but rather continue following the SUV. He did, however, alert Mac McKinney that something untoward had interrupted the procession.

"You know that we could have you imprisoned for that," Agent Black told the commissioner.

"I don't think that very likely," Whitemoor responded cockily. "You need me. And don't threaten me, boys, or I'll expose the whole scheme to *Hillary!*"

His bogus warning silenced the agents. And the bumbling Key West commissioner suddenly was aware of the powerful position in which he found himself.

Agent Gold scribbled a quick note on his notepad and passed it surreptitiously to Black.

*Leave him to the boys at the Bureau. They're going to cut his nuts off anyway— if he has any.*

The two agents exchanged grins as the SUV pulled to a stop in front of Whitemoor's home.

"Thanks for the ride, gentlemen," Whitemoor told the two as he stepped from the vehicle. "Now don't be strangers. You're both welcome for drinks any time! I can be quite the hostess, you know!"

"I really don't think he *does* have any," Black noted to his partner as the two pulled away, "Nuts I mean."

At Garrison Bight, John Hardin parked his Hummer and made his way out the dock toward Mac McKinney's houseboat. Mac was seated on the rear veranda waiting for him, cold beers in hand.

189

"You know I can't drink beer on a houseboat, Mac. I get seasick real easy."

"I dropped a Dramamine in it," Mac joked.

"Oh, okay then."

"Did you find out what they jettisoned?" the reporter asked.

"No. The agents told the officers to look for contraband— an envelope. But I'm pretty sure whatever it was is sleeping with the Tarpon in Cow Key Channel."

"And when they dropped Tommy off, he was alone?"

"Yep. So were the agents. Whoever was in that meeting left on that C-130 transport."

"Shit," Mac observed.

"Why don't you call Whitemoor and ask him who was there?" Hardin questioned his friend. "Isn't that what you reporters do?"

"Not when we're dealing with assholes. I'll probably place a call to him so I can honestly say I did. He won't return it because he hates me as much as I hate him. Then I can report that 'Commissioner Whitemoor failed to return calls for comment.' That leaves me free to speculate. Gonzo journalism 101."

"Sorry I couldn't get you more information," Hardin apologized.

"It'll all come out soon," said Mac. "If I know Whitemoor, he's on the Net to all his pals right now."

"You know, you're probably right— betcha he's all over Instant Messenger. Gotta go. I might have a date with a city commissioner."

Sergeant Hardin leapt hastily from the houseboat onto the dock.

"You forgot your beer!" Mac called after him. "You want it in a go-cup?"

"Hell no, we have an open container law in this town!" Hardin called back.

"That's why you're my hero!" the reporter shouted to the large figure quickly disappearing down the Garrison Bight dock. He meant it.

190

## CHAPTER THIRTY-FIVE

# *The Peacock Grooms*

The reporter's instinct had been correct. Whitemoor was on the internet like white on rice as soon as he had rid himself of the government agents. He was desperate to contact his friend Raúl Castro to inform him that his personal note had been "lost." In truth, he was anxious to find out what had been contained in the note.

Whitemoor tried Instant Messenger first, but the messaging system showed **RAÚL** "offline." He then e-mailed the Cuban president:

*Raúl... IM me, ASAP!*

Frustrated, he punched Victoria Pennekamp's number into his cell phone.

"Vicky! We have to do lunch tomorrow!" he instructed her. "It's important and has to do with the Cuban business and the big idea I told you about."

The Chamber head was in no mood for the ramblings of the insane commissioner.

"Listen, Tommy, I'm up to my tits in this 'Sink Week' business. The Vandenberg leaves the cleaning facility today and the tow boats will start dragging it down here. Press from around the world will be here for the sinking next week."

"Screw your rusty old battleship!" Whitemoor shouted. "This is more important."

"It's not rusty," Pennekamp retorted. "They just cleaned it. You can't have a rusty artificial reef. And how's your little Cuban party more important than the $5.7 million the county and the city have sunk— no pun intended— into this sinking? We've been trying to pull this stunt off for nearly four years now."

"It's rusty," Whitemoor insisted. "And furthermore, it's loaded with all sort of toxic chemicals and residue from all that war crap. But listen, that's not the point. What's important is, I really need your help with my Cuban project. Christ, we're talking about the opening of Cuba here!"

He can be such a drama queen! Pennekamp thought.

But Whitemoor was, after all, a city commissioner— just one more cross she had to bear in her capacity as Chamber of Commerce president.

"Okay, okay," she agreed reluctantly. "Lunch tomorrow. Call me in the morning."

"Good."

"You're paying, though."

The commissioner was going to argue but the thought was forestalled by the little yellow IM man racing at the bottom of his screen.

*PETER14 is Instant Messaging...*

Whitemoor unceremoniously hung up on Pennekamp and quickly logged on to Instant Messenger as *PEACOCK.*

*HI, Peter!* he typed. *Where you been? I've been IM-ing for weeks!*

*Busy with schoolwork.*

*Oh, of course. That's cool.*

*How about you? Wassup with you? PETER14* typed.

*Just work. Being grown up is hell!*

*What kind of work?*

*Oh, a little of this and a little of that.*

*PEACOCK* was answering obliquely. That didn't surprise *PETER14's* alter ego.

*That's no answer,* Whitemoor's young correspondent pressed. *What do you do?*

*I swim a lot. And I snorkel. Nude, of course. How about you?*

*PEACOCK* was pushing for titillation.

*Yeah, I like skinny-dipping, too. Kinda hard to do where I live, though. I mean, most of the nude beaches are full of dirty old men.*

*You have nude beaches where you live?*

*Sure. You don't? You sure you live in Florida?*

192

Hardin knew that nude beaches were plentiful on the mainland, but none existed— at least officially— in the Keys. *PEACOCK* had slipped.

*How about sending me a pic of yourself? Whitemoor typed, changing the subject.*

*I'd have to know you better.*

*You could come down here and go swimming nude with me... then you'd know me better.*

"...down here..." *PEACOCK* had slipped once again. Hardin wondered if he should continue to bob and weave or go for the K.O.

*You in SoBe or the Keys? He typed cautiously.*

There was a long pause before *PEACOCK's* response.

*Yeah, I'm in the Keys.*

It was a candid response the sergeant had not expected. Clearly, his subject was becoming careless, probably desperate.

*So when you gonna come down and see me? Whitemoor persisted. School's out in a couple of weeks, isn't it?*

*Yeah. I'd have to explain it to my mom, though. And I may have to go to summer school anyway.*

*I could send you a plane ticket, you could come down for a weekend.*

*Why? I don't even know what you look like. You might be 60 and ugly as hell.*

*I told you, I'm 29. I'm blond and I have a great bod!*

*Yeah, sure! Send me a pic.*

*Not 'til I've seen yours.*

Hardin had a file of stock boy photos he could use to represent *PETER14* and he decided the time was right to offer his subject further temptation. He chose a handsome, blond boy aged about 14 years. The boy was dressed in wrestling tights and holding a trophy. He would be *PETER14*.

*Where do I send it? Hardin typed.*

*PEACOCK1@SafeMail.com*

*Hold on a sec.*

Hardin made a note of the SafeMail account for "the boys" at the FBI and proceeded to send an e-mail with the photo attached to *PEACOCK*.

*Done. PETER14* typed.

Whitemoor hurriedly opened his SafeMail program and was delighted to see that he, indeed, had e-mail from *PETER14*.

*Damn, I'm good!* Whitemoor thought. He then clicked on "attachment" to view the photo.

*Wow!* He typed. *You definitely have to come down here this summer!*

*LOL! PETER14* responded. *I've shown you mine, now show me yours.*

*You sure that's you? You never mentioned wrestling.*

*You never asked.*

*LOL! You're right. Anyway, you're looking good in that pic! So send yours.*

*I'll have to dig one up. It'll take me a day or two.*

The subject was stalling. Hardin knew it would take many more IM's before he'd ever see a photo. But he needed that proof. He would bide his time.

*Hey, you never told me what you do! You're not a cop or anything?*

*Hell, no!* Whitemoor replied. *Of course I could play one on TV.*

*You an actor?*

*Well I have been on stage a lot.*

The pieces were coming together in Hardin's mind. He was getting closer to positively identifying his subject.

The yellow man again danced at the foot of Whitemoor's computer screen and the familiar IM bell tone alerted him: *RAÚL* is Instant Messaging you...

*Gotta go, Peter...* Whitemoor typed hastily. He hated to abandon his young target in mid-grooming, but he was anxious to hear from Raúl.

*I'll IM you later.*

*K... PETER14/Hardin* replied.

*PEACOCK* had already signed off.

*RAÚL!* Whitemoor typed. *It's great to hear from you. I just got out of the meeting a while ago.*

*And how did it go, my friend? Were you impressed with my prime minister?*

194

*Oh, yes! And that Otto Torres— he's very handsome, and such a dresser!*

*LOL! Indeed. They are my closest confidantes, Tommy. And tell me, was your government impressed? Did it go well?*

*I think so, Raúl. They excluded me from most of the important political stuff, but they all seemed to like my ideas for the opening. By the way, I still have to tell you about that.*

*Felipito has already told me of your plans, Tommy. And I am thrilled! A grand parade and a cruise ship from Disney— what an event! Surely it will overshadow the negative images the Miami Mafia will try to generate. I look forward to welcoming you and your city administration to Habana!*

*Just promise me a nice hotel suite when I arrive, Raúl. Of course I might be bringing a new YF with me— his name's Peter.*

*LOL! Don't worry, my friend. You and your YF will be staying at the presidential palace.*

*Ohmigod, I'll be the envy of every queen in Key West!* Whitemoor replied excitedly. *Oh, there is one thing that went kind of wrong...*

*Oh?*

*Yes, that personal note you sent through Roque. The Secret Service agents wanted to seize it. But I refused to give it up. I threw it out the car window. I hope it wasn't terribly important.*

*LOL! You should have surrendered it to the agents— it was merely an autographed photo of myself! I can be very vain sometimes.*

*Damn, I'd liked to have had that, too.*

*Do not worry, my friend. I will autograph one for you in person when you arrive in October. And speaking of things gone wrong, I have reason to believe that our correspondence here has been compromised.*

*Huh?*

*I have been informed by my technical advisors that our IM is being monitored. I suspect that the surveillance is on your end, as few here have access to IM.*

*Shit. Do you know how long this has been going on, Raúl?*

*No, I don't. Not long, I think. Still, I feel we must abandon this channel of communication. Someone there— someone I trust—*

*will contact you soon with a secure cell phone number through which you can contact me. And don't worry too much about what might have been said here, Tommy. We are moving closer to renewed diplomatic relations— thanks in great part to your efforts. I do not think that your government will choose to derail our negotiations over some IM conversations— no matter how lurid!*

*LOL! You're prolly right, Raúl. In the meantime, I'll wait for the cell number and I'll be looking forward to sharing a Mojito with you!*

*Bacardi, my friend... I'm strictly a Bacardi drinker. But I will see to it that you are served the best Mojito in all of Habana! For now, adios mi Amigo. I remain grateful for your efforts on behalf of myself and the people of Cuba. And I look forward to the arrival of yourself and the mouse boat!*

**RAÚL** signed off IM.

Whitemoor immediately clicked on the *PETER14* icon in his buddy list, but it flashed "offline."

*All in good time, my pretty,* he mumbled to himself.

196

# CHAPTER THIRTY-SIX

# *Tap-Dancing*

Mac McKinney had to do a lot of tap-dancing around facts— of which he knew few— and depend heavily on unnamed but reliable sources— factual or fanciful— in order to construct a news story based on the Boca Chica meeting. But he knew that the meeting had occurred. He knew big stuff was happening. And he knew that the public needed to know. To Mac, the end story justified the means.

**CUBAN INVASION?**
**TOP SECRET MEETING HELD AT KEY**
**WEST AIR BASE**
*By Mac McKinney*

While Key Westers share city streets with uniformed, armed soldiers dutifully protecting residents from a feared influx of Cuban immigrants following the death of Fidel Castro, a Cuban invasion may have already occurred— behind our backs.

In the early morning hours on May 1, air traffic was inexplicably halted in and out of Key West International Airport (KWIA). At the same time, a C-130 air transport, escorted by FA-18 fighter jets, secretly landed at Boca Chica Naval Air Base. The base was sealed to prevent any entrance or exit— save for one heavily escorted black SUV, which was admitted to the base shortly after the transport landed.

Sources inside city government told *The Reporter* that the unmarked transport carried high-level Cuban officials bound for a top secret meeting with representatives of the U.S. government. Some political observers speculated that the meeting may have been an attempt to smooth the way for the eventual resumption of diplomatic relations with the Communist nation of Cuba. Those sources told *The Reporter* that "following Castro's death, the opening of Cuba to U.S. travel is almost inevitable."

*The Reporter* has also learned that one passenger in the shadowy, black SUV was, in fact, the often flamboyant City Commissioner Tommy Whitemoor— a seeming paradox at a high-level, top secret geopolitical power meeting.

Commissioner Whitemoor did not return *Reporter* phone calls requesting comment. It is known, however, that Whitemoor recently sponsored a resolution calling for the city of Havana, Cuba to be named a "sister city" of Key West. When first proposed by Whitemoor, the resolution was met with virulent opposition from other commissioners. Curiously, the same resolution passed unanimously in a subsequent commission meeting.

U.S. government officials and Naval spokespersons for Boca Chica have declined to confirm or deny any meeting or even the closure of Key West airspace on May 1. An air traffic controller at KWIA called the hour-long closure "routine, a matter of testing our security systems."

Further details regarding the top secret Boca Chica meeting were unavailable at press time. Stay tuned.

—

"Don't tell me who your 'sources' are," Mac's editor told him when he reviewed the piece. "I don't think I even want to know."

Conrad placed the news story under a "EXCLUSIVE" banner, in its own bold-outlined mortise, page one, above the fold.

As soon as the edition hit the streets, the boys from the FBI were on the phone to Mac demanding to know the identities of his sources.

"Can't tell you, boys," he replied. "Freedom of the press, confidential sources and all that, you know."

*Gadfly 1, Feds zip,* Mac chuckled to himself.

## CHAPTER THIRTY-SEVEN

# *"Let us listen, the bugle blow"*

From the comfort of a daybed in his extravagant La Concha Hotel room, Manuel "Manny" Caballero guzzled a chilled Hatuey beer as he watched intently the dramatic Telemundo network coverage of Fidel Castro's funeral in Havana.

The *Democracia* operative had just finished reading Mac McKinney's piece on the Boca Chica meeting. While speculative, he thought, it did mesh with what he had been able to learn from his friend, Juan-Carlo Valdez and from sympathizers in the ranks of the U.S. Navy.

On a crowded, noisy street corner at the Malecon in Havana, Raquel Zavala clung tightly to the starched collar of her son's white Pioneer shirt as the two began to weave their way into the giant, rolling length of human fabric which had become Fidel's funeral procession. An anxious young Fidelito could not hear his mother's desperate pleas of "stay close, Fidelito" over the peripatetic and percussive shouts of "Viva Fidel!" and "Viva Raúl!".

Raquel craned her head and stood on her toes as she walked, in an attempt to see over the hundreds, maybe thousands of heads before her, hoping to see Raúl or perhaps even Fidel's flag-draped caisson. But even though she had managed to enter the cortege very near the head, it had already grown to fill the entire width of the Malecon. It was all Raquel could do to hold on to her son.

Telemundo helicopter-mounted cameras broadcast clear, overhead images of the procession which its announcers described as "now exceeding two million Cubans— a sea of humanity which stretches the length of Havana's Malecon!"

*Impressive,* Caballero thought as he watched the coverage.

Even he, one of the staunchest, most dedicated of *Democracia* followers, knew that no regime could pay for or coerce so large an outpouring of emotion. He could see it in the faces of the Cuban people as close-ups of crowd-members flashed across the TV screen— his people loved this devil, this Fidel. Obviously, he thought, they had not had their land stolen from under them in the Revolution. Obviously, they knew no better.

The unprecedented, wall-to-wall news coverage of Castro's funeral marked a bittersweet moment for Mac McKinney. He knew that with the interment of Fidel, his brother Raúl would feel free to cut a political deal with the U.S. to open Cuba. That eventuality could, for Mac, mean the realization of his lifelong fantasy— to move to Havana and publish an English weekly newspaper. At the same time the "opening" would bring with it yet another "Americanization" of Cuba. Hotel chains, Las Vegas nightclub syndicates and oil conglomerates would move in overnight to once again steal the land— and the souls— of the Cuban people.

Just as the dictator Fulgencio Batista, Raúl Castro would never be able to resist the appeal of the powerful Yankee dollar. Everything Fidel and his band of ragtag revolutionaries had fought for would be lost, forgotten.

Tour trains and trolleys would crowd the Malecon. And the quiet, charming streets of La Habana Vieja would become lined with countless T-shirt shops, operated by the same avaricious merchants who had sullied Key West's Duval Street with their obscene merchandise and less-than-reputable business practices.

The Telemundo heli-cams hovered close to the caisson carrying Fidel's Cuban flag-draped casket, then pulled back to reveal the substantial line of dignitaries who led the procession following Fidel's body as wound its way toward the Plaza de la Revolución. At the center of the line, Raúl Castro marched arm-in-arm with young Elian Gonzalez and Venezuelan president Hugo Chavez. Raúl was dressed in his uniform as head of the Cuban army. Chavez wore a traditional white Guayabera shirt with dark pants.

And Elian was dutifully outfitted in his Pioneer uniform. The three marched silent and stone-faced.

Represented on either side of the trio were members of the Council of Ministers, first vice presidents and vice presidents, as well as a number of Ruz and Diaz-Ballart family members. Behind the line of officials followed an incalculable number of ordinary Cuban mourners.

Mac took note of the presence of Hugo Chavez in the line-up of dignitaries. Chavez, he knew, had made significant strides in establishing a new Socialist movement in his own Venezuela and his influence was growing throughout Latin-America. He wondered if Raúl and Chavez might have a surprise in order for a U.S. president anxious to leave the opening of Cuba as a legacy.

The same thought crossed the minds of several of those watching the proceedings in the Situation Room at the White House.

"There's the real reason we can't delay a deal with Raúl," John Negroponte told the others gathered in front of the big-screen, plasma TV. "While a quick deal is certainly going to be politically advantageous to us, the fact is, if we screw it up, Chavez is poised to back Raúl with all the oil money at his disposal— and that's a lot of money."

The president agreed.

"You're right, John. We need to fast-track this. What's our current time-table?"

"We're talking about an announcement of the opening by the end of the summer… with an official opening in the fall, probably October."

"That's the Key West connection?" the president wondered.

"Yes. To divert Miami Mafia opposition."

"Do it, John. Get 'er done."

As the heli-cams circled around the José Martí monument at the Plaza de la Revolución, viewers saw the first images of Fidel's final resting place. A massive, marble, permanent catafalque had been added to the base of the monument. Atop the catafalque rested a polished Plexiglas viewing vault, in which Fidel's body would be entombed.

Raúl Castro had outdone himself. His brother and his revolution would be eternally aligned with Cuba's most revered savior, José Martí. Raúl's eyes became teary as he caught sight of the glistening Plexiglas vault reflecting dramatic shafts of Havana's bright, morning sunlight up onto Martí's powerful bronze likeness.

As the huge procession entered Revolution Plaza, a military band played and soldiers led Raúl and the front line of dignitaries onto a platform erected adjacent to Fidel's vault. The Cuban people were choreographed into a large circle surrounding the entire plaza. Most of them waved small Cuban flags. Many old women wept openly.

When the crowd had been fully organized, the military band began to play a funeral dirge as eight dress-uniformed soldiers serving as pallbearers respectfully and carefully removed the Cuban flag from Fidel's casket. The flag was folded in military fashion, and passed to Raúl on the speaker's platform.

Then a hush and pall fell over the assembled throng as the pallbearers unexpectedly removed the lid from the casket, revealing the Cuban leader's dead body. Fidel was dressed in his familiar green military uniform. His arms were crossed above his chest. Resting comfortably in one hand was a Partagas cigar with a gold band bearing the State seal of the Republic of Cuba.

With careful precision, the pallbearers lifted and began to slide Fidel's casket into the viewing vault. As a tearful Elian Gonzalez placed a ceremonial seal at the foot of his "Uncle Fidel's" vault, the band began to play the *Hymn of Bayamo*— the Cuban national anthem, composed in Bayamo in 1867, at the height of the fracas of Cuba's battle for independence.

Raúl Castro, the dignitaries and the Cuban people sang:
*Charge to combat, bayameses*
*Proudly our motherland watches you*
*Do not fear a glorious death*
*Because to die for our country is to live*
*To live chained, is to live*
*Under affront and opprobrium submitted*
*Let us listen, the bugle blow*
*To arms, braves, charge!*

At the conclusion of the anthem, Fidel's close friend, Venezuelan President Hugo Chavez spoke to the crowd.

"The voice of Cuba has been stilled," he began, "but it has not been silenced. For Fidel's voice continues to resound loudly and forever will resound in the hearts of the Cuban people. His life-long message of revolution and independence is the very heart of the Republic of Cuba. May it resound forever throughout the world."

"Viva Fidel!" echoed throughout the crowd and flags waved in unison.

Raúl Castro embraced Chavez and assumed the speaker's podium.

"I am not the eloquent speaker my brother was," he said. "As you know, Fidel could speak for hours, not from notes, but from his heart.

"My message of eulogy for Fidel, and for you, the Cuban people, is a simple one... derived from his own words... words he often broadcast from a small radio in his rebel camp, hidden deep in the Sierra Maestra... from the very beginning of our struggle for freedom from the illegitimate and inhumane Batista regime.

"They were words he broadcast to you and your forebears who hid from Batista's secret police in the streets of Habana, even as he hid in the mountains... they were words of reassurance, of confidence and of promise for the suffering citizens of Cuba... they were words which defined the revolution, and defined Fidel. They were words which awakened the desire for independence in the hearts of the Cuban people when Fidel spoke them.

*'You are us, and we are you.'*"

The shouts of "Viva Fidel!" and "Viva la Revolución!" from thousands of Cubans gathered at Revolution Square to say farewell to Fidel were deafening. Raúl waved his arms above his head as the Hymn of Bayamo once again rose from the band. He was joined by Hugo Chavez, young Elian and the other dignitaries on the platform.

Deep within the crowd of onlookers, Raquel Zavala wrapped her arms around her son, kissed his head and whispered in his ear, "Always remember him, Fidelito. He is you, you are he."

At the La Concha Hotel in Key West, Manny Caballero watched the display with disgust. At the same time, he felt a twinge of loss. It was a feeling he could not explain to himself.

# CHAPTER THIRTY-EIGHT

# *But Will It Float?*

As Tommy Whitemoor walked the short distance from his home to Kelly's, he noted a significant increase in the number of armed troops and white Homeland Security vehicles patrolling Duval Street following Castro's funeral. He wondered if and when hordes of Cuban refugees might arrive in Cayo Hueso. The thought of thousands of lustful Latin men roaming the streets delighted him.

For the moment, all he noticed were throngs of young sailors crowding the doorways of the multitudinous, tacky tattoo parlors which had recently replaced multitudinous, tacky T-shirt shops when the City Commission revoked— under threat of yet another costly lawsuit— its ordinance banning tattoo parlors in the southernmost city.

Whitemoor had voted with the Commission majority in overturning the ordinance— on instructions from the Bag Man. That meant, he knew, that there were big money payoffs involved. He wondered if he'd be seeing any of that money.

Victoria Pennekamp was already seated, sipping a glass of white wine, at a corner table below a spreading Banyan tree, as Whitemoor strolled merrily into the garden at Kelly's.

"Vicky, Darling!" Tommy announced as he approached the Chamber bigwig and adorned her with a number of flighty air kisses. "So good to see you, dear!"

"Now *I know* you want something, Tommy," Pennekamp responded. "Sit down and tell me what it is so I can get back to work. The Vandenburg has already left the Norfolk shipyard and we're three days away from the Sinking Ceremony."

"All in good time, my pretty… all in good time. I have a lot to tell you. But yes, I do need your help."

"Okay, what's it all about? that Cuba thing of yours?"

Not one to be rushed into things, Whitemoor took time to order himself a frozen mango margarita and a bowl of chips and salsa.

"Here's the story," he began. "The U.S. will resume diplomatic relations with Cuba this October…"

"And just how do you know that?" Pennekamp interjected.

"I just know. Trust me."

"Go on."

"Key West will be the focus of a major celebration of the opening of Cuba."

"You're going to compete with Fantasy Fest?"

"No, Fantasy Fest will be part of the celebration! I've already arranged with Ann Richardson to have the theme changed to *Cayo Hueso/Cuba Libre!* The Fest will be a celebration of the opening of Cuba, you see. We'll be positioning Key West as the 'Gateway to Havana.'"

"Okay, sounds pretty good. Sounds like you've got it all arranged. Why do you need my help?"

"There's more, darling, there's more. Ohmigod, it's so exciting! The Prime Minister of Cuba— Felipe Perez Roque— will be here as Grand Marshal of the parade, along with a delegation of Cuban dignitaries. At the end of the parade, they, along with representatives of our City Commission, will board the Disney *Magic* for an overnight cruise to Havana… to officially open Cuba to U.S. travel!"

"You've got all this arranged? Are you crazy? How do you think you can pull all that off? The *Magic*? Yeah, you are crazy!"

"Well, you wanted to know why I need your help. That's why. I need that cruise ship. I'm confident you and Lively— and maybe the Bag Man— can accomplish that."

"Yep, you're crazy. Do you know how much it would cost to rent an entire Disney cruise ship— I mean even if they would even entertain the idea?"

"What's money? Hell, you raised five and a half million to sink a ship. Listen, there will be media from around the world here to broadcast this event. The publicity is worth a fortune. And besides, this will guarantee Disney the first U.S. shot at the cruise business in Havana. I'll bet they might even give us that ship for free."

"You *are* dreaming. Why not just use a huge yacht or something like that?"

"Well, the Cuban government is expecting the Disney ship."

"Oh, I see now," Pennekamp chuckled. "You told them you'd already arranged this."

"They may have gotten that impression," Tommy admitted. "So now you've got to help me pull it off. You can do it. You deal with the cruise lines every day. You suck them into Key West. I'm just asking for one little cruise ship here, Miss Vicky!"

"Just one 85,000-ton Disney cruise ship," the Chamber head corrected the errant commissioner.

Victoria Pennekamp noshed on chips and salsa and ordered another white wine as she mulled over what she'd just heard.

"I'll make some calls," she told Whitemoor. "What I'll most likely find out is how impossible this idea of yours is. But I'll make the calls. I'll also talk to Ted. With his tour business, he'll probably have more gravitas with these cruise ship magnates than I will. By the way, do we have Commission approval for all this yet?"

"Picky, picky, picky," Whitemoor protested. "Since when do I need Commission approval to do anything? But, I'll be proposing it soon. Don't worry, I'll have enough backing to push it through."

"By the way, who's going to be on this cruise, aside from yourself, the commission and the Cubans?"

"Oh, just personal friends... like yourself, of course... and Ted and maybe the Bag Man. And of course we'll want the Mouse, and the whole entourage, Goofy and the whole brat pack. We'll let Disney handle that. Then..."

Whitemoor's guest list was interrupted by the ring tone of Pennekamp's cell phone.

"Excuse me, Tommy," she said, answering the call. "This is Victoria Pennekamp.

"Hi, Julie. I'm in conference right now. Can this wait?

"What? It *what?* You're shitting me! Oh, Christ! Oh, fuck!"

208

Pennekamp had pushed back from the table, stood erect and was screaming at the top of her lungs.

"What the fuck happened? How the shit could this happen? How could they do this to us?"

Whitemoor had never witnessed "Pantyhose" at the height of her fury. He was delighted at the display, and couldn't wait to hear the dirt.

Pennekamp threw her cell phone onto the table in a fit of rage.

"Something wrong?" Tommy asked.

"Wrong? Wrong?" the hysterical Chamber leader cried. "Not a thing wrong, just the damn ship sank, that's all. The damn thing sank!"

"The Vandenburg?" Whitemoor wondered, innocently.

"Yes, the Vandenburg. It fucking sank!" Pennekamp replied angrily.

"I thought it was supposed to sink," he said.

"Yes, Tommy, it was supposed to sink. It was supposed to sink three days from now, seven miles off Key West… not today, five miles off Nags Head, North Carolina!"

"That's trouble, huh?" Tommy wondered.

"That means we're fucked," Victoria answered. "Five and a half million dollars worth of fucked."

Downing the dregs of her white wine, Victoria Pennekamp threw her middle finger to the skies, turned on her trademark red high-heels and stormed out of the garden.

"Shit happens," Whitemoor muttered to himself.

## CHAPTER THIRTY-NINE

# A Slip Of The Ship

The news of the Vandenberg's untimely sinking reached Mac McKinney early Thursday morning— press day— just in time to make it into Friday's *Reporter*. He wouldn't be able to scoop the *Citizen*, but at least the story would hit the streets at the same time in both papers. The *Citizen*, of course, would decry the premature sinking as a great financial, even cultural loss to Key West and Monroe County. Mac had other plans for his piece.

From the first reports that the county was considering an artificial reef project, to be conducted by "professionals in vessel sinking" and being pitched by yet another group of snake oil salesmen— backed of course by the Tourist Development Council (TDC)— McKinney had warned editorially of just one more very costly "Spiegel Grove" debacle. The Spiegel Grove, a similar derelict, mothballed vessel, was sunk "by professionals" to great fanfare off Key Largo in 2001. Unfortunately, one of the "professional" engineers in charge was definitely not smarter than a fifth grader. Instead of sinking horizontally, as planned, the vessel decided to sink vertically. As a result, half of the Spiegel Grove underwater diving attraction remained above the water for weeks. There it sat, sticking ass-up, just off Key Largo— a testament to "professionals."

McKinney's objections fell on deaf county ears. That didn't surprise him. The county had, after all, hired a land use attorney who openly remained chief counsel for the county's largest developer.

*Not our problem— let the County Commissioners be hoisted with their own petard,* Mac figured.

210

But when funding for the new artificial reef project, the sinking of the Vandenberg, which was to be provided by a combination of State and County funds, was coming up close to $2 million short, a mysterious referendum item titled "a referendum in support of the sinking of the vessel Vandenberg as an artificial reef" quietly appeared on the Key West City Commission agenda. One of the scheduled speakers on behalf of the referendum was Chamber of Commerce president Victoria Pennekamp. Mac knew what that meant— the City would end up forking over two million taxpayer bucks to sink some rusty piece of nautical jetsam off Key West in the name of increased dive tourism.

The enraged reporter immediately launched into an editorial tirade unlike any since his notorious, and successful, battle against "jet ski pirates," a band of unscrupulous merchants who had persisted for years in illegally renting wave runners off Key West beaches. It was a red badge of journalistic courage for Mac that he had even been threatened with a blow to the head with a tire iron by one of the pirates. Fortunately, the City listened to his outcry and ran the scoundrels out of town — or at least into City-sanctioned franchise deals— before Mac met with any physical damage.

Unfortunately, the City Commission failed to see any wisdom in McKinney's warnings about the Vandenberg and proceeded to subsidize county and state funding for the sinking with $1.7 million in City funds. The vote in favor of the funding was clearly the result of heavy lobbying by the TDC and the Chamber's Victoria Pennekamp.

So it was with a great deal of personal satisfaction and an equally great sense of payback that Mac sat at his computer and pounded out his eulogy for the Vandenberg's premature plunge.

### THE VANDENBERG:
### SINK, SANK, SUNK
*By Mac McKinney*

The plan was a grandiose one. "Sink Week," this very week, promised to draw media from around the world to celebrate the sinking of the mothballed Naval vessel, the USS Gen. Hoyt S.

211

Vandenberg, six miles off Key West. It would become a watery Mecca for tropical fish, coral growth and, not incidentally, hordes of tourist divers, who would flock to fill thousands of hotel beds.

A glorious flotilla of boats was to carry the media, State officials, County officials and City officials out to the site of the final immersion. That immersion, that sinking, according to representatives of State government and the Florida Fish and Wildlife Conservation Commission, no less, would be executed by "professionals."

Late Tuesday night— even as representatives of the international media were checking into their hotel rooms and partying hearty at Hog's Breath Saloon and enjoying lap dances (along with a number of city officials) on Duval Street— the Vandenberg left a Norfolk, Va. Shipyard bound for the celebration and her final berth, deep in the waters off Key West.

But, early Wednesday afternoon, the Vandenberg decided to make a pit stop— a final one. Inexplicably and quite unceremoniously, she turned belly-up and proceeded to sink, about five miles off the coast of North Carolina— somewhere near Nags Head.

The "professionals" towing the Vandenberg barely managed to sever the massive steel tow cable before the plunging behemoth could drag their own vessel down with her.

The Vandenberg, where she now lies off the coast of North Carolina, is irretrievable.

Upon hearing the news of the Vandenberg's sinking off his state's coast, North Carolina Governor Bill Wilson immediately dashed off an email to the State of Florida, Monroe County and the City of Key West.

"The citizens of the State of North Carolina would like to thank the State of Florida, as well as the Monroe County and Key West City Commissions for their generous donation to the coastline of North Carolina. We would never have been able to afford such a great addition to our coastal marine environment on our limited state budget."

A spokesman for the Manteo County, North Carolina Chamber of Commerce also sent an email.

"We here in Manteo and Nags Head are grateful to the people of Monroe County and Key West for this tremendous addition to our list of tourist attractions. Finally we have something to promote besides the Wright Brothers, a light house and some sand dunes!"

The mayors of Monroe County and the City of Key West were, reportedly, not amused.

Early investigations of the accidental sinking being conducted by— go figure— the Maritime Administration, point to human error at the Norfolk shipyard where the Vandenberg underwent her environmental cleaning. Spokespersons for the Administration told *The Reporter* that a worker at that shipyard may have failed to fully seal one of the sizable openings left when the vessel's massive propellers were removed for salvage. Further details were unavailable at press time.

The cost of the environmental cleaning of the Vandenberg, its transport to the waters off Key West, and its ultimate sinking "by professionals": $5.7 million. Monroe County government will now pay $2 million of that cost. The Monroe County Tourist Development Council (TDC) will provide an additional $1 million. And the nondescript Maritime Administration has said it will pay $1.25 million. The remaining $1.45 million—thanks to the Key West City Commission— is now owed by the taxpayers of the City of Key West.

But the Vandenberg now lies off the coast of North Carolina— according to officials, irretrievable.

"Sink Week" is sunk, though a number of those international media representatives continue to party hearty at Hog's Breath Saloon, Sloppy Joe's and BareAss Bar. At least a few Duval Street lap dancers are still profiting from the city's $1.45 million dollar investment.

According to Acting City Attorney Michael Savage, the City has little hope of recovering any money from the State of North Carolina.

"We effectively made them a gift of the Vandenberg," Savage told *The Reporter.* "The law has ruled that if someone sends you an unsolicited gift in the mail, you're under no obligation to return it— or pay for it. It's the same with the Vandenberg. It's theirs now and we remain obligated to pay all of the expenses we agreed to prior to the accidental sinking.

"In fact, we may consider ourselves lucky if we don't get charged with environmental damage."

Savage said that the City could seek recompense from the Norfolk shipyard if negligence can be proven.

"If we're able to prove negligence on their part, it's certainly possible we could win a lawsuit and recover some money. But frankly, the time and expense involved hardly seems worth it. We're probably better off to just write off the whole sinking business as a lesson learned."

Fact is, the only lesson we've learned is that the Key West City Commission must stop caving under pressure from the Tourist Development Council and the Chamber of Commerce.

The Reporter editorialized repeatedly against the City funding the costly sinking of an artificial reef off Key West. This newspaper was joined by a number of local residents and voter activist groups in that opposition. But the Key West City Commission isn't interested in the opinions of newspapers, residents or even voters. Commissioners have proved once again that they only have ears for the voices of the Chamber, the TDC, developers and business interests.

And so we continue to sink... as the Vandenberg sank. The people of Key West are sunk.

—

Mac wondered for a moment if he might have editorialized just a bit too much.

*Nah, let's just label it "Commentary,"* he reconsidered.

# CHAPTER FORTY

# *Apparition In Cayo Hueso*

Juan-Carlo Valdez and Manny Caballero joked nervously in Spanish as they awaited the arrival of José Castillo at an early morning meeting at El Siboney, the popular Cuban restaurant.

"You will find José to be a man of the highest integrity and a splendid dresser, my friend" Caballero told the Key West city manager. "But he has no sense of humor."

While Valdez had been recruited years earlier by Castillo's operatives, and the two men had exchanged correspondence, he had never met Castillo in person. The man was legend in the Cuban-American community, even in the far reaches of Cayo Hueso. The superstitious among Cubans claimed that he appeared only as an apparition, that he was in fact a Santeria deity.

But it was no apparition that appeared at their table at El Siboney that morning— it was Castillo himself. His sudden, silent appearance aroused the same hush and curious stares which were always attendant with his appearance in Miami bodegas and cantinas.

"Buenos Días, gentlemen. May I join you for a Cuban coffee?" he asked politely.

Castillo presented his usual imposing presence— tall, stocky and dressed to the nines, wearing a blue pin-striped suit and resting his weight on an ebony cane topped by an ivory lion's head figure.

Valdez stood immediately to introduce himself.

It's so nice to meet you, Señor Castillo," he announced, briskly and firmly shaking the Cuban's hand. It was all part of the "Meeting New Associates" chapter in the motivational program he had studied and brought to City government. It was the sort of motivational political correctness that had resulted in Personnel becoming Human Resources and city workers being re-titled as Associates. So much ho-hum, so much hoo-ha. Valdez, though, bought the whole package and was quite proud to lead his business and personal life according to its dicta.

"The pleasure is mine, Juan-Carlo Valdez," Castillo answered with decorum. "Please call me José. And now, my friend, let us sit, enjoy some warm Cuban bread and talk of important matters… or unimportant matters as the occasion presents itself."

With a casual wave of his cane, reminiscent of an Obi Wan Kenobi, Jedi Knight gesture, conversation resumed in the crowded restaurant and curious stares ceased. And the shadowy Miami Mafia head sat with his two Key West operatives.

As Castillo adjusted his chair, Valdez was taken aback as he caught a glimpse of a Glock 9mm, semi-automatic pistol couched in a shoulder holster beneath the Cuban's pin-striped suit coat. Apparently, the city manager warned himself, this man of "highest integrity" also packs heat.

"We have important news for you, José," Caballero began.

"Otherwise, I am sure you would not have summoned me to this Cayo Hueso meeting, my friend," Castillo responded considerately.

"Indeed. While we still do not know all of the details of who was present at the Boca Chica meeting…"

"*We* know," Castillo interrupted. "Present were Cuban Prime Minister Felipe Perez Roque and Otto Rivero Torres, vice president of the Executive Committee of the Council of Ministers— Raúl's money man, and a promoter of future alliances between Havana and Hugo Chavez."

Valdez was impressed. This guy was like a Mac McKinney on steroids.

"Well," Caballero continued somewhat uncomfortably, "that ties in with the additional, new information that we have learned. I will let Juan-Carlo tell you of the most recent developments."

"Please, Juan-Carlo, tell me of your news," Castillo said.

"Yes, sir."

The "sir" usage was also part of Valdez's motivational practice. He used it with the lowliest of city "associates," as well as inquisitive and bothersome reporters.

"I was approached two days ago by one of our city commissioners, Tommy Whitemoor, to include a new resolution on the agenda of an upcoming commission meeting. The content is explosive for the Democracia movement, I believe."

"This is the commissioner who was present at the Boca Chica meeting? The friend of Raúl?" Castillo asked.

"Yes, sir," Valdez answered.

"The sexual deviant?"

"Well, he is homosexual," Valdez responded, careful to be politically correct in his town which lived by the nebulous motto, *One Human Family.* "And, well, also a drag queen."

"His deviant activities include much more, as do those of Raúl, my friend... but let us save that for later. For now, please continue."

"Well, sir, I suppose that the best way to explain would be to read from Whitemoor's proposed resolution itself... 'A resolution authorizing the extraordinary use of Mallory Square for the overnight docking and necessary city services required for the cruise ship Disney *Magic* on the night of this year's Fantasy Fest parade; Providing for the payment of hotel accommodations for a delegation representing the Republic of Cuba, including his eminence Prime Minister Felipe Perez Roque; Providing for the expenditure of city funds for travel aboard the *Magic* and Havana hotel accommodations and per diem expenditures for a number of Key West city officials, those officials to be determined by the Key West City Commission; Allowing for the City's participation in Fantasy Fest activities, newly-themed *Cayo Hueso/Cuba Libre.*'

"Commissioner Whitemoor asked me to fine-tune the verbiage and sit on the resolution until he authorizes me to place it on the commission agenda."

Valdez and Caballero waited for a response from the furtive leader of the so-called Miami Mafia.

"This is truly excellent Cuban bread," Castillo said. "Your local bakers must be from the families of expatriates. And the café con leche is the best I've tasted outside of Habana."

The enigmatic Cuban elder sipped his con leche and gently thumped his cane on the polished Dade County Pine floor as he absorbed what the Key West city manager had just related to him.

"This is truly disturbing news," Castillo said. "Your commissioner would not be requesting these items had not the U.S. government already approved the public presence of Roque at a major event in Key West. The import of that fact is that a rapprochement has already been agreed to. Frankly, we thought our Washington lobbyists had more time.

"When does this Fantasy Fest parade occur?"

"Halloween weekend, the end of October," Valdez answered.

Again Castillo paused to gather his thoughts.

"I think that I will extend my stay in Cayo Hueso, Juan-Carlo," he said, following a long delay. "I would like to take a tour of your town. I would like to see this Mallory Square, as well as the buildings along the parade route..."

"That's not a problem, Señor Castillo," Valdez said. "Actually, the parade goes down Duval Street. The reviewing stand is right in front of the La Concha Hotel... where Manny is staying."

"A short distance from the San Carlos Institute," Castillo added, anxious to be of help.

"That is good. The San Carlos is now under the control of parties favorable to our cause."

"Would you like me to make contact with them?" Castillo asked.

"No, not at this point. There is much planning to be done. For the moment, I will check into your hotel. Then I will spend some time as a tourist here."

"Would you like me to arrange a tour for you, José?" Valdez asked. "I can take you around myself, or have the assistant city manager conduct a tour for you."

"Thank you for your gracious offer, Juan-Carlo, but as I said, I would rather be a tourist, and see things for myself. Also, no one is to know that I am here. Further, my friend, we did not meet here today. In fact, you have no knowledge of José Castillo. And he has none of you.

219

"This is important for you to remember, Juan-Carlo. For we have passed beyond the point of lobbying and of diplomacy. Frankly, you may not wish to join us in the arena into which we now advance. That will be your choice. If you do wish to join us, I will call upon you to provide us with certain services and personnel which may be required to achieve our end."

"I'll do whatever I can for the movement, José," Valdez answered.

"Do not rush to the precipice, my friend. When you are needed, you will be called upon. You may help us, or you may deny us. Your help will be valued and not forgotten. A denial will not be held against you, ever, my friend. For our business now is dangerous— very dangerous."

A pall had once again fallen over the Cuban restaurant. Every ear seemed tuned to the table at which the "apparition" who was José Castillo sat.

"It appears that we have drawn attention to ourselves," the Cuban said, smiling. "Perhaps it is time that we finished our con leche and moved on."

"Would you like a ride to the La Concha?" Valdez asked anxiously.

"No, my friend, I prefer to walk. I see more that way."

"It's a long walk from here, José— at least a mile," Caballero noted.

"Compared to the distance we have traveled and the distance we have yet to travel, it is but a heartbeat in time," Castillo replied, slowly, gracefully raising his large frame from the table. "And don't let the cane fool you, my friends. I can still do the mambo with the best of Cubans."

All three men laughed heartily. And El Siboney resumed its normalcy, or at least appeared to do so.

As they left the restaurant, Castillo shook Valdez's hand, returning the vigorous handshake with which he had been greeted.

"Gracias, my friend," he said. "What you do, you do for Cuba. You are joined in the spirit of our great leader, José Martí. It is in his memory that you serve. Again, *gracias!*"

Valdez left filled with a growing sense of pride. He felt as though he might be involved in something truly important, for the first time in his life— something which didn't involve motivational bullshit or underhanded political deal-making. Then he remembered the specter of the semi-automatic secreted beneath the old Cuban's suit coat and wondered if he might not be in over his head.

As Manny Caballero was preparing to leave, Castillo took him by the arm and spoke quietly with him.

"I want you to take a cruise, my friend."

"A cruise, José?"

"Yes, I want you to book a cruise on this Disney ship, the same one which docks here in Key West. Take your grandchildren. It will be paid for by the movement. Also, take a camera, take pictures— like a normal tourist. I want to know everything about the ship. Ingress, egress, security procedures— I want to know it all."

"When, José?"

"Now, today. Return to Miami and have our office book the trip for you. I will remain here in Key West. There is much for me to do here."

Several cars away, on the other side of the street, a figure in a parked Hummer snapped digital photos with a telephoto Nikon. Sergeant Hardin knew that he was on to something big.

# CHAPTER FORTY-ONE

# *"We Knew That"*

Hardin knew the routine— ignore the numerous cameras leading to the unmarked FBI office on the third floor of the Federal Building. Knock three times and wait for the familiar ca-chunk of the dead-bolt being dislodged after he was recognized through the peep-hole.

Nothing about the way the boys conducted business ever surprised Hardin. But he was surprised to see a new face in Special Agent Tim Smith's office— that of the local Homeland Security Director, Ron Kilpatrick.

"Please, have a seat, John," Smith greeted him. "You know Agent Jill Andrews... and this is Ron Kilpatrick, our D.H.S. man here in Key West."

"Sure," Hardin said, nodding in Kilpatrick's direction. "He's given a few briefings to the department. Good to see you again, Director."

Hardin felt in his pants pocket to make sure that the memory card was still there, then sat in the chair offered him, opposite his three would-be interrogators.

"Your message said you have something to show us," Agent Smith began. "This have to do with Whitemoor?"

"Indirectly," the sergeant answered. "But this is really more about the Cuban business he's involved with."

"You mean the sister city stuff?

"No, bigger," Hardin answered gruffly. He was not ready to be toyed with.

"Okay, John, fill us in."

"Surely you guys know that Whitemoor is somehow a go-between for the Cuba opening— he's being used by the U.S. government and the Cuban government to help make it a clean deal."

"We knew that," Agent Andrews answered quickly.

Hardin doubted any such knowledge on their part.

"Actually, John, we have known for some time that Whitemoor has been in contact with Raúl Castro," Agent Smith added, honestly. "We're still unsure about all aspects of the deal, however. Any information you have for us will be welcomed."

Hardin welcomed the small crumb of candor.

"I have some photos of a meeting which took place this morning at El Siboney. I think that it was a significant meeting."

He reached into his pocket, retrieved the memory card and handed it to Agent Smith.

Smith inserted the card into his computer and uploaded the file. Kilpatrick and Andrews huddled closely over his shoulders as the images began to appear on the screen.

"Juan-Carlo Valdez," Jill Andrews announced.

"Correct," Hardin allowed.

"The other two?" Agent Smith asked.

"I've seen the guy in the suit," the Homeland Security director noted. "He's from Miami... something to do with the Democracia movement."

"He's the dark side of the movement, more correctly the Miami Mafia Cell," Hardin informed the agents and the director. "That's José Castillo... Chief Señor, Numero Uno enforcer guy."

"He looks like an aging Cuban gigolo," Jill Andrews observed.

"Or a cigar salesman," Kilpatrick added.

*Our tax dollars at work,* Hardin thought to himself.

"The third man, we have a file on," Agent Smith said. "Manny Caballero, small-time gopher for Democracia. We don't see him move from Miami much, though."

"He's been here in Key West since the Boca Chica meeting," Hardin informed the FBI agent.

"Do me a favor, John. Give us your take on this," Smith said.

"I think that the U.S. has secretly agreed to an opening of Cuba," Hardin answered frankly. "I think that Tommy Whitemoor is being used as a pawn to facilitate that opening, and that the Miami Mafia is not very happy about the whole deal. That's why Castillo is here in Key West. He's here to stop it."

"What about Valdez?" Jill Andrews queried.

"Good question," Hardin replied. "I can only guess that he has some connection to Democracia, and he's the one who's ratting out Whitemoor, and, I guess, Raúl Castro."

"Let me ask you another question, John," Agent Smith said, leaning forward over his desk to look the KWPD officer in the eye. "Where do you see this going? How far do you think Castillo will go?"

Hardin took a moment to think. He studied the countenances of the three federal officials who were studying his own countenance.

"I think that José Castillo and the Miami Mafia will stop at nothing to prevent an opening of Cuba over which they have no control," he answered sternly.

"You view this as a national security threat?" the D.H.S. director asked.

"I think that you've got a couple hundred National Guard troops carousing with bimbos in Duval Street bars and getting tattooed in our new tattoo parlors, while supposedly watching for Cuban refugees. Behind their backs, and yours, José Castillo and his Miami terrorist Cell is planning something bigger than 9/11. That's what I think."

A macabre silence crept into the room— across the drab gray government-issue carpet, up the drab gray government-standard walls. And the three federal officials exchanged grim glances.

Hardin took advantage of the awkward moment to quickly peruse the expansive third floor enclave of the local FBI. During none of the several visits he had made to the office, never, had he been offered even a cursory tour. And every time he left, he realized that he could not even remotely describe the office which he had just visited.

Hardin's trained detective's eyes meticulously scanned the area open to his view. There were a number of gray computer monitors, all with screensavers featuring the famed FBI seal. In one corner at the far end of the office there stood a bank of electronic equipment which appeared to be of a communications nature, but was otherwise nondescript.

None of the few desks in sight were occupied. There were no flowers on the desks, no family pictures. Suddenly Hardin realized that in all his visits, he had never seen anyone but the two feds with whom he regularly dealt. Maybe, he thought, the whole FBI office was like a Hollywood storefront— so much façade with little structure behind it.

"Anything to report on Whitemoor's pedophile activity?" Agent Smith asked, interrupting the sergeant's panoramic visual tour.

"I'll be giving you some more transcripts soon," Hardin answered. "I engaged him again recently— or *Peter14* did. He's becoming careless. I think he's ready to break. He's ready to invite the boy to meet him."

"That's good," Smith said. "The D.O.J. is poised to convene a Grand Jury. We may be able to use that to pull Whitemoor off the streets if this Cuban business gets to be too much of a threat."

"You wouldn't do that without all the goods?" Hardin questioned.

"We could take what we have and use it to get him to flip on others involved in the Cuban deal," he said.

"You mean give him immunity?"

"It's one of our most effective tools, John. The deal goes to the first guy through our door. The others are left out in the cold.

"And if there's no Cuban threat, there's no threat from the Miami Mafia."

Hardin went stone silent, reflective—

*The boys never tell me anything, now suddenly they're telling me everything. And I don't like one bit of it. These guys would let a pedophile walk so they could look good.*

"You do what you have to do I guess," he answered.

"Don't worry about possible deals, John, just keep up the good work you've been doing. See if you can trap him. And keep us advised."

"Sure."

"One other thing, do you mind if we hang on to this memory card?"

"Would it make a difference if I said yes?" Hardin asked.

"Not really, John. You know it's material evidence and we're required to seize it."

"I kind of figured that," Hardin answered.

"And of course you made a backup?"

"Hey," the sergeant replied, smiling, "If I told you that, you'd have to shoot me."

The agents laughed. Agent Smith removed the memory card from his computer and slipped it into his desk drawer.

*Our tax dollars at work,* Hardin again thought.

# CHAPTER FORTY-TWO
# *"Chickens, Rats and Mice"*

Influential Island Tours owner and developer Ted Lively and the ubiquitous Bag Man joined Tommy Whitemoor at the Chart Room for a clandestine meeting prior to the Commission session at which Whitemoor planned to publicly announce his Cayo Hueso/Cuba Libre cruise ship plan. While the clandestine label may hardly have qualified for any meeting between at least two of the most notorious and controversial figures on a two by four mile island, the figures present knew that Chart Room bartenders and waitpersons were noted for their discretion.

The Bag Man was not thrilled with being forced to do business once again with Whitemoor, but Lively was one of his plumpest cash cows. An ebbing tide lowers every boat, he figured. Financially speaking, the Bag Man went with the flow.

"Pantyhose spoke with me about your cruise ship plan," Lively began the conversation with Whitemoor.

"Pantyhose?" the Bag Man wondered aloud.

"Oops, reading too much Mac McKinney," Lively laughed.

"Vicky Pennekamp informed me of your plans," he corrected himself.

"Good," Whitemoor replied. "I was hoping you'd be able to help."

"It was no easy feat, Tommy, I assure you. But with a little tap-dancing and some long-term profit promises, I've been able to convince the mouse people to provide the *Magic* on the night of Fantasy Fest and to conduct the cruise to Havana the following morning."

"Awwesome!" Whitemoor shrieked.

The Bag Man shielded his face with a copy of the *Reporter* as heads throughout the small bar turned in his table's direction. Ironically, a photo of a former county mayor found guilty of taking bribes from developers graced the cover of that issue.

"Understand, Tommy, you're not getting the whole ship for yourself and your entourage... they're just going to reserve a number of staterooms for you, and reschedule the itinerary of a previously-scheduled cruise."

"That's perfect," Whitemoor answered excitedly. "That will be fine. That's just great. And if there's anything I can do for you, anything at all, you've got my vote!"

Lively displayed a small grin.

"You've always been a team player, Tommy. I expect you'll remain so when I ask the Commission for exclusive control of any future Key West to Havana ferry business. I'll be looking for a 30-year franchise deal with the City, something I can take to the bank."

"As I said, you've got my vote, Ted. Of course I can't speak for the other commissioners. You know they don't really like me very much."

Again Lively grinned.

"That's why our friend, the Bag Man is here," he said. "He will deliver Mayor Dailey, as well as Henry Becker and Carmen Burana. With your vote, that adds up to four Commission votes— you and your cruise are home free."

"But Becker positively *hates* me!" Whitemoor argued.

"He will protest," the Bag Man interjected. "He will hem and haw. He will put on a very dramatic show of his disgust for you and your plan. Then he will vote for it."

"You're sure?" Whitemoor begged sheepishly.

"It's already been arranged," the Bag Man answered softly.

As Tommy Whitemoor celebrated his pre-arranged victory with his confidantes and co-conspirators at the Chart Room, Mac McKinney was booting up his laptop at the press table at Old City Hall, sharpening his journalistic wit for what promised to be a noteworthy City Commission meeting— a rarity in Key West. He was not disappointed. After the meeting ended and the dust had settled, he wrote one of his favorite Commission Reports ever.

**COMMISSION REPORT:**
**OF CHICKENS, RATS AND MICE**
*By Mac McKinney*

While the agenda for Tuesday night's City Commission meeting contained only two potentially entertaining items, City Clerk Josephine Woods found herself serving as Ringmaster at a multi-ring circus of political juggling and literally death-defying acts involving chickens, rats and mice!

For your amusement, we present our first act of the evening: Kathy Banshee, known locally as "The Mother Hen"— breeder, promoter, protector, and defender of the much maligned and recently much propagated Key West poultry population.

*[**Voiceover, Sideshow Barker:** She walks with chickens, she talks with chickens... if you cluck at her, she'll lay an egg for you!]*

The self-proclaimed Mother Hen appeared before the Commission as part of a chicken discussion item sponsored by Mayor Jimmy Dailey— a politician known previously for simply not having all his ducks in a row.

Once introduced to the commission, Banshee offered a hypothesis for the disappearance or mutilation of hundreds of chickens and roosters over the last year— replete with a computer-aided, power-point presentation.

"For the longest time we thought people were poisoning the chickens," the Mother Hen squawked. "But we have not come upon evidence that many of the deceased poultry were fully or partially eaten."

With a click of her remote, Banshee's computer flashed a photo of a pile of sun-bleached bones and bloodied feathers on a screen just to the right of Commissioner Carmen Burana.

229

A pall fell over the commission audience.

*Chickens... **eaten!***

Commissioner Burana virtually gagged.

"I suppose you're going to blame the eaten chickens on the homeless at Higgs Beach?" Commissioner Becker queried Banshee.

"Make light if you will, Commissioner," the Mother Hen chided him. "But we are in dire danger of losing our entire chicken and rooster population!"

"Is that a *promise?*" a catcall came from the audience.

Her feathers unruffled, Banshee continued her morbid presentation.

"In addition to the eaten and mutilated chicken corpses, we have also discovered numerous nests with eggs crushed and consumed!"

For emphasis, Banshee displayed a photo of a hen's nest with crushed egg shells, clearly stained with the remnants of what could only be described as... *yolks!*

Again Commissioner Burana gagged.

"Someone fond of three-egg omelets," Becker observed, tapping his pencil on the dais impatiently— his trademark signal that the speaker was rapidly running out of both credibility and time.

"The real culprit, as we have now discovered..." the Mother Hen continued, "is pictured here."

On the screen appeared a close-up of a huge, toothy rat, seemingly smiling like, well, the rat who'd eaten the chickens.

A collective, audible gasp arose from the dais and from the audience.

"A rat has been killing our chickens?" Burana asked.

"That's not just any rat, that's a Gambian giant pouch rat— an invasive African species which grows up to nine pounds and reproduces at an alarming rate…"

"Like chickens," Becker quipped.

"And it wasn't just one Gambian rat," Banshee noted. "Monroe County wildlife officials have confirmed to me that a significant number of the rats have migrated down the keys to Key West from their original home in Grassy Key. Estimates are there may be as many as 100 rats in Old Town, and they are reproducing at a rate of 20 per week."

"What is it you would have this commission do, Ms. Banshee," Mayor Dailey asked.

"If we are to save our chicken population, we must immediately bring in a professional exterminator, someone familiar with this particular species," the Mother Hen pleaded.

"I now see the seriousness of this matter," Commissioner Becker intoned. "Mister City Attorney, with the approval of the rest of the commission, I suggest that you take the following action…"

"Yes, sir?" City Attorney Michael Savage responded quickly.

"Please prepare an RFP [Request for Proposals] for a Pied Piper."

The laughter and subsequent applause from the commission audience was the most hearty and immense ever seen by this reporter. Becker had outdone himself. He leaned back in his leather chair, a smile of self-satisfaction on his face.

The Mother Hen, on the other hand, flushed an infinite number of shades of red. She appeared as though she might self-immolate on the spot.

The mayor pounded his gavel in a futile effort to halt the frivolity.

*"Order!"* he called. "Order in the commission chamber or I'll have this chamber cleared!"

The raucous laughter and accompanying tittering among the crowd continued unabated until, mercifully for the mayor, Commissioner Becker raised his hand for silence and spoke once again.

"Mister mayor, with all respect due to Ms. Banshee, I would suggest that this body has more important matters to consider than rats eating chickens— even if they're fat African rats eating chickens. Have the city manager hire an exterminator and let's get on with city business."

Another, more controlled round of applause followed Becker's judicious remarks.

"Move to approve Commissioner Becker's suggestion and close discussion," Commissioner Burana motioned.

Her motion was unanimously approved. The Mother Hen slunk off, her tail feathers dragging behind.

Residents are, however, warned to be on the alert for fat African rats romping amongst the omnipresent poultry on Duval Street.

## JUST ANOTHER MICKEY MOUSE RESOLUTION?

Like Daniel entering the lion's den, Commissioner Tommy Whitemoor dared to disregard the smoldering corpse of the Mother Hen to propose what he considers a very significant resolution— the city's co-participation in a grand party for a possible opening of the Communist nation of Cuba.

As reported previously in this newspaper, sources have indicated that Whitemoor has had extensive, surreptitious contact with Cuban representatives and possibly U.S. government officials regarding the possibility of such an opening of relations with Key West's neighbor, a mere 90 miles from our shores.

City Clerk Josephine Woods read Whitemoor's resolution to the commission:

*A resolution recognizing and applauding the imminent opening of diplomatic relations with the Republic of Cuba, together with our Sister City, Havana, Cuba; further authorizing the extraordinary use of Mallory Square for the overnight docking and necessary city services required for the cruise ship Disney Magic on the night of this year's Fantasy Fest parade; Providing for the payment of hotel accommodations for a delegation representing the Republic of Cuba, including his eminence Prime Minister Felipe Perez Roque; Providing for the expenditure of city funds for travel aboard the Magic and Havana hotel accommodations and per diem expenditures for a number of Key West city officials, those officials to be determined by the Key West City Commission; Allowing for the City's participation in Fantasy Fest activities, newly-themed* **Cayo Hueso/Cuba Libre.**

Surprisingly, there was no clear audience reaction following the reading of Whitemoor's resolution. Most probably didn't understand the import of what was being said. That might have been due, in part, to the fact that media information packets, normally issued by the City Clerk's office at least three days prior to Commission meetings, were inexplicably delayed until the morning of the meeting— too late for most media press times. The public were simply not informed on what was being proposed. Go figure.

Commissioner Whitemoor— wearing his trademark, obnoxious Florida shirt— leaned forward to his microphone, tentatively, to explain his resolution. If the other commissioners held true to form, he knew, the other commissioners would blast him and his resolution out of the water, as they did with most of his feeble attempts at being a "serious" commissioner. [We cite his most recent resolution supporting the Hillary Clinton/Barak Obama Democrat ticket for the presidency, as well as his infamous resolution calling for importing alligators to the island as "a tourist attraction."]

"Mister mayor, fellow commissioners... before discussion of this resolution, I'd like to present the Commission with this formal document officially naming Key West as a Sister City of Havana, Cuba," Whitemoor declared, dramatically pulling a large, gold-framed scroll from beneath his space on the dais.

"It is signed by now-Cuban president Raúl Castro Ruz, as well as vice president Carlos Lage and Prime Minister Felipe Perez Roque."

But Whitemoor never really presented the framed document to anyone, he merely replaced it from where he'd produced it. Perhaps he intends to sell it on EBay.

"Now we have the opportunity to position Key West as the 'gateway to Havana,'" Whitemoor continued. "Cuba is about to open up to travel by Americans— I have that on good authority."

An audible *harrumph* emanated from Commissioner Becker's spot on the dais.

Whitemoor pretended to ignore Becker's cynicism and continued with the explanation of his complex and convoluted proposal.

"*Cayo Hueso/Cuba Libre*— Key West/Cuban Freedom is now the official theme for this year's Fantasy Fest, thanks to Fest Director Ann Richardson. It has the full support of the Fest organization. The theme and related activities,

234

which I propose tonight, also have the support of the Key West Chamber of Commerce, thanks to the foresight of Chamber Director Victoria Pennekamp [Vicky Pantyhose for you regular *Reporter* readers]. I can also tell you that the concept has the full support of both the U.S. and Cuban governments."

At that point, City Manager Juan-Carlo Valdez took the unusual step of interrupting a city commissioner in the middle of a presentation.

"Excuse me, Commissioner Whitemoor, but I feel it necessary to point out to the Commission that neither the U.S. nor Cuban governments have contacted the City of Key West regarding this proposal, its appropriateness or even legality— given that the U.S. embargo of Cuba, to this date, remains in effect."

"The embargo is going to be lifted!" Whitemoor yelped.

"I think we need a clarification from the city attorney," Mayor Dailey suggested. "How about it... is what Commissioner Whitemoor proposes tonight legal?"

City Attorney Michael Savage smiled and shrugged his shoulders.

"To tell you the truth, Mister Mayor, I don't really know because I'm not sure exactly what the commissioner is proposing. If he wanted to bring Cuban leaders to Key West today, with the embargo in effect, it would be patently illegal. But if the embargo were indeed lifted, then the law would depend upon what restrictions the government chooses to impose or not impose at that point.

"Passing his resolution tonight will not subject the commission as a whole, nor individual commissioners, to prosecution, even under the current embargo provisions— unless acted upon. His resolution is, in effect, moot, given those provisions. In other words, it's harmless... at this point."

"May I proceed, Mister Mayor?" Whitemoor squeaked.

"Go ahead, Commissioner."

"Thank you. My proposal is that several Cuban leaders will be guests of Key West for the Fantasy Fest parade. In fact, they will be Parade Marshals. Of course, I'll ride in the parade with them."

Another *harrumph* arose from Commissioner Becker.

"But the really big idea is that on the day of the parade, the Disney Cruise ship *Magic* is now scheduled to arrive in Key West to participate in the festivities. The ship will remain in port at Mallory Square until the conclusion of the parade, at which point the Cuban leaders, together with a delegation of our own city leaders, including myself, will board the ship and set off on a truly magic cruise to Havana... the first official U.S. visit to a Cuban port in more than forty years! It will signal the official opening of political relations, as well as travel and trade between the U.S. and Cuba.

"Media from around the world will be here to cover that opening, and in the process will provide invaluable publicity for Key West, presenting our island as 'the gateway to Havana.'"

Whitemoor spread his arms in the air as though he were motioning to the heavens and expecting rousing applause. To say it was an anticlimactic moment would be hyperbole.

"I cannot support this," warned Commissioner Raimundo Hernandez— whose family fled to America from Cuba shortly after Castro's revolution. "You are talking about a Communist government. I cannot support it."

"The worldwide publicity part of the proposal interests me," Commissioner Burana noted. "I'm not sure what we'd have to lose."

"That's a good point," Mayor Dailey agreed. "If this 'opening' does come about, we'd sure be at the forefront of things."

"I haven't been persuaded," Becker demurred. "Commissioner Hernandez is right, we're talking about a Communist country. I can't support that."

"They're not Communist, really, they're Socialist," Whitemoor pleaded. "And besides, I believe that Raúl Castro is soon going to announce democratic elections. It's just weeks away."

Were Whitemoor not a political nitwit, that pronouncement might have been a news bombshell. Instead, he was basically ignored.

"I still maintain we have nothing to lose," Burana reiterated. "If Fantasy Fest has already changed its theme, why not go along? If by some miracle the opening happens and the cruise ship shows, fine... if not, we've lost nothing. I move to approve."

"Do we have any scheduled speakers?" Mayor Dailey consulted the city clerk.

"Yes," Josephine Woods answered. "Key West police Sergeant John Hardin has signed up to speak on the issue."

The respected KWPD officer presented a dignified and authoritative presence at the speaker's podium.

"Mayor and commissioners, the politics of this issue are of no interest to me or my officers. However, I cannot support Commissioner Whitemoor's proposal because of the inevitable increase in security risks which would be presented by the presence of Cuban officials and hordes of international media in the narrow streets of Key West.

"Fact is, we don't have enough manpower to handle the 60,000 to 70,000-strong crowds we normally have to deal with during Fantasy Fest. On the night of the grand parade, all of our main streets are blocked— to both police and emergency vehicles— even though some are pre-positioned near Duval Street. As it currently stands, should a major disaster occur, a riot or bomb threat or whatever, I can tell you that our response time would be slow at best. We simply can't guarantee the safety of our residents or visitors if you add to that a major security risk such as the one proposed by Commissioner Whitemoor. Again, commissioners, I cannot support it. And I encourage you to reject this resolution as unmanageable."

At that moment, a red-faced, fuming KWPD Chief "Cuz" Dillard appeared from the wings, marched to the podium and fairly pushed Hardin to the side.

"That's a lot of *bullshit!*" Dillard screamed into the mike.

"Chief Dillard, you were not registered to speak," the mayor cautioned him.

"I don't give a damn, mayor. Sergeant Hardin is out of order— he never consulted me on this. He does not represent my department— I do. And I can assure you that the Key West police department is fully prepared to handle any size crowd which Fantasy Fest produces, with or without Whitemoor's Cubans!"

It was *Law and Order* gone amok.

"Thank you for your comments, Sergeant Hardin, and you for yours, Chief," Mayor Dailey sought to cool the heat of the moment. "Now,

Commissioner Burana has a motion on the floor and I second that motion.

"Ms. Woods, please poll the commission."

Despite all his protestations and harrumphs, Henry Becker voted in favor of the resolution, as did Burana and Dailey— giving Whitemoor a four to three victory.

As a result, it appears that we are now all going to be celebrating *Cayo Hueso/Cuba Libre* at this year's Fantasy Fest. Look for a lot of Che Guevera and Fidel costumes.

At *The Reporter,* we're just wondering whether or not we'll be granted free passage on the cruise to Havana. We're guessing not.

But the City Commission was not done with its mischief. One item remained on the agenda— a few minor amendments to the development agreement between the City and the developers of the Pirate World theme park, already under construction on Wisteria Island.

Appearing on behalf of the owners was attorney Tim King (a.k.a. Timmy, the developers' pal), who had won development rights by threatening to sue the city— a ruse which, in recent years has become so easy it's a bar-room, hand-slap ritual among local lawyers.

"These amendments are really just a few housekeeping items," King told the commissioners.

*Ah, the old housekeeping items!*

"That's verbiage that doesn't sit well with this commissioner," Henry Becker warned the blustering attorney. "'Housekeeping' was how Truman Annex went from a simple development agreement for a largely affordable housing and market rate mix into 600 amendments and a gated, high-end, transient rental bonanza for absentee landlords and the developers.

239

"I want to hear what you're really up to, then we'll decide on whether you'll be allowed to do it."

"I appreciate your candor, Commissioner Becker," King said in his most sincere voice— the one which patted his opponent puckishly on the cheek while stabbing him in the back. "Let me assure you, sir, that we have no intention of significantly increasing our number of transient units— well maybe just a few."

"What's a few?" Mayor Dailey asked.

"We need to add another 10 or 20 units to Morgan's Castle to offset the cost of the new marina complex where we'll be docking our fleet of replica pirate ships. And we're going to need to sacrifice a few more acres of endangered flora for an expanded Booty Slide area."

"You're out of ROGO units," Becker growled. "And you ain't gonna get any more from this commissioner! I've already told you what you can do with your Booty Slide!"

"Well, sir, we're transferring some units from the developers' properties on North Roosevelt Boulevard, which were temporarily transferred to their Northside Drive project, then sold to another developer, but repurchased for use on our Pirate World project just a week or two ago."

*Jeez, no tap-dancing or deception there!*

"You see, sir, it's all completely legal, ROGO-wise, through Transfer of Development Rights. We simply need an amendment or two to the original development agreement— that little housekeeping matter of which I spoke— to make everything Kosher, as it were."

"TDR's!" Becker snarled, "goddamned TDR's— I rue the day we ever allowed the wool to be pulled over our eyes with that legal larceny!"

*[Regular readers of the Reporter will recall
that we railed against Transfer of Development
Rights more then ten years ago when the idea was
first presented to the Key West City Commission.
Maybe, just maybe, we were right.]*

There ensued much screaming and hollering,
legal wrangling and tangling. Tim King seemed to
float above it all, agreeing and schmoozing, as
well as continually commenting on how lovely
Ms. Josephine Woods hair looked that evening.

And, in the end, the developers got their
amendments— the first few of many we're certain we'll witness before Pirate World on Wisteria
Island (Oops, Skull & Crossbones Island) sees its
first rosy-cheeked little pirate butt slide down the
much-heralded new Booty Slide.

All of which concludes our Commission
Report— from chickens to rats, to Mickey Mouse
and some Mickey Mouse lawyering. Who said
Key West is going to the dogs??

—

Mac emailed his copy to Dennis Conrad at the Reporter
office the following morning. Shortly thereafter, he received a
return email:

*Well, you've done your usual hatchet job— a great and inim-
itable hatchet job— on the commission. Love it!*

*Of course, I'll label it "Commentary" in hope of saving one
or two advertisers.*

## CHAPTER FORTY-THREE

# *Captain Mac*

The gentle sway of his aging houseboat and the creaking of its deck-boards comforted Mac McKinney as he awoke from a particularly disturbing nightmare. It was not so much the content of the dream— those details dispersed like fireflies fleeing the dawn as he opened his eyes to the brilliant glow of a full moon over Garrison Bight. Rather, it was the recent increasing frequency of discomforting nightmares that gave him pause.

Mac lay in bed, long beyond his normal 4 a.m. rising time, contemplating both the moon and where he was in life. Once he did force himself from the comfort of his bed, he continued to defy routine by ignoring the TV and the Svengali-like allure of its early morning news shows. Instead of reaching for the TV remote, as was his wont, Mac slipped into his Weejuns and retreated to the day bed on the second floor balcony of the houseboat. He did not even bother to turn on the lights. The palpable feeling of the darkness on the bight, accentuated by the lustrous moonlight on its waters, was welcoming and refreshing to him.

The darker side of Mac McKinney was kept carefully concealed, unseen by anyone but himself. His personal life was one of highs and lows, one of immense mood swings. He might find himself elated for no reason other than the sight of a soaring frigate bird at one moment, and cast into the depths of depression with even less impetus minutes later.

Mac knew that any number of clinical psychotic classifications might apply to him— anything from manic depression to paranoid schizophrenia or a bipolar condition. But Mac never allowed himself to think in such deep, clinical terms. He knew the truth, and it was a simple one. As with Shakespeare's Hamlet, the world was too much with him.

From childhood, he had been the serious one. At age six, he lay on the floor in front of the TV watching neither cartoons nor westerns, but was rapt instead with *Meet The Press*. By age eight— already a seasoned reporter for William Fox Elementary School's' paper, *Fox Tales*— his Christmas wish was for an electric type-writer.

From his earliest years, there had existed two irrefutable truths in Mac's mind. One, he would— in some form or fashion— be a writer. Two, he would never live past the age of 30. He had been half right. And when he continued to partake of life well beyond his self-allotted 30 years, he attributed it to unclean living and was duly grateful, though he remained dubious about any extended lifespan.

Mac stared through the balcony railing onto the shadowy fig-ure of his little sailboat, *Front Page*. It had been months since she had stirred from her moorings. There seemed to be a plaintive look about her resting there, lifeless, in the water. Mac's depression transfigured to guilt. He decided it was time to take his *Front Page* out for a sail. This was no small decision, as Mac was far from the most accomplished single-handed sailor. In fact, he had taken *Front Page* out alone only once before— which had resulted in running her aground before he even left the confines of the Bight. Ever since, he had sailed only with one or more friends serving as crew.

Captain McKinney packed an ice chest with two cheese sandwiches and a six pack of Bud. He stowed the cargo, along with a carton of Marlboros, below and set about preparing *Front Page* for sea. He would motor out of the Bight, but raise the mainsail so he'd have one less thing to do once he arrived in the main channel. He started the engine, left it in neutral, then loosed the bow line and scrambled back to release the stern line. There was a gentle port wind as he pulled away from the dock and he could feel its effect on the mainsail. Once in the harbor, Mac killed the engine and strode forward to raise the jib. The entire process of leaving Garrison Bight had been uneventful, which was energizing for Mac.

As *Front Page* glided gently past Fleming Key on a port tack, Captain Mac trimmed the sails on his small boat until he had gathered the wind in to form a nice belly in both the main and foresail. He headed up into a fresh breeze and quickly found himself and *Front Page* on a healthy heel. He stared up into the belly of the mainsail, which formed the largest cloud in his sky at that moment.

*This, my man, is sailing!*

Mac's nautical exhilaration was short-lived, as he discovered he had rapidly entered the main channel of Key West harbor and was about to broadside the Disney Magic. The 11-deck, 85,000-ton cruise ship was doing a turn-around, aided by her powerful bow-thrusters, in the middle of the channel. The ship was headed on her way to another port, but at the moment, she towered stories high above, mere yards away from Mac and *Front Page*.

*Shit, this is not sailing!*

Noticing that a sea gnat was about to squash itself on one of its port holes, the liner belched out a deep, prolonged wail of warning. There was little more the massive vessel could do.

Mac thought quickly— it was all he could do— turning the helm to the wind and throwing *Front Page* into a shuddering jibe, away, ever so barely, from the face of the rising wall of the soaring mountain. Even though his tiny boat was comfortably falling off, he could feel the pull of the whirlpool the cruise ship created around itself as it turned in the channel. It was truly frightening.

*Fifteen years ago… this channel wasn't dredged so deep as to allow this monster entry… then it was only the graceful schooners, and the hard-working shrimp boats… and the sponging boats…*

Instead of reveling in the life which he had just saved— his own— through relatively incredible sailing prowess, Mac was thrown right back into his depression. His glass always seemed half empty, he mused.

Mac's immediate thought was to return to the security and safety of Garrison Bight and his houseboat.

*Wuss!* He chastised himself. *Captain Wuss!*

Emboldened by the sight of Magic speeding off toward the horizon, Mac once again trimmed *Front Page*'s sails, pointed her bow to the wind, and set his course for Sand Key— a tranquil six nautical-mile cruise away. It was a course he had sailed hundreds of times on the schooner *Constellation*. He didn't even need to glance at the compass. All he had to do was follow the horizon and its relation to the out-islands.

*Front Page* was an obliging craft. Her comfortable weather helm allowed Mac to lean back and steer her with one mere finger, even with her nose pointed squarely into the wind. While he had no electronic indicators, Mac could feel that he was doing about 12 knots... a nice little clip for *Front Page*.

His depression was slowly swept away, like the waves under the bow, and was supplanted with the old love he held for the sea, for solitude and for sailing.

It was a gentle cruise all the way to Sand Key. It took less than an hour. Along the way Mac spotted two giant loggerhead turtles and a legion of dolphins, many of which had swum playfully alongside *Front Page* for a good portion of the sail.

As Mac approached the floating buoys just offshore of Sand Key, he maneuvered so that the sails were directly into the wind, settling his craft "into irons," motionless. That allowed him to dash forward and hook a mooring line onto one of the buoys. Many careless sailors simply dropped anchor, damaging the sensitive coral beds below.

Mac was grateful that he had ventured out so early. None of the numerous "head boats" filled with hordes of wide-eyed, riotous tourists had arrived yet. The tiny spit of sand called Sand Key was completely free of human life. The contemplative reporter cum sailor liked that.

The water was calm, glassy, inviting. Mac stripped off his shirt, donned his snorkel and mask and dove into its 82-degree warmth. Instantly he found himself surrounded by swarms of colorful parrot fish, crowds of curious barracuda and a pack of anxiously circling nurse sharks.

The unnatural gathering startled Mac. Then he realized why they were there. They were waiting for the tourists with their bread crumbs, potato chips and Cheez Whiz; they were waiting to be fed. As the tragic fox in Saint-Exupery's *The Little Prince*, they had been *tamed*.

Thrown once again into his funk of depression, Mac climbed back onboard *Front Page*. Lighting a Marlboro, he lay on his back in the cockpit and stared up at the morning sky. Frenetic gulls, madcap terns and majestic frigate birds circled above, flying in and out of his view. Mac wondered if they, too, might be waiting for the tourists.

As he stared into the blue, Mac engaged in some self-analysis. He tried to figure out which one concern was prompting his current bout with depression. As usual in such exercises, he could arrive at no single answer. It wasn't the unnatural gathering of fishes. It wasn't the tourists and their Cheez Whiz. And it wasn't his contretemps with the cruise ship in Key West harbor. It was all those things, and more.

Retrieving his laptop from below, Mac opened it and began to make a list of contributing factors.

*Too many chickens, for too many years, and the city commission ignores the problem.*

*T-shirt shops ripping off tourists and displaying obscene merchandise, for too many years, and the city commission ignores the problem.*

*Too many bums, palm-frond weavers, wizards, painted human statuary and other derelicts on the streets and the city commission either ignores them or issues them licenses as "street performers."*

*Ever-increasing numbers of lap-dancing parlors, "gentlemen's clubs," and tattoo parlors and the city commission ignores them or issues them licenses with stern warnings such as "y'all be good now and don't go within 250 feet of a church, or proliferate."*

*Ever-increasing numbers of cruise ships— when the city commission had promised "two or three a week at most" when giving approval to the first ships a decade before.*

Mac paused for a moment to consider what he was doing. This was not helping his mood, he thought. Still, he continued the exercise.

*City Commissioners, County Commissioners, County Attorneys and developers who break the law and get influential friends to write letters for them so pals in the judicial system let them go, or they never even get charged.*

*Businesses that get special consideration from the city commission because they retain one of the commission-approved attorneys.*

*Developers who— well, there's a volume unto itself. Begin with developers who use "affordable housing" as a bugaboo to build more and more while making less and less housing affordable.*

*Developers who manipulate the Land Development Regulations through Transfer of Development Rights to bypass ROGO restrictions— with the full knowledge, or maybe a wink, from the city and county commissions.*

*The Department of Community Affairs (DCA), which operates as toady (perhaps butt-boy would be more appropriate) for developers.*

*Every city commissioner, county commissioner, attorney, businessman or "street performer" who knows precisely what's going on and continues to walk the streets as if their hands were clean and their crap didn't stink.*

*The Bag Man— the man we all know and love; the man we hate to love.*

Mac had to stop. The list was getting too long, though he had just scratched the surface. But, in a way, it had worked. He was no longer depressed. He was angry.

The anger was fleeting. It turned quickly into a familiar feeling of frustration. There was nothing he could do about it. He was one of the most powerful journalists in the county. He could influence some votes, limiting jet skis and the like. But when push came to shove, when a mega-developer wanted something, he could do little more than delay commission action on it. Nine times out of ten, one of his close sources (most of whom were close friends) would call and say "Please lay off so-and-so because he's a really nice person, and besides the vote's already been decided." He might bitch and holler, but he knew all of his editorial power was useless against the bubba system.

And, Mac wondered, if he felt frustrated even with all his editorial power, how frustrated must average citizens— those without his metaphoric barrels of ink— feel?

Captain Mac's self-analysis and his musing was interrupted by the arrival and the attendant clatter and chatter of the first tourist head boat of the day— a large catamaran teeming with more middle-age flab, bulging cellulite and teenage tits and ass than should be allowed on one boat.

Mac simply sighed. He didn't really blame the tourists. He couldn't begrudge them the beauty of the ocean and of the reef. He, too, had been drawn to Cayo Hueso by the same beauty. And at least, he figured, the developers had not yet managed to transfer development rights six miles out to Sand Key. But he knew that the day would come.

He lifted the line from the mooring buoy, raised *Front Page's* mainsail and jib, came about and set off on a starboard tack toward Key West harbor.

One day soon, Mac thought, he would not come about. He would head south, toward Havana. He hoped it would be soon enough to beat Ted Lively's tour trains.

## CHAPTER FORTY-FOUR

# *Politics and Paradigms*

Given commission approval, Fest organizers began to fast-track the incorporation of the Cayo Hueso/Cuba Libre theme into advertising and promotion for the upcoming event. A competition among local artists to design artwork for the Fest was under way. And locals were beginning to openly, actively discuss the possibility of Cuba opening to travel and the possibility of Cuban leaders riding in the Fantasy Fest parade.

While Key West's Cuban community was significantly smaller than that of Miami, the subject of Cuba opening was no less contentious. Tempers were flaring over many an otherwise peaceful game of dominoes. At the same time, Key West Cubans seemed to be more liberal than their counterparts on the mainland. Many welcomed the possible opening— regardless of how democratic it might be. Most simply wanted to be able to return home again, or to have their relatives be able to visit them in Cayo Hueso for the first time in more than 40 years.

The national media had already begun to pick up on the story. Imus was talking about it on the Trump network. As he watched and listened intently, Mac McKinney still could not believe that the plan could possibly have ever been the brainchild of Tommy Whitemoor— walking, talking dimwit. Yet there it was. People were talking about it. It appeared to be happening.

*Well, a lot of talk doesn't bring democratic elections to Cuba,* Mac thought. *Harrumph,* he added to himself for emphasis, à la Commissioner Becker.

Mac stopped thinking heavy thoughts and smiled as yet another "Breaking News" banner flashed on the TV screen.

*Another car chase in California?* Mac wondered.

"This is a Trump News special report," the onscreen news reporter began. "We are awaiting a press briefing from the U.S. State Department regarding Cuba. We take you live now to Washington, where Deputy Secretary of State John Negroponte is about to speak."

With little fanfare, a stone-faced Negroponte approached the podium.

"With the passing of Cuban dictator Fidel Castro, much has changed in the Communist nation of Cuba," Negroponte began. "Much still remains to be changed. Still unaddressed are the fundamental issues of democratic elections and human rights, including the freeing of political prisoners. But representatives of the U.S. Department of State have been in contact with representatives of the Raúl Castro government. And I believe that while a great distance remains to be traveled, there may light at the end of a long political tunnel.

"While the United States is not prepared at this point to resume normal diplomatic relations with Cuba, we are prepared to take one positive step in that direction. Acting as Commander-in-Chief, President Bush today ordered that the U.S. military base in Guantanamo, Cuba be decommissioned and closed within one year. The president has ordered further that the land and buildings comprising the U.S. base in Guantanamo will be ceded to the government and the people of the Republic of Cuba."

*Interesting,* Mac thought. *Bush sends Negroponte out to spin for him. He reaps the larger political benefits without having to face the outrage of the Miami Mafia.*

"The people of the United States should have no fear that the closure of our facility at Guantanamo Bay will negatively impact our continuing war on terrorism," the Deputy Director continued. "Suspect terrorists being legally detained there will be shifted to other U.S. military facilities."

*"Legally detained..."* Mac noted the weasel-wording. *No political prisoners held in U.S. prisons!*

The deputy secretary declared the presser ended and stepped from the podium, waving and smiling to reporters as he left the State Department briefing room.

Mac understood fully what he had just heard. The handwriting was on the wall. The Bush administration was paving the road to renewed diplomatic relations with Cuba. That was something that he knew had not occurred overnight. Obviously, as Negroponte had indicated, there had been extensive top-level negotiations underway for some time— probably even prior to Fidel's death. He then understood the purpose of the Boca Chica meeting in Key West. As the southernmost city had been center stage during the missile crisis in Cuba, it would be similarly positioned in the opening of relations with Cuba. Someone, Mac knew, was one hell of a political Spinmeister— and it sure as hell wasn't Tommy Whitemoor.

*Raúl,* he thought. This all came from *Raúl.*

From all reports that he had seen and heard, Mac knew Raúl Castro to be an alcoholic and possibly a pedophile. He had feared his ascension to the Cuban throne. He had considered Raúl's political acumen pale and inadequate by comparison to his elder brother, Fidel. It appeared as though he might have been wrong, at least as far as his political assumptions were concerned.

While Mac feared the Americanization of Cuba, he knew that the people of Cuba needed U.S. trade and, God forbid, even U.S. tourist dollars. If Raúl could be an effective conduit for renewed diplomatic relations with the U.S., then Mac felt that he could ignore the new president's personal quirks. After all, he himself lived in a town that tolerated free-roaming chickens and lap-dancing city managers.

He could not and would not, however, lend public editorial support to a dimwit like Tommy Whitemoor.

Mac determined to develop a new editorial/political paradigm— one which could support the Cayo Hueso/Cuba Libre effort, without supporting its perceived sponsor. In political essence, the sound of one hand clapping.

Change, big change, was clearly on the way. Mac had never felt so close to it. And he could see that Key West would be at the heart of that change. The impact on the small island would be greater that that of the missile crisis or the Mariel boatlift. He hoped that somehow the crazy, odd, idiosyncratic and unpredictable residents of the southernmost city might rise to the occasion, rather than trip on their own, well, put politely— feet.

At any rate, the possibility of Cuban leaders riding in a parade down Duval Street was a notion which amused the reporter.

*If it happens, it's going to make for one helluva Fantasy Fest,* Mac thought. *I wonder if Katie Couric will have her body painted for the Evening News?*

## CHAPTER FORTY-FIVE

# *"Hot, Hot, Hot!"*

Tommy Whitemoor, you've outdone yourself! the flamboyant city commissioner observed inwardly as he surveyed the delightfully bizarre scene in his lush garden at Casa Whitemoor. He had managed to organize the self-indulgent fete champetre— to celebrate his first big commission victory— in less than 48 hours.

Spicy Latin Salsa, performed by a 20-piece Cuban orchestra recruited from Miami, rumbaed throughout the garden, adding to the natural heat of the midsummer Cayo Hueso night.

A host of simply-too-pretty pool boys, wearing spandex Capri pants and colorful, frilly, silk blouses with puffed sleeves, paraded about shaking castanets and serving Mojitos to the invited gathering of notables and notorious.

Duval Street drag queens chattered about and gasped over the latest Paris Hilton gossip while clusters of county and city commissioners exchanged pleasantries and discussed agenda items, comforted by darkness, away from any nasty "sunshine."

It was all too much for the normally-ostentatious twin peacocks, Bogey and Bacall, which cowered in a darkened corner behind a Bougainvillea bush.

At the center of it all— the focus of everyone's attention— stood the party's host, Tommy Whitemoor. He was in the spotlight, and he loved it.

The commissioner wore simple white Bermuda shorts accented by a pink Guayabera shirt— for him, almost an understatement. His freshly Lady Clairol Blonde-treated hair was done up in a high pompadour and when he waved his hands to gesture—

253

which he often did— sparkles of glitter shone from the dazzling pink polish on his fingernails.

"Now *there's* a piece of work!" Juan-Carlo Valdez whispered to Michael Savage, directing his city attorney's attention in Whitemoor's direction.

"Yeah, kind of makes you wonder just what the voters were thinking," Savage concurred.

"Obviously, they *weren't* thinking," Valdez said, chuckling as he sipped his Mojito and patted the rear end of a passing female city worker.

In a more secluded corner of the garden, attorney Tim King busily schmoozed Mayor Jimmy Dailey— an individual joked about locally as being several elevator stops short of the top floor.

"Now, Jimmy," he purred, "Once we get Pirate World up and running on Wisteria— I mean Skull and Crossbones Island— you can rest assured that there will be a condo reserved for you at Morgan's Castle."

"Condos?" Dailey asked naively. "I don't recall any mention of condos."

"Oh, just a little housekeeping detail we'll bring before the commission in a few weeks," King replied, deftly brushing off the introduction of condominiums as yet another amendment to the Wisteria Island development agreement.

"Oh," Dailey said, grinning. "I get it. Can I have another Mojito?"

The Cuban orchestra played *Hot, hot, hot!*

Island Tours czar Ted Lively shared a poolside chaise lounge with Chamber of Commerce standard bearer Victoria Pennekamp. Lively thought her especially voluptuous in the low-cut, satin evening gown she was wearing. It was, naturally, fiery red— to match her high heels.

As Lively stroked her lower back, Pennekamp purred and leaned her head against his shoulder. He considered briefly a one-night stand with her, but thought better of it. For one thing, she was too easy, and he preferred challenges in life. She also bore the personal brand of Mayor Dailey, someone he couldn't afford to antagonize. And most importantly, he didn't want to end up reading his name in Mac McKinney's paper listed as yet another man "intimately involved with Vicky Pantyhose."

"I suspect you're the real power behind this deal," Pennekamp told Lively. "I know that Whitemoor could never have pulled it off by himself."

"Not really," Lively answered, edging away from the lady in red. "You're right that Whitemoor is just riding the coattails of this event. But someone else is pulling the strings, not me."

"Who then?"

"You'd be surprised at how many people are involved in this Cuba business— and on how many sides."

"You're saying you have no interest in it?"

"Oh, of course I do. Cuba means big money to me, but all my plans were in place long ago. I'm not the driving force behind what's going on now. But I do welcome it. The timing is good— Key West is built out. Even worse, the Bubba regime is either selling out or dying out.

"It used to be easy to buy a variance to the land use regulations. It used to be easy to buy a commissioner. Hell, it was easy to buy a judge. But now there are too many newcomers— too many bases to be covered. Too many chances to get caught with your hand in the cookie jar, if you know what I mean."

Pennekamp understood.

"Tell me about it. Chamber membership is down and so are the tourism figures."

"Even worse, the D.A.'s actually starting to *prosecute!*" Lively added.

Both laughed riotously. Pennekamp pinched the butt of a passing pool boy.

Boldly venturing from the safety of the Bougainvillea bush, Bogey nipped at the heel of KWPD Capt. Andy Toler. Little did the bird know that his beak was within mere inches of the .38 Toler kept secreted in an ankle holster.

"Hey, what the hell?" Toler barked. "Get away from me, you faggot bird!"

Kicking his leg violently, the captain drove Bogey back to the bushes with his soul mate, Bacall. Toler's companion, Chief Cuz Dillard was greatly amused at the whole scene.

"Careful," Dillard warned Toler. "The Peacock Civil Liberties Union could bring you up on discrimination charges. Not to mention the use of excessive force!"

"Probably not far from the truth," Capt. Toler agreed.

"Back to Sergeant Hardin—" the Chief continued a discussion he was having with his close confidante before the peacock attack. "I want him up on charges before Fantasy Fest. I don't care what you do. He's a threat to all of us. He's fighting me on security for the parade. He's after Whitemoor. And I know he's been ratting to the Feds."

"Problem is," Toler said, "he covers his ass. He's damn near married to the attorney for the Police Benevolent Association."

"Screw the PBA," Dillard said. "If they give me any shit, I'll pull the department's contract with them. Meantime, get me whatever you can on John Hardin. It's important that he not be around when all this Cuba business goes down."

Tommy Whitemoor was busy downing Mojitos and flattering Fest Director Ann Richardson.

"I tell you, Ann, this is going to be the greatest Fantasy Fest ever! Did you see the news? They're closing Guantanamo. The 'opening' is next. And it's all going to come down right here in Key West! All the networks, I mean *all* the networks will be covering this, Ann. We could never buy this kind of publicity!"

"I hope you're right, Tommy. The board of directors gave me hell for changing the theme at the last minute. It's cost us a bundle in overtime. If anything happens to screw this up, I'm toast."

"Don't worry, dear," Tommy reassured her. "We've got the Cuban president on our side. This is going to go off perfectly. Honey, it's going to be as delicious as black beans and rice!"

With that pronouncement, the commissioner left her in the company of several Woman's Clubbers and directed his attention toward the pool bar for yet another Mojito, and perhaps a pool boy. But he was sidetracked by a gentle tap on the shoulder.

"Hello, Tommy," a familiar voice said.

He turned to find himself face-to-face with the Bag Man.

"Nice party."

"Thanks," Whitemoor replied.

He had invited the noted dignitary, but never expected him to actually attend.

"I can't stay, I just wanted to bring you this," the Bag Man said, pressing a piece of note paper into Whitemoor's hand.

"It's from a friend. He said you'd been expecting it, and he apologized for the delay. Something about communications problems."

Whitemoor unfolded the paper and read the name *RAÚL*. Beneath the name was a cell phone number.

"This is great!" he exclaimed, looking up from the note. "I *have* been expecting this, and..."

The Bag Man was gone.

*So he was the "contact" Raúl had spoken of,* Tommy realized. But what was the connection, he wondered. How did he know Raúl... or Fidel?

*Oh well, no matter,* he thought, *I have the number now. I'll call him first thing in the morning. Right now, time for another Mojito, and perhaps that pool boy!*

## CHAPTER FORTY-SIX

# *Raúl— A Cingular Leader*

Tommy Whitemoor's hand shook nervously as he attempted to tap Raúl Castro's cell phone number into his i-phone. The trembling was not a symptom of anxiety, but rather a symptom of a serious hangover from too many Mojitos consumed the previous evening.

Following several distant ring tones, the commissioner was surprised to hear a recorded message, in English: *The Cingular customer you are calling is unavailable... you may leave a message at the tone.*

*Raúl has Cingular?* Whitemoor wondered. He chuckled to himself at the irony, and dutifully left a cryptic message: *Raúl... it's your Cayo Hueso cutie... call me if my cigar order is ready!*

Cat-calls from the courtyard below his bedroom window forced him to leave the comfort of his bed, attempt to walk upright, and step onto the balcony. The screeching arose from Bogey and Bacall, both of whom were anxious for their overdue morning feeding.

Recalling a classic Peter Lorre line, Whitemoor muttered to himself... *One day, one seed will be cyanide.*

He was about to force himself down the stairs to feed the monsters when his phone rang.

*Cayo Hueso cutie?* a voice asked in Spanish.

*Raúl!* Whitemoor responded.

*I see that our mutual friend has supplied you with my number, Tommy.*

*Yes,* Tommy said. *I wanted to ask you about that. How do you know him?*

Raúl laughed.

258

*He is well known in many circles, my friend. He had much contact with Fidel— during our 'special period' in the 1990s — on behalf of certain parties in your town. He now works closely with my prime minister, Felipito Roque, still on behalf of those parties.*

*I'm not surprised,* Whitemoor said. *He's very influential here, though he keeps a very low profile. Locals call him the Bag Man.*

Raúl again laughed.

*Yes, he is secretive and all business— with little time for humor,* Raúl replied. *We here call him el empresario de pompas funebres— the undertaker.*

Whitemoor sniggered.

*Tres approprié, mon ami.*

*Que?* Raúl asked.

*Oh, sorry, mixing my languages. Listen, Raúl, the commission has approved everything. We're all set for Cayo Hueso/Cuba Libre at Fantasy Fest in October. And I've secured the Disney cruise ship. I will be on the ship headed for Havana right after the parade!*

*This is great news, Tommy! Things here are proceeding well, too. You have heard of our arrangement with your government regarding Guantanamo Bay?*

*Yes, it's all over the news, Raúl.*

*Another major announcement will be coming from my government very soon, my friend. Be prepared for even bigger news,* Castro informed him.

*Nothing you do surprises me anymore, Raúl. I'm so delighted that you're president now! I can't wait to sit and talk with you regarding our mutual interests.*

*It is something I look forward to as well, my friend. But let me ask you, are you receiving adequate protection from your government?*

*Huh?* Whitemoor asked, his brain suddenly awakening from its alcohol-induced slumber. *Protection from whom?*

*My agents in Florida tell me of increased activity among the Miami Mafia. I am informed that one of their most powerful leaders has, in fact, traveled to Key West and is currently operating there. His name is José Castillo.*

*Here? Is he dangerous?*

*Yes, he is there, and he is very dangerous,* Raúl answered ominously. *Many, many years ago, Castillo was a friend. He was a gentleman of culture, highly-educated and refined. He moved in the highest circles. But he was also one of Havana's most successful entrepreneurs— something which Fidel despised. His land and business interests were appropriated by the State and Castillo fled, swearing revenge against the Castro regime. Over the years, he has grown even more bitter, and even more dangerous. He is now one of the most powerful leaders in the Miami-based Democracia movement.*

*And you're sure he's here?*

*Yes. Please, Tommy, secure protection from your government as soon as possible.*

*Well, Raúl, I'm not real popular with 'my government,' especially the Secret Service, but I'll talk to our police chief about it.*

*Good. Now, I must go, my friend. I look forward to hearing from you again soon.*

*Adios, Raúl! And by the way, **Cayo Hueso/Cuba Libre!***

Raúl chortled.

*Indeed, my friend, indeed!*

## CHAPTER FORTY-SEVEN

# *A Bum Rap*

As Mac McKinney strolled casually down Caroline Street toward his preferred meeting place, Kelly's, he was taken aback to see two armed National Guardsmen posted outside the garden gate. He had become accustomed to a military presence on Duval Street, at Mallory Square and Old City Hall. But Kelly's? It occurred to him that Homeland Security had increased its presence in Key West since the announcement of the closure of Guantanamo. He was of the opinion that the situation— basically a relaxation of tension between the U.S. and Cuba— would instead have called for a decrease in that presence. But then he didn't run Homeland Security. Nor was he interested in the job.

*Just so much smoke and mirrors,* he figured.

Mac offered a friendly salute to the young guardsmen as he strode past them into the garden.

"Good evening, sir!" one of the soldiers replied, returning the reporter's salute.

McKinney chuckled to himself.

Chablis, the news hound, sprung to her feet as McKinney entered the bar. The genial lab knew a sure petting when she saw one. Mac never disappointed.

"Hey, Chablis!" he greeted his editor's dog. "Good to see you."

"What, I'm chopped liver?" David Conrad asked from the comfort of his regular seat at the bar.

"You want to be petted too?" Mac asked.

"Naw, just gimme a good lead story!" Conrad snapped, semi-seriously.

Mac settled himself at the bar, gratefully accepting his usual cold beer from his favorite bartender.

"Well, David, we have a veritable cornucopia of lead stories from which to choose this week!" he announced, equally semi-seriously.

Chablis settled herself on the floor between the two journalists and lifted one hind leg to scratch behind her ear.

"Give me a sample," Conrad said, sipping his Canadian Club.

"Okay, I've now documented that of the 1,235 transient rental licenses being offered for sale around town, only 235 are legitimate, as defined by the Comprehensive Plan," Mac told his editor. "The others exist on paper only— if that. They've been created our of thin air, and yet they're being traded with abandon and being sold about town, willy-nilly, for an average price of $65,000 apiece."

"Hey, that's a good lead!" Conrad said, beaming. "I'll buy you a beer on that one!"

"That's not all," Mac noted.

"There's more?"

"Yep. Juan-Carlo's been caught in another lap-dancing saloon— this time he had a commissioner with him. Of course, the commissioner owns the saloon."

"Good source?" Conrad asked.

"The usual one," his reporter answered.

"Sergeant Hardin?"

"Yep."

"Okay, that'll be page one, below the fold."

"That means you're buying me *two* beers?" Mac asked.

"Then I couldn't afford Chablis' steak tonight," Conrad argued.

The lab's ears perked up at the mention of her name in conjunction with steak.

"Cheap screw," Mac groused to his editor.

A familiar U2 musical ring tone alerted Mac to his cell phone.

"Excuse me," he said, answering the call.

"This is Mac."

"Yeah.

"Yeah.

"Yeah. They found *who??*

"You're shitting me! My gawd, it's too hilarious!"

Conrad's ears perked up. He could smell a story.

"Okay, I'll take the water taxi over and get some photos. Thanks, John!"

"Hold the presses!" Mac announced to his editor. He loved saying that, even when he only had a small puff piece. It was *so* journalist. "We've got a new lead. I've gotta run grab a water taxi over to Wisteria Island. You won't believe who they found out there!"

With that, he chugged his remaining Budweiser, patted Chablis on the head, disappeared into Kelly's lush garden foliage and darted out the back gate.

"Wait! Tell me..." Conrad said to no one but Chablis.

*Hell,* he thought, *here's another one that's gonna come back and bite me in the ass! Kiss another advertiser goodbye.*

## "PIRATE WORLD" DEVELOPERS
## UNCOVER REAL BURIED TREASURE
### *By Mac McKinney*

The controversial development of Wisteria Island— a.k.a. Christmas Tree Island— which has resulted in the clearing of the last refuge for several endangered species, including many aged Jack Kerouac devotees, may have proved to be a blessing in disguise. While digging the foundation for the "Booty Slide," touted by developers as the feature attraction of the island's soon-to-be "Pirate World," construction workers uncovered the skeletal remains of one of Key West's most notorious historical figures— the legendary Bum Farto.

Farto, a former Chief of the Key West Fire Department, mysteriously disappeared in February, 1976, following a drug conviction. Farto had been using the city's fire station to sell

263

drugs— in mass quantities— from the trunk of his car. Reports of Farto sightings in various venues, from the Bahamas to Venezuela, have occasionally surfaced over the ensuing years.

All the speculation was laid to rest Tuesday when Farto's skeleton— still clad in his blue KWFD windbreaker— was unearthed by frontloaders on Wisteria Island. The identity of the remains has since been confirmed by the Monroe County Coroner's office.

One local Conch, who wished to remain anonymous, suggested that Farto might have been hiding out on the island since the 1970s.

"He's been out there all these years, poor guy, just getting by on grits and grunts!" he told the *Reporter*. "Hell, he was prob'ly smoking' dope out there, too!"

Tim King, attorney and spokesman for Pirate World theme park, said that the developers might take advantage of the unique find.

"We may file suit claiming ownership of Bum's skeleton," King told the *Reporter*. "We'd like to wire it together and hang it over the top of the Booty Slide. It'd make a great attraction!"

Yes, *Reporter* readers, developers have been bemoaning the fact for years, and now we know it to be true— they do, indeed get a Bum rap.

—

David Conrad chuckled as he pasted McKinney's Farto piece onto page one, above the fold.

*Screw the Pirate World ads,* he thought to himself. *I've got the best damn reporter on the streets.*

# CHAPTER FORTY-EIGHT

# *Goofy Pictures*

Careful not to stay in one place too long— and thereby be traceable and observable— José Castillo moved from the La Concha Hotel to the home of Álvaro Rafael, the curator of Key West's San Carlos Institute. The Institute had once belonged to the nation of Cuba. It was from the balcony of that ornate edifice that José Martí had plead for American funds to help finance the Cuban Revolution against Spain.

Rafael was a *Democracia* sympathizer and vehemently opposed to returning the Institute to Cuba and the hands of any Castro regime— Fidel's or Raúl's.

In addition to a welcome in Rafael's home, Castillo also received a small office at the San Carlos building. Located in the wings behind the Institute's theater, the office was small and dimly-lit, but served his purposes well. The radical Cuban expatriate's furtive associates from Miami could come and go without being questioned by anyone in authority.

"I was really beginning to like *El Siboney,* José," Manny Caballero said as he forced his rotund frame into a small, wooden chair in Castillo's backstage office. "Great Cuban bread."

"Indeed, my friend," the elder Cuban agreed. "But it is not good to become a 'regular' at any establishment when one is engaged in shadowy activities. That is better done, Manuel— in the shadows.

"Now, my friend, tell me of your cruise. What did you learn?"

"I brought pictures!" Caballeiro announced excitedly.

He spread scores of color photographs out on the desk before Castillo and began to describe his favorites as he pointed to each.

"Here, this one's my grandson, Manuelito, posing with Goofy! Such a good boy that one, he's 12 now, you know.

"And here's Consuelo— my wife— with both the grandkids on the waterslide. José, you can't believe how much fun that ship is! Consuelo wants to go again next summer."

Castillo rapped the desk with the fingers of one hand and shifted his cane on the floor with the other. Manny could tell instinctively that he was growing impatient.

"Oh, you want to know about the security!" he said.

"That was the purpose of the cruise, Manuel."

"Well, here, look at this one..."

He shoved a dark, poorly focused photo under his superior's nose.

"What is it?" Castillo asked.

"Metal detectors. They have them on the gangway, where you enter the ship."

"That's it?"

"Well, no. Baggage is checked in at the port of departure. I think they have sniffer-dogs there. So it'd be risky to pack anything suspicious."

"Such as C-4 explosive?" Castillo asked rhetorically.

"Exactly. And everyone is issued an I.D. card with a magnetic strip. You have to have it to get on and off the ship."

"And once you're onboard the ship," Castillo pressed, "you would call the security..."

"Not much," Manny answered. "A lot of uniformed baby-sitters."

"That is a good piece of information, Manuel. That is the sort of detail I need to know."

"I brought a brochure, too. It shows all the decks and activities."

"Thank you, my friend. But we have already studied technical schematics of the ship, including each of its decks, as well as it's engine specifications and power stations— downloaded from the internet."

"So the movement has committed?" Caballero asked.

"Nothing is written in stone," Castillo answered, almost pensively. "Everything is mercurial. All depends on the twists and turns of events. But then life is such. Is that not so, my friend?"

"I suppose, José," Manny answered, somewhat confused. "I mean, yes— life is like that. But I sure hope I can take Consuelo on another cruise. Maybe we'll go without the grandkids."

"That would be nice, Manuel. Nice, indeed."

# CHAPTER FORTY-NINE

# *Fishing for a Predator*

*Have you ever heard of Fantasy Fest, Peter?* Peacock typed.

John Hardin's heart raced. It was his twenty-fifth IM exchange, over a three month period, with the cloaked pedophile he felt certain was Tommy Whitemoor. And he sensed strongly that it was about to be the pivotal one.

*Yeah, I've heard it's a big party.*

*A big naked party!* PEACOCK corrected PETER14.

*Kewl, I guess.*

*You'd like it.*

*I dunno.*

*Trust me, you'd like it. It's coming up in October—Halloween weekend, you know. Hey, how about coming down? I'll pay for everything. And I may even take you on a cruise. I'll get you drunk. Ever been drunk? Then we'll get naked and...*

Sergeant Hardin sighed as *PEACOCK* described in ugly detail what he planned to do with *PETER14*. He was so immersed in his onscreen persona that he could feel the emotions of a real 14-year-old boy being solicited on the internet. It sickened him and he felt cyber-violated.

*That's a lot to do with a guy I've never seen...* Hardin typed, always fishing for the big catch.

*Suppose I send you a pic?* PEACOCK responded. *I've found one.*

*Patience,* Hardin whispered to himself. *Patience.*

*You've got my email addy,* PETER14 answered cryptically.

*Pic's in the mail,* PEACOCK typed.

*Standby, lemme check...* PETER14 replied.

Hardin had never felt so sure of anything. He knew whose photo he would see. Whitemoor had become overconfident with his recent political success and had transferred that hubris into his onscreen personality.

He minimized the IM screen and opened *PETER14's* email site. There was the email from *PEACOCK*... with a jpeg attachment. Anxiously, he clicked on the attachment icon.

A blurred photo materialized. It pictured a smiling, blond-haired man standing on a boat, wearing a wet suit, proudly holding up a spear gun with a yellowtail impaled upon its tip.

Although the photo was blurred and was clearly at least ten years old, there was no doubt about the identity of the subject. It was Key West City Commissioner Tommy Whitemoor.

*Gotcha!* Sergeant Hardin thought to himself. But he would not make Whitemoor's mistake of overconfidence. Nor would he show his hand. He would remain in character and set the hook. He would not celebrate any victory until he saw Whitemoor on the front steps of the Federal building— in shackles.

*Kewl, you're okay. That a yellowtail? PETER14* typed.

*You know your fish, Peter. I can tell we're gonna have a lot of fun when you come down here!*

*Maybe, PETER14* answered. *I just have to figure out what to tell my 'rents.*

*I'll figure out a story for you. Don't worry. I'll handle everything, PEACOCK* boasted.

*Kewl, I gotta go, though. Lemme know what's up, Peacock.*

*I can't wait to see you... and touch you, PEACOCK* typed. *I'll try to control myself 'til then...*

*CYA, PETER14* ended the IM exchange.

Hardin quickly downloaded a transcript of the conversation and a copy of the jpeg to a portable flash-drive. Then he placed a call to Special Agent Tim Smith's private cell phone number.

"I need to see you tomorrow," Hardin told the FBI agent. "I've got some evidence to show you."

"Nine A.M.," the agent responded. "Knock three times."

## CHAPTER FIFTY

# *Given The Evidence...*

Special Agents Tim Smith and Jill Andrews closely studied the photo alleged to be Commissioner Tommy Whitemoor.

"You see any doctoring?" Smith asked his associate.

"No. It's a clean photo," Andrews answered.

She then pulled up a current Bureau photo of Whitemoor on the same computer screen, for a side-by-side comparison with the jpeg which Sargeant Hardin had brought them.

"You're the expert in this area, Jill. What's your opinion?" Smith asked.

"I think it's clearly Whitemoor," the agent answered confidently. "Of course we'll have to seize his computer and verify that the jpeg was generated from that hard drive. Otherwise anyone with a grudge against him could have sent this to Hardin."

"And, of course, there's always the chance Hardin dug the photo up himself," Agent Smith suggested.

Jill Andrews bristled at the suggestion.

"Jesus, Tim, you're thinking like an FBI agent. I hate it when you do that. Damn it, we've known John Hardin for five years. We've checked him out from top to bottom. Hell, we even know what size boxers he wears.

"Hardin's as clean as they come. And he's provided information that's led to the conviction of half a dozen pedophiles and one county attorney."

Smith chuckled and patted Agent Andrews on the shoulder.

"That's why we maintain a two-man office here, Andrews. So you can keep me in line. You're right, of course. Call it my Bureau training— I just have a hard time believing that *anyone* is as clean as John."

"Nature of the beast," Andrews answered. "Now, how about the transcript? What's your take?"

"I think we've got enough evidence to convene a grand jury," Agent Smith replied. "I'll contact the prosecutors and see what we can schedule. In the meantime, we should encourage Hardin to continue the correspondence."

"It would be good to have Whitemoor commit to a meeting time and date," Andrews suggested.

"Yep. I'm also worried about how much court time the prosecutors can offer us on this, given everything we've already placed on their plate." Smith said.

"You mean *Operation Greene Street?*"

"Yeah. Juggling seven RICO indictments at one time is keeping them and the judges pretty busy."

"Well, that's gonna take 'til the end of the year, at least," Andrews observed. "This case is pretty clear-cut. They ought to be able to slip it in during court recesses."

"And there's one other problem," Smith told her. "I'm not sure the boys upstairs want us fooling with Whitemoor right now. It's a very politically sensitive time, given the Cuban business he's involved with."

"We're supposed to let a pedophile walk because he's buddy-buddy with Raúl Castro?" Andrews asked indignantly.

"Chill, Jill. I have no intention of letting him walk. I'm just talking about pushing any arrest back 'til after October, after the parade and the opening and all that. That way we'll get less interference from the Bureau bosses."

"Better not tell John Hardin that," Agent Andrews recommended.

"No intention of doing so," Smith agreed. "In fact I'll let him know we're convening the grand jury based on his evidence. That'll keep him on the case."

"Good," Andrews said. "I like having him on the case. Shit, I wish we could get him through Bureau training."

"Naw, not a chance," Smith said. "No way the Bureau would ever accept him as an agent."

"Too old?" Andrews asked.

"No, too law-abiding," Special Agent Smith answered.

271

## CHAPTER FIFTY-ONE

# *On The Brink*

The announcement came like a bolt from the blue. Mac McKinney was watching Fox News' Special Report with Brit Hume. Mac referred to Hume as "the Mummy" because he delivered the news so expressionlessly— be it news of a mass murder or of a cat stuck in a tree— that he must have died and been mummified three thousand years ago.

*No need to "dumb it down" or "tart it up" with Brit,* Mac thought. *You can't beat news delivered by a dead man!*

"Huh?" Hume muttered, holding his hand to the audio device in his ear and glancing uncharacteristically off-camera. "Repeat that, please, producers…"

*What is this?* McKinney wondered. *Signs of life?*

"Okay, got it… get me hard copy asap," Hume barked to the voices in his ear. "Well, for our viewers, you're watching truly breaking news. Fox news producers are telling me that Cuban President Raúl Castro announced moments ago that he will be holding an international news conference in 24 hours.

"While the text of Castro's announcement is still being translated, Castro has apparently invited representatives of all major U.S. commercial and cable news networks to the presser— to be held in Havana's presidential palace. That would be an unprecedented event."

A bodiless and unidentified hand appeared on camera, placing copy on Hume's news desk.

"Alright, we're getting more details now," Hume vamped as he scanned the fresh news copy.

A photo of Raúl Castro appeared in an on-screen mortise.

"Cuban President Raúl Castro has invited representatives of American news networks to a news conference in Havana, where he will deliver what he terms 'an announcement of momentous importance to the people of both the United States and of the Republic of Cuba.'"

"Well," Hume said, removing his tortoise shell half-glasses and staring intently into the camera, "We can certainly only speculate about what Raúl Castro might have to discuss with the American people... and what the U.S. government will have to say about the prospect."

The bodiless and unidentified hand placed another piece of paper in front of the reporter. Hume again donned his reading glasses and quickly perused the fresh copy.

"This may *indeed* be a 'momentous' announcement," the reporter extemporized, reading his latest update. "The Associated Press is now reporting that U.S. Deputy Secretary of State John Negroponte has issued a statement encouraging American news outlets to attend and to *broadcast live,* the Cuban president's news conference."

Once more, Hume removed his half-glasses and gazed stoically at the camera lens.

"It looks as though a new geopolitical stage may be set. We're going to take a break now to gather more details and give you, our viewers, time to absorb what we've learned so far..."

Mac went to his refrigerator and secured a cold Bud. This would be, he knew, a long, amusing night of talking heads debating the pros and cons of allowing Raúl Castro to speak to the American people about anything at all.

Republican Senators would pander to the Miami Mafia and decry any dealings with Raúl. Democrat Senators would prattle on, professing the humanitarian and economic benefits of renewed relations with Cuba.

The only variable in the formula debate was the apparent backing of renewed relations by the Republican administration, which was— save for the statement by Negroponte— declining comment, allowing the electorate to read what they wished into the silence.

Before the onscreen debate even began, Mac knew that the fix was in. Still, he relished the gaggle of heads talking which did, indeed, ensue for the remainder of his evening. It was a five-beer night of political entertainment for him.

José Castillo was not so amused as he watched the news coverage in the dark confines of his small, secluded office space at the San Carlos Institute. As he watched the commentators, he made call after call to his Miami contacts.

"I want forces in place here," he commanded. "Send me Lopez and Fernando. They are the best at what we need. Also, send instigators for the parade route. Have them bring signage— you know the wording necessary. And… make sure they bring arms."

"I have reserved rooms in the Inn of a collaborator here."

Speaking with another contact, the old Cuban barked, "Two months… if things go as I expect, we have two months. I want demonstrations all over Miami. Put things in motion now. Drop some incentive to Ros-Lehtinen and the politicos, as well. Get them on-camera denouncing Raúl and the Bush administration.

"As soon as Raúl begins to speak his lies to the Americans tomorrow, I want them ready to respond."

Ensconced in the restored presidential palace in Havana, President Raúl Castro Ruz spoke quietly and confidentially with his prime minister, Felipe Perez Roque.

"This is Cuba's hour of victory," he boasted, holding his tumbler of Bacardi up, in the fashion of a toast, to a giant portrait of Cuba's national hero, José Martí.

"What Fidel was never able to achieve," he told Roque, "you and I will soon see accomplished, Felipito!"

"You are ready for the speech tomorrow?" Roque asked, trying not to reveal his hidden fear that Raúl might appear live on American TV more than a little tipsy.

"Do not worry, my friend. I have seen the first draft and my speech writers have outdone themselves. Fidel himself could not have done better. Longer, Si. Better, No. And I assure you, Felipito, I will drink only coffee from the morning on."

Roque laughed uncomfortably.

"That was never of concern to me, Raúl," he lied.

274

"I know you better, my friend. But of no matter. Tonight I celebrate. Tomorrow, I approach soberly our realignment with the United States, and all the benefits which will surely follow— *for us,* Felipito."

"You have spoken with Chavez?" the prime minister asked.

"Yes. Hugo is well-briefed. We will enter into our dealings with the Americans as a united Latin-American Socialist power. His oil primes us with the stature and security needed to play in the same ballpark with the Americans.

"When the time is right, we will exercise our Socialist power. For now, we democratize, my friend. We *democratize.*"

"Democratic Socialism," Roque suggested.

"Let us only hope that the Cuban people will elect us," Raúl said, the hint of a faintly Machiavellian grin present on his lips.

A grin spread across Roque's face, as well.

## CHAPTER FIFTY-TWO

# *"A Forgiving People"*

By sunrise the following morning, satellite trucks from numerous Florida television stations were lined up at the front gate of Key West's Boca Chica Naval Base. They had traveled overnight from Miami, Ft. Lauderdale and Tampa to take advantage of the Navy's extraordinary offer to fly their broadcast vehicles to Havana onboard a C-130 transport.

By Noon, Cubans were witness to a media spectacle unseen before in Old Havana. Men, women and children lined the streets to wave and cheer as a procession of American TV satellite trucks wended their way from José Martí International Airport, through the narrow streets of the decaying capital, toward Cuba's presidential palace. Each of the spirited onlookers waved small flags— astonishingly, both Cuban *and* American flags.

Watching taped coverage of the day's events from a comfortable hammock on the deck of his houseboat, Mac McKinney was amazed at the display of patriotic duality.

*No flies on Raúl,* he thought. *This boy knows how to spin.*

As 8 p.m., the announced time of Raúl's speech, approached, the cavernous presidential palace ballroom filled to overflowing with cameras and reporters from around the world. The walls of the ballroom were covered with red velvet and lined with giant oil portraits of Cuban heroes— Martí, Fidel, Che, and even Raúl— each posed valiantly, if out of proportion, atop the Sierra Maestra, clutching staffs with giant Cuban flags waving in the breeze.

In the Situation Room at the White House, the president, the Secretary and Deputy Secretary of State and a number of senior presidential advisors sat relaxed, mostly in shirt-sleeves, at a lengthy conference table and watched N.S.A. CCTV coverage of the event on a large-screen plasma TV. Picture-in-picture frames featuring coverage by each the major U.S. networks lined the bottom of the screen.

"Look at all that red velvet kitsch!" President Bush exclaimed. "Looks like a god-damned whore house!"

The president slapped John Negroponte on the back and bellowed his trademark Texas horse laugh. The other officials present dutifully laughed in response.

"Whatcha think, John? This damn dog gonna hunt?"

"I think so, Mr. President. Raúl's given us all the necessary assurances. And I've read and approved the text of his speech. Basically, it's everything Prime Minister Roque promised us at the meeting in Key West."

"Well, I'm reserving judgment," the president responded. "The sonofabitch better not screw us... or he'll wind up with a nuclear cigar up his butt."

"Shhh," Condi Rice chastised the president, "Raúl's entering the room."

Mac McKinney noticed it immediately from his hammock. Raúl Castro was clearly staggering as he approached the podium.

As if scripted to emulate the famous fall taken by his brother Fidel two years before, Raúl took one step to mount the raised platform and immediately fell to the floor in a lump.

"Sonofabitch is shit-faced!" Bush shrieked to his staff.

Castro's interpreter, already in place on the platform, hastily helped Raúl to his feet and steadied him at the podium. Castro muttered a few words to the interpreter.

"Ladies and gentlemen of the press, President Castro wishes me to convey his apologies for his clumsiness. The president has been suffering from a case of the flu and is experiencing side effects of heavy medication. But he bravely appears tonight despite his illness because of the significance of the event."

Castro flashed a sheepish smile to the gathered reporters and cameras.

"Flu my ass. The Sonofabitch is crocked!" the American president reiterated.

277

Deputy Secretary of State Negroponte buried his face in his hands.

Following several moments of uncomfortable uncertainty, Castro seemed to compose himself. He shuffled the papers before him, faced the cameras and began to speak, in Spanish. The interpreter followed each line read with the English translation.

"To the citizens of the United States of America, I send you warmest greetings from the Cuban people this evening.

"I would like to thank President George Bush and his administration, as well as the American television networks for being given the opportunity to speak with you tonight.

"I will speak briefly, I hope, and candidly."

"Damn," President Bush observed, "he must've snorted some of that strong Cuban coffee while he was on the floor there—he talks like he's almost sober."

Raúl adjusted his heavy reading glasses and continued to deliver his speech.

"There was a time, my friends, when Cuba and America shared amiable diplomatic relations. American travel to our friendly island nation was commonplace, and welcomed by the Cuban government and the Cuban people.

"Following the glorious Cuban Revolution, led by my late brother Fidel, in 1959, those relations began to sour. The reasons were many and varied, including tensions caused by the U.S. cold war with the former Soviet Union."

"You approved this, John?" President Bush pressed his deputy secretary of state. "Sonofabitch is trying to blame everything on us!"

"But the Cuban people are a forgiving people," Castro continued.

"Forgive *this!*" Bush shouted at the TV screen, flashing a bold middle finger at Raúl's image. He then stormed out of the room, leaving Negroponte and the other staff members wondering if they still had a deal with Havana, or whether they even still had jobs.

On the screen, blissfully unaware of the U.S. president's gesture of disapproval, Castro continued with his remarks.

"Tonight I am announcing the first steps on the part of our government to restore diplomatic relations with the United States.

"It is our wish that the Republic of Cuba move forward toward a Socialist Democracy. Not since 1948 has our nation seen a presidential election. Such an election, my friends, is what I am here to announce tonight.

"Currently, Cuban general elections are held every five years, to elect Deputies to the National Assembly and delegates to the Provincial Assemblies of People's Power.

"We plan to establish a Cuban Republic National Party— a nationalist party— which will be faced by an opposition party, the Cuban Democratic Party. Both political entities will present candidates for Deputies, Delegates, First and Second Vice President and President of the Republic.

"By choice of the current Council of Ministers, I, Raúl Castro Ruz am honored to be the first candidate of the Cuban Nationalist Party for President of the Republic. The opposition candidate will be freely elected by delegates to a national convention of the Cuban Democratic Party.

"In a general election, voting will be open to all Cuban citizens, in all provinces. And, significantly, the process will be open to scrutiny by invited U.S. and United Nations representatives.

"In effect, this will be the *democratization* of the Cuban election process."

"Word for word what Roque promised in Key West," John Negroponte pointed out to the staffers still present in the Situation Room.

"In addition to this bold political step, my government would like to respond to the closure of the U.S. Naval Base, the removal of its political prisoners, and the return of the property to the Cuban people, in kind.

"Any 'political' prisoners now detained in Cuban prisons will, as of tomorrow morning, be freed. They will be offered free passage to the United States, or assimilation back into the Cuban community, provided that they have not been proven guilty of murder or sexual crimes against children."

"My friends in America— the Cuban government is making these courageous, innovative changes in the hope of reuniting families which have been separated for more than 40 years. Our expatriate Cuban brothers and sisters will be welcomed home with open arms. And we will welcome all Americans to our shores, in a shared spirit of democracy.

"The next step on this road to democratic brotherhood is in the hands of the U.S. government. The elimination of the travel and trade embargo against Cuba is that next step. We anxiously and confidently await the announcement of that action by the United States Congress.

"*My American friends*— the Cuban people sincerely wish to extend to you a gracious invitation to visit and enjoy our island nation."

With a recorded, rather tinny-sounding flourish of trumpets, two giant flags— one Cuban and one American— descended dramatically from the ceiling behind Castro.

*The boy knows theater,* Mac McKinney observed, smiling inwardly.

Raúl Castro stepped carefully from the podium and disappeared through a rear door. The American television network reporters began their boilerplate, on-camera wrap-ups. And then the talking heads back in the mainland studios began the Democrat versus Republican debate which would consume the remainder of the evening.

Deputy Secretary of State Negroponte cautiously, tentatively rapped on the inner door of the Oval office, then warily stuck his head inside the seat of American government.

"Am I welcome?" he asked.

"Is it over?" Bush asked, grimacing.

"Yes. He promised free and open elections and the release of all political prisoners.

"Do we still have a deal?" Negroponte asked, sidling closer to the president's massive desk.

"I'll wait for the overnights," the president responded. "I wanta see the opinion polls."

Mac McKinney opened a cold Bud and toasted Raúl Castro on a nice piece of political theater.

In a dark and quiet Havana, Raúl Castro retired to his bed chambers, poured a stiff Bacardi and called for his houseboy.

## CHAPTER FIFTY-THREE

# *The Opening*

The White House remained silent regarding Castro's announcement for nearly a month. Lifting the decades-old embargo against Cuba was not something the administration was anxious to do. But democrats were running away with the '08 presidential election. The president's favorable opinion rating was in the toilet. And virtually the entire U.S. citizenry stood opposed to both the old war in Iraq and the new war in Iran. The nation needed good news, senior political advisors told the president. And while renewed relations with Cuba might cost republicans the State of Florida in the November election, the advisors felt strongly that the move would provide at least the semblance of a positive legacy for the administration.

"We may even be able to pull out Florida come election time," John Negroponte told the president and a team of high-level administration officials. "Democracia and other anti-Castro groups have been demonstrating in Miami. It's begun to irritate a lot of locals and it's being read as negative. At the same time, the event we have tentatively planned for Key West is going to generate a lot of positive press. Even the Disney cruise ship will be there— and hell, you can't get any more positive than Mickey Mouse!"

The Oval Office assemblage anxiously awaited a response from the angst-ridden president.

"Well, y'all seem set on this, so I'll go along with it," President Bush said grimly. "But I'll tell y'all one damn thing— I ain't gonna go on national TV and kiss Raúl Castro's ass."

The announcement came in a simple, declarative statement issued by the State Department:

*By Executive Order, the Trade and Travel Embargo imposed upon the Republic of Cuba by the United States is lifted, effective October 15, 2008. Full diplomatic relations with the New Republic of Cuba may be established upon the fulfillment of promises made by President Raúl Castro Ruz to release all political prisoners from Cuban prisons and to hold free democratic elections.*

Understated as the brief pronouncement was, it nevertheless set in motion epic events extending from Washington, D.C. to Miami, to Key West— and 90 miles south of the Conch Republic to Havana.

Liberals in Congress hailed the move toward renewed relations with Cuba as "historic." Conservatives, still tentative and gun-shy about backing the president on any issues other than traditional family values and right-to-life, were more restrained, saying the announcement was "progressive and significant."

Upon hearing the news, South Florida Representative Ileana Ros-Lehtinen went on Miami TV and suffered a bloodcurdling meltdown. Flailing her arms and virtually pulling out her hair, the public official— who had once said that she would not be unhappy were Fidel Castro to be assassinated— called on all Cubans in Miami to "rise up and resist American surrender to Castro's communist lies!"

Miami's Democracia movement was happy to oblige, hastily organizing and staging even more marches and demonstrations throughout Miami. There was chaos in the streets unseen since the Elian Gonzalez confrontation.

Among politicos in Key West, however, the reaction was— as with most geopolitical affairs— more *laissez-faire*.

"Generally, I think it's a good thing," Mayor Jimmy Dailey told Mac McKinney in an interview for the *Reporter*. Figuring then that readers might like something more comprehensive, he quickly added, "There's probably a lot of good stuff in it for us."

In a somewhat more scholarly statement, Island Tours Chairman Ted Lively noted, "This opens the doors to great economic opportunity for Key West. I feel certain that this will mean increased tourists flowing through our city on their way to Havana. I'm sure anyone in the ferry business will do well."

Lively neglected to mention that he had already incorporated "Island Tours of Havana" and secured three 200-person ferry boats, which were already being delivered to the Key West Seaport. He had also enlisted the services of the Bag Man to make sure that the City Commission gave him an exclusive franchise.

"We at the Chamber are thrilled," Chamber of Commerce president Victoria Pennekamp said. "It will definitely increase tourism. Of course, I have been working toward this— with Commissioner Whitemoor's help— *for months!*"

While Tommy Whitemoor declined to be interviewed by Mac, he was effervescent speaking before a tea at the Key West Woman's Club.

"Oh yes, dears, this announcement is the result of everything that I— with the help of my good friend Raúl Castro, of course— have done for Key West. No need to thank me, though. Just remember me when nominations come up for club president!"

There was good-natured giggling among the elderly matrons, accented by some serious sniggering among the smattering of younger Debs.

At City Hall, City Manager Juan-Carlo Valdez called for an executive planning session to discuss logistics for the upcoming Fantasy Fest parade and the contingent visit of Cuban officials.

"It looks as though this is going to be the largest Fest we've ever been tasked, as a city, to handle," Valdez told McKinney. "I want to be sure that all the parties involved, from Fest organizers to city workers, to the KWPD, are all reading from the same script."

In his dimly-lit, backstage office at the San Carlos Institute, José Castillo huddled and planned with a growing number of Miami operatives who had descended upon a sleepy, unsuspecting Key West.

"The operation is called *Magic*," he told his gathered troops. "And we are now committed to it."

The gravity of the old Cuban's words caused the hair on the back of Manny Caballero's neck to stand on end. The stage setting in which he found himself seemed appropriate, and disturbing, for he knew that he was now inexorably playing his part in a drama which could only end in tragedy.

## CHAPTER FIFTY-FOUR

# "Their Reason for Being Here is Malevolent"

Mac McKinney was surprised to find himself invited to the city manager's planning meeting. Reporters were traditionally left out of the loop until all the i's had been dotted and t's crossed. Even then, word always went first to some sycophant at the *Citizen*. But never one to look a gift horse in the mouth, Mac showed up at the City Hall conference room promptly at 8 a.m., the designated meeting time.

Naturally, 8 a.m. in Key West Time translated to 8:30-ish, or 9-ish, so Mac passed the time schmoozing about the feral chicken problem and the giant Gambian rat problem with City Clerk Josephine Woods, the only other human being on time for the scheduled meeting. Time well spent, Mac figured. Woods was the only person in City Hall with an ounce of genuine integrity and the only one he found worthy of respect.

Woods gave Mac a copy of the meeting agenda and of the scheduled attendees. His eyes fell first on the name Commissioner Tommy Whitemoor. Next on the invitation list was Chamber prez, Victoria Pennekamp.

*Yikes!* he thought. *Wrong meeting— get me out of here...*

But scanning the other names on the list, Mac decided it might just be fun to stay and enjoy the carnival. There might be games and prizes.

Police Chief Ray "Cuz" Dillard greeted Mac with a cold har-rumph as he entered the conference room and took a seat as far away from the reporter as possible.

McKinney's paper had never been friendly toward the Chief. Mac liked to refer to him as either Barney Fife or "the cop who not only can't shoot straight, but is afraid to shoot at all."

Of course, being seated a scant five feet away from the guy, Mac was pleased, for once, to see that the Chief was *not* armed.

But Chief Dilliard was not nearly so scary to Mac as his chief nemesis, Vicky Pantyhose, who entered the room moments after Cuz Dillard.

An icy chill filled the air. The seditious reporter was convinced that he had died, gone to hell and was being forced to pay for his sins.

Mac grinned at the Chamber slut and nodded his head in greeting. Pennekamp ignored him completely, refusing to make even eye contact. Her attitude amused Mac because he knew its genesis. Years before he had editorially forced Pantyhose to open up Chamber financial records which revealed not only a gargantuan, secret slush fund, but receipts for numerous pairs of red highheels and massive quantities of makeup paid for with Chamber credit cards, as well.

*Damn, I love being a muckraker,* he reflected.

Fortunately for Mac's self-esteem, his good pal, City Attorney Michael Savage showed up for the meeting. Immediately he strode toward the reporter, gave him a big bear hug and sat beside him.

"Mac-man!" Savage greeted him. "What the hell you doing here?"

"Well, thanks… good to see you too, pal."

The affable city attorney laughed and slapped his friend on the back.

"You know I'm glad you're here, Mac. Just wondering how they dragged you into this den of thieves."

The Chief and Pantyhose exchanged glances of disdain and raised eyebrows.

Suddenly the tiny conference room was full as a cheery Juan-Carlo Valdez charged into the room (as was his wont), followed by Fest Director Ann Richardson and a suited gentleman who Mac vaguely recognized as a high-level Homeland Security official.

"Good! We're all here!" Valdez voiced his excitement to the diverse gathering. "Well, almost of us. Commissioner Whitemoor called and said he'll be a little late— he's tied up with some important business..."

"The beauty parlor was crowded?" Michael Savage asked sardonically.

Sniggers filled the room. Even Chief Dillard could not conceal a chuckle at the city attorney's droll remark.

"Now be nice," Mac nudged his friend. "You know Tommy doesn't go to beauty parlors... he uses Lady Clairol."

"Okay, okay, let's get started," the city manager suggested, rapping his Waterman pen on the conference table. "I think we all know each other. But some of you may not know Ron Kilpatrick."

Valdez motioned toward the well-dressed, dour-faced official seated next to him. Kilpatrick, a man in his mid-forties who appeared to be graying early, nodded in greeting to those assembled around the table.

"Ron is the Director of the Key West office of the Department of Homeland Security. He's going to be giving us background and assistance on security issues surrounding the visit of the Cuban officials during the event.

"I'd also like to mention that I personally invited Mac McKinney, of the newspaper, *The Reporter*, to be here today."

Pennekamp chose that moment to kick off her high-heels to be more comfortable... with seemingly deliberate clatter as the red shoes fell to the floor.

"Sorry," she purred, smiling demonically.

"Mac is here," Valdez continued, "because we're going to have a lot of information that we're going to need disseminated to the public quickly. We'll be issuing press releases to all the media, of course, but it seemed a good idea to have one central media contact any of us could contact for relatively instant communication with the public."

Mac straightened in his chair and did his best to appear responsible, a quality anathema to his basic character.

At that moment, Tommy Whitemoor fairly danced into the room.

286

"I'm here, people!" he declared as he gingerly squeezed his outsized rear into a vacant chair directly opposite McKinney.

"What's *he* doing here?" the pompous commissioner demanded.

"Mac's my date," Michael Savage ribbed Whitemoor.

"I was just explaining, Commissioner, that Mac is here as a central media representative," Valdez interjected. "It's something I think we need, given the scope of what you've managed to pull together."

Valdez knew that a little cocoa butter could go a long way with Whitemoor.

"Fine," Whitemoor snorted. "Let's move on, then."

"Great," the city manager said. "Moving on... Ann, why don't you get us started. Most of the event will be handled as in past years, though we're expecting a much larger crowd. It's really parade day— Saturday, October 27— we're concerned about, when the Cuban dignitaries and the cruise ship may be in town. Tell us what you have scheduled."

Fest Director Ann Richardson read a time-line based itinerary for parade day, beginning with the street fair on Duval St. and ending with passage by the reviewing stand of the 45 registered floats.

"In truth, I don't see any real problems from our end," Richardson said. "The name change— to *Cayo Hueso/Cuba Libre*— was our biggest headache. Now that seems to be working. The artwork is done and the posters will be going on sale in a few days. In fact, there seems to be increased excitement about the Fest thanks to the Cuban aspect.

"There may be a few thousand more spectators. That we'll handle with increased parade monitors and, hopefully, increased police presence. That's the Chief's department, of course. And the county sheriff's office will supply officers. Plus we'll have off-duty ATF officers, as usual.

"As far as the Cuban dignitaries, we'll place them in cars at the head of the parade and they'll serve as this year's grand marshals. That's about the extent of Fest involvement."

"I think you may be underestimating the security risks involved here," Ron Kilpatrick interjected. "We're talking about controversial Cuban officials visiting a small, relatively unprotected venue just a couple hundred miles south of the heart of the Democracia movement. A few extra police officers will not be able to provide adequate security in the event of a serious terrorist threat."

"Ron— are you suggesting that Democracia is a terrorist organization?" Valdez asked, with noteworthy indignation.

"I'm suggesting that *any* organization interested in preventing the opening of diplomatic relations with Cuba will view this event as a great opportunity to make a significant statement— and no, I don't rule out a terrorist attack of some sort."

"This is Key West, not New York," Whitemoor snipped. "The only terrorists we have here work for the newspapers."

*That's two, Tommy,* Mac noted.

"And this is Fantasy Fest," he continued. "It's always fun, and it's going to be even more fun with my friends from Cuba here. We're going to have Camparsa dancing, Latin bands and— God knows— a lot of Mojitos. And I personally don't want a lot of uniformed soldiers carrying AK-whatevers interfering with our fun."

"I have to agree somewhat with Commissioner Whitemoor," Chief Dillard said. "I believe that— given the advance time we now have— we can provide adequate police coverage for any increase in either crowd size or security concerns."

*Jesus, did these people ever hear of 9/11?* Mac wondered.

"I don't mean to insult your department's professional ability, Chief Dillard," the DHS director said. "But I would respectfully suggest that our office has had a good deal more experience in dealing with terrorist threats. And I do very much see a terrorist threat presenting itself with an event of this nature in the current political climate."

The DHS director turned to Whitemoor.

"Commissioner Whitemoor, can you tell me exactly who Cuba will be sending to the event and when they plan to arrive?"

"Indeed I can," Whitemoor responded without delay. "In fact, that's why I was late for this meeting. I was on the phone with Raúl Castro, firming up just such details.

"Felipe Perez Roque— I call him Felipito, he's the Cuban Prime Minister— will be coming. With him will be Otto Rivero

Torres— vice president of the Executive Committee of something or other there. He's like Raúl's number one or two vice president."

Ron Kilpatrick wrote down the two names. He was familiar with both.

"They will be arriving at the new Jimmy Buffett International Airport on Friday morning."

"Can we bring them into Boca Chica Naval Air Station?" Kilpatrick asked. "We'd have much more control there."

"Okay by me," Whitemoor said. "As long as you provide the national media access to their arrival."

"We can maybe work that out," the director answered. "What about housing Friday night?"

"I thought we'd put them up at the La Concha Hotel. Something wrong with that?"

"It's too accessible, right on Duval Street," Kilpatrick told the commissioner. "I'd rather see a more remote location."

"How about Sunset Key?" Juan-Carlo Valdez suggested. "Only the hotel launches have access to the island."

"Sounds good," Kilpatrick agreed.

"Could be a political problem," the city attorney noted, remembering the flap over the proposed development of neighboring Wisteria Island.

"I'm not concerned about local political problems," Kilpatrick countered. "We've got to think globally when potential terrorism is involved."

*Globally?* Mac thought. *Really, globally?*

"Fine," Savage said. "Just don't invite any city commissioners to dinner over there."

"Are we supposed to escort these Cuban officials?" Chief Dillard asked.

"Actually," Ron Kilpatrick answered before anyone else could, "I should tell you all that we at DHS have already had a Joint Interagency Task Force assigned to this event. It will be comprised of our agents, as well as agents from the U.S. Secret Service, the NSA, the FBI, and the U.S. Coast Guard.

"The task force will be assigned to provide security for the Cuban officials and, in addition, the Disney cruise ship while it is berthed here."

Chief Cuz Dillard was clearly not pleased with a know-it-all bureaucrat stealing his thunder.

"Is there *anything* you'd like from the KWPD?" he asked huffily.

"Yes," Kilpatrick answered seriously. "Crowd control."

*Whoa— one for the DHS guy!* Mac observed to himself. While the natty government administrator thought just a little too globally for his taste, he liked his style.

"What about the cruise ship, Commissioner Whitemoor?" Kilpatrick asked. "When does it arrive and depart? And who's scheduled to be on board?"

"All the details have not been completely finalized," Whitemoor answered. "But it looks like the *Magic* will arrive early Saturday afternoon— the day of the parade. Following the parade, the Cuban dignitaries and I will board the ship— along with any city officials who care to go— and the ship will then leave for Cuba. The timing will depend on the length of the parade. Again, there's a lot still up in the air regarding the cruise ship."

"That's enough for us to go on for now," the DHS director said. "But keep me informed as plans become more finalized."

"I have a concern," Victoria Pennekamp said, leaning forward for both dramatic emphasis and to reveal her plenteous cleavage.

"What is it, Vicky?" Valdez asked, trying to appear genuinely interested in her opinion.

"Well, it's kind of like what Tommy said— about all the soldiers. I'm worried that we're going to have too many of those alphabet agency types— I mean FBI, NSA and all that— roaming all over town and scaring the tourists.

"As Tommy said, this is Fantasy Fest. People expect a party— not an armed encampment. I know that most of you here will remember the infamous *helicopter* incident..."

Mac remembered. The "helicopter" incident occurred in the mid-nineties. Responding to a series of shocking photos taken on parade day by a Bible-toting activist— which Mac delighted in publishing in his paper— the City Commission banned nudity and body painting of any sort. No large, erect, latex members were allowed. And to enforce the rules, the City flew a black helicopter— replete with high-power searchlight— in the sky up and down the parade route all night. People were blinded. Young children ran in fear— in even more fear than that caused by the large, erect, latex members.

Mac thought it was the greatest Fantasy Fest ever.

"We certainly don't want that again," Pennekamp concluded.

"Most of the security will go unnoticed," the DHS director promised. "Their job is not to interfere with your event, but rather to protect it from terrorist attack."

"Pardon me, Ron," McKinney said, "How serious do you view the terrorist threat? And may I quote you?"

"I would prefer that I not be quoted for now," Kilpatrick answered. "But we have received intelligence reports that operatives from the so-called Miami Mafia are already in place here in Key West. I have no doubt that their reason for being here is malevolent. Their objective is to at least create a disruption during this event. At worst... well, I'd rather keep those details confidential at this point. Does that answer your question, Mac?"

"Yup," the reporter answered. "Thanks for the warning. And you're off the record."

"Thanks," Kilpatrick said, smiling.

Ever true to his word, Mac would not quote the Homeland Security director. But he would sure as hell cite his omnipresent, always dependable "reliable source" while reporting precisely what the DHS director had asked him not to report.

*The informed citizen is the cornerstone of democracy,* he quoted Jefferson to himself.

There ensued two more hours of nitpicking over parade routes, the virtues and/or evils of body painting, armed soldiers and open container laws.

The DHS director promised to continue to brief Chief Dillard. The Chief promised to continue to brief Ann Richardson. Ann promised to brief Vicky Pantyhose whenever possible. And Vicky promised that her Chamber of Commerce would have the best float in the parade.

Mac observed that Commissioner Whitemoor appeared to sleep during most of the meeting.

291

## CHAPTER FIFTY-FIVE

# *Key Evidence*

*PEACOCK's* grooming of *PETER14* had grown into an almost daily affair. Whitemoor had become perilously careless in his IM's with the "boy," dropping nearly all his defenses. He was now totally convinced that *PETER14* would be visiting him in Key West and traveling with him in his stateroom on a cruise to Havana. He had already painted a "romantic" picture in his mind. And he had luridly described that picture to the "boy" in his latest IM's— damning evidence.

Whitemoor pressed daily for the boy to use a webcam or to contact him by phone. He even supplied his cell phone number— information which Sargeant Hardin considered the final nail in the commissioner's coffin.

Hardin had gone as far as he could go. *PEACOCK's* demands for phone calls and commitments had to be answered or Whitemoor could smell a rat and bolt. He decided to IM the commissioner one last time to keep him hooked while he supplied his newest evidence to the FBI.

*My grandmother died and my parents are taking me to Denver for the funeral. I'll be gone for a week. Will IM when I get back. May have a webcam by then! CYA.*

The sergeant knew that the promise of a webcam image of the boy would keep *PEACOCK* on the line.

Having sent the IM, Hardin downloaded transcripts of all of his latest IM's with Whitemoor to CD, then placed a call to Special Agent Tim Smith's cell phone.

"Come on down," the agent told him. "We've been waiting for your call."

Hardin carefully stuffed his evidence into a manila envelope and drove to the federal building on Simonton Street. Upon arrival at the imposing structure, he was approached in the parking lot by Special Agent Jill Andrews. She greeted him, shook his hand firmly, and the two engaged in a brief conversation.

"John, I want to thank you for all you've done to help us with this case," Andrews told the sergeant. "You know, we're supposed to remain distant and ask questions more than make statements... but this sort of case affects me personally. My younger brother was sexually abused by a priest when he was 12."

Hardin wasn't sure how to react to such a candid revelation by a federal agent. He reacted instinctively, sincerely, embracing the agent tenderly in his arms.

Andrews welcomed the gesture.

"Thanks," she said. "For that and for your help."

"Let's just put the sonofabitch away," he said.

The two separated and shared an elevator to the secretive third floor FBI office.

It was the first time Hardin had not had to follow the ritual three-time rap on the door. Agent Andrews simply slid a blue, plastic card emblazoned with the FBI logo into a small silver slit by the door handle. Hardin had never really noticed the opening before, but there it was. With the sound of an electronic beep, the door opened and the agent led Hardin into the office.

"Hey, John! Good to see you!" Special Agent Smith greeted the KWPD officer. "Come, have a seat. Can I get you anything?"

"How about one of those neat blue key things?" Hardin quipped.

"Ha! Why not? You're here often enough! Hell, Jill wants to hire you."

"I appreciate the confidence," Hardin said. "But to tell you the truth, I'm just about burned out on law enforcement. You bust one and another one just crawls out of the woodwork."

He sat in the chair opposite Tim Smith and lay the manila envelope in front of the FBI agent.

"These are the final transcripts," he said. "Whitemoor tells the subject what he wants to do with him sexually. And he provides his real-life cell phone number. That should be enough for you guys to hang him."

Agent Smith slipped the envelope into his desk drawer.

"To tell you the truth, John, we've already seen the IM conversations. Our technicians hacked into his system and downloaded the entire contents of his hard drive. Under the current national security rules we can do that. In addition to your transcripts, we found a sizable collection of kiddie porn."

"So you didn't need this?"

"Yes, John, we do need it. It's proof that he sent the IM's to the subject. I'd also like to ask you if you'd bring in your laptop so we can document Whitemoor's ISP and such, for evidentiary purposes."

"Why not just download it from here?"

"We don't treat our friends that way, John. And you're one of our best friends."

"That's good to know."

"We also have some very good news for you, John," Agent Andrews said. "Downstairs, in Courtroom C, a Grand Jury has been convened and is hearing evidence— mostly yours— and in a week or two we expect them to return federal indictments for solicitation of a minor and possession of child pornography against Whitemoor. He faces 30 to 50 years in prison and will be labeled a sexual predator for life."

Hardin breathed a grateful sigh of satisfaction. It was a sigh that had been a long time coming.

"Thanks," he said simply.

"No," Agent Smith corrected him. "Thank *you,* John."

"We do need your help on something else, John," Andrews said. "The U.S. Attorney needs your testimony. Tomorrow, if you can."

"Sure, no problem," Hardin told her. "I can call in sick."

"Would a subpoena help, John?" Smith asked. "I know that Dillard is after your ass and it would look better on your record if you were issued a subpoena."

"You cover all the bases, don't you, Tim?"

"We try."

"You're right, let's do the subpoena thing then."

Agent Smith picked up the phone from his desk and dialed three digits.

"Watkins? This is Special Agent Smith. We're gonna need a subpoena for Sergeant John A. Hardin, KWPD, for an appearance in courtroom C tomorrow— Case #USDOJ1112-0908. Can you have one of your people bring it up for service now? Thanks."

Smith replaced the phone in its cradle.

"That's done, John. We'll have you serviced in no time."

"Great," Hardin said with a laugh. "It's been a while since I've been serviced."

"We do what we can," Smith said.

"Now tell me, how long is all this going to take?" Hardin asked. "I mean when do you see this going to trial?"

Agent Smith paused, glanced at Agent Andrews.

"Like Jill said, we expect an indictment in two weeks at most. With your testimony, maybe less. Once prosecutors have the indictment, they'll probably issue a warrant immediately."

"Probably?" Hardin asked. "I'm just wondering because we're less than a month away from Fantasy Fest. And, you know, Whitemoor has made himself kind of a star in this whole *Cayo Hueso/Cuba Libre* deal. His arrest will sure throw a wrench into those works."

"I promise you, John, it won't bother me one bit to lock him in cuffs right in the middle of the parade."

"How about the prosecutors?" Hardin asked.

"I can't speak for them," Agent Smith answered honestly. "But I don't think they'll be influenced by the Cuban deal. These are hard-nosed prosecutors. I know 'em all personally. They want Whitemoor behind bars as much as you and I do."

"Let's hope so," the sergeant said. "Let's hope so."

Hardin heard three knocks at the FBI office door behind him. Agent Andrews opened it and escorted a young man in a pin-striped suit into the office. He was a junior attorney working in the U.S. Attorney's office. He handed Hardin a subpoena and a receipt of service acknowledgement form.

"Could you please sign this for me, Sergeant Hardin?"

"I guess I don't have a choice," Hardin teased the young attorney.

"No, sir."

Hardin signed the paper, folded the subpoena and stuffed it in his uniform shirt pocket.

Agent Andrews showed the attorney out of the office.

"He doesn't have a blue key," Sergeant Hardin noted.

"Nope," Agent Smith said. "But you do."

The agent reached into his desk drawer and pulled out a blue, plastic card key, replete with the FBI logo, which he handed to the officer with much ceremony.

"Really? Thanks!"

"No problem, John. Truth is, it's a blank."

"It won't get me in, huh?"

"Not even the men's room," Agent Smith replied. "But it'll make you a nice souvenir."

Hardin laughed and stuffed the card key into his pocket with the subpoena.

"See you in court," he said.

## CHAPTER FIFTY-SIX

# *Terrorism Exposed*

Ever in search of headlines, David Conrad was heavily pressuring his star reporter to write a lead story about what he'd learned from the DHS director in the Fantasy Fest planning meeting.

"I can't, I promised," Mac pleaded.

"You promised?"

"Yes. The best I can do is dance around it."

"So the readers are supposed to follow Arthur Murray footprints on the floor?" Conrad prodded.

"Well, the facts don't have to be *that* occluded, but I don't want to point to Kilpatrick or the DHS as a source."

"Fine, give me what you can," Conrad grumbled as he gathered up Chablis, the newshound, and left the pre-press day summit at Kelly's.

Mac remained to nurse a Budweiser and consider his journalistic options. He decided to pursue the story in his weekly humor column.

**THE NAKED TERRORIST**
***By Mac McKinney***

If you're a regular reader of this newspaper, you're aware that this columnist has forever and a day decried the rampant nudity which inevitably rears (sorry) its ugly head at Fantasy Fest. My reasons for this position (sorry again) have always been twofold. For one thing, it makes no sense to arrest people for indecent exposure if they flash something untoward 354 days a year, but then allow them to bare it all, willy-nilly, on Fantasy Fest weekend in so-called "party zones." It smacks (no S&M intended) of selective enforcement. For another, we're not talking about "Spring Breakers Gone Wild." It's more like "Grandmas Gone South."

[The words *clothing optional* should be surgically removed from the frontal lobes of any human, animal, vegetable or mineral over the age of 50.]

As Fantasy Fest approaches this year, we face an additional quandary. With the opening of Cuba and the scheduled arrival of Cuban officials in our town, the annual event has taken on a unique and notable political significance. In fact, reliable sources have told this reporter that there is a high risk of a terrorist attack during the week-long festival.

*The quandary? How to uncover a naked terrorist?*

Nudity is, after all, the great equalizer. Osama Bin Laden is nearly seven feet tall and sports a 12-inch… beard. But would we recognize him without his turban, cloak and walking staff?

Harley bikers could be plotting terrorist action against a former Key West mayor who referred to them as "those people." But between the pot bellies and the tattoos, how do we distinguish a physician exhibiting his midlife crisis from a Harley terrorist?

Speaking of tattoos, now that there are tattoo parlors located conveniently adjacent to every Duval Street bar, who's to tell Grandma after a few Miller Lites from a member of the Miami Mafia?

Then there's pirates. Arrrrrr, matey. We have pirates on every corner in Key West— even when it's not Fantasy Fest. But can we tell a naked pirate from a terrorist? No, we're all staring at the peg leg.

All kidding aside (well, sort of), we should take this year's *CAYO HUESO/CUBA LIBRE* celebration a little more seriously. Follow that TSA guideline— *If you see something, say something.* That does not apply, of course, to glimpsing our city manager enjoying a lap-dance at a popular Duval Street night spot. We're talking about something out-of-the-ordinary.

If you see something crooked and it's not a nude dude wearing a Bill Clinton mask, tell a cop. Of course, pick a cop wearing a uniform and carrying a gun— not our Police Chief.

The terrorism threat is real. Still, there's no reason to let it detract from the customary ludicrousness which has become Fantasy Fest. Feel free to engage in whatever animalistic behavior you choose. Just remember to follow the standard safety rules:

•Buy Viagra only from known, local sources

•Never accept a date with an inflatable woman

•Think twice about an invitation to a keg party at the Anchors Aweigh Club

—

Mac emailed his piece to Conrad. He got an email in return which read, "Osama Bin Laden naked? There goes my publishing career."

299

# CHAPTER FIFTY-SEVEN
# The Making of a Good Cigar

As the CAYO HUESO/CUBA LIBRE celebration rapidly approached, events moved quickly. In the early morning hours of October 1, Cuban President Raúl Castro announced that Cuba's first national democratic election would be held on July 26, 2009. In a lengthy, written statement, Castro also renewed his offer to both U.S. and U.N. observers to oversee the election process. In addition, he revealed plans to return to the U.S. government the building and property that once housed the U.S. embassy.

"It is our wish that American representatives once again occupy that embassy— as we begin to enjoy the restoration of diplomatic relations between our two countries."

By nightfall, the U.S. Department of State issued a statement responding to Castro.

*The United States is gratified that the people of the New Republic of Cuba will soon enjoy the benefits of democracy. We are also grateful for the return of our embassy on Cuban soil. A Cuban Embassy is to be restored in Washington, D.C., and plans are underway for a mutual exchange of ambassadors on Oct. 15, the official date of renewed diplomatic relations between our two countries.*

In Key West, members of the city commission were so impressed with the positive international developments that they passed a resolution authorizing the City to purchase the San Carlos Institute— which José Martí once called *La Casa Cuba*— and return it to Cuban ownership.

The resolution outraged José Castillo, revolutionary-in-residence at the Institute. But he was even more enraged when he read the full text of Raúl Castro's written statement. Following the paragraph in which Castro returned the U.S. Embassy property, there was an italicized clause, in small type, which had gone completely unreported by the U.S. media.

*"Ownership of the United States Embassy property shall be the sole property ceded to U.S. interests by the government of Cuba. Any lands and/or businesses, chattels, etc. expropriated and/or nationalized under the Cuban Agrarian Reform Act of 1959-1960 shall be held and remain, in perpetuity, in the ownership of the New Republic of Cuba."*

With the tacit acceptance of that caveat by the United States government, Castillo knew, the members of his movement, as well as hundreds of other Cuban expatriates in Miami, had lost a nearly half-century battle to recover their valuable lands and businesses.

*It is merely a battle, not the war,* the old Cuban thought to himself.

José Castillo knew that such inspiring axioms were the rhetoric of younger, more heroic days. He had seen too many battles, too many revolutions. They had carved the lines in his face, the furrows in his brow— created the coldness in his heart. But, ultimately, it was that coldness which would fortify the old Cuban to lead his final revolution— to make his final statement.

*Magic* was in motion, and even in the air. In the wings of the darkened San Carlos theater, Castillo met all night and into the early morning hours with Diego Lopez and Fernando Aguilar, his primary operatives. Their hushed but defiant voices soared to the ornate ceiling of the edifice and mingled, surely, with the moldering yet still rebellious echoes of Martí and the political insurgents of his time, long past.

When the work was done, Castillo fell asleep in the high-back leather chair at his desk. His rest was short-lived, as he was awakened, aptly, by the clarion call of the oft-maligned Key West roosters— audacious fowl which were descended from Cuban roosters, originally brought to Cayo Hueso for their cock-fighting prowess.

*Let us listen, the bugle blow...* the old Cuban chuckled to himself, recalling the essence of the Hymn of Bayamo.

*...To arms, braves, charge!*

Castillo's desire for a strong Cuban coffee and warm Cuban bread overcame his patriotism. He phoned Manuel Caballero and asked that he join him for breakfast at El Siboney. Before leaving the San Carlos, Castillo opened a desk drawer and retrieved two items— an envelope and a vial of pills. He placed both in a larger manila envelope, switched off his desk lamp and left for breakfast with his old friend.

Never one to miss a meal, Manny Caballero was already seated in a secluded, corner booth and munching heartily on Cuban bread when Castillo arrived at the cafe.

"It is good, my friend?" Castillo asked, seating himself.

"Si, bueno!" Caballero replied earnestly.

Castillo ordered coffee and bread, then peered warily at the faces which peopled the popular venue. Satisfied that no one more unsavory than himself was present, he felt comfortable speaking.

"It is done, my friend," he began.

*"Magic?"* Caballero asked.

"Yes. I met with Lopez and Aguilar last night. The necessary materials have been delivered and will soon be in place."

"You met without me?" Castillo asked dejectedly.

The old Cuban pulled a Partagas from his vest pocket and lit it— slowly, deliberately— twisting and turning it above the flame to achieve just the right burn.

"To make a good cigar, my friend," he illuminated, "you need ripened filler tobacco and a seasoned, mature leaf wrapper. Lopez and Aguilar are the filler. You are the wrapper."

Manny wasn't sure that he followed the metaphor, but was contented with the trust couched in Castillo's voice.

Under cover of the table, Castillo passed the manila envelope to his friend.

"There is an envelope inside," he said. "It contains travel reservations for you and Consuelo. You will be sailing on the Disney ship on Oct. 26. The following day, you will arrive here in Key West."

"Wait, José... is it safe for my Consuelo to board this ship with me? My life belongs to the movement. But I will not place her in the way of harm."

"Nothing will happen on your way here," Castillo assured him. "Whatever may be planned will occur after both you and Consuelo are safely disembarked in Key West."

"Am I to place something on the ship?" Caballero asked.

"That will be handled by other hands," the old man said. "But your presence on the ship will make it possible for those hands to do their work."

Caballero felt uncomfortable with his mentor's circuitous word play, and with his lack of candor.

"I want to know the part I play, José," he said.

"In the manila envelope you will also find a vial of pills," Castillo said. "The vial is labeled as prescription Prozac— prepared by a pharmacy in Miami. But it is not Prozac. Upon the ship's arrival at Mallory Square— and only then— you are to take one pill. The remainder you must have Consuelo flush down the toilet."

Caballero fingered the manila envelope and, indeed, felt the hard form of a prescription container. Then he wondered about what Castillo had said. Why would Consuelo have to dispose of the remaining pills?

"Will the pill kill me, José?" he asked frankly.

Castillo sipped his Cuban coffee and took a long puff of the Partagas.

"Yes, my friend, it will kill you."

Stunned at the frankness of the answer, Caballero could only stare at the old Cuban in disbelief.

"More accurately, it will give the appearance of your imminent death," Castillo added.

"The *appearance?*"

"A very convincing appearance," Castillo said. "But you must trust me, my friend, I would never give you up— not even for the liberation of our homeland.

"Remember this... *Lazaro* will be your savior."

Again the word play. But despite the fogginess of Castillo's plan, Manny Caballero did trust the old man with his life. In fact, had José asked him to die for the movement, he would have done so with no reservations. Still, the involvement of his wife, Consuelo, troubled him.

"So the pill is not Prozac," Manny said, looking to lighten the atmosphere and cheer himself at the same time, "I don't suppose there's any chance that it's really *Viagra?*"

José Castillo laughed openly and louder than Manny had ever heard him. It was a laugh the timber of which bolstered Caballero's high regard for the man. And it did, indeed, lighten the atmosphere.

"Were it not so early, I would buy you a Hatuey, my friend," Castillo said. "for I believe, judging from the wealth of children and grandchildren for whom you are responsible, a hearty Cuban beer has been far more productive for you than Viagra ever could be."

As the two stood to leave, José Castillo uncharacteristically embraced Caballero and whispered in his ear.

"Remember, my dear friend... Lazaro will be your savior."

## CHAPTER FIFTY-EIGHT

# *A Grave Discussion*

With Key West's Fantasy Fest only two weeks away, Mac McKinney sensed an enthusiasm in the island community which had, in his opinion, been lacking from the event for at least a decade. Gathering background for a feature piece on the festival, Mac walked the length of Duval Street, taking photos and making notes.

He was pleased with the fact that, once again, storefronts were constructing impressive facades to tie in with the *CAYO HUESO/CUBA LIBRE* theme. The practice of dressing storefronts had dwindled of late. But this year, even the old *Strand* movie theater— now a tacky Walgreen's— was erecting an elaborate recreation of the Mariel boatlift atop its still-remaining theater marquee.

Mac was also pleased to see that most of the T-shirt stores had replaced their cheap shirts bearing obscene remarks and their illegal drug paraphernalia with Fantasy Fest posters and Cuban flags.

While the City was not banning body painting, it was discouraging the ritual and hoping to limit the number of seedy booths (and seedy airbrush artists) offering such adornment.

Expecting hordes of expatriates from Miami, the tattoo parlors, which had— despite feeble attempts by the City Commission to limit their numbers— sprung up in storefronts next to every bar on Duval Street, were offering special prices on Cuban flag tattoos. Full renderings of Fidel, however, remained a high-ticket item.

The reporter was about to snap a photo of Fast Buck Freddy's window display featuring Castro's triumphant march from the Sierra Maestra when he was startled by the screech of a

305

police siren directly behind him. The siren was followed by a loud, very official pronouncement on a raspy patrol car loudspeaker.

"Drop the camera and put your hands in the air!" a stern voice boomed.

Mac turned and immediately recognized a clearly amused John Hardin at the wheel of the KWPD patrol car. The officer rolled down the passenger window as Mac approached his vehicle.

"Jeez, Hardin," Mac chastised the cop, "you nearly made me piss my pants! I thought it was Cuz Dillard come to lock me up for calling him a gun-shy weenie."

"Get in, pal," Hardin said. "Let's go for a ride."

"Right here on Duval Street?" McKinney wondered. He was accustomed to meeting the sergeant surreptitiously, never on crowded streets and never going for rides.

"Is this legal?" Mac asked, securing himself in the passenger seat of the patrol car. "Don't you have to call dispatch and let them know you've got a civilian in the car?"

"I don't do a lot of things I'm supposed to," Hardin answered. "And I do a lot of things I'm not supposed to."

"Very true, Sarge," Mac observed as the patrol car turned off Duval and down Fleming Street. "Where we going?"

"Nowhere in particular," the sergeant answered. "I just wanted to brief you on a couple of things."

"You're not worried about Dillard or his boys seeing you with a dreaded reporter in the car?"

"Naw, not much," Hardin said. "Dillard has I.A. guys following me all the time, but he doesn't really have the cojones to follow through on anything. Besides, I'm history after Fantasy Fest."

"What?"

"Yeah, I'm buying the ranch, literally— a little piece of land out in Colorado."

"Brokeback Mountain time, huh?" Mac quipped.

"Only me, the wife and a few horses," Hardin answered longingly.

"You'll be missed, pal," Mac said.

The patrol car wound its way into the historic and colorful Key West Cemetery, located in the very heart of Old Town. In the past it had been one of Mac's favorite spots. He would spend hours there reading headstones and listening to the profound silence. But after 15 years in Key West, he had come to know personally too many people residing there amongst the warmness of fragrant frangipani and the coldness of polished marble. They had been people he had walked with, laughed with, drunk with; people of political renown and of political infamousness. They had been friends, confidantes, even enemies. Through the years, their numbers had so increased, so surely, that walking among them— or *above* them— made the reporter too uncomfortable with his own mortality.

The patrol car came to a stop in front of Wilhelmina Harvey's imposing tomb. The former Monroe County Mayor and grande dame of Key West had designed and contracted construction of the shrine to herself— replete with decorations and awards honoring her political offices and accomplishments— years before her actual death. "Wild Willy" as she was known by old Conchs, liked to plan ahead.

Contemplating Willy's mausoleum, Mac thought warmly of his most lasting memory of her. It was her response to any group before which she spoke or at any location in which she found herself.

"Why, I'm just so *glad* to be here!" she would declare with a distinct Conch intonation.

Mac had to chuckle, thinking that the Key West Cemetery was surely the last place Wild Willy where would be *glad* to be.

"I miss the old girl," Hardin said wistfully.

"Yeah, me too," the reporter agreed. "She was a good friend— and always a great source."

"Speaking of sources, I have two pieces of information for you," Hardin told the reporter. "One I'm going to ask you to sit on. The other I hope you'll run with now."

"You're the guy with the gun," Mac said. "What you got?"

"Well, your favorite city commissioner is about to be indicted by a federal grand jury and will likely face 30 years to life."

"TOMMY?"

"Yep, Tommy."

"No shit? What's the charge? Are you sure?"

"I'm sure. I just spent two days testifying before the grand jury. I heard all of the testimony— and it's damning. He's going to be charged with solicitation of a minor and possession and distribution of child pornography."

"Damn!" McKinney responded. "I'd heard rumors. Hell, I even heard he tried to hit on the Bag Man's young son years ago. But I had no idea he was that involved with pornography. Who was the kid he solicited?"

"Me," Hardin said with a grin.

"No shit? You lured him online?"

"Yep. I posed as a 14 year-old boy."

"And that was your testimony before the grand jury?"

"Basically, yeah. I've been working with the FBI boys on his case for almost a year now."

"Cool! That's the story you want me to break now?" Mac asked hopefully.

"Naw, that's the one I hope you'll sit on, at least for a week or two until an arrest is made. When that happens, you'll get the first call. In the meantime, I'll give you all my background files, including manuscripts of online conversations. So you'll have a big advantage over other reporters."

"Okay. I can live with that," Mac agreed. "But why the wait?"

"Because Tommy is so involved with this Cuban business and with Fantasy Fest right around the corner, I'm afraid that the feds may be forced by higher-ups to shove this indictment— or at least an arrest— to the back burner. They don't want anything to go wrong with those Cuban dignitaries in town.

"If that happens, then I'll give you the go-ahead to run with the story. That will force their hand."

"A bit of 'cover your ass,' huh?"

"Exactly."

"Okay, John, how about the other story? I hope it's just as juicy."

"Well, it's more political, but almost as important," Sergeant Hardin answered. "It involves the DHS and the City. You attended the planning meeting that Valdez conducted, right?"

"Yeah. The DHS guy warned everyone there about a terrorist threat during Fantasy Fest. It went pretty much ignored."

"I saw your piece about it," Hardin said. "But it goes a lot deeper than that. After that meeting, the DHS informed Valdez and Chief Dillard in a private meeting that they had formed a Joint Inter-Agency Task Force to deal with the threat. Among the recommendations of that task force were that the Key West Harbor be closed to all traffic, that the airport be closed and U.S. One blockaded while the Cuban dignitaries are in town. Their plan was to have soldiers at every intersection during the parade."

"Better safe than sorry," Mac observed.

"I agree. Of course, a lot of the stuff they were proposing was overkill, but I can sure support any help we can get to police the parade route, even armed soldiers. Initially, Valdez and Dillard agreed to their plans. But then Valdez informed Vicky Pennekamp at the Chamber. She went ballistic— even threw one of her red high-heels at him, or so I heard."

"I'm not surprised. Pantyhose freaked in the meeting at any suggestion of armed military scaring our valued, naked tourists."

"Well, the story is that after Pennekamp's blowup, Valdez called DHS and told them, basically, to stuff it. Chief Dillard backed him up. Bottom line, the City has officially disinvited the Department of Homeland Security from any participation in the event."

"Jeez, that's freaking stupid!" Mac said.

"Yep. Dillard has gone so far as to instruct officers not to cooperate with any DHS officials. And he wants us to use a different radio frequency on parade night— which will just add to the mass confusion we face normally during the Fest."

"Every time I think they can't get any dumber," Mac said, shaking his head, "they just get dumber."

"A lot of the DHS stuff they can't do anything about," Hardin told Mac. "The Coast Guard is still going to block the harbor as soon as that Disney ship has docked. And increased national guard troops will be here— all over Mallory Square and along the parade route. Only thing is, the City won't cooperate and we'll all end up looking like assholes… especially if anything terrorist-related should happen."

"CITY REFUSES HOMELAND SECURITY HELP," Mac previewed the headline for the officer. "That sound okay to you?"

"Sounds good," the officer replied. "Now where can I drop you?"

"Make it Kelly's— I feel like a beer," Mac answered.

Hardin drove slowly, respectfully through the narrow lanes of the cemetery toward the Margaret Street exit, as if in the lead of a funeral procession. A gentle breeze rustled through palm fronds and seemed to whisper to Mac McKinney the names of those friends who had left him alone to deal with the absurdity that was Key West: *Ted Strader, Josephine Parker, Marion Stevens, Norman "Captain Outrageous" Taylor, Emery Major, Tom Sawyer, Merili McCoy, José Caballero, Jack London, Charlie Ramos. And Wilhelmina Harvey, dear Wild Willy.*

For a moment, Mac envied their easy escape. Then he reconsidered.

*"You haven't escaped anything, my friends— one day, with the help of a clever land-use attorney, they'll come and dig up your bones to make way for a high-rise condo project. And you'll have no more to say about it than the living."*

310

# CHAPTER FIFTY-NINE

# *Lazaro*

City Manager Juan-Carlo Valdez was speeding down North Roosevelt Boulevard on his vintage Harley— he considered it a display of his second childhood, rather than a symptom of midlife crisis— on his way to work when his cell phone vibrated and displayed an incoming call from the San Carlos Institute. Valdez pulled to the side of the road and took the call.

"We need to meet, my friend," the voice on the other end said solemnly.

He recognized the cultured, Cuban-flavored voice as that of José Castillo.

"No problemo," Valdez answered. "Let me get to the office and clear my schedule. Shall I meet you at your current location? And when?"

"Yes, at this location— soon, my friend. I will have hot Cuban coffee waiting for you here."

The city manager hung up and raced toward his office, virtually flying over the Garrison Bight bridge at near 70 in a 35 zone. He was in no particular hurry to meet with the old Cuban, but the speed was exhilarating to him— it helped to clear his mind.

"What've I got this morning?" Valdez asked his assistant, Cheri.

"Eight o'clock meeting with Ron Kilpatrick, DHS... nine o'clock with Kathy Banshee..."

"Oh hell, the *Mother Hen*. I don't need to listen to her whining about all those horrible young hooligans chasing chickens and giving them heart attacks. Scratch her.

"And scratch the Homeland Security guy, too. Tell him some pressing commission business came up. No, tell him that the City will be handling security issues on its own."

"You sure?" his assistant asked. She was astute and protective, and always tried to point out a potential political faux pas to her boss.

"I'm sure," Valdez said sharply. "The City won't be cooperating with DHS. That's the way the Chief and I want it."

"Okay," Cheri replied, making the requested changes on the city manager's morning schedule. "Scratch Homeland guy, scratch Mother Hen."

"Good, thanks," Valdez said as he threw his laptop on his desk, then turned to leave the way he'd come in— quickly.

"I'll be at the San Carlos for an hour or so— meeting with some appraisers to secure that property at the request of the city commission," he informed his assistant as he cleared the main office door and bounded down the central staircase at City Hall.

"But..." his assistant called after him. But... the city manager was gone.

Juan-Carlo was surprised to find the massive wooden doors of the San Carlos open so early in the morning. He wondered for a moment if perhaps some of the Duval Street vagrants who usually camped all night in front of the edifice might have made their way inside. But as soon as he pushed open one of the doors, he was greeted by the San Carlos' curator, Álvaro Rafael.

"He's waiting for you," Rafael said. "I'll take you there."

The foyer of the Institute was in near-darkness. The footsteps of the two echoed off the polished marble floor as they made their way toward the rear of the theater. Valdez could hear the arrogant crowing of a Key West rooster from somewhere outside the building.

*Gotta do something about those damn fowl,* he thought to himself. He was pleased that he had canceled his meeting with the Mother Hen.

The stage area in the theater was completely dark, save for one bare bulb on a simple metal stand placed center stage— a theater tradition. But in the wing, stage left, Valdez could see the glimmer of a green-shaded desk lamp.

"Come in, my friend!" the old Cuban called out to him.

"I'll leave you, then," the discreet curator said, directing Valdez toward José Castillo's small office.

Stepping cautiously into the small cubicle, Valdez shook Castillo's hand firmly and sat in a straight-back wooden chair opposite his desk.

"Buenos Días, José," he greeted the Cuban.

"Good morning, Juan-Carlo. Thank you for coming so swiftly. I know that as city manager, you must have a busy schedule. I appreciate your attention to my meager affairs."

The words poured smoothly from the old Cuban's lips like fresh-cut, sweet cane syrup. But Valdez feared that the business that Castillo had to discuss with him would have a much more bitter taste.

"So, what can I do for you, José?" he asked warily.

"Do not fear, my friend. I will not involve you in dark and nefarious activities. I have only one small request of you."

Valdez waited for the other shoe to drop.

"I have a friend who needs a job," José Castillo said.

*That's it?* Juan-Carlo wondered. *It couldn't be that simple.*

"It is *most important* that my friend get this job," Castillo further clarified himself.

Castillo then pulled a folder from his desk drawer and handed it to the city manager.

"His name is Lazaro Menendez," he told Valdez. "Doctor Lazaro Menendez."

"I see," Juan-Carlo said, opening the file.

"You are holding his résumé, the résumé you will use to get him a job as an EMT with the city's contracted ambulance service."

"He's a doctor and he wants a job as an EMT?" Valdez asked, immediately regretting the question.

"He has his reasons," Castillo replied. "We have our reasons.

"I am sorry, but I will not tell you more, for your own protection. You simply need to know that Lazaro must be employed by the city's ambulance service and he must be on duty on October 27."

"The day of the Fantasy Fest parade," Valdez observed.

The old Cuban fondled the silver handle of his cane and smiled at the city manager.

"I do know that Lazaro has always enjoyed a parade," he said, flashing only briefly the hint of a malevolent grin.

"You and the ambulance service will find that the résumé is completely accurate, all the references genuine and superior in nature," Castillo continued. "Anyone would jump at the chance to employ such an Emergency Medical Technician."

"I will see what I can do, José," Juan-Carlo said.

"I have every confidence in you, my friend. The movement has every confidence in you."

"You mentioned hot Cuban coffee," Valdez said.

"Perhaps I lied," Castillo replied. "It's a nasty habit."

Taking pleasure in the old man's sarcastic streak, Valdez laughed.

"Well, hell, we gotta have Cuban coffee!" he said, standing and tucking the file under his arm. "Let me take you to El Siboney for a nice con leche, my friend."

"I would enjoy that, Juan-Carlo," Castillo answered. "But we must be quick. There are many things to be done in a very short time.

"We would not want the parade to pass us by."

## CHAPTER SIXTY

# *Goombay Cubano*

Fantasy Fest week arrived in spirited style with the Goombay Festival. Always a favorite with locals, Goombay was hosted annually by the black, mostly Bahamian-descended residents of Bahama Village. Many Village residents also had roots deep in Cuban soil. So the *CAYO HUESO/CUBA LIBRE* theme was both fitting and welcomed by the hosts as well as the celebrants.

Cuban Prime Minister Felipe Perez Roque— a wizard of public relations— arranged for *Los Van Van*, Havana's hottest *orquestra*, to perform at Goombay. They were joined by the Afro Cuban All Stars, primo crowd-pleasers who exemplified the Cuban big band sound and the rhythmic Cuban music form called *son*. The repetitive beat of wooden sticks called *claves* resonated through the narrow, teeming streets and quickened the heartbeats of Bahama Villagers.

Both bands were stalked by Commissioner Tommy Whitemoor, who danced from stage to stage during the event proclaiming his gravitas in bringing the two hot Cuban groups to Key West. Occasionally, he would give a small amount of credit to his *close friend,* Raúl Castro— simply for the egocentric benefit of name-dropping. Never once did he bother to mention Prime Minister Roque or his role in the musical coup.

Petronia Street quickly filled with Key Westers, Bahama Villagers and Cubans visiting from Miami. Most of the Cubans carried small Cuban flags and laughed and danced the mambo with the local girls.

Some Miami expatriates set up food booths where they served, among other traditional Cuban dishes, *moros y cristianos—*

a blend of black beans and white rice, which aside from being a good and hearty staple, has always been a symbol of cultural union between Africans and Europeans (mainly the Spanish who imported them as slaves to work the sugar cane fields) in Cuba.

As night closed in on the celebration, and a gentle, tropical breeze began to stir, the spicy blend of Cuban smells and sounds seemed to transport Mac McKinney 90 miles across the Florida Straits to *Habana!* It was the best Goombay ever, he surmised— and they were always great.

Every year, McKinney made it a practice to chronicle Goombay from the comfort of a wooden stair-step in the earthy, and dusty, courtyard of Ricky's Blue Heaven restaurant. From that chicken-level roost— which he always reserved early in the afternoon— he could enjoy the constant parade of Key West's glitterati, literati and nobodi passing through the see and be seen hot spot. He could also enjoy the constant company of a cold long-neck Budweiser. He could get a good buzz and keep a low profile at the same time. Mac always tried to follow his attorney, Michael Savage's boilerplate, universal advice: *Keep your head down.*

Onstage at Blue Heaven (which is to say up on the platform affixed to the old water tank), the much-beloved Bahama Village Junkanoos played with typical gusto their classic, off-color crowd-pleaser, *Who Put the Pepper in the Vaseline?* Two members of *Los Van Van* sat in and added the distinctive rhythm of Cuban son. It was a musical marriage made in the Caribbean.

A clearly cultured, older Cuban man wearing a white suit and sporting a white Panama hat, danced in the middle of the garden with a sultry, cinnamon-colored girl with glistening black hair and radiant red lips. He held the fiery young beauty with one hand and kept beat in the air with a silver-tipped cane in the other. Two large Partagas cigars also danced in the breast pocket of his suit coat.

Mac marveled at the skilled and artful— almost graceful— dance steps of the old Cuban and wondered who he might be.

The old Cuban was, in fact, José Castillo. His work was nearly done, and he was celebrating *Carnaval* early.

The reporter focused his telephoto camera on the old man and snapped several pictures. He envisioned a feature piece aptly titled, *Goombay Cubano!*

316

As the festive throng grew through the evening, the reporter noticed that the number of armed National Guardsmen grew, exponentially. The crowd was also peppered, Mac noticed, with blue-shirted Homeland Security agents. While he knew that a threat was a serious possibility, it seemed to him that the terror-mongers were intent upon throwing a wet blanket over the entire Fantasy Fest event.

Mac ignored the militari — who were trying their best to blend in anyway— and continued to people-watch rapaciously from his stair step.

He observed Vicky Pantyhose slip onto the earthen dance floor wearing a flashy pair of red, retro pumps sprinkled with glitter, a very tight-fitting and very short strapless red dress, and a colorful cloth head wrap, festooned with wax fruit, reminiscent of those made famous by '50s icon, Carmen Miranda.

Her presumed partner for the evening, Mayor Jimmy Dailey, was, as usual, making a fool of himself— reaching up (a necessity given his diminutive height) for the wax fruit as he danced what appeared to be some version of the antiquated *frug* to the vibrant, *now* beat of Latin *son*.

Mac felt sorry for the mayor's wife— not because she was being cheated upon, but because she suffered the misfortune to be married to him at all. Still, he thought, Vicky and Jimmy did make a cute couple. He figured that they might have done well on *American Bandstand*.

Mac zoomed his lens in for a tight shot of Pantyhose and Jimmy. He would never use the photo in a news feature, but he could always hold it in reserve for political blackmail.

"Nice shot," Ann Richardson observed, peering over the reporter's shoulder at the digital display on his camera. "I wonder if Jimmy might want to use it in his next campaign?"

"He'll have to pay dearly for the rights," Mac replied, turning his head to greet the Fantasy Fest Director. "I'll want at least a couple of ROGO units and some Transfer of Development Rights."

"How about free access to Truman Annex?" Richardson maintained the line of political humor.

"Hell, the U.S. Navy can't even get *that!*" Mac replied, laughing.

Mac liked Richardson. She was a pro at what she did. At the same time, she was always a lady, demure and proper. For Goombay, she wore khaki shorts and a blue on white pin-striped Ralph Lauren shirt, accented by a lei of official Fantasy Fest beads. It was her show, but she was there as simply another participant.

"Good to see you, Ann," Mac said. "Goombay's just great this year! I hope the rest of the week goes as well!"

"Me, too," Richardson concurred.

"But tell me, on the record, how are you feeling about the Fest and this *CAYO HUESO/CUBA LIBRE* theme?"

"Honestly?" the Director asked. "Well, when Tommy Whitemoor— and at some point Vicky Pennekamp— first approached me with the idea, I was furious. I mean, between you and me, Tommy can be a bit of a flake. And we had prepared a lot of promotional materials, artwork, etc. based on another theme. I was not anxious to make a huge change like that."

"It had to create internal chaos!" Mac agreed.

"Indeed. But now that I see how everything has come together, almost serendipitously— I mean the actual opening of Cuba and now all these people from Miami and from Cuba here in Key West— well, I have to admit that it has worked out very, very well. I'm extremely pleased.

"In fact, I can only say... *Cayo Hueso!* And *Cuba Libre!*"

Ann was always the consummate P.R. artist, Mac observed.

"How about all the military presence?" the reporter pursued the impromptu interview.

"It doesn't really bother me," Richardson answered. "We had National Guard troops in town after Hurricane Georges and everyone was glad to have them when we were without power for two weeks. I think people are just as happy to have them now, given the post-9/11 atmosphere."

Mac hurriedly snapped several photos of the Director for his feature before she made her way off into the crowd. She would make an appearance, however brief, at every event during the week-long Fest. It was her job, and she enjoyed it.

More members of the *Los Van Van* group had joined the Junkanoos and Mac was anxiously taking photos of them when he saw Sergeant Hardin wandering through the crowded courtyard.

Hardin, too, was doing his job— scrutinizing each and every reveler. Mac figured the sergeant was worth at least a dozen Homeland Security agents.

The reporter waved fervently until he caught the officer's attention. Recognizing his friend, Hardin made his way through the still-growing crowd to the wooden stair-step, where he sat down beside him.

"Taking filthy pictures?" Hardin joked.

"Hey, you're close, pal," Mac said. "I got a great photo of Vicky Pantyhose dressed as a fruit salad, dancing with Jimmy!"

"Jeez, that sounds kinky— lemme see!"

Mac held his digital camera up so Hardin could see and pressed "review."

"There's Ann Richardson," he noted.

"She always looks good," Hardin said.

"Yeah. And, here's the fruit salad."

"My God, she looks like Carmen Miranda!"

"Yeah, that's what I thought," Mac said.

"What the hell's Jimmy doing with his arms in the air like that?" Hardin wondered.

"He's either reaching for a cherry or doing the *frug*," Mac suggested.

Hardin laughed riotously.

Mac pressed the review button again.

"Now here's a couple who could really dance!" he said. "That old Cuban guy and the babe... they were hot!"

"Wait a second," Hardin said, examining the frame more closely. "You got any close-ups of that Cuban?"

Mac pushed review again, revealing a close-up of the old man's stern face.

"Yep, that's him," Hardin said.

"Him? Him who?" Mac asked, curiously. "You know him?"

"Sure do," the officer answered. "So do the boys at the FBI and your Homeland Security guys."

"So who is he?"

"His name is José Castillo. He's reputed to be the leader of the Miami Mafia."

"What's he doing here?" Mac wondered.

"Good question," Hardin replied. "I had him under surveillance about a month ago when he was staying at the La Concha Hotel. The feds picked up on the surveillance but told me that had checked out and left town. Looks like he's back... or maybe he never left."

"You know the babe?" Mac asked.

"No. But she's playing with fire," Hardin said ominously.

The crowd was beginning to press in on the two men. Conversation at a level below screaming was becoming difficult.

"You mind if I borrow your memory card for a few minutes and upload it to the computer in my patrol car?" Hardin asked.

"Sure, go ahead," Mac said, ejecting the card from his camera. I've got a spare here. Just get that one back to me. I was planning on running a feature piece with maybe a photo of Ann Richardson. But if what you're saying is true, then maybe we've got a bigger story."

"Good possibility," Hardin answered. "After I upload this, I'm gonna run it by the DHS guys to make sure they're aware he's in town. It's not a good sign."

"Okay!" Mac shouted, trying to be heard over the intense frivolity. "Just don't lose it!

"And try to find out who the babe is... she's *hot!*" Mac shouted a prurient afterthought.

The reporter inserted a spare memory card in his camera and continued taking candid shots of revelers boogieing to the rhythmic beat of hot Latin *Son*. Mac never boogied publicly. But he was damn tempted by the atmosphere at *Goombay Cubano*.

# CHAPTER SIXTY-ONE
# *Parade Eve*

By Friday, Oct. 26— Fantasy Fest parade eve— more than 100,000 souls had descended upon the southernmost island of Key West. Most were middle-aged partiers driving RV's or campers, desperately seeking a cheap or free spot to park their oversize vehicles. Some were Parrot-heads, desperately seeking Jimmy Buffett. There were bikers, desperately seeking more beers and more tattoos— both of which were now plentiful on Duval Street. A number came in armored vehicles and Blackhawk helicopters— Homeland Security agents, desperately seeking terrorists or perhaps a few illegal Cuban rafters. There were ATF (Alcohol, Tobacco & Firearms) agents and DWF (Dept. of Wildlife and Fisheries) agents— desperately seeking something to do besides taking payoffs for ignoring borderline-legal alcohol sales, writing citations to tourists fishing without a license or trying to abscond with live Conchs.

One surprise visitor was singer Britney Spears, still desperately seeking to revive her career following her infamous performance at the MTV awards. After having her request to serve as celebrity parade grand marshal declined, the former star reportedly was seen drowning her sorrows over fistfuls of frozen margaritas at Sloppy Joe's. One bartender was quoted as saying, "Man, what a cheap tipper!"

The number of Fest visitors had increased by an astounding 40,000 over previous years, at a time when— due to the number of hotels, motels and inns converting to time-shares or condo-hotels— the number of available hotel rooms totaled a meager 1,897. Those rooms were rented strictly on a four-night minimum

321

basis, at a rate of $1,000 per night. The roots of piracy ran deep in Cayo Hueso.

Given the shortage of accommodations, every park, every beach and even shopping mall parking lots had been converted into visitor bivouacs of some sort. Bayview Park had become a muddy mess, packed tightly with more than 150 RV's. For the first time in recent memory, the park was free of bums, er, homeless. They were understandably irate at having been ejected. Park neighbors were unsure whether they preferred the bums or the RV's.

Reporter Mac McKinney received numerous, unsubstantiated reports of some of the errant visitors chasing, netting and (gulp) cooking up a sizable number of Key West's feral chicken population. Kathy Banshee, a.k.a. "Mother Hen," cried *fowl*!

On Duval Street, scheduled to begin at Noon, day one of the two-day street fair was already in full-swing by 9 a.m. Fest Director Ann Richardson, near heart failure due to the unexpected crowd size, had, perforce, authorized the early opening. She had no choice. Anxious partiers, lining the entire length of Duval Street shoulder-to-shoulder, had begun demanding beer at dawn.

Mac McKinney was astounded when he arrived at the street fair— at the appointed time of Noon— and witnessed the massive throng.

*This cannot be good,* he thought to himself.

Two blocks north of the reporter, KWPD Sergeant John Hardin stared at the swelling mass of merry-makers from the comfort of his patrol car.

*This is not good,* the officer thought to himself.

The non-stop chatter on Hardin's police radio revealed an alarming state of confusion among the department hierarchy regarding crowd control and safety procedures.

"It's not even parade day and we can't get ambulances anywhere near Duval!" came one call from a clearly distressed motorcycle cop.

Hardin had warned them. And warned them. And warned them.

Mac, too, was distressed. He hated crowds. He disdained human touch. Raucous merriment made him nauseous. So the reporter sought refuge on the front porch of the Woman's Club, which overlooked Duval Street and provided him a safe, semi-private vantage point. Between him and the writhing blob of inhumanity stood a protective line of matronly blue-hairs, avariciously emptying keg after keg of Budweiser to thirsty tourists at $5 a cup. Profits from the borderline-legal alcohol sales would fill their Club's coffers to overflowing.

Deliberately avoiding, or trying to avoid, the prurient, perverse and pervading nudity amidst the passing horde, Mac focused his telephoto lens on uniquely-costumed participants. Most popular among this year's costume choices appeared to be various impersonations of the late Fidel Castro. Scattered among the crowd were also a number of Che Guevera masks. And Carmen Miranda look-alikes were also abundant. But Mac was most surprised by the multitude of individuals— obviously locals— dressed as Gambian giant rats and Key West chickens.

One thing Mac always admired about Key Westers: they were always able to laugh at themselves and their problems. Hell, he thought, they had to.

While the claustrophobic, nauseous reporter nervously monitored the street fair from his perch at the Woman's Club, a Navy Lear jet was landing at the Naval Base at Boca Chica. Aboard were an excited Cuban Prime Minister Felipe Perez Roque and a dubious Otto Rivero Torres, vice president of the Cuban Executive Committee of the Council of Ministries, together with a small diplomatic entourage.

The two dignitaries were greeted by U.S. Deputy Secretary of State, John Negroponte, who shared with them a limousine, as well as a police/Secret Service/FBI/Homeland Security/DWF escort into Key West. The motorcade, replete with sirens, flashing lights and Blackhawk helicopters buzzing ominously overhead, sped down North Roosevelt Boulevard, turning onto Bertha Street by Garrison Bight, which morphed into Palm Avenue, and cut through the Key West Bight to avoid the mob on Duval Street.

The motorcade arrived safely at the entrance to the Westin Marina, where the U.S. and Cuban politicos were quickly shuffled onto a launch to remote Sunset Key, across the harbor from the main island. The launch was escorted by two Coast Guard vessels bearing 60 mm machine guns manned by attentive, young

Coasties. Other CG vessels formed a cordon around the small out-island and two Homeland Security Blackhawk's droned dutifully above.

Negroponte, the two Cubans and their diplomatic entourage were secured in separate, private cottages on the pricey and exclusive resort. Shortly after sunset, the Deputy Secretary hosted a welcome dinner for the Cuban delegation at Latitudes, the resort's restaurant— known by locals to be second only to the Chart Room as the most popular meeting place for surreptitious political deal-making. They sat on the beach, enjoying genuine Cuban cigars, Bacardi Rum and the dancing display of searchlights emanating from the grand opening of Pirate World on adjacent Wisteria Island. The multi-hued, neon tube-lighting which outlined the entire length of the "Booty Slide" was impressive, and promised to far outshine the fabled "green flash" so anticipated by many devoted viewers of Key West's famous sunset.

"Neon beats nature!" Pirate World attorney Tim King had bragged to the planning board and the Key West City Commission when he thanked them for yet another variance *(item: variance to code of ordinances, neon)* to the Pirate World development agreement. He then took them all to dinner at Latitudes.

In a small stateroom aboard the Disney cruise ship *Magic*, Manny Caballero stared blankly out the oversize porthole at a calm sea and a bright, full moon. In a sweaty palm he held tightly the brown prescription bottle bearing a pharmacy label reading, *Prozac*.

Peering over a giant Cuban flag hung from the ornate balcony of the San Carlos Institute— once used by José Martí to stir the first Cuban revolution— three darkened figures watched and listened to the unrestrained and boisterous activity taking place below them on Duval Street.

"Eight p.m.," José Castillo said to his associates, Fernando Aguilar and Diego Lopez. "Twenty-four hours from now, our work is done.

"Let us hope that they enjoy the fireworks."

324

## CHAPTER SIXTY-TWO

# Cayo Hueso/Cuba Libre: The Parade

Face to the wind, alone, at dawn on the pool deck, and troubled by a sense of foreboding, Manny Caballero still thought that there might never have been a more beautiful morning, as a radiant sun rose behind the giant red smoke stacks of the cruise ship, *Magic*. The Cuban expatriate stared up, awe-struck, at the towering stacks, each emblazoned with shining white images, in relief and iconic proportion, of Walt Disney's trademark mouse, Mickey.

His mood lightened as he recalled searching the massive cruise ship with his grandchildren for all the "hidden Mickeys." They were everywhere— carved in burled banisters, buried in nautical wallpaper patterns. But the kids' favorite had been the huge bronze statue in the ship's atrium lobby, called "Helmsman Mickey." It was a manifestation of a heroic Mickey, wearing a captain's cap, standing nobly at a giant ship's wheel. In a bizarre way, it reminded Caballero of the communist-inspired portraits of Che and Fidel— always heroic, always triumphant.

Manny wondered if he would ever see his grandchildren again. He wondered if he might one day be able to walk with them up the beautiful hills of the Sierra Maestra, in his true homeland.

He took a deep breath of the cool, autumnal air. There was an odd smell of smoke on the breeze. Manny wasn't sure exactly where the ship was, but he supposed its location to be somewhere between Miami and Key West. He wondered, wistfully, if the slightly acrid smell might be wafting northward from Cuba, born of the annual burning of the harvested sugar cane fields.

Manny hoped to see one more cane harvest.

On fabled Duval Street, in Key West, as the second day of the Fantasy Fest street fair and the much-awaited Bacardi Parade dawned, anxious vendors were already at work, hurriedly stocking their small tents with hot dogs, hamburgers, ribs and beer— *mucho* beer. Complicating their efforts were wandering clusters of rowdy, costumed revelers still drunk from the night before. Many of the men— and a few of the women— sported freshly-inked "Fidel" tattoos, $50 specials offered in fly-by-night tattoo parlors which had sprung up along the parade route.

Mac McKinney, out early with his camera to document the epic day, could only shake his head.

"Hey, pal!" the reporter called to one of them. "Were you drunk when you got that tattoo of Fidel on your forearm?"

"Drunk?" the man replied in a slurred voice, "Hell yes I was drunk! This is damn *Key West!*"

The tattooed man threw one arm around his bare-chested girl friend and the two staggered down the street in search of the any bar open at six a.m.

As Mac made his way up Duval from Greene Street, he noticed that emergency vehicles— ambulances and fire rescue trucks— were already parked at every other intersection. Obviously, he thought, Police Chief "Cuz" Dillard was responding to Sargeant Hardin's warning that emergency vehicles would never be able to get near Duval Street on parade night. It was a good idea. The Chief was thinking ahead. The only problem Mac saw was, how the hell would they ever be able to get out?

The reporter chuckled to himself.

Stationed at the corner of Front and Duval Streets was an ambulance manned by paramedics Bubba McCoy and Lazaro Menendez. The two had been partnered for two weeks. Bubba knew that Lazaro had been hired on orders from the city manager, but that didn't bother him. Hell, that's the way things work in Key West, he figured. Besides, judging by what he had seen so far, the new guy was one hell of a paramedic.

"If I didn't know better, I'd think you were an MD!" McCoy had told the new man following his astute diagnosis of a ruptured spleen resulting from an auto accident to which the two had responded.

Lazaro liked Bubba, as well. The young, fifth-generation Conch was not the sharpest pencil in the box, but he was an adequate paramedic and good company on bad business. Bubba had asked no questions when Lazaro slipped an extra piece of equipment into their ambulance that morning. His only concern was who would buy the doughnuts.

By 10:00 a.m., the noisy, burgeoning crowd had already grown to the point at which Mac felt compelled to once again retreat to safe isolation on the veranda of the Woman's Club. The reporter attached his telephoto lens and shot candid photos of the passing host of sundry costumed, near-naked, fully-naked and tattooed partiers. Parade day produced more Fidel's and Che's than Gambian rats, he noted. The Gambian rats, however, displayed better breasts.

As payment for his prized position on the Woman's Club porch, Mac was forced to engage in small talk with, and take many not-flattering photos of the attendant WC matrons. A small price to pay, he considered. His only hope was that Matron Number One, Tommy Whitemoor, would not show up on the veranda.

By noon, the crowd on Duval Street had already grown, in Mac's opinion, beyond control. That opinion was shared by the hierarchy of the KWPD. Cuz Dillard, his top Captains and City Manager Juan-Carlo Valdez had gathered in the EOC—Emergency Operations Center— to engage in a group head-scratching on how to deal with the urgent situation— a potential public safety crisis.

"We've got close to 100,000 people in town and it looks like most of them are already on Duval Street," Valdez informed the Chief. "And at three, that cruise ship is going to dump another 2500 more— including children— out there."

"It's under control," Dillard answered. "Yeah, it's bigger than we expected, but I've already got emergency vehicles in place and I've got officers coming from the Monroe County Sheriff's office. We'll be able to handle it."

"You'd *better* handle it," a panicky and irate Valdez growled. "One kid from that Disney ship gets trampled and your ass is gonna be writing parking tickets in Bahama Village."

The atmosphere was much more serene on genteel Sunset Key, where Tommy Whitemoor had gathered with the Cuban dignitaries and his friend, the Bag Man, for a celebratory luncheon. Also present were several island movers and shakers, including Victoria Pennekamp and Ted Lively.

But there was little celebrating at the luncheon. There seemed to be an all-consuming pall of apprehensiveness hovering over the affair. The gloom was oppressive.

Prime Minister Roque and Vice President Torres seemed nervous and uncomfortable. Perhaps it was because they were the first Cuban leaders to walk freely and openly in America in nearly a half century. Both men glanced fretfully around the beachfront restaurant while they ate, as if fearing an unannounced visit from police officials— theirs or ours— at any moment.

Vicky Pennekamp was worried about the huge military presence— as well as the surprising enormity of the crowd which was assembling, even as she sipped her vichyssoise, for the parade on Duval Street. With the loss of so much Key West "character" due to unbridled development, she knew that the tourism balloon was in danger of bursting at any moment. Any negative press whatsoever could serve as a catastrophic pin prick in the fragile membrane of that metaphoric balloon.

Her uneasiness was reflected in her friend, Ted Lively's mood. Although the Island Tours baron did, predictably, attempt to caress Vicky's leg with his beneath the table, his thoughts were in reality consumed with the necessity of a successful launch of his tour operations in Havana. He had lately been warned by his attorneys that federal restraint of trade charges might be looming. And the payment of various lawsuit settlements, combined with the falloff of tourist dollars, had left his empire in the shadow of bankruptcy. He needed Havana desperately. He was more than willing to trade Key West for it. He was, after all, a Conch.

The shroud of dread seemed to envelop even the normally gregarious Tommy Whitemoor. While he laughed and waved his hands in the air at appropriate moments, the commissioner seemed oddly distant. In fact, he was becoming concerned that he had not heard from the young boy known to him as *Peter14*. The plan had been, he was certain, for the boy to call him before departing for

Key West. There had been no call. Still, Whitemoor was sure that *Peter14* would meet him at his home just before the parade, as planned. He would ride in the lead car with Whitemoor and the Cubans. Then Tommy would escort him to the cruise ship and a specially-selected suite— a private one, mid-ship, with a *heavenly* view. Together they would sail off to Havana together. Tommy believed the dream. He knew that it would come true. He worried only about practical things like time and tide. But worry he did.

Only the Bag Man seemed completely at ease, even cheery. He flitted about the intimate dining spot whispering in the ears of various politicos and friends. He cajoled the Cubans with humorous anecdotes of Ante-Castro Cuba, when Batista ruled the roost. And he made them promises of Post-Castro Cuba— promises of prosperity which he would help deliver. They were promises the Bag Man would keep. Because, regardless of what might happen, he always came out on top, unscathed.

While the politicos were dining in high style on Sunset Key and Gambian rats and Fidel look-alikes were partying down on Duval Street, two Special Agents with the FBI were questioning a Cuban expatriate named Fernando Aguilar in their secretive chambers in the federal building on Simonton Street. Aguilar had been picked up for questioning at Mallory Square by Homeland Security agents.

At the FBI office, he was not read his rights. He was not given the opportunity to have a lawyer present. Given the high probability of an imminent terrorist attack on the U.S., Special Agents Tim Smith and Jill Andrews were operating under the liberal guidelines of the Patriot Act. Agent Andrews noted for the record that the interview began at 1:00 p.m.

The interview did not go smoothly. The subject refused to speak English, even though the agents knew through a records search that he had lived in Miami for 25 years and had even served in the U.S. Navy Seals— as an explosives expert.

The subject would speak only his name, *Fernando Aguilar,* and the Spanish phrase, *Patrio o muerte! Venceremos!*— Fatherland or death! We shall be victorious!

"We know everything about you," Agent Smith told Aguilar. "We know that you live in Miami, that you are an explosives expert... and that you are here with José Castillo and the so-called Miami Mafia. We want to know why."

*"Patrio o muerte! Venceremos!"*

"Have you placed explosives here in Key West?"

*"Patrio o muerte! Venceremos!"*

Agent Smith regretted— if only for a moment— that the special freedoms of interrogation under the Patriot Act stopped short of torture.

Then Agent Andrews whispered something in his ear which caused him to change his tack.

"At this moment, agents from our Miami office are with your wife, Angelina and your daughter, Rosita. My associate tells me that they are being more cooperative than you."

"Angelina would *never*..." Aguilar started, rattled by the FBI agent's claims.

Agent Smith had broken the faux language barrier. It was a beginning. The intense interrogation would continue for five hours.

At 2:45 p.m., the colossal, colorful cruise ship *Magic* glided silently past waving sun-bathers and swimmers snorkeling at Fort Zachary Taylor, at the southwest tip of the island, slowing its forward speed as the ship neared its appointed berth at historic Mallory Square. The ship was escorted, quite conspicuously, by two fortified Coast Guard vessels on either side, and one heavily-armed Homeland Security Blackhawk helicopter circling ominously overhead.

In Cabin 5400, square amidships, Manuel Caballero sat pensively on the foot of his bed with Consuelo, his wife of 30 years. In one hand he clutched the prescription bottle given to him by José Castillo.

"We don't have to do this, Manny," Consuelo pleaded. "We can throw that vial overboard and walk away."

The aged freedom fighter mulled her words.

"Yes, we can do that," he replied. "But can we walk away from our homeland— away from the hundreds, the thousands who suffer daily, hourly oppression and deprivation?

"Can we walk away from *them*, Consuelo?"

"But there will be freedom now, Manny. Free elections!" his desperate wife argued.

330

"Do you really believe that, dearest one? Do you believe Raúl? Do you not remember how the man we called the Beast ruled with his military? And do you think we will ever again own the land that once was ours?"

The tiny, gray-haired Cuban woman knew that argument with her husband was hopeless. He had determined his course, and would not be swayed. All she could do was respect his decision, and love him for it.

"Is it time, then?" she asked.

"Yes, my dearest, it is time."

Manuel Caballero whispered sincere prayers to the Santeria deities *Eleggria* and *Oya*. The he nervously took one oval pill from the brown vial and hesitantly placed it on his tongue. Drinking from a glass of water retrieved from a bedside table, he swallowed the pill. His wife placed her hands over her eyes and sobbed softly.

Thunderous and forceful bow thrusters growled as they churned the harbor waters below, easing the giant cruise ship against the docking dolphins at Mallory Square. Line handlers in small boats retrieved the ship's lines, whose girth exceeded that of their own arms, and secured the Magic comfortably in her Cayo Hueso guest berth.

As the ship's horn blared out, citywide, its signature arrival tune, "When you wish upon a star," Manny Caballero, in his cabin below, felt a piercing pain and gripped his chest.

His heart began to beat with an irregular rhythm. Boom... boom... stop. Boom... stop... boom. Each constrained compression of the major muscle echoed in his ear and burned through his veins.

Every light entering his eyes began to dim, and all about him became but a blur.

"The remaining pills... in the toilet," he struggled to instruct his wife. "Call... ship's doctor."

From their privileged position at Front and Duval Streets, Bubba McCoy and Lazaro Menendez were enjoying the view of the Street Promenade, which consisted primarily of near-naked or body-painted ladies, when a call crackled across their ambulance radio:

*UNIT FOUR, UNIT FOUR... RESPOND TO MALLORY SQUARE— THE CRUISE SHIP MAGIC. SIXTY-TWO YEAR OLD MALE SUFFERING SEVERE CHEST PAINS. CALLED IN BY SHIP'S MD... PRELIMINARY DIAGNOSIS, ACUTE ARYTHMIA. RESPOND, SEND ECG STRIP AND TRANSPORT. DISPATCH TIME: 1300:15.*

Before the call was even completed, Bubba McCoy had hit the siren switch and hot-wheeled the vehicle into the midst of a scurrying crowd on Front Street. Although Mallory Square and the cruise ship were only two blocks away, Lazaro Menendez felt it necessary to secure his seat belt. He was familiar with Bubba's driving.

Upon arrival at the Mallory Square dock, the ambulance and the two paramedics were waved past security and allowed to pull their vehicle right up to the disembarkation ramp.

Bubba and Lazaro leapt from their seats, ran to the rear of their vehicle and swung open the doors. Together they pulled the collapsible gurney from the ambulance and secured it in its unbending position. Bubba quickly placed a metal case containing a portable ECG unit and another containing medical supplies onto the gurney. Lazaro hurriedly but coolly added a third metal case to the gurney.

"Backup ECG," he advised Bubba casually.

Bubba took no notice.

The two paramedics quickly wheeled their gurney into the Magic's boarding area, where the stainless steel, wheeled stretcher and medical cases immediately set off the ship's metal detector. They were waved on by security and entered the impressive Atrium Lobby where they sped past "Helmsman Mickey" toward the elevators.

The doorway to Cabin 5400 stood open, with two *Magic* security guards standing outside discouraging curious gawkers. The paramedics brushed past them, wheeling their equipment into the cabin, which was already frantic with activity.

On the king-size bed lay Manny Caballero, his shirt unbuttoned and his chest bared to a stethoscope wielded ponderously and methodically by a middle-aged man who was obviously the ship's doctor. He was dressed professionally in gray slacks, a

Ralph Lauren shirt accented by a blue and red regimental tie, and a blue sport jacket emblazoned with an embroidered image of Mickey Mouse on the breast pocket.

Two nurses in white uniforms, also bearing the MM logo, peered over the doctor's shoulders.

Manny's wife, Consuelo, knelt on the floor at the bedside, holding her husband's hand.

Manny himself was barely conscious. His chest was visibly heaving from pain, and he was covered in sweat.

The doctor removed his stethoscope from his patient's chest and turned to greet the two paramedics.

"Dr. Leslie Rhodes," he introduced himself to the emergency medical technicians.

"Menendez and McCoy," Lazaro replied, brushing past the physician to gain access to the patient's chest.

"Mind if I send a strip?" he asked the doctor rhetorically as he removed portable ECG monitor from the gurney and threw it onto the bed.

Not waiting for a response, Lazaro swiftly applied conductive lubricants and electrical contacts to Caballero's chest.

"He's presenting symptoms of acute arrhythmia," Dr. Rhodes informed Lazaro, impressed with the efficiency of the paramedic.

Lazaro powered up the ECG. As it began to whir and display digital analyses, the doctor turned paramedic pressed his own stethoscope to Caballero's chest. He gripped the patient's wrist and measured his pulse. He lifted his eyelids and looked for anomalies.

Consuelo Caballero watched his every move as she continued to hold her husband's hand and comfort him.

Lazaro was worried. Perhaps the dose of Corazol had been too much for the old man's heart to bear. He had picked it for its obscurity, a drug unlikely to be quickly identified by U.S. hospital labs. It had proved fatal in some human tests, but the mortality rate was relatively low. Also known as Pentylenetetrazole, Corazol was manufactured in Bulgaria and used primarily to induce seizures in rats. The FDA had banned its use in the U.S.

The ECG strip had been sent via modem to Lower Florida Keys Hospital. But Lazaro was not waiting for instructions.

333

Reaching into the medical case, he inserted a syringe into a small vial of liquid.

"I'm administering Streptokinase," he advised the ship's doctor without turning to look for signs of approval.

"Clot-dissolver, Mr. Menendez?" the doctor asked, nervously. "Are you sure that's advisable? We could be dealing with pericarditis or simple esophageal irritation."

"I'm sure," Lazaro replied, pushing the syringe into Caballero.

It was clear to him that Caballero suffered from pre-existing arterial blockage— and the Corazol had helped bring on myocardial infarction.

Confident that Caballero's condition was, for that moment, stabilized, Lazaro turned to his associate.

"Bubba... gurney. Let's transport."

Lazaro removed the second metal case, the backup ECG, from the gurney, making room for the patient. He placed the case by the bed.

The nurses stood by, lost in the moment, as the two paramedics carefully but promptly lifted Caballero onto the stretcher.

Consuelo never let go of her husband's hand during the process. She did think to grab her purse from a dresser-top for a trip to the hospital.

As the paramedics prepared to leave the cabin with their patient, Lazaro picked up the metal case containing the actual ECG. In the haste and confusion of the transport, no one noticed him forcefully but gingerly slide the second metal case far under the bed with his left foot.

The gurney was almost at the door when Bubba halted its forward motion with one hand.

He turned to his partner and said, "Didn't you forget something?"

"Huh?" Lazaro, wondered, sweat forming on his brow.

"Leave a copy of the physician witness statement. The doc can fill it out and send it to us later."

"Oh yeah, sure," Lazaro said, relieved.

He fumbled through forms in the medical case and handed one to the Mickey Mouse physician.

"Thanks for you help, Dr. Rhodes," Lazaro muttered as he and Bubba wheeled Manny Caballero out the door and down the hallway to the elevators. Within minutes, the three, along with Consuelo Caballero, had been escorted off the ship without incident and were speeding their way, siren wailing and lights flashing, toward Lower Florida Keys Hospital.

Following routine procedure, after the paramedics, the patient, Dr. Rhodes and the nurses had left the room, ship's security officers sealed the cabin.

No one on board would ever detect the Casio portable alarm clock, attached to two interface circuits and two electronic detonators, surrounded by 12 pounds of C-4 plasticized explosive— in a stainless steel case secreted beneath Caballero's bed.

Cabin 5400 was sealed, as was the fate of the *Magic*.

Once the ambulance had cleared the dock area, anxious passengers and some crew members were allowed to disembark for their tours of Key West and a night's merriment at the Bacardi *CAYO HUESO/CUBA LIBRE* parade. They were scheduled to return to the cruise ship for their departure for Havana following the parade. With them would be Commissioner Whitemoor, several city commissioners, and the Cuban officials.

Back on Duval Street, the pre-parade celebrants continued to swell in number, increasing Mac McKinney's feelings of paranoia and claustrophobia exponentially. The anxious reporter decided it was time to abandon his perch at the Woman's Club and withdraw to the less-crowded, more convivial clime at Kelly's Caribbean Bar and Grill.

But the moment Mac ventured from the hallowed ground at the WC, he was instantly swallowed up by an undulating mass of masked flesh. It seemed to have a life all its own, ebbing and flowing, heaving and surging to the rhythm of some unscored orchestration.

It took him 20 minutes to cross the street and trudge a half block to the corner of Caroline and Duval Streets. The experience reminded Mac of struggling to walk a half block down wind-swept Michigan Avenue in Chicago, in the midst of a blizzard.

When he finally did round the corner, the first person he saw was KWPD Sargeant John Hardin, seated in his patrol car.

Mac pounded on the passenger window.

"Any chance I can get in out of this blizzard?" he called.

The sergeant opened his passenger door and Mac crawled in. "It's a mess, isn't it?"

"I've never seen anything like it," Mac answered. "And it's just four o'clock. We've got three and a half hours 'til parade time. What's it gonna be like then?"

"Uncontrollable," Hardin replied darkly. "And at this moment, that cruise ship is dumping another 2500 onto the streets, including a lot of kids."

"Jeez!" Mac said, shaking his head. "Glad crowd control's your job, not mine. I'm on my way to Kelly's for several cold beers. Wanna join me?"

"I'd love to, but like it or not, I *am* on duty."

At that moment, a low-pitched alert tone sounded on Hardin's patrol car radio, followed by a stern dispatcher's voice:

*ALL DUTY OFFICERS... THIS IS A BOLO... BE ON THE LOOKOUT FOR THOMAS A. WHITEMOOR— AKA KEY WEST CITY COMMISSIONER TOMMY WHITEMOOR... OFFICERS INSTRUCTED TO APPREHEND AND HOLD. SEE ATTACHED WARRANT NOW BEING POSTED ON YOUR IN-UNIT COMPUTER. DISPATCH TIME: 1600:04.*

"What the shit?" Hardin said, and Mac thought.

As Mac watched, the officer fingered the icons on his patrol car computer screen until the image of an arrest warrant appeared.

"Damn," he said, quickly reading from the screen, "They've really issued a warrant for the sonofabitch. Solicitation of a minor and possession with intent to sell child pornography.

"Hell of a time to issue a warrant, though."

"I thought the Chief was his pal," Mac observed.

"Me, too. That's what's so odd about the timing. The boys at the FBI must've arranged this with the court so that Cuz Dillard wouldn't have time to pull any strings."

"Guess this means you won't be joining me for a beer?" Mac asked.

"Naw, I know where Whitemoor is. He's at his house waiting for a kid named *Peter14*. I'm gonna go bust his ass before the Feds get there."

"Mind if I tag along?" Mac asked.

"Better not this time, pal. But let me give you something for your front page."

Hardin pressed the print key on his computer and ran off two hard copies of the warrant. He handed one to the reporter and held one for himself.

"I'm sure no other reporters will see that for days," he said.

"Thanks, guy," Mac said, clutching the copy of the warrant. "And call me on my cell as soon as you've got him in cuffs. I gotta have a photo of that for the front page!"

"You got it, Mac," the Sergeant Hardin answered, shooing the reporter unceremoniously out of his vehicle.

Parade monitors and city workers were doing their best to clear the crowds onto the sidewalks and set up barricades for the big event, just a few hours away. It was an opportune time for the KWPD officer to attempt to maneuver his patrol car across Duval Street without killing or maiming scores of drunken partiers. Still, the crossing took lights, sirens and 10 full minutes. And the sergeant was sure he'd severed the long, rubber tail of at least one Gambian rat.

At the bar in Kelly's, Mac McKinney proudly flashed the warrant at his editor. David Conrad nearly wet his pants. Then he bought Mac two beers.

Sergeant Hardin approached Whitemoor's house with his blue lights turned off and his siren silenced. He suspected strongly that the arrogant commissioner was a "runner" at heart. He wanted the element of surprise.

The officer brought his patrol car to a stop in the rear of the Whitemoor compound. He saw bright lights and could hear raucous activity in the commissioner's lush garden. Clearly, the commissioner was unaware of anything untoward and was partying with friends as he awaited the arrival of his young conquest and the parade activities to come.

Warrant in hand, Hardin began to step from his vehicle.

At that moment, another low-pitch warning tone sounded on his radio.

*ALL DUTY OFFICERS... BE ADVISED... A WARRANT PREVIOUSLY ISSUED FOR THOMAS A. WHITEMOOR— AKA*

*KEY WEST CITY COMMISSIONER TOMMY WHITEMOOR— WAS ISSUED IN ERROR AND HAS BEEN RESCINDED. REPEATING... THE WARRANT HAS BEEN RESCINDED. OFFI- CERS ARE INSTRUCTED TO DISREGARD THE PREVIOUS BOLO AND ARREST WARRANT. REPEATING... THE ARREST WARRANT WAS ISSUED IN ERROR AND IS INVALID. OFFI- CERS SHOULD ACT ACCORDINGLY. DISPATCH TIME: 1600:30.*

John Hardin's heart sank. Someone had gotten to the Feds. They had quashed the warrant under political pressure.

From within Whitemoor's garden, the sound of unconcerned laughter and merry-making sickened him. He had been so close to putting an end to Whitemoor's illicit, perverted activities. And he'd been stopped short on someone's political whim.

Hardin grasped his cell phone and placed a call to Mac McKinney.

"You still at Kelly's?" he asked.

"Yeah, what's up?" the voice on the other end of the line replied. "You got him?"

"That offer of a beer still stand?" Hardin asked, somberly.

"Well... yeah, sure. Come on over, pal."

Deep in the bowels of the federal building on Simonton Street, FBI Special Agents Tim Smith and Jill Andrews intensified their interrogation of the Democracia operative, Fernando Aguilar.

"We have found your van in the parking lot behind the La Concha Hotel," Agent Smith told the subject.

"It's a crime to have a van?" Aguilar replied with an attitude.

"It is when it's filled with bomb-making materials," Agent Andrews replied, with an attitude of her own.

"We've also picked up your partner, Diego Lopez," Smith pressed Aguilar.

Sweat began to bead on the subject's brow.

"He's in an interrogation room just down the hall," the agent continued. "And he's talking."

It was not merely a clever FBI technique designed to per- suade Aguilar to talk. His partner was, indeed, just down the hall being questioned by two other agents. But he was telling them no more than Aguilar was telling Smith and Andrews.

338

Agent Smith glanced nervously at his watch. Fifteen minutes past five. The parade would be stepping off in a little more than two hours. More than 100,000 people— including women and children— would be lining the street along the parade route. And Smith was sure as hell that Aguilar and Lopez had planted a bomb— a large bomb, judging from C-4 residue found in the subject's van— somewhere. He just didn't know where.

The agent continued his questioning, with an added sense of urgency.

"Listen, Aguilar, we know everything about you and your partner. We know your affiliation with the Miami Mafia. We know when you arrived and how long you've been here. And we're sure you've placed an explosive device along tonight's parade route."

"You're wrong, my friend," Aguilar answered, smiling.

"Wrong about a bomb or wrong about where it's placed?" Jill Andrews asked.

"You're just wrong," came the subject's cryptic reply.

Agent Smith began to pace the floor. He walked to the office window, which overlooked Simonton Street. He could hear the din of Duval Street two blocks away.

"Okay, Fernando," he said, turning, "I'm going to make you the standard Bureau deal. Both you and your partner are going to go to prison for life for a terrorist attack. If an explosive device goes off and any people are killed, you will both be executed."

Aguilar stared, expressionless, at his interrogator. But, based on his years of interrogation experience, Agent Smith was sure the subject was about to break. He could feel the shift of power.

"The Bureau opens one door to the two of you. Whoever steps through it first— giving us the information we need— will be labeled by us as a 'cooperating witness.' That can mean a lot in your sentencing.

"That door is open to you now. But I'm about to close it."

Agent Smith again turned toward the window, deliberately removing his attention from the subject. That *was* a Bureau technique, designed to isolate the subject, to press him or her, to induce a feeling of desperation.

After a long period of silence, Aguilar began to speak.

"Is there protection for my family?" he asked.

339

*Bingo!* Smith breathed a sigh of relief to himself.

He turned to face Aguilar. Reaching for a chair, he sat directly in front of the subject. He wanted to present an air of sincerity.

"We can place your family in the Witness Protection program," he answered. "That can be done the minute you tell us what we need to know. I can give you my personal assurance that no harm will come to them."

Again Agent Smith glanced at his watch. Half past five p.m. Perilously close to parade time.

"There is a bomb," Aguilar said bluntly. "A big one."

Agent Smith could feel sweat beading on his forehead.

"How big?"

"Around 12 pounds of C-4," Aguilar replied.

"Where?" Agent Smith wanted to know. "The La Concha? The San Carlos?"

"No," Aguilar replied.

"Where?"

"The cruise ship," the subject answered, his head slumped.

"Shit!" Jill Andrews cried aloud. "That's a Disney ship. You wanted to kill *kids?*"

"We wanted to stop a deal between Bush and Raúl Castro," Aguilar replied angrily.

"Okay, okay," Tim Smith tried to calm the atmosphere. "What we need to know now is *where*. Where is the bomb on the ship?"

"I don't know," Aguilar replied. "I didn't place the device. I only prepared it."

"Who placed it? Wait... hold that. When's it set to go off?"

"Eight p.m. tonight," Aguilar replied confidently. "Casio travel clock— they're very reliable."

"Jill, get Kilpatrick at Homeland Security on the radio," Smith shouted to Agent Andrews. "Let's get that ship evacuated... I mean everybody— passengers, crew, wharf rats... and let's do it *NOW*."

"What about the parade?" Andrews wondered.

"I don't know what we can do about that," Smith replied. "I think it's too late to stop it. Given the size of the crowd, we'd probably cause uncontrollable panic if we let this get out. A lot of people might get hurt. All we can do is evacuate the ship, clear the waterfront area, and watch the fireworks.

"At least, that's the advice I'd give to DHS."

Within minutes of receiving the FBI warning, Ron Kilpatrick had donned his bullet-proof vest and mobilized every Homeland Security agent available to him. He dashed out of the DHS home office and sprinted toward a Blackhawk helicopter waiting in the parking lot. As he strapped himself in the chopper, he used his radio to enlist the help of the Navy and the Coast Guard. Finally, with some reluctance, he called KWPD Chief Cuz Dillard at the EOC.

"We've got a situation involving the cruise ship at Mallory Square," he told the Chief. "It's a bomb."

Chief Dillard was struck dumb.

"We're going to be closing the harbor and sealing off Mallory Square. Your people can best be used along the parade route exercising crowd control. Also, send me 20 officers to Mallory Square. I'll need them to evacuate the hotels in that immediate area. For the record, a state of national emergency exists— your officers are now under the command of the Department of Homeland Security.

"Another thing, Chief, keep this off the airwaves. We can't have panic with a crowd the size of that you have on Duval Street. Two-thirds of them are drunk… we don't know what the hell could happen.

"Got it?"

"Got it, sir." Dillard responded blankly.

The Chief was not sure how to tell the Homeland Security Director that 20 officers constituted more than half the total force he had on duty that night. The city commission had refused to allow more, citing excessive officer overtime costs.

At the bar in Kelly's *Reporter* Editor David Conrad was edifying Sargeant John Hardin with his philosophy of political campaigns.

"What most politicians don't understand is, it's easy to get my paper's endorsement. All they have to do is run an ad."

Mac had heard it all before. But suddenly Hardin and Conrad had become fast drinking buddies. It was the first time Mac had ever seen the officer drink, especially in uniform, and in public. The cancelled warrant had obviously broken his spirit completely.

Chablis, the news hound's ears perked up as a low-pitched warning tone sounded on Hardin's shoulder radio.

*SIGNAL 52— REPEAT SIGNAL 52— ALL OFFICERS SWITCH TO SECURE CHANNEL.*

Hardin put down his drink and switched the channel on his radio. He stood up and moved to an isolated corner of the bar, so that he might hear better.

*SIGNAL 52— AVAILABLE OFFICERS RESPOND TO MALLORY SQUARE, THE CRUISE SHIP MAGIC... SIGNAL 52 CONFIRMED ABOARD THE VESSEL. OFFICERS ARE NOW UNDER THE COMMAND OF HOMELAND SECURITY. REPEAT... OFFICERS ARE UNDER COMMAND OF HOMELAND SECURITY. DISPATCH TIME: 1800:30.*

Sergeant Hardin's wits kicked swiftly back into cop mode. He darted out the rear garden of Kelly's without so much as a goodbye to the two journalists. He leapt into his patrol car and, switching on his blue lights and siren, whipped a U-turn in the middle of Caroline Street and turned down Whitehead toward Mallory Square, just blocks away. Fortunately, the street had already been cleared— as well as possible— for the parade.

A bomb, Hardin thought. Damn, I warned them!

The officer could not believe what he saw when he slammed his patrol car to a stop in the red brick parking lot at Mallory Square.

The air above the cruise ship was filled with circling helicopters. There were three DHS Blackhawks with agents hanging off the runners, as well as four Navy and Coast Guard choppers. A sheriff's chopper had landed in the parking lot. And DHS Director Ron Kilpatrick was just stepping out of another DHS Blackhawk.

National Guardsmen with automatic weapons were forming a cordon around the entire Square. Armored military vehicles were sealing off all the entrances. Vehicles with giant spotlights were being wheeled up to the dock area.

From the belly of the massive cruise ship flowed a steady line of clearly alarmed passengers, crewmembers and ship's officers. Many of the passengers were children, some of them wearing mouse ears. The steady line of evacuees was being hurried along toward the safety of the perimeter by anxious military personnel shouting marching orders.

In the harbor, Coast Guard vessels with manned weapons mounted on their bows and sterns were clearing all pleasure craft from the area. The harbor was being sealed to all traffic.

The hastily-positioned searchlights flashed on, illuminating the Magic with a brilliance that leant majesty to its shining ebony-painted hull. From the prow of the ship, a giant gold image of Mickey Mouse peered out at the scurrying pack of humanity running frantically from his company, like rats deserting a sinking ship.

Sargeant Hardin was the first KWPD officer on the scene. He pulled his vehicle up to the Blackhawk where Ron Kilpatrick was barking orders to his agents.

"Hardin, KWPD, sir," he announced.

"Hardin, good. You're in charge. I'm gonna tell you this once... we got a bomb. It's timed to go off at eight p.m. We don't have time to search this entire cruise ship. So we're pretty sure it's gonna *go off* at eight p.m.

"We need to clear these hotels. Send your officers in teams to this one on the left, what is it the Ocean Key House? And more to the one on the right here... the Westin. I want 'em empty in 30 minutes. I mean empty... no people, none. No guests, no management, no busboys.

"Got it, Hardin?"

"Got it, sir. What about Sunset Key and Pirate World, I mean Wisteria Island?"

"No time. The harbor's sealed. They're on their own."

Hardin drove his patrol car to the perimeter, where black and white KWPD vehicles were beginning to arrive. He stood in the headlights of his car and began to bark his own orders.

"You two, Ocean Key House... clear it now.

"Jack, you and Tom, Westin... clear it.

"Don't take time to argue with them, just get them out... tell them there's a fire, whatever..."

Sergeant Hardin shined his duty flashlight on his watch. Seven p.m. The parade would step off in 30 minutes. In 60 minutes...

That was when the idea struck Hardin.

"Thomas, you're in charge... clear these hotels!" he shouted to a fellow officer.

He jumped into his patrol car, eased his way past the guards at the perimeter, and sped back up Whitehead Street toward Fleming Street, where the parade was preparing to kick off.

Members of the KWPD motorcycle escort waved casually at Hardin as he sped past them, screeching to a halt beside the parade's lead car, a shiny, pink 1959 Cadillac. The Caddy had been Whitemoor's idea— his impression of Cuba. While saying nothing, Cuban Prime Minister Roque had expressed his disgust at the choice privately to members of his delegation and to Deputy Secretary of State Negroponte. But he did not protest riding in the car. It would be an insult to his hosts, he felt.

Commissioner Whitemoor was just stepping into the Cadillac, positioning himself in the front seat, next to Negroponte.

Sergeant Hardin reached his hand over the seat back and fumbled around on the back seat of his patrol car for the piece of paper he had discarded there. Retrieving the paper, he placed it on the dashboard, then exited his vehicle.

His hand pointedly poised on his gun holster, Hardin slowly approached the passenger side of the pink Cadillac. No one in the car seemed to notice him.

"Commissioner Whitemoor," he said, leaning on the car door, "I need to speak with you, sir."

"Huh?" Whitemoor started, turning to face the officer. "Sergeant, we're about to have a parade here. Is it important?"

"Yes sir, it is very important."

"Very well, then. Speak."

"I'd appreciate it if you'd join me in my patrol car, sir. It is a matter of some importance."

"Oh, bother!" Whitemoor screeched. "If I must!"

As the two walked to his patrol car, Hardin glanced once more at his watch. Fifteen minutes past seven. Time was becoming critical.

344

Tommy Whitemoor sat, quite unhappily, in the passenger's seat of the patrol car. Hardin turned on the overhead light, lifted the paper from the dashboard and handed it to the commissioner.

"What's this?" Whitemoor asked, indignant.

"It's a warrant, Commissioner. It's a warrant for your arrest."

"What in hell... what the hell is this?" Whitemoor shrieked.

"Sir, you've been charged with felony solicitation of a minor and possession of, with intent to sell, child pornography."

The arrogant commissioner was enraged.

"This is outrageous!" he shouted. "This is absurd! I've done no such thing. Who's responsible for this? Was it those damned Secret Service people? I won't stand for this... I want my attorney! I want Michael Savage here right now!"

"I believe the boy's nick is *Peter14*," John Hardin calmly told the irate commissioner.

Whitemoor became silent. He was flushed and began to shake, almost uncontrollably.

"Listen, Commissioner," Hardin said, attempting to calm Whitemoor, and gain his confidence, "Chief Dillard sent me here to help you. There's a BOLO out... there are other officers on the way to pick you up."

"But the parade..." Whitemoor protested weakly.

"Forget the parade. You're looking at 30 years in prison. I'm here to help you get out of this, to get away."

"You can do that?" Whitemoor asked.

The commissioner was panicked. He was caught, and he would do anything to save himself.

"I'm going to get you safely onboard the cruise ship," Hardin told him. "You can wait there until the parade is over, then you'll travel to Cuba. Your friend Raúl won't let the Feds pursue you there."

Whitemoor's mind was addled, racing 50 miles an hour.

"That makes sense. I've got my boarding pass."

He reached in his pocket and pulled out a plastic card bearing an image of the Disney *Magic*.

"See? That'll get me on, for sure. You'll help?"

"That's why the Chief sent me," Hardin answered.

"Thanks," Whitemoor said, beginning to sob like a little girl.

Hardin glanced in the rearview mirror to make sure that the wide grin of self-satisfaction he felt was not perceptible on his face.

The officer placed his car in reverse, backed away from the Cadillac filled with Cuban and U.S. dignitaries, and sped north up Whitehead Street.

Along the way, Whitemoor actually leaned out the passenger window and waved to the crowd lining the street.

As Hardin's vehicle approached the Mallory Square perimeter, it was clear to him that the DHS director had done his job.

The helicopters still hovered in the air, but hovered a safe distance from the *Magic*. The Coast Guard vessels had pulled away to either end of the harbor. All military personnel had withdrawn to the perimeter area. And the cruise ship floated alone, abandoned, in the brilliant light of military floodlights.

The barking of orders had ceased. And an eerie silence filled the Square. Everything that could be done had been done. It was then all about waiting.

Hardin neared the armed guardsmen with trepidation. He was not sure he could execute his plan.

Figuring he had nothing to lose, he switched on his blue lights and moved his vehicle forward.

Surprisingly, the guardsmen smiled and waved him past.

"What's all this?" Whitemoor asked nervously. "Where is everyone?"

"Security for the Cuban delegation," Hardin answered, matter-of-factly.

"Oh."

Still amazed that he was not being pursued by trigger-happy Homeland Security agents with lethal weaponry, the KWPD sergeant brought his patrol car to a stop directly in front of the boarding ramp of the *Magic*.

"Run!" Hardin instructed the commissioner. "Run now. Run to your cabin, and stay there."

Still confused, but desperate, Tommy Whitemoor did as instructed. He bolted from the patrol car and headed straight for the open loading port of the cruise ship.

346

As he stepped onboard, Whitemoor turned to Hardin's patrol car and yelled, "Thanks!"

Sergeant John Hardin smiled. His work was done. And, he knew, his job was finished.

When he returned to the perimeter, the officer's car was surrounded by soldiers and DHS agents with automatic weapons pointed at his head.

Ron Kilpatrick approached his vehicle window.

"Who did you just let inside that vessel?" he wanted to know.

"Nobody, sir," Hardin answered. *"Nobody."*

The sergeant was pulled from his car and placed under arrest.

Inside the *Magic*, Tommy Whitemoor found his way to the atrium lobby and the elevators.

*Where is everyone?* He wondered.

He examined his boarding pass.

*Cabin 5500,* it read.

The commissioner took an elevator to Deck Five and found his way to the appointed cabin. He entered the cabin and was delighted with what he saw. There was a great view of Mallory Square and there were "hidden Mickeys" everywhere. He lay down on the comfy double bed and felt safe.

The Fantasy Fest *CAYO HUESO/CUBA LIBRE* parade stepped off, sans Tommy Whitemoor, at its scheduled time, 7:30 p.m.

From the lead car, Felipito Roque and John Negroponte waved to the hundreds of smiling faces, masked Fidel's, Che's, chickens, and Gambian rats, as the parade wound its way down Whitehead Street.

Directly behind them followed the first float, a tribute to Cuban Son, featuring *Los Van Van*. Behind that, another float featured the *Afro-Cuban All Stars*.

The sound of hot Latin rhythm preceded the parade as it rounded the corner of Front and Duval Streets at 7:45 p.m. The crowd, grown then to beyond imagining, went wild. People were dancing in the street alongside the musical floats.

From the reviewing stand, opposite the La Concha Hotel at Fleming and Duval Streets, Victoria Pennekamp could already see the blue lights and hear the sirens of the police motorcycle escort leading the parade route. And the Latin music already wafted into her ears. She could barely contain her desire to dance. Controlling her impulses, she satisfied herself with rhythmically rubbing Mayor Dailey's leg with hers.

Surely, the Chamber of Commerce head thought, this was the best Fantasy Fest ever!

The other dignitaries, commissioners and power brokers on the reviewing stand craned their necks in the direction of the steadily approaching lights and music.

The tropical night air was intoxicating. And a *parade* was coming!

For the first time in its decades-old history, the parade reached the reviewing stand on time— *at exactly 8:00 p.m.*

Cuban Prime Minister Felipe Perez Roque stood up proudly in the halted Cadillac and raised his hand in a dignified salute to the officials on the reviewing stand.

Above him, above the crowd, above the bars and tattoo parlors of Duval Street and the entire southwest quadrant of the island of Cayo Hueso, the night sky instantly, stunningly turned to blazing daylight.

Those on the reviewing stand, and most of the onlookers on the eastern side of the street, were temporarily blinded.

Seconds later came the deafening sound of an explosive blast, emanating from Mallory Square.

A shuddering, percussive shock wave followed, shattering T-shirt shop windows up and down Duval Street. At the lower end of Duval, near Mallory Square, large shards of glass and flying strips of metal sliced indiscriminately through the bodies of revelers in the street and on the sidewalks.

Huge parade floats were blown apart by the percussion or turned over onto screaming, horrified spectators.

At the reviewing stand, Vicky Pennekamp, along with many in the crowd, collapsed in a faint.

Prime Minister Roque fell back in his seat and the Cadillac was swiftly diverted by the motorcycle patrol down Fleming Street and out of sight. Many parade onlookers were simply run over in the process.

At Mallory Square, Ron Kilpatrick watched, from the safety of an armored vehicle, in disbelief and shock as the cruise ship Magic creaked, groaned and buckled mid-ship, then split in two, sinking slowly to the bottom of the harbor— stern and bow straight up in the night sky, in opposed directions. It took just minutes.

Minor explosions continued at odd intervals throughout the derelict hulk of the ship.

The blast had occurred square amidships. The resulting concussion and shock wave had blown away all the docking dolphins and most of the dock itself. Every window at the two closest hotels was imploded.

Across the harbor, on Wisteria Island, the Booty Slide at Pirate World had shuddered twice at the impact, then collapsed in a heap of steel and shattered neon tubing.

Late into the night, sad, tattered felt mouse ears and torn, floppy Goofy ears washed up on the shores of both Sunset Key and Wisteria Island.

A gaseous, caustic cloud hung over the entire harbor, and over the island called Key West.

The parade was over.

—

While watching, from the balcony of the San Carlos Institute, the fireworks he had ignited, José Castillo was handcuffed and arrested by federal agents.

In the Cardiac Care unit at Lower Florida Keys Hospital, Consuelo Caballero never left her beloved husband Manny's side as he slowly recovered.

Felipe Perez Roque and his delegation returned on the next flight to Havana, where he and Raúl Castro met two days later with Venezuelan President Hugo Chavez to discuss a Socialist alliance between the two countries.

John Negroponte resigned from his position as Deputy Secretary of State.

Victoria Pennekamp forced Mayor Jimmy Dailey to leave his wife and the two moved to New Jersey, where they planned to open a tattoo parlor.

KWPD Sergeant John Hardin was acquitted of all charges and subsequently replaced Cuz Dillard as Chief of Police.

349

And, finally, reporter Mac McKinney loaded up his small sailboat, *Front Page,* and sailed her 90 miles south to Havana, Cuba. He planned to start his own newspaper. And he planned never to return to Key West.

That was his plan.

# Epilogue— *Part One*

Mac McKinney's Key West press credentials got him into Havana. In truth, a $100 bill slipped to the proper official at Marina Hemingway could have done the same. But the credentials allowed him to stay in Cuba following the political fallout which resulted from the *CAYO HUESO/CUBA LIBRE* debacle.

The expatriate reporter stayed for a month in a Havana hotel which catered primarily to Canadian tourists. That translated to English-speaking and cheap. He used the time to familiarize himself with the city and to enroll in a crash course of Spanish, self-taught.

The language came to him easily, if not quickly, through friends he made at local bars and bodegas. These were the people Mac had come to Cuba to meet: the real Cuba. They invited him to their homes, shared their food and wine with him. They accepted him into their families and made him feel welcome, never asking for one peso.

Mac sold his small sailboat, *Front Page,* to a visiting American businessman who had become trapped in Havana following the local political crackdown on tourism. He gave the land-lubber some old nautical charts, explained the difference between a jib and a mainsail, and pointed him in the direction of Key West.

The transaction signaled Mac's commitment to remain in Cuba, and also added $5,000 in American cash to the bankroll he had brought with him to Havana. It was cash he would need to possibly purchase a small homestead and to publish the newspaper he dreamed of.

Mac quickly learned that, given the political climate in Havana, publishing any sort of English newspaper there presented more obstacles than he cared to attempt to surmount. So he bought a 20 year old scooter with totally bald tires for $15 and began to make day trips to smaller, outlying towns.

Seventy-five miles east of Havana— on one of the longest treks he had dared make on his decrepit scooter— he found the small city of Cardenas.

Home to both horse-drawn carriages and Elian Gonzalez, Cardenas was known as La *Ciudad del Cangrejos,* "City of crabs." It was also called Cuba's "Flag City," as the first Cuban national flag had flown atop the town's *La Dominica* Hotel.

Conducting intense research in several local bars, Mac learned that many foreigners lived in Cardenas and worked in the tourist industry in Varadero, a short distance away. His fifth Hatuey beer convinced him that he could publish his paper in cozy Cardenas and have it distributed it in the more cosmopolitan Varadero.

"Lucy, I'm ho-ome!" he exclaimed aloud in a lame Ricky Riccardo impersonation.

"You look for a home, amigo?" a voice to the left of him in the dimly-lit bar responded.

"No, that's not what I meant," Mac explained. "Well, actually I guess I *am* looking for a home— or a house or an apartment…"

"I am Jorge," a gnomish, slightly sleazy-looking Cuban, seated on a bar stool taller than he was, introduced himself. "I deal in the real estate."

Mac tried to look beyond Jorge's 1950's-style wide pinstripe suit and slicked-back, Pomade slathered, shiny black hair.

"Nice to meet you, Señor," he said.

Jorge smiled. And Mac knew instinctively that it was not an "I've got a bridge I'd like to sell you" smile. Rather, it was a genuine smile, the sort he'd seen on the faces of so many of the Cuban people.

The next day, Jorge— Mac never, ever learned his last name— drove the would-be publisher to a house, which he had described as "a palace fit for Fidel."

Mac suspected the description, knowing that Fidel Castro had lived most of his life in a very commonplace bungalow, recognizable as El Presidente's residence only by the number of soldiers guarding it.

A bumpy ride in Jorge's 1959 Buick down a dirt road winding through a burned out sugar cane field did little to bolster the reporter's hopes. But when the ancient vehicle came to a stop at the end of the road, Mac saw that Jorge's description of the house had been accurate. In fact, it was not a house, but a large, white, Spanish villa, replete with an adobe tile roof, a central garden and ornate fountain. It was, indeed, a palace fit for Fidel.

"Plus 20 acres!" Jorge announced proudly. "You can raise cane!"

Mac thought that his well-worn but always well-pressed Ralph Lauren shirts might have misled the Cuban.

"Did anyone ever tell you, Jorge, that *all* Americans are not rich?" he asked. "I could never afford something like this. I probably couldn't even afford to rent it!"

Jorge smiled.

"The taxes, my friend. You pay old taxes to the government and it is yours," Jorge told the American. "Plus a small fee for Jorge, of course."

"How much?" Mac wondered, visions of a Cuban sugar plantation lifestyle dancing in his head.

"Eight thousand dollars, American," Jorge answered, again smiling. "Including my small fee."

Mac had done dumber things in his life than purchase a million-dollar Spanish villa for $8,000.

"Times are hard for the government," Jorge told him. "They need American dollars."

Mac was trying hard not to do anything foolish. He had $15,000 in cash. Buying the house would consume more than half that amount. And he needed money to start his newspaper, and to live.

*Living here costs nothing,* he told himself. *And I have a laptop with a PageMaker program installed. That and a printer are all I need to publish.*

Mac also knew that when Cuba did open up and become inevitably Americanized, his $8000 purchase could make him wealthy overnight.

"How does this work?" Mac asked his new friend in the real estate. "Do I get a legitimate deed and all that?"

"We appear before the regional magistrate, you hand him the money and he hands you the deed— yes, a legitimate one, complete with the seal of the Revolutionary government," Jorge answered. "Then, my friend, you move in."

The ensuing transaction was, incredibly, as easy as Jorge had informed him, although the regional magistrate appeared nearly as sleazy as the real estate agent himself.

Dressed in a bright yellow Guayabera shirt, slumped over an old wooden desk cluttered with ash trays overflowing with cigar butts, the aging magistrate's appearance provided Mac little confidence in the legitimacy of any deed that might be handed to him. But then he had seen far less legitimacy in many of the "transfer of development rights" deals he'd witnessed amongst Key West developers.

At Jorge's instruction, Mac withdrew a wad of American dollars from his pants pocket and handed it to the magistrate. Bill by bill, the official carefully counted the money, then stuffed it into a battered metal lockbox which he then slid under his desk, glancing toward the doorway as if to make sure no one was watching.

From under one of the myriad filled ash trays, the magistrate produced an old, yellowed document. With a pen he scratched out what appeared to be a former owner's name.

"Your name, Señor?" the magistrate asked.

"McKinney, your honor. Mac McKinney."

The magistrate looked up from the paper and gave Mac a stern look.

"You are American?" he asked.

"Yes, your honor, well I was…" Mac answered awkwardly, fearful that his nationality might queer the deal, or worse, land him in a Cuban prison.

"Well," the magistrate said, scribbling Mac's name on the deed and affixing his official Revolutionary government seal, "Welcome to Cardenas and to Cuba, my American friend."

He handed Mac the yellowed deed and shook his hand.

Mac wondered if the American dollars would go to the government or to the magistrate's cigar maker.

The reporter cum sugar cane plantation owner moved into his Spanish villa, feeling only the slightest guilt that he might be stealing land from the Cuban people, just as Batista's American friends had done before the Revolution. It was a guilt he could live with.

Soon Mac had ingratiated himself with many of the hoteliers and businessmen in Cardenas and Varadera. With the promise of their meager advertising revenue, he published the first edition of *Las Noticias Nuevas De Cuba*— The New Cuban News.

Not having fallen off the papaya truck yesterday, the reporter was careful to avoid political controversy in his new paper. He focused instead on the beauty of the countryside and of the people of Cuba. A year passed quickly, and his journalistic stance had won him favor with the local government and even landed him an interview with Elian Gonzalez, the young hero of the Castro regime. The interview was subsequently picked up by the AP in America— a first for Mac since leaving Chicago years before.

Following the publication of the interview in America, he received a note of congratulation from President Raúl Castro, enhancing even further his credibility among the movers and shakers in Varadero.

But the life of a Cuban publisher was no bed of frangipani. His ads were paid for in Cuban Pesos, which afforded him little more than money for transportation, limited products or services, such as juice or pizza in the streets or Hatuey or Cristal beer in hotel bars.

Still, Mac McKinney was happy— happier than he had been in many, many years.

Then he received the phone call.

"Hey, Mac! It's David Conrad."

His former editor was calling from Key West.

"David? That really you?"

"Yeah, I had a helluva time finding you. Where the hell's Cardenas anyway?"

"East of Havana," Mac answered. "Flag City, home of Elian."

"Yeah, I saw your Q and A piece picked up by AP."

"That why you're calling?" Mac wondered. "Or are you looking for Cuban cigars?"

"Naw, I've got an assignment for you… Page One, above the fold stuff."

"You want me to write something about Cuba?" Mac asked.

"No, I want you to come back and cover the biggest story to hit town since the *Magic* sank."

"You've got to be kidding. Why would I come back? Hell, I don't even know if they'd let me back in the country.

"*What* story?"

Mac's journalistic curiosity got the better of him.

"The feds have indicted some city commissioners on RICO charges," Conrad answered.

"Commissioners, plural? How many?"

"*All of them,*" Conrad answered with a sinister chuckle.

"You're shitting me."

"Nope, they've charged the entire Key West City Commission with racketeering, plus indictments pending for six former commissioners and mayors. It's all going to trial in two weeks. They're calling it Operation Greene Street."

"Christ, the *ultimate* Bubba Bust!" Mac observed.

"And no one could cover the trial like you," Conrad said, shamefully stroking his former star reporter's ego. "You know all the players."

It was true. No one could cover such a story like Mac McKinney. Conrad knew it, and Mac himself knew it.

"Shit, David. I'm happy here. I've got a pretty successful paper and friends and a nice house— hell, a plantation. I just can't leave all this for one story in Key West."

"I'll pay your airfare and put you up in a hotel for a month," Conrad offered. "And I'll cover your tab at Kelly's."

*Shit, a tab at Kelly's. Now there's an offer that's hard to refuse.*

As a politician can never quite cure that itch to run for office, a journalist can never pass up a really good story.

"Let's say I'll consider it," Mac told his friend and former editor. "But I'll have to talk to Raúl and make sure I can get back in if I leave."

"Shit, you know Raúl Castro?" Conrad was impressed.

"Let's just say we're on a first note basis," Mac joked.

"So I'll hold Page One for you, then?" Conrad pressed.

"All of them indicted, huh? The *whole commission?*"

"Every one but Tommy Whitemoor," Conrad answered. "They couldn't find enough of him to arrest."

Mac laughed.

"Send me a plane ticket," he said.

# Epilogue— Part Two

*"America's greatness has been the greatness of a free people who shared certain moral commitments. Freedom without moral commitment is aimless and promptly self-destructive."*
**John Gardner**

McKinney could smell political blood in the air the moment he stepped off the Cubana Airlines plane at Key West's Jimmy Buffett International Airport. *Citizen* newspaper racks in the terminal screamed it with banner headlines: COMMISSION INDICTED! TRIAL LOOMS OVER CITY POLITICS!

*What? Like no one ever knew what was going on?* Mac pooh-poohed the scare headlines.

The subject even dominated the reporter's cab ride from the airport to his hotel.

"You here on vacation?" the driver asked Mac.

"Naw, business," he answered, wishing not to become involved in any sort of conversation until he had his hands on a beer. Flying was not one of his favorite things, especially with Cuban pilots.

"Guess you've heard about the trial? The feds have busted our city commission, you know."

"I heard," Mac answered.

"Won't do any good," the driver continued, unfazed by Mac's obvious desire for isolation. "They'll just get a bubba judge to hear the trial. The whole gang of 'em will walk."

"Think so?" Mac wondered.

"Listen, bubba, this is Key West," the driver responded. "That's the way things work."

Mac feared that the driver was likely correct in his analysis of the situation. He'd seen it happen too many times before. Commissioners indicted get a bubba judge and walk. High-profile attorneys get a bubba judge and walk. The current trial would probably end up no differently.

*Same circus, different clowns.*

"Forget the hotel, take me to Kelly's," Mac instructed the driver.

Two days later Mac was seated in Courtroom A in the federal building on Simonton Street observing the formal arraignment of seven city commissioners and one former mayor. He listened attentively, and with some personal pleasure, as each was instructed by U.S. District Court Judge Shelton H. Smith, interestingly, brought down from Miami and allegedly highly independent, "You have been indicted by a federal grand jury under Title 18 of the U.S. Criminal Code."

After explaining the racketeering charges and hearing pleas, the judge ordered each to surrender their passport and proceed upstairs to be photographed and fingerprinted.

"Speaking of passports..." a voice from behind Mac whispered in the reporter's ear. "We'd like to see yours."

He turned to recognize his friend, FBI Special Agent Tim Smith.

The agent laughed.

"Just kidding, of course," he said. "But I do hear you've been away for a while."

"Yeah, visiting family out of the country," Mac answered with a grin.

"I hope you brought me some cigars."

"That would be illegal," Mac advised the agent.

"Indeed."

The two stepped out into the hallway where they could speak openly.

"Hey, Tim, is this your bust? Were you guys involved?"

"We've been working on it with federal prosecutors for two years," the agent said. "Operation Greene Street."

"What's your read?" Mac wondered. "Does it stand a snow-ball's chance in hell?"

"Normally I'd say unlikely," the agent answered honestly. "But this time we've got 'em by the short hairs. We've got our own 'Deep Throat.' These boys— and girls— are going down.'"

"How about this judge? You're sure the bubbas haven't gotten to him?"

"Between you and me, Mac, he's a freaking hanging judge! He's a strict moralist with a real thing about corrupt politicians. Hell, I don't think he's ever even had a beer."

"Well for sure he's not a bubba, then," Mac observed.

"Gotta run," the FBI agent said. "I want to watch the finger-printing— just to intimidate 'em a little bit."

Mac chuckled.

"By the way, who's this 'Deep Throat'?" he called to the agent, who was halfway to the elevator bank.

"Everything I said is off the record, Mac," Agent Smith called back. "Or I'll check that passport for real."

The trial lasted two weeks. Mac McKinney was present for every court session. He had never seen so many defendants and so many lawyers in one court room. Most of the defendants were cocky and most of the defense lawyers were incompetent bubbas more familiar with land use law than criminal defense.

The reporter took notes as Commissioner Becker was charged with accepting a new Cadillac every year from a high-pro-file developer in exchange for favorable commission votes on his real estate developments.

He heard prosecutors accuse Carmen Burana of using her political influence to garner clients for her public relations firm.

Prosecutors tried to shake former mayor Jimmy Dailey's confidence with charges of taking bribes to ignore illegal transient rentals. He remained stoically defiant, smiling only when he turned toward the audience to wink at Victoria Pennekamp, who had become his omnipresent court follower.

One by one defendants were charged by federal prosecutors with crimes of bribery, fraud and racketeering.

Near the end of the second week of the trail, Mac wrote in his notes that while the prosecution case was thorough, comprehensive and cogent, it lacked a "smoking gun." He feared that, once again, the feds would prove themselves incompetent to garner a conviction.

And then came the final day of the trial. With it came Mac's story.

## THE MORAL IMPERATIVE
### By Mac McKinney

When the Key West City Commission— yes, the *entire commission*— was indicted under the Racketeer Influenced and Corrupt Organizations (RICO) Act, some thought it unprecedented. In fact, it was merely 1984 redux. In that year, the Key West Police Department— yes, the *entire department*— was declared a Criminal Enterprise under federal RICO statutes. Deputy Chief Raymond Cassamayer was arrested on federal charges of running a protection racket for illegal cocaine smugglers. And the City hung its head in shame.

On Tuesday, the trial of our City Commission ended in the conviction of all the defendants.

But the story to be told is not of the trial itself— for much of it was lackluster and bordered on prosecutorial incompetence. Rather the story came in the dramatic finale, and in the sentencing statement which thundered down from on high in the voice of District Judge Shelton H. Smith.

Throughout the historic trial, federal prosecutors presented their case against each defendant matter-of-factly. One could say it was, well, dull theater. But on the final day, with little fanfare, they shocked the court audience, reporters and the defendants and their lawyers as produced their Deus Ex Machina.

"The prosecution calls to the stand Rod Aberten."

A dignified, gray-haired gentleman, dressed conservatively in a blue blazer and gray slacks, accented by a silver and maroon regimental tie, appeared from the wings of the courtroom and stepped slowly into the witness booth.

Sweat appeared on the brows of several defendants.

"Would you tell the court your name, sir?" the prosecutor asked.

"Rod Aberten," came the answer.

"And have you also been known as the *Bag Man?*"

Commissioner Becker visibly cringed, as if he could feel the burn of handcuffs on his wrists.

"I have been called that," the Bag Man answered, aware that he had been granted immunity from prosecution in exchange for his testimony.

As if conducting an opera, the prosecutor led the witness through aria after aria of testimony against each defendant, punctuating the score with admissions of political payoffs, bribery and coercion on behalf of Key West's robber baron Gemeinschaft.

Following four hours of devastating testimony, the Bag Man stepped down from the witness stand and left the courtroom. Not one defense attorney dared direct or cross examination. There were, they knew, simply too many skeletons that could have still been exhumed.

The jury retired and took 30 minutes to reach a verdict: Guilty of each count for each defendant.

The Key West City Commission was convicted, en masse, of racketeering.

Judge Smith did not adjourn court and set a date for sentencing.

"I will pronounce sentence now," the 72-year-old, crusty adjudicator informed the defendants and the courtroom.

"The defendants will rise."

The rogue's gallery formerly known as our City Commission stood, quaking, and faced the judge.

"You, the defendants, have been found guilty under Title 18 of the U.S. Criminal Code— you have been involved in a criminal conspiracy, with an established pattern."

The judge paused, removed a handkerchief from beneath his judicial robes and wiped his glasses.

"As a body, you test my judicial temperament," he continued, glancing down the row of defendants and glaring deliberately at each of them.

"You have violated your public trust. You have stolen from your constituents their most precious possession— their vote, which is their confidence— and pawned it for avaricious self-aggrandizement.

"You and even many of your predecessors on the city commission have conspired to exclude the many and reward the few— the landed and the moneyed.

"You have ignored land use laws or amended them to favor developers.

"You have taken money and or favors in exchange for your vote, a vote sworn to your constituents."

Again Judge Smith paused. It appeared as though he might be wiping a tear from one eye.

"When you took your oath of office, you accepted personal accountability and liability for your legislative actions," he continued. "I am about to hold you accountable.

"Before sentencing, I should tell you that I have received a number of heart-warming letters and emails from individuals describing what wonderful human beings each of you are. The writers urge leniency in sentencing.

"Well, ladies and gentlemen, here's a wake-up call. I am not a 'bubba judge.' There is no wool over my eyes, and I will not be hoodwinked.

"The letters and emails I received came from some of Key West's most influential citizens, the town's movers and shakers... which is precisely the reason I will ignore them. In fact, given the authority, I would indict each of them on the same charges of which you have just been convicted. Ladies and gentlemen, not only will they not save you; they are the reason you stand here today—convicted criminals."

Former Commission Henry Becker clutched his chest, groaned and collapsed on the courtroom floor.

Judge Smith called a five minute recess while paramedics were called to attend Becker and carry him out on a stretcher.

The interruption may have prevented the judge from continuing his stern lecture of the defendants for days on end. Instead, he chose to move directly to sentencing.

"Under the Criminal Statute, I am allowed to sentence each of you to 20 years in federal prison," the judge informed the defendants left standing. "And that's just what I'm going to do."

A collective gasp rose from the courtroom audience.

"It is so ordered," Judge Shelton H. Smith pronounced.

"Now you and your bubba attorneys can go seek a bubba appellate judge to overturn that sentence.

364

"The defendants are remanded to custody. Court adjourned."

The judge's gavel echoed not only through the courtroom, but throughout the Florida Keys, sending the message that political corruption may not be dead but has been severely wounded.

*The Reporter* will follow the inevitable appeals to Judge Smith's sentencing. Another reporter, however, will pen those stories.

—

*El fin*

# *ABOUT THE AUTHOR*

A resident of Key West for 15 years, Michael Ritchie has served as a reporter and associate editor of *Key West The Newspaper.* He was also editor of the *Key West Morning Star,* which he helped found with island legend Hilario "Charlie" Ramos, Jr.

Ritchie remains a freelance reporter and occasional author.